Hem & Maxine

NALINAKSHA BHATTACHARYA

Hem & Maxine

JONATHAN CAPE
LONDON

First published 1995

1 3 5 7 9 10 8 6 4 2

© Nalinaksha Bhattacharya 1995

Nalinaksha Bhattacharya has asserted his right
under the Copyright, Designs and Patents Act 1988
to be identified as the author of this work

First published in the United Kingdom in 1995 by Jonathan Cape
Random House, 20 Vauxhall Bridge Road, London SWIV 2SA

Random House Australia (Pty) Limited
20 Alfred Street, Milsons Point, Sydney,
New South Wales 2061, Australia

Random House New Zealand Limited
18 Poland Road, Glenfield,
Auckland 10, New Zealand

Random House South Africa (Pty) Limited
PO Box 337, Bergvlei, 2012 South Africa

Random House UK Limited Reg. No. 954009

A CIP catalogue record for this book
is available from the British Library

Papers used by Random House UK Limited are natural,
recyclable products made from wood grown in sustainable forests.
The manufacturing processes conform to the environmental
regulations of the country of origin.

ISBN 0–224–04237–8

Printed and bound in Great Britain by
Mackays of Chatham PLC

To
Rachael
&
Lavinia

Author's Note

Most of the characters and situations in this book are imaginary and they bear no relation to any real person or actual happening. Miss Muller, the educationist, Lady Ranu, the Calcutta socialite, Madame Blavatsky, the clairvoyant and her able successor, Henry Foulke are however real people. So is Miss Van Tassell and her spectacular parachute jump from the balloon.

Acknowledgements

I am indebted to Ms Monica Redwich for her very informative book *Everyday Life in Britain* which helped me to construct much of Maxine's early life, and *The Statesman* for some excellent vignettes appearing in their '100 years ago' column, a few of which found their way into my book in a garbled manner.

One

The Rani Jhansi club was practising the "dribble-pass-dribble" when I reached the Maidan opposite Birla Planetarium. I was very surprised that Tama was not there and the only girl I could recognize in the team was my old enemy Damba. Paromita had insisted on accompanying me to the Maidan to fight it out with Miss Nag if she opposed my entry into Rani Jhansi, but I had assured her that as long as Tama, the former captain of our school team, was in Rani Jhansi I wouldn't need any additional support. But now, as I watched Miss Nag working a new batch of girls, I felt shy of approaching her directly and slunk behind a raintree to watch the practice for a few minutes.

I was in awe of Miss Nag because of her strict regimen and her Marxist claptrap, which kept all the unfit and apolitical elements off the field. And yet, I had been lucky enough to pass her bizarre tests and might have found a berth among the top sixteen of the then newly-formed Rani Jhansi club if Damba hadn't fouled up my chances at the crucial moment. We had been sworn enemies ever since that violent charity match between Chetla High and Champaboti in which the Chetla girls, led by the pugnacious Damba, had attacked in revenge for the humiliating defeat we had inflicted on them in an earlier match. Nine of our team, including Tama and myself, were seriously injured. In fact that skirmish put the seal on my brief footballing career as the acquisition of my second scar below the nose (the credit for the first one, at the corner of my lips, went to my mother) made me look so hideous that my parents promptly married me off against my wishes to a Writers' clerk. But football was in my blood and I returned home within a month of my marriage, after a battle with my mother-in-law, to join the trials camp of Rani Jhansi. But, as ill luck would have it, Damba was already there to ensure my exit from the team.

But why should I blame Damba alone for my present pariah status in the world of soccer? Everyone had done his or her bit to keep me out

1

of the game. Mother conspired with my charlatan uncle to send me back to the widow and her nagging, Oedipal son Babu and that was when I found myself degraded from a player to a plaything. Mother and Mother-in-law — both veteran players in the domestic circuit — kicked me back and forth between their goals till Uncle entered the arena to seduce Mother-in-law with his tantric mumbo-jumbo and elope, pinching my jewellery on the way, leaving me behind with my raving husband. Babu bashed my head against the wall to add a new scar to my collection and then plummeted into the dark abyss of infantilism, forcing me to play the doting mum. Even the renowned psychiatrist Dr Nandy failed to give back Babu his precious twenty-six years. Penniless, yet afraid of seeking shelter in my parental home, I sold my furniture, worked as a housemaid and finally begged on the streets to support my surrogate son who clung to my bosom like an unweaned baby of six months. The constant pressure of playing my assigned role pushed me to the brink of madness and I really started behaving like Babu's mother! That was when Mother abandoned her striker's boots and stepped into the referee's shoes to bring a semblance of order to my chaotic life, for she belatedly realized that, between themselves, she and my mother-in-law had knocked the stuffing out of me. She threw Babu into the mental ward of B.R. Sen Hospital and lugged me home. There I found myself relegated to the smoky confines of the kitchen where I was expected to waste away my life as an unpaid domestic. I fled home one morning and, to my good luck, found shelter in the cottage of my Gandhian friend Paromita, who had had a soft spot for me right from our school days, though she had always shunned soccer for its inherent violence. No wonder she devoted all her precious time and energy to Swadhikar, an organization that worked for the rehabilitation of the deserted and the battered women in the bustees. It was in Paromita's "ashram" (that's what she called her mud-and-thatch hut that stood defiantly against the backdrop of her industrialist father's palatial house) that I first tasted freedom, picked up the pieces and eventually felt the urge to put on a football jersey again. Paromita, of course, had to confer with her Inner Voice before she could allow me to return to my flock, and before I started for the Maidan, she warned me: "Don't be swayed by Miss Nag's Marxist bilge."

There was however no bilge in what Miss Nag was trying to accomplish with her stopwatch and whistle. I watched in fascination as she gave two sharp blasts on her whistle to freeze the girls in midplay, drawing everyone's attention to the players in poor positions, and then reconstructed the play, timing the girls on her stopwatch, first in slow motion and then at match speed. Most of the girls, however, failed to keep pace with Miss Nag's delicate, balletic exercises and fumbled with the ball, revealing their rawness. I felt quite confident that, even after staying away from the game for about a year, I could do better than some of them. I took a deep breath, patted my stomach which I had managed to reduce substantially during the past two weeks by skipping and jogging, and approached the field with a grim determination. "I have come back, Miss Nag," I decided I would say, "and you have to give me a chance. I am sure I can do better than most of these greenhorns."

Surprisingly, Miss Nag didn't recognize me; she ignored me completely and went on with her practice while the girls eyed me with curiosity. It was Damba who finally broke away from her group and came running to meet me. I clenched my fists as I remembered the nasty fight we had had at the trials. Miss Nag had been so angry with us she had called us "unevolved primitives" and had expelled both of us from the team, snatching away our Manifestos. Damba had somehow managed to stage a comeback, but I hated her all the same. As she came nearer, I drew my breath sharply, wondering if I would be able to beat the formidable, former Chetla half-back in a hand-to-hand fight if she pounced upon me without warning.

"Hem! What a surprise!" cried Damba cheerfully. "Never expected to see you near a football pitch again."

"Really?" I tried to sound sarcastic.

"Yes. Tama told me all about your disastrous marriage. Do you still live with that loony boy?"

"None of your business," I snapped and wondered why of all persons Tama should confide my misfortune to this rogue, or was she lying?

"Come on, Hem. Let bygones be bygones." Damba edged forward and placed her hand on my shoulder. I flinched a little, half-expecting her to throw me off my feet, but when nothing happened I lowered my guard and enquired, "Where is Tama?"

"Must be at home, nursing her sprained ankle. Have you seen our New Improved Miss Nag?"

"Yes. I can see she has acquired a stopwatch and some new techniques."

"And lots of statistical information on diet and nutrition as well. She picked them up from the Hungarian coach at the National Institute of Sports, where she has recently undergone a three-week reorientation course for football coaches."

3

Obviously, Damba was not in a fighting mood, so I arranged my facial lines to express friendliness and bonhomie and said:

"I wonder if Miss Nag would take me back in the team."

"There!" cried Damba and pressed my shoulder. "Ever since my right eye started fluttering this morning I knew there must be some good news for me today. Come on Hem, let's talk to Miss Nag."

When Damba took me over to Miss Nag, she narrowed her eyes to have a close look at my face and then nodded. "Yes, of course. I remember that nasty fight you two had last year. Sworn enemies become fast friends and vice versa; that's Historical Materialism, comrades. We badly need some football fiends to storm the enemy's citadel. Peel off your sari, Hem, and join the battle. We start at five sharp. Right?"

"Thank you very much, Miss Nag," I said, overwhelmed by my speedy acceptance into her proletarian commando.

"You should be thanking our former president Mrs Sarkar for your easy entry," someone whispered in my ear even before Miss Nag had turned her back.

"Why do you say that?" I asked the tall, curly-haired girl whom I had seen clowning between the goalposts when the ball was at the other end of the field.

"Esha is right," said Damba. "You must be brought up-to-date."

Rani Jhansi, I learnt, had fallen into bad days after it had been knocked out in the semi-finals of the previous year's Hazrat Mahal Cup. Miss Nag was held partly responsible for the debacle because of her unorthodox coaching methods and she was bundled off to Patiala for rigorous re-training. A more serious development, however, was that Mrs Sarkar, the president and the principal financial backer of the club, declared that henceforth she would no longer be associated with Rani Jhansi in any capacity and the club would have to fend for itself. Some of the girls who had embraced soccer in the hope of earning at least their pocket money left the club and some committed footballers like Tama and Damba started skipping practice to play hockey or volleyball for their college teams or B grade clubs because they knew that was the only way in which they might get a decent job in the Railways or in a nationalized bank.

"We are now playing for a club that can't even provide us with a daily tiffin of bread and butter, let alone boots and blazers," grumbled Damba. "Just imagine! Professionals playing barefoot football on empty stomachs."

"Let's hope we can earn something from next month's exhibition matches in the districts," said Ira, the massive, square-jawed Rani Jhansi captain, who sported a headband and a pair of steel bangles.

"Even if we do, it's like giving a blood transfusion to a dying patient," pointed out her gloomy companion. "We can't survive without a rich patron or sponsorship from a good company."

"You are probably right, Leena," nodded Damba." Picking up a few thousand rupees from the districts won't solve our problems. Even if we somehow go up to this year's Hazrat Mahal Cup matches, we'd definitely be trounced once again by Kerala or Manipur and then the club will have to wind up."

*

That evening, when I told her about Rani Jhansi's miserable condition, Paromita was shocked. "A football club that can't even provide a good tiffin for its players shouldn't be allowed to disgrace the Maidan," she observed, scowling through the powerless glasses she occasionally put on to look solemn and censorious. I told her about the fund-raising tour, but she had serious doubts about the outcome. "I don't think people in the districts are fool enough to fritter away their hard-earned money just to see a bunch of emaciated, barefoot girls running about with a tattered ball like a pack of circus clowns. Why doesn't Rani Jhansi operate a brothel so that its players can earn enough at night to provide themselves with boots and blazers during the day?"

*

I hadn't kicked a ball for over a year now, but once I joined the daily practice sessions I regained my speed and reflexes and re-learnt the basic skills and tricks of the game pretty fast. Miss Nag was happy that I had scraped through a hopeless marriage and she quoted liberally from Engels' *The Origin of the Family, Private Property and the State* to console me that ever since society turned patriarchal, marriage had been an instrument of torture and oppression. In an ideal State, where the dictatorship of the proletariat was firmly established, the bourgeois institution of marriage would be replaced by healthy, state-sponsored communal alliances between the sexes in which a girl would be free to change her partner whenever she found him wanting in any respect. I found myself nodding vigorously at Miss Nag's vision of the ideal

Marxist society and was promptly included in the first group of five players chosen to practise the flick pass within a tight space of a hundred yards. Between coaching sessions Miss Nag tried her best to dispel our doubts about the club's bleak future by retailing suitable anecdotes from Marxist lore. Her favourite one was about Lenin who, isolated and outnumbered in a meeting by the vociferous Mensheviks, counted his own shadow as an ally. "That's the spirit, comrades," she said, clenching her fist. Few seemed convinced by her anecdote, but none dared to say so to her face.

Every one of us, however, admired Miss Nag's courage and combative spirit when she harangued Mrs Mookerjee, our cross-eyed treasurer, and Mrs Chaudhury, our fat, ever-smiling general secretary, about the utmost necessity of a protein-rich tiffin whenever those two functionaries came to watch our performance.

"Miss Nag, I think we should practise by playing seven-a-side rather than wasting our precious time on those slow, balletic exercises," suggested Mrs Mookerjee one afternoon.

"Yes, and I think we should also practise one-touch football to increase the fitness and speed of our girls," joined in Mrs Chaudhury, her effusive smile plastered on her face like a mask.

"One-touch football isn't meant for girls running on empty stomachs, Mrs Chaudhury," Miss Nag reminded her haughtily and promptly opened her fat notebook to read out the high calorie diet followed by a German women's football club. The girls cried "Shame! Shame!" and Mrs Chaudhury was forced to cough up fifty rupees from her own pocket for a modest tiffin of toast, bananas and omelettes at a pavement tea stall.

One afternoon, Paromita turned up unexpectedly to assure herself that I had properly rehabilitated myself in the team. She was instantly drawn into a fierce verbal duel with Miss Nag.

"You are talking rot, Miss Sen," retorted Miss Nag when Paromita suggested that all the players should fast one day a week in order to keep violence off the field. "You are trying to sabotage my good work on the field by preaching your obsolete Gandhism. Football isn't your peaceful satyagraha, it's hard work. It needs a lot of energy, it needs . . ."

"Revolutionary spirit, huh?" quipped Paromita, "and an intense hatred for the bourgeoisie? Am I right? Come, all ye proletarians, I'll feed you today so that you have enough strength to hate me tomorrow like a true Marxist."

The girls greeted Paromita's offer with joyous shouts which drew a sharp admonition from Miss Nag, but the forces of reconciliation were already afoot and Miss Nag was soon heard muttering, "Well, Miss Sen, I join my team under protest in the interests of football. After all, there is no harm in exploiting a bourgeoise." As if to add a comic note to this uneasy truce between the two, the bells of nearby St Paul's cathedral pealed thrice.

We crossed Chowringhee Road, threaded our way through the hawker-infested pavement and finally turned into S.N. Banerjee Road where, opposite the USIS library, Anadi Restaurant, famous for its mughlai parathas, was doing a brisk business with the peak-hour crowd. There wasn't a single vacant table inside but the proprietor promptly borrowed a few benches from the nearest teashop and laid them out on the pavement to accommodate us.

The aroma of crisp, delicious mughlai paratha activated our salivary glands and when the dishes finally arrived, we attacked them like a pack of wolves; Paromita, a strict vegetarian, sipped her tea and looked on with a benign expression like a mother feeding her starving brood. Miss Nag set an example of proletarian appetite by finishing her paratha before everyone else and wondered aloud if she could count on her bourgeois friend for a second helping.

After we had had our fill of mughlai parathas, Paromita flung a hundred-rupee note at the pot-bellied proprietor and said majestically, "Distribute the change equally among the three urchins who served us."

"God bless you, didi!" cried the smallest of the three boys, who had a runny nose and a dirty towel flung over his shoulder. "Come here every day."

"And give you a generous tip every time, hun?" said Paromita, ruffling his untidy hair affectionately. "But blow your nose occasionally, my dear, or some day the cook will end up mixing your mucus with the flour instead of eggs."

"The imperious scrap-iron merchant's daughter," grunted Miss Nag as she stifled a belch on our way to the bus stop. "Showing off the filthy lucre her bourgeois dad has squeezed out of the toiling proletariat. Have you any idea about the Theory of Surplus Value?"

I shook my head.

"I'll explain it someday."

"What did she whisper in your ear when we came out of the restaurant?" Paromita asked me later.

"Theory of Surplus Value."

"The usual Marxist garbage."

I nodded, even though I felt a little apprehensive. I respected Miss Nag as a coach and adored Paromita as a friend, but how could I maintain a good relationship with these two antagonistic creatures when they were constantly fighting like a snake and a mongoose? I feared that if Paromita met Miss Nag too often and they quarrelled over controversial issues, the time was not far off when I would have to leave Paromita if I wanted to play football under Miss Nag's coaching. The only way to avoid this catastrophe was to keep my Gandhian friend away from the Maidan, so I tried my best to convince her that she was wasting her valuable time on a hardcore communist while those poor battered women were pining for her help and guidance. Paromita cut down her visits, but she refused to stop them altogether. Apparently, she enjoyed sparring with Miss Nag and the latter enjoyed the lavish treats her adversary offered, and it was therefore difficult for me to keep the two apart. Thus, Paromita continued visiting the Maidan once a week and took us to Anadi or to a fruit-chaat shop she had lately discovered behind the Metro cinema. Miss Nag invariably joined us, declaring that she had no qualms about exploiting bourgeois benevolence. She would always take a second helping and then routinely abuse Paromita who retaliated with all the acerbity a Gandhian could muster. I scrupulously avoided taking sides, and later Paromita would chide me for not supporting her cause and Miss Nag would quote Lenin to remind me that petit-bourgeois fence-sitters were worse than rank reactionaries.

A week before our district tour, Paromita, who had been so keen to see me rehabilitated in the team, ironically precipitated a major crisis in my brief football career by pushing me into a direct confrontation with the club authorities. The treasurer and the secretary had arrived, as usual, in a taxi with their files and papers, just like two fussy government officials on tour, and had promptly set up their temporary office under a jamun tree with two folding chairs and a folding table. There couldn't be an odder pair in Calcutta: Mrs Mookerjee was dark, short, cross-eyed and intimidating, while her companion, Mrs Chaudhury, was tall, flabby, fair-complexioned and ever-smiling, though her smile often baffled us as it conveyed nothing. On this particular occasion Mrs Chaudhury had, however, a bit of good news in her bag to justify her smile. Amidst vigorous claps and shouts of "Three cheers for Rani Jhansi!", she announced that the club had received a small donation from a football lover (who would like to remain anonymous) and from now on each player would receive a tiffin allowance of three rupees per day during the entire football season. Miss Nag was not very happy with this pittance, but she condescended to arrange a game of one-touch football to show off our skills and stamina.

After the practice, Mrs Mookerjee doled out our three-rupee allowance for the day and then briefed us about the tour, fixing her gaze on the horizon in order to establish eye contact with the girls. She assured us that we would be accommodated in decent hotels with clean bathrooms, flush latrines and twenty-four-hour water supply though, for economy's sake, four girls would have to share one double-bed room. She advised that each girl should carry a mosquito net, a torch, a padlock and key, candles, matchbox, a penknife (for self-defence) and a good length of stout coir rope (purpose undisclosed).

"Please note that you are not supposed to mix with the local girls and issue gate passes to all and sundry," cautioned Mrs Mookerjee. "The price of the tickets has been kept sufficiently low, fifty paise to be specific, to attract a good crowd. And remember, these exhibition matches have been arranged to provide you with proper football gear, so you must maintain austerity at every step to save as much money as possible. Play well, draw crowds and raise funds — that should be our motto. Now, our general secretary would like to tell you a few words about the forthcoming matches."

"Women footballers are a rare commodity in the sports world," began Mrs Chaudhury in a pompous manner, flashing a meaningless smile at us. "Rani Jhansi is proud of its dozen and a half jewels. . ."

It was at this precise moment that Paromita, who had been quietly sucking on an orange, decided to heckle the club authorities.

"I am afraid your arithmetic isn't quite correct, Mrs Chaudhury," she said coolly as she spat out the pips. "Are you aware that at least half a dozen of your precious jewels are being lured away by basketball and hockey just because your club can't feed them properly and assure them of any regular income?"

There was a stunned silence which was broken by a fierce grunt from Mrs Mookerjee. "Miss Nag, is that true?" she demanded.

"Can't help," said Miss Nag with a shrug. "We shouldn't forget that we are mostly dealing with petit-bourgeois elements and as we have seen during the Russian and the Chinese revolutions, this class often veers towards . . ."

"Stop spouting Marxism and give me a list of those black sheep who are using our club as a springboard," thundered Mrs Mookerjee.

Mrs Chaudhury's smile almost vanished; Miss Nag grimaced and gave a rebellious toss of her head. "Everyone for herself, comrades," she said, looking meaningfully at Tama, Damba and Ira, but the trio refused to meet her gaze and turned their faces away. A few other girls who missed soccer practice to play hockey or volleyball cast down their eyes and exchanged covert glances among themselves.

"Give me the list within two days and then we shall see what disciplinary action we can take against the offenders," threatened Mrs Chaudhury.

"But it's not going to solve your problem, Mrs Chaudhury," said Paromita, spitting a lump of the chewed orange on the grass. "As they say, the cow that gives milk also gives you a kick now and then. Why don't you open a brothel so that your jewels can earn enough to buy their own tiffin and football kit, freeing the club authorities from all responsibilities except speechmaking?" The suggestion was so outrageous that even Miss Nag looked shocked, though I heard a few girls giggling and twittering.

"Who are you?" shouted Mrs Mookerjee, trembling with rage. "How dare you make such a dirty proposal? We don't need outsiders to advise us on our affairs."

I didn't like Mrs Mookerjee's intimidating tone and felt that I should stand by Paromita at this crucial moment. "My friend may be sarcastic, madam," I piped up, "but she speaks the truth. We can't go on like this. We need money, and the three rupees you have just sanctioned for us do not buy a decent tiffin these days for hard-working footballers like us."

"Who is this new girl?" asked Mrs Mookerjee, scowling. "Miss Nag, I don't think you have asked our permission to include her in the team."

"She is a friend of Tama's, a Champaboti veteran," said Miss Nag. "I must say she has shaped up very well."

"She has shaped up very badly indeed," snapped Mrs Mookerjee. "Bringing along a heckler to agitate sensitive issues which can't be decided instantly by shouting. We don't want such dangerous elements in our team."

"And I don't want to play for a club which can't even kit me out in a pair of socks," I declared haughtily and stormed out of the gathering Miss Nag, Tama and a few other girls tried to bring me back but Paromita grabbed my arm firmly and dragged me away, shooting one of her poisonous arrows at the girls over her shoulder: "Keep quiet, you proletarians, if you don't want to lose your precious three rupees."

"I will fix you up with the Bengal team, Hemprova," consoled Paromita when she found me slouching in a corner of the veranda with a martyred expression. "A communist coach, a cross-eyed, tight-fisted treasurer and a non-functioning secretary. Why, Hemprova, you ought to thank me for saving you from yet another disaster."

I didn't respond, for it was no use telling her that the Bengal State team took only seasoned players and couldn't be coerced into accepting me by non-violent Gandhian tactics.

"You promised me a compost pit and a hedge when you came to live with me," Paromita reminded me when she found me still sulking two days later. "Yes!" I wanted to shout, "and you promised me football!" Paromita recognized my foul mood from the way I bit my lips and twitched my brows. She came and sat by my side, throwing her arm affectionately around my shoulders. "Come on, Hemprova, don't be so grumpy," she said. "If you really miss football so badly, I don't mind prostrating myself before that cantankerous treasurer and that idiotic general secretary to plead for your re-entry."

"Don't!" I cried, trying to choke back my tears. "I will soon learn to live without football." And to prove that it was not a false promise, next morning I borrowed a spade from the mali of the big house and started digging a compost pit at the back of our hut. But after digging about three feet I had to abandon the pit when my spade struck a solid layer of rock. Comparatively, the hedge was an easy job as the good mali helped me out with the plants and a pair of shears.

"Excellent!" praised Paromita after a cursory look at my day's work. "I can see that you have a creative bent. The hedge seems to have wavered a little here and there like my father's footsteps approaching the big house after a cocktail party at the Grand, but I like it all the same. Now, why don't you do something artistic with that dug-out earth from the unfinished compost pit?"

I thought for a while and suggested, "We could build a multi-layered earthen platform and plant a tulsi sapling on the top. Just like they do in the villages."

"Capital! An ashram without a holy tulsi plant in the courtyard is inconceivable."

So, for the next two days I kept myself busy mixing earth with gravel and cow-dung and carefully built the platform, layer by layer, narrowing the base gradually with each layer as it went up till the structure culminated in a one-foot-square peak with just enough space to plant a twig of basil. Paromita planted the tulsi sapling, pouring a pot of water at its root while I recited an incantation (a jumble of words I learnt from my mother though I could never decipher their meaning) to complete the ceremony. Later, in the evening, Paromita lighted a wicker lamp under the tulsi plant and it flickered for about ten minutes before being extinguished by a gust of wind. My friend was ecstatic. "You have done a wonderful job, darling," she gushed, hugging and kissing me. "It's such a holy experience. I can gaze at it for hours and get in touch with my Inner Voice." I made appropriately enthusiastic noises, for she would have been shocked if I'd told her that I hated living in her ugly mud hut and would attain my moksha only if I could somehow transport myself to the lavish comforts of Mr Sen's air-conditioned house.

I had finished planting a line of brinjal saplings and was preparing a bed for marigolds when, one afternoon, a freak hailstorm broke over Calcutta, bringing down the temperature by a few degrees and giving us a foretaste of the winter which was still two months away. The hailstones hit the roof and the hard-baked earth like bullets and soon there was a thick white layer of them on the courtyard. I braved the storm to collect a few hailstones in a bowl and darted back to the veranda to press them around a toothpick to improvise an icecream. As the ice slowly melted in my mouth, I felt a surge of loneliness welling up inside me. I wished Paromita had at least taken a day off from her onerous work for the battered women and kept me company on this bleak, stormy afternoon. God! How would I live the rest of my long life pottering about this drab mud hut, planting brinjals and suffering interminable lectures on Gandhism and the *Gita* when all my tainted soul hankered for were creature comforts and an uninterrupted access to football? The recurrent thought of poor Babu languishing in the mental ward of B.R. Sen Hospital only made me more miserable. I looked wistfully at Mr Sen's big house and sighed. If only Paromita were a little more sensible . . . I closed my eyes and tried to visualize a scenario in which, prompted by the dictates of her Inner Voice, she would abandon Gandhi, spinning wheel, homespun cotton and her battered women and return to her father's big house, taking me with her. She would instruct the cooks and bearers to treat me as an honoured guest. I would promptly install myself in that airy, south-facing room on the first floor. It had a small, ornamental balcony where I often found Mrs Sen, Paromita's mother, drying her tresses in the sun.

My daydream was shattered by a shrill, high-pitched cry: "Hem! Go inside and stuff your things in a bag double quick!" I opened my eyes with a start and saw Tama pushing open the wicker gate with her umbrella.

"Tama!" I gasped and in three big leaps crossed the slushy courtyard to meet her at the gate. "What's the matter? What are you doing out in such foul weather?"

"No time to answer your queries, Hem," said Tama, puffing and panting from exhaustion. "Hurry up! A taxi is waiting at the gate and we have to rush to catch the five-thirty Midnapore local."

"But I can't play for the club, Tama. Not after that showdown with Mrs Mookerjee."

Tama fished out a crumpled chit from her pocket and thrust it in my palm. I unfolded it and read this missive: "Dear Hem, I apologize for my rude behaviour on that day. The club needs you. Do come back."

"This is incredible! Mrs Mookerjee apologizing to me!"

Tama gave an impatient jerk of her head and pushed me towards the house. "Be quick, Hem, or we will miss the train."

Ten minutes later, as the taxi splashed through the waterlogged S.P. Mukherjee Road, Tama said, "You aren't that dumb, are you? Guess what prompted Mrs Mookerjee to eat humble pie?"

"A couple of girls must have dropped out at the last moment to play hockey or volleyball and put her in a rather difficult position. Right?"

"Absolutely. I can't tell you how happy I am to see you back in the team."

"So am I," I said and thanked my stars for giving me yet another chance to play the blessed game.

Two

Our much-publicized district tour was a disastrous flop. We drew huge crowds everywhere but our pickings from the ticket sales remained very low because of heavy gatecrashings. Some sightseeing had been promised in between the exhibition matches but this mostly turned out to be visits to the nearest Shiva or Durga temple, the local bazaars or occasionally the ruins of a Zaminder's palace infested by snakes, monkeys and hordes of Bangladeshi refugees who made the place stink like a Calcutta bustee. Mrs Mookerjee's promise to accommodate us in decent hotels with clean bathrooms and comfortable beds was also a hoax as the rooms allotted to us were invariably small and dirty. The old, lumpy, coir mattresses were veritable storehouses of bugs, the bathrooms stank of male urine and the food was overspiced or undercooked. To make matters worse, I had to share my bug-infested bed with three other girls — Leena, Namita and Utpala — each one having her own little quirks and oddities. I avoided Leena on and off the field for her persistent gloom and dark prophecies, but I enjoyed the company of Namita for her cheerful disposition and her readiness to lend me Miss Brinda Bagui's five-rupee College Romances in which buxom, doe-eyed freshers displayed a mind-boggling array of seduction techniques to hook the bright young dons on the campus within the space of a hundred pages. The real menace to our menagerie was, however, Utpala, who had a penchant for converting her every little curiosity into three penetrating questions. This was obviously a hangover from her primary school days when each and every lesson had to be made lucid through three or more pointed questions: 1. Why did pussycat go to London? 2. What did she do there? 3. Who is the present queen of England? On a few occasions we did enjoy Utpala's little eccentricity, but most of the time we had to stifle her inquisitiveness, literally, by clamping her mouth shut with our palms. Perhaps we would have shown a little more tolerance if our district tour had not been such a total wash-out.

Without any real contest from our opponents, the exhibition matches degenerated into a farce, sometimes even worse. Our far-flung sisters were no match for us; most of them were casual, weekend footballers who had practised for a fortnight or even less under some local coach before they were let loose on the field.

In our first match of the series against Midnapore Maids we pumped in ten goals, allowing everyone except our goalkeeper to go up and score. The crowd booed the local team and cheered us and we responded to this noble gesture by making a lap of honour after the match, waving at the enthusiastic crowd and picking up a few marigold garlands thrown on us from the stands. Back in the hotel, Mrs Mookerjee dampened our jubilant spirits with the shocking news that half of the cheering crowd had either obtained passes from the local organizers or had gatecrashed, reducing our share of the gate money to less than five hundred rupees.

It was worse at Purulia. After we had trounced Victoria XI by nine goals before the lemon break, the school kids started throwing stones at us, shouting in a chorus "Go back, Rani Jhansi!" We returned to the hotel in a police van, but the boys chased us all the way, shouting filthy abuse, and started hurling stones at our rooms. After two panes of glass were shattered, the manager politely asked us to leave before his hotel was reduced to rubble. Mrs Mookerjee and Mrs Chaudhury shoved us into a hired mini-bus and we left for Bankura, our next port of call, hungry and distraught, like a pack of refugees escaping their riot-torn homeland under cover of darkness.

"Two hundred rupees thrown down the drain for commuting less than a hundred miles!" groaned Mrs Mookerjee as the bus hit the highway and everyone sighed in relief. "Mrs Chaudhury, if we have to flee like this from one district to another in hired buses, I am afraid we won't be able to provide our girls even with a pair of socks, let alone boots and blazers."

"We shall have to economize a bit at Bankura, I suppose," observed Mrs Chaudhury, her silly smile still intact. "We can cut the egg from our breakfast and add a banana. Miss Nag, I seek your expert opinion about this dietary change. Surely, banana is as nutritious as egg?"

"It's very filling too," pointed out Mrs Mookerjee cheerfully.

Miss Nag promptly consulted her fat notebook and said, "No, madam, I can't approve banana as a substitute. The protein content of banana, ripe, is 1.2 grams per hundred grams of edible portions, whereas in egg, hen, it is 13.3 grams."

"I am told that pulses and legumes, particularly soya beans, are rich in proteins," observed Mrs Mookerjee. "Suppose we cut the egg and introduce a delicious soya-bean item?"

The girls protested in chorus: "No egg, no play."

Miss Nag again consulted her notebook and said, "Pulse proteins have little biological value, Mrs Mookerjee. They lack the essential amino acid methionine though they are rich in lysine. In my opinion, only cheese can replace egg."

"Cheese!" cried a shocked Mrs Mookerjee, holding tight her money-bag as if we were going to snatch it away from her to buy cheese. "Miss Nag, why, you might as well suggest prawn cutlets or mutton chops for breakfast. No, let the good old egg continue. But the question that has been nagging me, Miss Nag, is do our girls really need to burn so many of their precious calories just to defeat those ragtag outfits?"

"I think we should arrange our games in such a way that the local spectators do not harbour hard feelings towards us after the match," observed Mrs Chaudhury. "I suggest that we should make our games more interesting and well-contested by beating our opponents by just one or two goals. The score board should read 6–5, 5–4 or 3–2."

"Occasionally, we should also show our little weaknesses and pull a draw," suggested Mrs Mookerjee. "I am sure goals can be arranged for either side during the last few minutes of the match to provide a bit of drama. In short, we need exciting but friendly contests to keep the local crowd in good humour."

Again, there were angry protests from the team. Ira, our captain, declared that she wouldn't take the field if fair competition was reduced to a farce. Miss Nag took up the cudgels on our behalf and fought like a true revolutionary to keep football untainted by financial considerations, but she had to capitulate after some sharp verbal exchanges with Mrs Mookerjee when the latter pointed out that fair competition being an alien concept in the districts, it would be a sheer waste of time and energy if we stuck to our high principles. Mrs Chaudhury tried to soothe our hurt feelings, reminding us that when in Rome we shouldn't behave like Calcuttans.

But our new strategy of playing exciting football didn't improve the situation. We allowed Bankura's Ma Chandi to score three goals in a row in the first ten minutes of the match and drew loud applause from a partisan crowd of twenty thousand, but when we decided to return those goals to make the game slightly more exciting, we met considerable resistance from an organized gang of hooligans in khaki shorts and black vests who distracted us by dancing a jig on the touchline, beating canisters and crashing cymbals like a group of frenzied tribals warming up for a battle. And as if this was not enough, the moment we entered Ma Chandi's penalty area the referee blew his whistle sharply to indicate offside!

"Don't try to teach me the rules, little girls," growled the bald, hairy gorilla with an intimidating glare when we challenged him. "Only those who can't dance blame the floor."

"This is not football," protested Ira during the interval. "I won't take the field in the second half, come what may." She started pulling off her boots and Tama and Damba followed suit. Those of us who played barefoot had nothing to pull except our faces. Sensing an imminent revolt, Mrs Mookerjee and Mrs Chaudhury rushed in to sort out the problem. They heard our grievances, conferred in hushed tones and then rushed back to the opposite camp to find an amicable solution.

"A deal has been struck, girls," informed Mrs Mookerjee cheerfully after the duo returned from their hectic parley with the Ma Chandi authorities. "We had a fair and open-hearted discussion as to how the game should be conducted in the second half without creating any ill-feeling between the teams. Now, listen carefully."

According to Mrs Mookerjee's bizarre scenario, in the first ten minutes after the break we would be spared frequent offside calls to help us equalize and, if possible, to get ahead by a goal or two. In return for this great favour, during the next twenty-five minutes Ma Chandi had to be allowed at least three more goals and the remaining ten precious minutes would be devoted to a real contest between the two teams, unhampered by canister-beatings and partisan refereeing.

"The organizers have promised to arrange an exciting sight-seeing tour for you in and around Bankura town which will, of course, include some famous terracotta temples and historical monuments. But, in return for that special favour you have to allow Ma Chandi to win by a goal," concluded Mrs Mookerjee with a puckish grin.

"It's not football!" protested our defiant captain.

"*It is football!*" asserted Mrs Mookerjee, glowering at me to upbraid Ira. "If a little compromise is necessary on the field to build up a solid fund, you shouldn't croak like a dying goose. Get into your boots and take the field. That is an order." Mrs Chaudhury, for once, switched off her smile and nodded, lending authority to her colleague's injunction, but we declared in one voice that we wouldn't play under such humiliating conditions. Surprisingly, it was Miss Nag who intervened to pacify us. She pointed out that even with all the degrading restrictions imposed on us, we could easily pump in half a dozen goals in the last ten minutes and win the match. "Let's take it as a challenge, comrades," she said, raising her clenched fist. "I don't think any of us will be interested in terracotta temples and refugee-infested feudal ruins."

We took the field amidst a torrent of boos and catcalls and outplayed the locals, scoring four goals in the first ten minutes allotted to us. Ira then passed on the word that we would not accept the degrading scenario laid down by Mrs Mookerjee and allow our opponents to score at their sweet will. The Ma Chandi girls were naturally infuriated when we frustrated their feeble attempts to get level and they started pushing and tripping us. We appealed to the referee and he promptly responded by awarding a penalty kick against us. Tama argued and got a yellow card; Ira cursed the hairy gorilla and was sent off. It was then that Damba slapped the rascal and he retaliated by declaring Ma Chandi the winner of the match! The jubilant spectators and the khaki-clad hooligans stormed the field and started stoning us. We ran pell-mell towards the police van which had been judiciously requisitioned by Mrs Chaudhury to pick us up in case of a mob attack. There was a mad scramble for the back entrance of the Black Maria and in this stampede I found myself lagging behind my nimble-footed comrades by a few paces. I ducked my head as the stones whizzed past, but one of those deadly missiles finally found its target on my face a little above the chin. I shrieked as the jagged stone cut open my flesh and blood oozed from the wound in a thin trickle. I saw those familiar bright stars flickering before my eyes, stumbled forward and then collapsed.

*

Six days and four more arranged matches (in which we resolutely lost by one or two goals to save our skins) later, we finally reached Burdwan, the last town on our itinerary. Considerably weakened by loss of blood, I had mostly kept to my bed, allowing the five stitches on my chin to heal, sleeping long hours under the spell of sedatives and waking up at odd hours to take medicines and flick through a few pages of one of Miss Bagui's College Romances, even though nothing penetrated my foggy brain. The day before we played our last match of the series with the Burdwan girls, I felt slightly better and went to the bathroom to peel the bandage off my chin and stare hard into the mirror to find out if I could now claim a mention in the *Guinness Book of Records* as the ugliest woman in the world. But, surprisingly, the image I saw in the mirror buoyed up my spirits because I noticed that the new scar in the middle of my chin had mysteriously lessened my hideousness a wee bit. The four scars, evenly spaced out over my face, had an intriguing symmetry. After an intense, narcissistic study of my face, I became almost convinced that I now looked much better, a bit sexy even, in a very unconventional way. To elicit public opinion on this exciting discovery, I rushed out of the bathroom and asked my roommates: "How do I look now, comrades?"

"You look like a potholed Calcutta street after the first monsoon shower," said Leena, the incorrigible pessimist. "Or, if you insist on a better comparison, I can tell you that you look like a witch with dark and mysterious powers."

"Oh no, Hem definitely looks very chic with her new scar," observed the plump and cheerful Namita. "I think if you put on a pair of sunglasses and pout just a wee bit, you'll look very sexy."

"Thank you, Namita," I said and affected a pout to look sexy.

"Answer my three questions," demanded Utpala. "One, when are you going to get your next scar to look more beautiful? Two . . ."

We clamped our palms tight on her mouth to bottle up her second question.

"Divine intervention, my dear," said Mrs Chaudhury when, at the breakfast table, I invited comments on my new look from my respected seniors. Mrs Mookerjee merely grunted and asked Miss Nag to pass the pepper pot; it seemed she was yet to recover from the trauma of shelling out two hundred rupees to a nursing home to patch up my face.

"Hem definitely looks better," observed Miss Nag as she spread a thick layer of pineapple jam on her bread. "We can see the inescapable Law of Dialectics operating here: quantitative change manifesting itself in qualitative change."

"Miss Nag, you'd better forget your Dialectics for a while and think up a good strategy to lose convincingly in tomorrow's match by at least three goals," said Mrs Mookerjee. "I hear that the Burdwan girls are well-trained, and that the home crowd won't be happy with a one-goal victory."

There was, however, no necessity to evolve a good losing strategy as the Burdwan girls put up a fierce contest and our weary, thoroughly demoralized team had to fight tooth and nail to repulse their relentless attacks. A record crowd of thirty thousand turned up to see the match, but Mrs Mookerjee was not at all happy because hardly any of them had paid to get in. The bulk of the crowd were actually peasants who had come to see a cattle fair on an adjoining ground and had included the match in their itinerary as they thought that the spectacle of bare-legged women chasing a ball would be as exciting as a circus show.

Watching from the touchline, I found the Burdwan girls giving our team, for the first time, some anxious moments on the field. They were even able to establish territorial supremacy in the first half and twice they came dangerously close to scoring but Esha, our tall, fidgety goalkeeper, managed to fist off the ball both times. Just before the half-time hooter, Binita, one of our most dependable forwards, des-patched a right-footed volley from inside the box that caught the entire Burdwan team on the wrong foot with their goalkeeper looking quite helpless.

The Burdwan girls threw everything into attack in the second half and earned an equalizer after about fifteen minutes when their nippy striker neatly tapped the ball in off a rebound. In the tie-breaker our team converted four out of five kicks while the Burdwan girls missed two shots, enabling us to win by one goal. The peasants roared and clapped and some of them even threw coins at us when our players took a victory lap around the stadium.

Immediately after we returned to our hotel, Mrs Mookerjee and Mrs Chaudhury summoned us into the latter's room to discuss the club's future.

"Now, let's tell them about our present financial position, madam treasurer," said an uncharacteristically grave Mrs Chaudhury as we trooped in and spread ourselves on the carpet. Mrs Mookerjee adjusted her reading glasses, consulted her notebook, cleared her throat and then directed her gaze at the ceiling to focus her eyes on us.

"I will submit a detailed account to you, madam, only after we reach Calcutta," she began. "At the moment, all I can say is that after the district tour we are left with a sum of nine hundred and thirty-seven rupees, which includes the one hundred and fifteen we picked up from today's match. From this amount we have to pay the daily allowance to our players, the hotel charges and our train fares to Calcutta."

"Thank God we won't have to sell our bangles and earrings to pay for our tickets," whispered Reba, the team's beauty queen who received more accolades for her good looks and fair complexion than for her prompt midfield clearances.

"I think we should wind up," said Leena, the pessimist. "No point in playing barefoot football in this jet age."

"We were certainly better off financially without this tour," observed Ira and many of us found ourselves nodding in agreement. Miss Nag tried to instil some hope in the dispirited ranks by her oft-repeated anecdote about a beleaguered Lenin counting his own shadow as an ally, but it drew only acid comments and sniggers from the girls.

"It seems that the only beneficiary from this disastrous tour is Hem," said Namita, my cheerful roommate. "She has added a neat little scar on her face and improved her looks."

Everyone laughed to lighten the situation, but soon the apprehension lurking in everyone's mind reared its ugly head as Mrs Chaudhury sought our vote on the motion "Isn't it the right time to disband Rani Jhansi?"

Five girls, including Tama and myself, voted against the motion, suggesting that a vigorous campaign should be launched immediately to pull the club out of its present moribund state. The others, however, believed that Rani Jhansi was already dead and that it should be given a decent burial. Miss Nag tried once again to boost our morale with the Lenin anecdote, but no one paid any attention. Mrs Mookerjee then heaved a heart-rending sigh, loud enough to be heard from the other end of the town, and handed her moneybag to Mrs Chaudhury. "Here, madam, I beg you to take charge of the money and relieve me of my thankless duties as a treasurer."

"Not yet, Mrs Mookerjee," said Mrs Chaudhury even as she accepted the leather bag. "We can't take a vital decision affecting the club's future here in a hotel room. Rani Jhansi is a registered club and there are certain formalities to be completed before it's wound up." She took a sweeping glance at our gloomy faces and then flashed her patent smile. "You girls definitely deserve a good reward from the club for your sterling performance in the exhibition matches." She took out a hundred-rupee note from the bag and handed it to Ira. "In our straitened circumstances this is all I can offer you at the moment. Now, girls, go and enjoy a movie and forget about the club and its bleak future for a while." Mrs Mookerjee looked stunned by Mrs Chaudhury's unexpected generosity and she expressed her disappointment and surprise with a shrug and an elaborate gesture of helpless surrender.

*

"There is good news for you, girls," said Mrs Chaudhury when we met the duo in the hotel lobby after the film. "The organizers of the Burdwan team have invited us to a reception tomorrow evening at the Ajanta, which I hear is the best hotel in this town. Mr Gour Basak, the MP for Katwa, is presently staying at that hotel and has graciously agreed to be the chief guest."

"Long live Burdwan!" cried Ira. "We have been receiving brickbats throughout this tour and now Burdwan has at last thrown us a party. How wonderful!"

"A terribly handsome fellow, this Gour Basak, isn't he?" said Namita, the purveyor of College Romance.

"Yes, he is," said Tama. "And a great womanizer too. This could be your chance, Reba. Who knows . . .?"

Reba the beauty queen fluttered her eyelashes as though she was preparing herself for a great seduction.

"Reba, dear, would you please see me in my room after dinner?" said Mrs Mookerjee with a honeyed voice, startling us quite a bit. We looked at her for a few more words but our shrewd treasurer preferred to remain inscrutable and merely turned her gaze at the ceiling to read the wall clock.

Three

Gour Basak, the MP for Katwa, ensconced in a deluxe suite of the Hotel Ajanta, kept us waiting in the lobby for over an hour without any valid explanation. Our repeated queries at the reception desk elicited only a curt reply that the honourable MP was busy in his room and was not receiving any outside calls. Mrs Bhandari, the rotund president of the Burdwan team, glibly consoled a distraught Mrs Mookerjee that it behoved an aristocratic MP of Mr Basak's stature to keep his guests waiting for a while. "But the girls are already famished, Mrs Bhandari," pointed out Mrs Chaudhury, her omnipresent smile waning by the minute. We appreciated Mrs Chaudhury's bluntness, for we were indeed ravenous and when a clever Burdwan girl, who had managed to sneak into the adjoining banquet hall to have a peep at the dishes, came back to report that prawns and chicken were eagerly awaiting our arrival, our hunger became quite acute. "Socialize, my dears," advised Mrs Mookerjee, who had wrapped herself in a gaudy, rustling Mysore silk sari for the great occasion. "Chat up your Burdwan sisters who gave such a good performance." "Circulate, my dears," chimed in Mrs Chaudhury. "Exchange news and views with your new friends." But we had already bored the Burdwan girls stiff with our superior knowledge about everything – from the current trend in designer saris to film actress Keya Tarafdar's latest romance – and they had wisely retreated to a corner to share an old joke or two among themselves, refusing stubbornly our half-hearted attempts at socializing. Even in our own ranks hunger had taken its toll, making everyone sulky, listless and uncommunicative. I found Namita staring blankly at a mural of the sad-looking Black Princess lifted from the Ajanta cave paintings, and weepy Leena looked so depressed even as she licked her third bar of chocolate icecream cadged from a teammate that I feared she might start howling at any moment if she was not provided with a steady supply of icecream and other delicacies. But it was Reba who drew everyone's sympathy. Mrs Mookerjee had persuaded our beauty queen to tart herself up in a see-through chiffon sari, heavy make-up and upswept coiffure and play the role of an apsara, a seductress, to charm Mr Basak and extract a handsome donation for the club. As she cooled her heels waiting for her elusive beau, Reba was shocked to find herself the cynosure of the hotel's male guests, some of whom whistled softly to attract her notice, probably mistaking her for a call girl on her nightly prowl.

One hour and ten minutes had already passed and the three wise heads of Mrs Mookerjee, Mrs Chaudhury and Mrs Bhandari had come together for the third time to confer in hushed tones whether the hungry girls should be allowed to sneak into the banquet hall, one by one, in a quiet and orderly manner and lift two fish fries and one mutton cutlet to prevent mass fainting, when Mr Basak, neatly dressed in sober grey tweeds, sauntered in through the glass door, mumbling an apology for being late. Mrs Chaudhury and Mrs Bhandari rushed to greet the tall and handsome chief guest and Mrs Mookerjee ordered both the teams to form two parallel lines to facilitate a quick introduction. I felt slightly offended when Mrs Mookerjee shuffled our girls and shifted me from the middle to the far end, bringing in Reba to fill my place, but I stomached this insult without any protest in the larger interest of the club.

Mr Basak first met the Burdwan girls, who were introduced by Mrs Bhandari rather loudly as if she was taking a roll-call in a class full of noisy schoolgirls. The chief guest shook hands, smiled and occasionally exchanged a word or two with a girl, reminding one of the Duke of Kent meeting the ball girls before presenting the Wimbledon trophy. The girls looked mesmerized by Mr Basak's towering height, handsome face, seductive moustache and rich baritone voice. I saw Namita clasping her hands in ecstasy and Reba discreetly adjusting her sari to expose her gorgeous cleavage.

After he had finished with the Burdwan girls, Mrs Chaudhury introduced our team to Mr Basak, starting with Ira, the captain. There was a palpable tension in our ranks as Mr Basak finally stood before Reba, who fluttered her eyelashes seductively and offered her finely manicured fingers for a handshake with a come-hither smile which she must have practised before a mirror. But, to our utter consternation, Mr Basak completely ignored Reba's devastating charms and moved on to meet the next girl in the line. I could hear Mrs Mookerjee's deep sigh of disappointment and realized that our club had lost its only chance of survival. Who could believe that a womanizer of Mr Basak's reputation would ignore our beauty queen?

Finally, as Mr Basak reached the end of the line to finish his hand-pumping session, Mrs Chaudhury introduced me perfunctorily: "Hem, our half-back." And then she added, "She is from your school, Champa-boti, sir." I made a little bow and smiled.

"Ah, so you have got two of my girls in your team?" said Mr Basak with a polite smile.

"Yes, sir, and they are very good players too. Assets, really."

"I am glad to hear that. *Jolie laide*, isn't she?" Mr Basak took my hand and pumped it three times, smiling and nodding.

"Isn't that French, sir?" asked Mrs Mookerjee who had sidled up to Mr Basak to hear what the great man had to say about me.

"Oh yes," said Mr Basak and crinkled his eyes which, I thought, were very mischievous. "How did you manage to get so many of them, dear?"

"Two from soccer, sir," I said, took a gulp, and then added, "The other two from domestic accidents."

"I see."

"We are thinking of plastic surgery to restore her face, sir," lied Mrs Mookerjee which shocked no one. "But Hem isn't very keen to get back her original looks."

"Really?"

"Yes, sir. She believes — and some of her friends agree — that she looks much better after she got her fourth one on the chin."

The girls twittered but Mr Basak didn't join them. "I think she is right," he said thoughtfully, fixing his big, slightly reddish eyes on my face for a few seconds. "You never know, she might win a Caesar with her very special look," he quipped.

Having finished the tedious introduction ceremony, Mr Basak led us, on the promptings of the three wise ladies, to the banquet room where, under the glittering brass chandeliers and a few more Ajanta murals, a sumptuous buffet awaited us. There were kebabs, fish fries, mutton cutlets, pilau, butter chicken and tiger prawns, the last item easily taking pride of place. Mr Basak stood at the head of the table and made a charming little speech, praising us for choosing a difficult game which had been so far dominated by men, and saying that he hoped that marriage and the compulsions of homemaking wouldn't deter us from playing this beautiful game. We clapped at the end of his speech whereupon our chief guest graciously took a plate, picked up a kebab and a piece of naan and formally invited us all to join the feast. The starving girls responded wholeheartedly and made a dash for the nearest table to fill up their plates with choice items. After fighting the Burdwan girls on the field we now found ourselves pitted once again against a strong rival in a fierce battle for fish and fowl. I heartily joined the fray and elbowed my way through the crowd to grab a boat of prawns. I retreated only after I had loaded my plate with seven of them, two of which I promptly bartered with weepy Leena for half a portion of butter chicken, another item for which there was a great demand. To avoid my friends' lusty gazes at my precious hoard, I quickly buried my treasure under a pyramid of pilau, decorated its peak with a spoonful of plastic papaya chutney and finally circumscribed my delectable mound with a thick border of golden, luscious mihidaana, the sweet for which Burdwan was so famous. I moved away from the greedy crowd, picking up a stool on my way, and settled in a quiet corner of the hall, just a few feet away from the gents.

I had gobbled the prawns and was savagely tearing at the chicken with my teeth when I became vaguely aware of a figure approaching me. I turned my head and stopped chomping as I saw Mr Basak regarding me with an amused look.

"Are you enjoying your food, dear?" inquired Mr Basak, playfully wrapping a white embroidered handkerchief around his wrist.

"Yes, sir," I mumbled, feeling very embarrassed at this discovery of my gluttony by the venerable president of my alma mater.

"Haven't I met you somewhere before?"

"No, sir." "But I have seen you in my dreams," I could have added, for it was true that in one of my adolescent dreams Mr Basak had appeared, in a tracksuit, as my coach and asked me to choose between him and soccer. In flesh and blood I had seen him a couple of times, though only from a distance, on Founder's Day when he used to come to give away the prizes and make his nice little speech.

"Hem . . . isn't that your name?"

"Yes, sir."

"Well, Hem, your face needs a bit of cleaning up."

"I am sorry, sir," I said, cringing in acute embarrassment. "I will go to the tap and wash my face right now."

"Let me clean it for you," said Mr Basak and before I could protest he stepped forward, unwrapped the kerchief from his wrist and then carefully wiped the grimy smears from the corners of my mouth. I noticed that while performing this very delicate job, Mr Basak's fingers grazed over my lips even though I had already licked them clean.

"I have soiled your hanky, sir," I said, still dazed by Mr Basak's kind gesture.

"Keep it," said Mr Basak, hanging his dirty kerchief on my arm like a piece of washing. "You will need it."

"Thank you, sir."

Mr Basak looked steadily at my face for a while and then smiled.

"You have good bones, my dear."

"Sir."

"Stop siring me, will you? Call me Mr Basak. Right?"

"Yes, si . . . Mr Basak."

"That's it. You have an excellent figure, Hem."

"Oh, Mr Basak!"

"And such a fine little nose."

"You must be joking, Mr Basak."

"I am damn serious, my dear. I like your angular face and your slanting eyes. I am rather biased against moonfaces and saucer-shaped eyes."

I felt slightly alarmed as I knew that Mr Basak was now trying to seduce me by singing my praises, but I had already heard enough rumours about his reputation as a womanizer and didn't want to end up as one of his numerous one-night stands.

"But it's those scars that make you so fascinating," persisted Mr Basak, *sotto voce*. "In Sudan young women ritually mutilate their faces to look beautiful, but here providence has done a marvellous job for you."

"Please Mr Basak . . ."

"In fact, you are one of the most attractive women I have come across in recent times."

The shock was so great that my hands shook uncontrollably and the plate slipped from my hand and broke with a crash, splattering some of the gravy on Mr Basak's trousers. Everyone in the hall turned and looked at us.

"I am extremely sorry, Mr Basak, I've spoilt your trousers," I said, half-expecting Mr Basak to frown and remind me of the necessity of observing good manners even outside the four walls of Champaboti. But Mr Basak took my gaffe in his stride and smiled. "Never mind, my dear," he cooed. "The hotel has recently installed a laundromat to take care of such minor accidents."

Mrs Mookerjee rushed in from nowhere to upbraid me: "Chee-chee! Dropping prawns and chicken on Mr Basak's pants! Is that how we should repay the kindness of our hon'ble chief guest?"

"It's entirely *my* fault, Mrs Mookerjee," said Mr Basak. "I said something which made Hem slightly emotional."

Mrs Mookerjee focused her eyes on an Ajanta mural to establish eye contact with Mr Basak. What she read there I couldn't fathom, but it certainly had a profound effect on her behaviour. She flashed a smile full of comprehension and complicity and said, "Sorry to disturb you, Mr Basak," and retreated to my curious teammates to explain (as I found out later) that the accident occurred because of a good joke from Mr Basak who apparently enjoyed the spectacle of young girls dropping their plates on his trousers!

"You'd better change your trousers, Mr Basak," I suggested. "Curry stains are hard to get off."

"I will cherish this particular stain," quipped Mr Basak with an enigmatic smile.

"No, no, you must change," I insisted. "It doesn't look nice, a chief guest going around in soiled clothes."

"You're right," nodded Mr Basak. "I appreciate your concern for my appearance. I'll take just about ten minutes. Please wait for me."

But as soon as Mr Basak left the hall I returned to my friends, only to face their hundred and one barbed queries, including Utpala's vital three, all of which hinted broadly at a possible romance. I was trying my best to fend off their questions when Mrs Mookerjee came unexpectedly to my rescue. She took me aside and asked, "Now, Hem, do tell me what actually happened there to make you so emotional."

"Actually, Mr Basak reminded me of a hilarious school skit in which I had played the role of a crooked landlady," I lied.

"I don't eat grass, girl," said Mrs Mookerjee, frowning. "You know jolly well how badly we need a donation. Reba has failed in her mission . . . Now if you can help me a bit, we may still save the club."

That broke my reservation. Of course we needed Mr Basak's lucre and, as Miss Nag had taught us all these days one shouldn't be squeamish about extorting a few thousand rupees from a degenerate aristocrat like Mr Basak if that helped the cause of women's football. So, I told Mrs Mookerjee how Mr Basak had praised my nose, my eyes and my scars.

"I guessed as much," said Mrs Mookerjee, her eyes lighting up. "Now do as I tell you."

Mrs Mookerjee's plan was that I should leave the hall before Mr Basak returned and wait at the far end of the corridor where she would eventually meet me along with Mr Basak and coax the latter in my presence into donating a handsome amount for the club. Mrs Mookerjee's plan seemed very innocuous, if not childish, but I suspected that there was more to it than met the eye.

I paced up and down the deserted corridor for about half an hour, waiting for Mrs Mookerjee and Mr Basak, but when no one turned up and my legs started aching, I flopped down on a settee and watched yet another voluptuous, bejewelled apsara dolefully staring at me from the opposite wall. Why should a beautiful woman possessing all those ornaments look so sad? I wondered. If I had even half of . . .

"Why, Hem! What are you doing here all alone when your friends are frantically searching every nook and corner for you?"

I turned my head and saw Mrs Mookerjee and Mr Basak striding towards me from the other end of the corridor. "Just trying to get a breath of fresh air, madam," I intoned, steeling myself for a few minutes of inspired acting.

"And a little rest perhaps?" said Mrs Mookerjee in a sickeningly sweet voice. "Poor thing! You know, Mr Basak, she lost a gallon of blood in that terrible accident and has become very weak."

"How sad!" said Mr Basak, planting himself squarely in front of me. He had changed into a light brown suit and the way he responded to Mrs Mookerjee's crocodile tears, it seemed that the two had already rehearsed their lines before approaching me. Mrs Mookerjee now sat by my side and affectionately brushed aside a strand of hair from my face. "I would have liked to pack her off to a hill station for some rest and recuperation, Mr Basak, but as things stand . . ."

"I quite understand your problem, Mrs Mookerjee," said Mr Basak and looked at my face with a fatherly concern which made me sick.

"I am perfectly all right, Mr Basak," I said and sprang to my feet. "And I don't like people chasing me along the corridor to spout sympathy when all I want is to be left alone."

"Hem, dear, that's not how one talks with a venerable chief guest," reminded Mrs Mookerjee and pulled me down on the settee with a firm grip on my arm.

"I appreciate your defiance and your strong sense of self-respect, Hem," said Mr Basak.

"The credit, of course, goes to the wonderful education they impart at Champaboti where Hem, I hear, was a brilliant student," rhapsodized Mrs Mookerjee.

"I think it's football in which Hem primarily made her mark," corrected Mr Basak, sensing my foul mood.

"She is an asset to our club, Mr Basak," gushed Mrs Mookerjee, placing her fat arm protectively around my shoulders. "A formidable half-back who, I am sure, will soon elevate herself to the forward line."

"If only Rani Jhansi isn't disbanded for lack of resources," I snapped, just to make Mrs Mookerjee's job easier.

"Don't say such cruel things, darling," cooed Mrs Mookerjee, even as she squeezed my shoulder approvingly. "We have survived bigger crises, haven't we? God willing, this one too will blow over."

Mr Basak suddenly started showing great concern about Rani Jhansi's future and Mrs Mookerjee lost no time in convincing him that only a generous donation from a genuine football-lover like Mr Basak could pull the club out of its present crisis. Mr Basak made sympathetic noises and then took out his chequebook and a shining black Mont Blanc pen from his pocket. "Well, Mrs Mookerjee, how much do you think . . .?"

Mrs Mookerjee squealed and threw up her hands in girlish confusion. "Oh Mr Basak, I am so innocent about money matters. Let your Champaboti girl decide the amount."

"Twenty thousand," I said firmly.

Mr Basak looked at my face and smiled. "No problem."

*

After we returned to our hotel, Mrs Chaudhury called me to her room where Mrs Mookerjee was also present.

"Mr Basak has graciously offered to put you up in a good Darjeeling hotel for a fortnight and arrange some sightseeing tours for you in and around the hill town," Mrs Mookerjee informed me.

"Lucky Hem!" chirped Mrs Chaudhury. "Just imagine! Seeing the sunrise over Kanchenjunga from Tiger Hill, visiting Tibetan monasteries, Batasia loop, orchidariums . . ."

In a flash I could see that Mrs Mookerjee had already sold me to Mr Basak before they had met me in the corridor to ooze their sympathy for my ill-health. "I am not a saleable commodity, Mrs

Mookerjee," I said firmly, "and you can't force me to go with Mr Basak."

"We are not forcing anything on you, darling," said Mrs Mookerjee in her honey-dripping voice. "You don't know how sick you look, my dear. You need plenty of rest."

"And some recreation too," chimed in Mrs Chaudhury.

"I am quite fit and I don't need rest or recreation," I declared bluntly.

"Come on, Hem, don't be a spoilsport," chided Mrs Mookerjee. "He fancies you. And there's no harm if we take advantage of that in the interests of our club."

"But we have already got a handsome donation, madam," I argued.

"Yes, darling," said Mrs Mookerjee. "But even that twenty thousand won't last for ever. We need his continued support. Do you understand?"

"Look, Hem, Mr Basak is an MP and he is on the Board of Directors of at least a dozen companies," reminded Mrs Chaudhury. "He can help us get sponsorship from a big company like the Tatas or MRF Tyres. We would very much like to rope him in as our President."

I could feel the noose slowly tightening around my neck and knew I must wriggle out of this dirty trap. "I can't go to bed with a man I don't love," I said firmly. "I know the Basaks pretty well, Mrs Mookerjee. A streak of lechery runs in the family. Sir Hiren, his grandfather, had a French mistress, Isobelle, and Mr Basak too has a mistress called Lola Mudgal who lives in Delhi and does bit parts in TV serials. I don't want to join Mr Basak's harem."

"You don't have to," assured Mrs Mookerjee. "All he desires is the company of a slim, young woman with very distinctive features. That's what I figured out from our little chat before we met you in the corridor."

"And mind you, he is an MP, a public figure," pointed out Mrs Chaudhury. "He knows pretty well that a sex scandal could cost him his precious seat in Parliament."

"Still, if he attempts a rape," said Mrs Mookerjee, noting my stubbornness, "you have enough strength to fend off his advances and rush to the nearest police station to file an FIR."

I nodded instinctively. Of course, I had a pair of strong legs and I could pack enough power in my kick to floor Mr Basak if he tried to get fresh with me.

"You now understand why I advised you girls to include a pocket knife in your luggage," said Mrs Mookerjee with a triumphant smile. "I

33

expect a club member to be fully prepared for a bout of self-defence, if necessary."

"But use your knife sparingly, my dear, if you must," cautioned Mrs Chaudhury, who looked slightly alarmed at the possibility of blood-shed. "Better to use your powerful legs to execute a half-volley on his behind. I think that will teach him not to trifle with the modesty of a Rani Jhansi girl."

"If it comes to kicking, please remember that the scrotum is the most vulnerable part of male anatomy," Mrs Mookerjee informed me know-ledgeably. "I think one light instep kick in that region would be adequ-ate."

"Thanks for your kind advice, madams," I said as I realized that after such detailed discussion about male vulnerability, refusing Mr Basak's offer would be an act of sheer cowardice. "I think I will travel in my tracksuit," I said, gritting my teeth. "I don't have the proper clothes for an outing."

"Borrow some from your roommates," suggested Mrs Mookerjee glibly.

"But I am pretty sure that Mr Basak will buy you some fashionable clothes once you reach Darjeeling," assured Mrs Chaudhury.

"Prefer diamonds to pearls if he takes you to a jeweller," advised Mrs Mookerjee.

Mrs Chaudhury nodded. "Diamonds are forever, my dear. The market is glutted with those spurious American pearls which have very little resale value."

"And here is something for your ultimate protection, Hem," said Mrs Mookerjee and dug deep into her capacious leather bag. I expected a small ladies' pistol but what came out from Mrs Mookerjee's bag was a foil of Mala-D contraceptive pills!

*

The approach road to the highway was clogged with hundreds of peasants returning home from the cattle fair. Mr Basak gritted his teeth and pressed the horn continuously, but the bullock carts and the herds of cows and goats ignored his frantic blasts and moved sluggishly, throwing up a thick cloud of dust which settled on Mr Basak's jeep.

"Shit!" hissed Mr Basak venomously and fumbled inside his glove compartment for his cigarettes and lighter. "Why don't these idiots take a bridleway to reach their village?"

"That's not fair, Mr Basak," I said. "They are your bread and butter."

Mr Basak shot me a sidelong glance even as he flicked the lighter and lit his Classic kingsize. "Chastising me, are you? What do you know about politics, you pretty monkey?"

"Nothing, except that it harbours some dubious people who thrive on long speeches and false promises."

"I like your tongue-in-cheek style but you are quite wrong in bracketing me with those degenerate politicians," said Mr Basak rather sanctimoniously and blew out a thin trail of smoke with a gentle twist of his mouth which, I presumed, was a mark of aristocracy. "For your information, I have spent the best part of a week in my constituency, Katwa, right among my voters, trying to solve their multifarious problems."

"Blessed are those who have chosen you for that big house in Delhi."

Mr Basak frowned and pressed the horn savagely. "Trying to be smart, eh? Well, if you are really interested in my work I can tell you that during my stay in Katwa I settled a dispute over canal water which had been dragging on for years."

"Quite an achievement, that. How did you do it?"

"I waved my magic wand," said Mr Basak and drove the jeep through a narrow gap that had suddenly appeared between two bullock carts.

"I didn't know you were a magician, Mr Basak," I said. "Why don't you take the car off the road and sail through the air like Mandrake and land safely on the other side?"

Mr Basak shot out his left arm and boxed my ear.

"Ooh!" I cried. "I am not a schoolgirl, Mr Basak."

"You are worse. Respect your president, girl, or I will make you kneel down."

"You are a terrible man, Mr Basak, but I am not afraid of you."

"You would certainly change your views about me if you knew what I did to those obstinate bumpkins who were fomenting trouble in my constituency. My men opened fire and wounded seven of them, two fatally."

I looked at Mr Basak's face, shocked and unbelieving. How could this tall, handsome man sporting Wrangler jeans and a stylish denim jacket, smoking Classic kingsize and exuding a musky perfume, open fire on poor, unarmed villagers? Mr Basak noted my alarmed look and smiled. "Politics is a dirty game, my dear."

"But why such violence? Gunning down poor peasants! Was it really necessary?"

"Absolutely. They belonged to the rival party and they had to be chastised because they were diverting water from the Government's irrigation canal to their own fields, depriving my supporters."

"But surely you could have settled the matter through negotiation?"

Mr Basak smiled wryly and shook his head. "Impossible. These are bad times, my dear girl. Earlier, people listened when one shouted, now they don't take notice till you open fire or throw a couple of bombs. Look at Punjab, Kashmir and Assam. But we needn't even go that far. There was this Gorkhaland agitation right at my doorstep, disturbing the peace of Darjeeling and its adjoining hills. Thank god, we can expect some respite from those unending bandhs and blockades after our Home Minister's assurance to Mr Ghising last week that the Government would consider his demands sympathetically."

I was going to ask what worthy politicians like Mr Basak were doing to stop the bloody secessionist wars all over India, but he suddenly swerved the jeep sharply to the left to drive through yet another gap. I was sure that in his impatience to get past the slow-moving caravan, Mr Basak had knocked down at least one stray goat before he reached the highway. Mr Basak was, no doubt, a cruel and ruthless politician with no consideration for common people or for mute helpless beasts. I felt the reassuring presence of the small knife in my pocket. It would have been better if I had worn my tracksuit to be in combat readiness, but I had changed my mind just before I started off and slipped into a pair of bell-bottomed trousers and a red and yellow V-necked sweater, both borrowed from Namita. Mr Basak had done nothing so far to frighten me except that, freed from the traffic jam, he now drove like a maniac. I felt slightly panicky as the needle of the speedometer jumped from thirty to fifty and then swung further, wavering between ninety and hundred. I turned my eyes away from the dashboard and looked outside where, in the brilliant November sunshine, I could see mile after mile of flat, brown, harvested fields and fleeting glimpses of thatched huts, haystacks, greenish ponds, banana groves and occasionally a few farm-hands toiling hard on a vegetable patch.

After about an hour Mr Basak slowed down and drove carefully through a haat, a weekly village market, that had spilled over the highway, leaving a narrow passage for traffic. He utilized this opportunity to light another Classic and croon "You don't mess around with Jim." My roving eyes rested on the trunk of an ancient, gnarled neem tree on which was pasted an advertisement that proclaimed: "Join Mr Kundu's English Academy! Learn to speek and write English flooently like an Ingrez and get job in a month." I wondered how many village youths who had learnt to "speak and write English flooently" in Mr Kundu's Academy had got jobs so far. Jobs! Why, I myself needed a job very badly and here was a rich and influential MP in love with me or my scars or both.

"Mr Basak, could you get me a job?" I said, afraid that once we crossed the haat he would speed up again and sensible talk would be quite impossible.

"What sort of job do you want, my pet?" asked Mr Basak with an amused smile.

"Any decent job will do. I won't mind working as a receptionist or a shopgirl."

Mr Basak laughed aloud and pinched my cheek with his free hand, clamping the cigarette deftly between his lips. "What would you do with such a petty job, darling?"

"I have liabilities, Mr Basak. A sick husband . . ."

"I have already learnt something about your past from Mrs Mookerjee and I don't want to hear it again," said Mr Basak with an impatient jerk of his head. "You have an excellent figure and a sexy face. Why don't you cash in on these assets?"

"Modelling? Oh no. Joking apart, I know I don't really possess a good frontage."

"But, my dear, you must at least aim for something higher than being a receptionist or a shop assistant."

"Thank you for the advice, Mr Basak. But how can a non-matriculate, scarface girl like me get a better job when graduates and postgraduates are not getting even clerical posts?"

"I can make you an excellent offer."

"So kind of you, Mr Basak."

"Would you like to be my mistress, Hem?"

I was so stunned by Mr Basak's proposal that I couldn't utter a single word for thirty seconds. "Thank you for expressing yourself so candidly, Mr Basak," I said at last with a cold fury. "Now, would you please stop the car and let me get down right here?"

Mr Basak shot a sidelong glance at my face and smirked. "Now, what's the trouble with you, darling? Do you want to pee?"

"I don't want to be your mistress, Mr Basak," I spat out. "And there is no point in my continuing this journey after your dirty offer."

"But I have already booked a room for you in the Snowview Hotel, my dear," said Mr Basak, changing gear.

"Cancel the booking!" I cried.

Mr Basak shrugged. "You are working yourself up unnecessarily, Hem. It's not an ordinary offer. Let me explain. I'll buy you a cosy two-bedroomed flat in a decent area of Calcutta and pay you a monthly allowance of two thousand rupees which, I suppose, is equivalent to the salary they pay to a junior officer in a bank or a Government office. You'll also get all those things you always wanted but could never afford: designer clothes and accessories, imported cosmetics, pearls and diamonds . . . any damn thing that tickles your fancy. You will have the full freedom to play football and I won't even object to your keeping a lover as long as he doesn't show up when I am in Calcutta which will be mostly at weekends."

"I am tempted by your very generous offer, Mr Basak," I said, "but I won't accept it. Now, please drop me at the next bus stop so that I can get back to Burdwan and catch the next train to Calcutta."

Mr Basak looked annoyed. "Why are you so scared of me? I won't touch you, if you don't want me to. That's a gentleman's promise. Okay? Enjoy your vacation in Darj and return to your flock with your virginity intact."

"But I don't want you to spend money on my vacation when I can't offer you what you want."

"I hate middle-class people because they are all sanctimonious hypocrites," fumed Mr Basak. "Look, my ancestors once wasted huge sums of money to build ghats on the Ganga for bathers, and for weary travellers they planted some of these shade trees you can still see on both sides of this highway. I haven't inherited their philanthropic zeal but I can still fork out a few thousand on the vacation of a chaste Champaboti girl, can't I?"

And with that edifying little speech Mr Basak pressed down on the accelerator with a vengeance.

*

Three long hours had passed without Mr Basak exchanging a single word with me. I knew he was furious and he wasn't making any effort to hide his anger. He had even stopped smoking to concentrate on his driving and it seemed that he was very keen to reach Darjeeling as early as possible, dump me in the Snowview Hotel with some money and forget the unwholesome episode with a stiff jolt of Scotch. I started feeling slightly guilty for hurting a man of Mr Basak's standing. Perhaps I could have turned him down with more tact and guile without causing any serious damage to his monumental ego. But now it was too late and I couldn't see how I could break the ice without compromising myself. The most awful consequence of this breakdown of communication was that I felt terribly hungry but didn't dare to suggest a brief halt for breakfast in one of the roadside tea stalls. I waited, hopefully, for Mr Basak to get hungry, but anger seemed to have killed his appetite and he drove like a man possessed. A cruel man! Could he do this to his own wife and children? I wondered.

At last, around twelve, when the jeep slowed down to bypass a road blockage caused by an overturned lorry, I opened my mouth.

"I am hungry, Mr Basak," I declared shamelessly.

Mr Basak threw me a long hard stare and a flicker of a smile crossed his lips. "Can't you wait for another hour, Mrs Mitra?" he said very politely. "There isn't a good restaurant on this side of Farakka bridge."

"I will drop dead before I reach Jalpaiguri," I moaned.

"I see. Well, then watch out for an eatery of any description on the road."

"Thank you, Mr Basak."

Fifteen minutes later, Mr Basak stopped in front of a tea stall and allowed me to have some toast, bananas and tea for a late breakfast.

*

Having lived eighteen long years amidst the filth and squalor of Calcutta and after roughing it for over three weeks in those stinking, bug-infested, provincial hotels, I felt quite dizzy as the straight road from Siliguri took a dramatic twist upwards and we were suddenly propelled into the enchanting greenery of the Darjeeling hills, full of majestic pines, feathery ferns and wild orchids. I was thrilled by the series of hairpin bends which Mr Basak negotiated with wonderful aplomb. Down below, I could see the picture postcard view of a fast-flowing river glinting in the afternoon sun.

Earlier in the day, while passing through New Jalpaiguri, Mr Basak had treated me to a nice Chinese meal — mixed fried rice, chilli chicken and an enormous pineapple sundae — at the Golden Dragon, while he himself had stuck to a bowl of Talumin soup and vegetable sandwiches. Mercifully, Mr Basak had regained his composure during the meal and had laughed heartily and tugged my braid playfully when I teased him that his Talumin soup looked like vomit tarted up with a garnishing of coriander leaves and shredded cabbage. "I think you should meet my precocious daughter, Teesta," he had said, flicking away a grain of rice from the corner of my mouth with his fingertips. "I am sure you two would get on famously."

"I'd love to meet her. Does she live in Darjeeling?"

"No dear, she is at St Catherine's, Kalimpong, but whenever I return to Rose Valley she somehow manages to hoodwink her teachers with some imaginary illness and comes home for a few days to keep me company."

Mr Basak seemed to be an indulgent father and I envied his clever daughter, for paternal love was something I had only read about in books. Mr Basak, after all, was not a bad sort, I had concluded after my sumptuous Chinese meal and had wistfully looked forward to my first ever journey to the hills.

But now, after absorbing lungfuls of clean, rarefied air and watching the unending hills chock-a-block with pines and ferns I felt an urge to flick a coin heavenward and shout: "Thanks for the good show, my lord, but I think you are laying out a bit too much for poor Hem."

"When will we reach Darjeeling?" I asked Mr Basak.

"Not before eight," he replied.

"I am feeling bored. I wish I could see some stretches of flat land, ripe corn, grazing cows and a few little huts with naked children playing in the courtyards."

Mr Basak laughed silently as he negotiated yet another hairpin bend at a crawling pace. "Bear with the greenery for another half an hour, dear. You'll soon see some shops, houses and children when we stop at Kurseong for tea."

But Mr Basak had to stop the car after fifteen minutes to make way for an army jeep that was coming down from the opposite direction. "You aren't going to Darjeeling, are you?" shouted the Sikh driver, sticking out his bearded face from his jeep, as Mr Basak slowed down.

"Of course we are going to Darjeeling, Sardarji," responded Mr Basak cheerfully. "Any landslides on the way?"

"Worse than that," said the Sikh as he carefully manoeuvred his jeep to the other side. "The Gorkhas have declared a forty-eight-hour bandh after a skirmish with our troops last night near the Gymkhana."

"Oh shit! This, after the Home Minister's generous offer of a negotiated settlement!" Mr Basak looked crestfallen and slumped over the wheel as if he had received a mortal blow on the head.

"I think you should drop me at Kurseong," I suggested. "Darjeeling will now be a ghost town."

Mr Basak slowly raised his head and glared at me. "Look, there are only four decent hotels in Kurseong, two on Hillcart Road and two on Tenzing Norgay Road. With the mass exodus of tourists from Darj, I don't think you will get even a square foot of space on the terrace in any of them. Why don't you be my guest at Rose Valley?"

"Oh no, I don't want to inconvenience your wife."

"Don't worry. Maxine is very accommodating and I am sure she would like to have a lady guest in this lean season." Mr Basak started the car with the comforting knowledge that he wouldn't have to drop me at Kurseong bus depot and tarnish the philanthropic tradition of the great Basaks.

"I have never met a pukka memsahib," I said after a while. "What shall we talk about?"

"Anything but football," said Mr Basak. "She hates it. She is an aristocrat, mind you, a close relation of the famous Trestletons of Mugbury and the Gumseys of Lupinsville."

"You are also an aristocrat, Mr Basak, but you don't hate soccer."

Mr Basak rolled his eyes significantly. "English aristocrats are a notch above us, my dear. Maxine has real Bourbon blood in her veins."

I had no idea how real Bourbon blood manifested itself in a mem-sahib, but I felt slightly apprehensive. "You better drop me at Kur-seong, Mr Basak," I pleaded. "I will spend the night in the waiting room and take the morning bus to New Jalpaiguri."

"Chickening out, huh?" he said teasingly. "I thought you were a brave girl."

"I won't take the bait, Mr Basak," I said. "Let me go back."

"Come on, baby. Be a good sport," coaxed Mr Basak. "You aren't really afraid of my memsahib, are you?"

"Why should I be afraid of an Ingrez woman? Her people don't rule us these days, do they?"

"Of course they don't. Maxine is a very nice woman, I assure you, and she will treat you lavishly as long as . . . " He broke off to concentrate on his driving as another hairpin bend loomed ahead." . . . as long as you know how to make genteel conversation about some of her pet subjects."

"But I am not aware of your wife's pet subjects, Mr Basak."

"I will tell you. Have you ever visited an exhibition of paintings or sculptures?"

"Never. Is your wife an artist?"

"No, but she runs an art gallery in Calcutta and is quite familiar with the artists and their works. Aslam Huda is, of course, her favourite. Don't

41

forget to praise Huda's abstract horse painting and also those colourful reproductions of Tibetan thankhas adorning the walls of our sitting room."

"I will remember that," I assured Mr Basak.

"Good. That will ensure you a warm reception. Do you have a horse sense? I mean, can you distinguish between a stallion and a gelding?"

"I am not a syce, Mr Basak, nor am I a race jockey. How can I . . .?"

"That will do. Do you know the game of golf, at least theoretically?"

I shook my head.

"Your reading habits, Mrs Mitra?"

"Diamond Comics, mostly. Recently, I read a few College Romances by Miss Brinda Bagui."

"Never heard that name. Barbara Taylor Bradford seems to be Maxine's favourite. May I presume you are equally innocent about Italian opera?"

"I don't think I have heard about it. Is that also a favourite of your memsahib?"

"Yes. Have you any idea about the Calcutta Ladies Club and its multifarious activities?"

"Slightly. Our Marxist coach, Miss Nag, once told us that it is a stinking vestige of the rotten Raj and she wondered why the Government has not yet disbanded it."

Mr Basak winced. "I advise you not to air your coach's strong and derogatory opinion on that hallowed institution. I am afraid you haven't got pass marks in my test, Mrs Mitra."

"I know. Well, Mr Basak, frankly speaking, I don't want to face your Bourbon wife. You better drop me at . . ."

Mr Basak shot a scorching look at me. "I don't expect my Champa-boti girls to quake like chickens before a storm."

"I am not quaking," I protested. "Try to put yourself in my position."

"That's what I intend to do to find a solution. Now keep your trap shut and let me do some serious thinking."

I made a face and closed my eyes. Mr Basak seemed to have a very high regard for his English wife and her accomplishments and he was overcautious not to hurt her delicate feelings. Well, let him rack his brains and find some way to make me palatable to his memsahib. If it suited me, I would give it a good try, otherwise I'd chicken out.

Mr Basak drove silently for about ten minutes and then said, "Listen carefully, Hem. You are a freelance journalist who has just got a modest contract to write a small, illustrated, easy-to-read book — in

Bengali, of course – on tea, which will contain all the basic information an inquisitive sixth grader might like to know from his class teacher."

"I am not a good actress, Mr Basak, and your wife is not dumb. How could you suggest . . .?"

"Patience!" cried Mr Basak. "I am not a fool. Maxine is as well-informed about the Bengali language and the Bengali press as you are about Italian opera. In fact, she was asking me the other day if I could put her in touch with a journalist working for the *Anandabazar* or the *Bartoman* whom she could persuade to write an article on her club. I have a hunch that she has an axe to grind. It's only natural that she would be delighted to entertain a young lady journalist who might do an article at her bidding. Does that make you feel better?"

I nodded, though I felt as comfortable as a battered soldier tiptoeing across a minefield. True, I had played the role of an unscrupulous landlady in a school skit called "To Let" but this was a completely different ballgame.

"To establish your credentials you need a few accessories," said Mr Basak.

"A fat notebook and a jotter," I suggested.

Mr Basak patted me on the back. "Fine. That shows that you have already got the hang of your chosen profession. I will only add a cheap Hotshot camera loaded with a roll of spurious Kodak film. We will get all these items at Kalimpong."

"Thank you, Mr Basak. I'd love to possess a camera. But don't you think I look too young to be a member of the fourth estate?"

Mr Basak gave me a critical look. "You are right, my dear. A pair of zero-power glasses will hopefully add five years to your age."

"You are a rogue, Mr Basak," I said, grinning.

"That's not how a Champaboti girl addresses her venerable president," chided Mr Basak, feigning a show of great authority, then he started crooning "Bad Bad Leroy Brown".

Four

I could feel the butterflies in my stomach as the jeep swerved sharply off the highway, crossed a cattle-bridge and finally climbed a gentle slope flanked on both sides by terraced tea gardens that stretched out for miles. Through the windscreen I could see a glimpse of Mr Basak's two-storey, red-brick bungalow which was well fortified by high, spiked boundary walls and had the awesome look of an impregnable fortress. Playing a crooked landlady in a half-hour school skit in front of an appreciative teenage audience couldn't be considered an adequate apprenticeship for impersonating a gung-ho freelance journalist before a highly accomplished memsahib, so I had been rehearsing my opening lines and adjusting my specs during the last lap of our journey from Kalimpong, even though these cursory exercises didn't bring much solace to my fluttering heart. I could almost hear it pounding against my ribs as the car slowed down before the huge iron gate and the stocky, bandy-legged Gorkha durwan scuttled out from his sentry box to push the gate wide open and execute a smart salute, clicking his heels sharply. Mr Basak raised his hand in benediction and drove in. In the dim light thrown by the antique-looking lampposts flanking the gravelled driveway, I could see a tennis court on my left and a well-kept garden on my right where a profusion of marigolds and dahlias were in bloom. Mrs Basak's passion for local flora was evident on the wide semi-circular veranda which was dotted with potted ferns and strung with a chain of baskets containing some more ferns (of smaller varieties) and a cornucopia of orchids.

"Now!" cautioned Mr Basak as he pressed the horn and pulled in right at the bottom of the stairs. Two bearers, one old and limping and the other young and sprightly, emerged from the house and greeted their master.

"All well here, Bhairon?" Mr Basak enquired of the old bearer.

"Well, sir, very well. Memsahib expecting you since morning."

"We have a guest — Mrs Mitra. Tell Sarla to fix up a good room upstairs, achha?"

"Yes, sahib."

Both the bearers greeted me with a little bow and a namaste, but I didn't miss the puzzled expression on their faces. Obviously, they were not used to entertaining dark-skinned, ugly-looking guests at Rose Valley.

"Where is memsa'b?" asked Mr Basak.

"She is taking her evening bath, sahib."

"Fine. Ask someone to bring tea for us in the sitting room."

The bearers hauled our luggage out of the jeep and carried it inside. We were still on the veranda when a plump and pretty girl enveloped in a loose kimono (or was it a maternity suit? I couldn't be sure) burst on the scene with a jubilant shriek, with a pair of black shaggy dogs treading hard on her heels. The girl and the beasts flung themselves on Mr Basak at the same time, making him stagger a little and grab a post for support. He hugged and kissed all three with equal fervour and then introduced me to his daughter, Teesta.

"Glad to meet you, Mrs Mitra," said Teesta cheerfully with a conspiratorial wink which intrigued me. Had she already seen through my game? I wondered. My suspicion became acute as she scratched my palm a little with her nail while shaking my hand. I was momentarily gripped by a fear that one of those two pug-nosed dogs would sniff out my false identity and start barking at me but, to my great relief, both of them let me off after a thorough sniffing of my feet.

I felt slightly relieved when Teesta led me to the large sitting room which was done up in a style that Mr Basak had taught me on the way to recognize as "Mix 'n' Match", though to my unartistic eyes the room appeared as a veritable antique shop with some gigantic, lavishly upholstered, Victorian sofas installed at the centre for effect. The items on view included a Louis XIV chair and a Regency table set in diametrically opposite corners, a low Tibetan side table carved with dragons and geometrical motifs, exquisite crystal, china and porcelain, and a few objets d'art arranged tastefully on the sideboard and mantlepiece, classical lamps, colourful and mysterious thankhas on the walls and, of course, my hostess' favourite Aslam Huda displayed very prominently right above the sitting area. My senses dazed by this powerful assault of art and artefacts, I slowly lowered myself on the sofa and wondered for the umpteenth time if I had made a blunder in accepting Mr Basak's invitation.

"Don't leave Mrs Mitra alone, darling," said Mr Basak to his daughter. "I'll be back in a few minutes." I looked beseechingly at Mr Basak, but he left me in the company of his suspicious daughter and the two exuberant dogs who now started sniffing my legs with renewed vigour like two determined sleuths bent on exposing my secrets.

"Dad is so naive, isn't he?" said Teesta, lowering her voice. "You know, Mrs Mitra, you don't look like a journalist at all, even with your powerless glasses. In fact, those specs make you look more dubious."

I was so stunned by my swift exposure that I fumbled for a suitable denial. To my great relief, a tall gaunt maid entered the room just at that moment and announced: "Memsa'b coming now!"

"Don't worry," whispered Teesta as the housemaid left the room as dramatically as she had entered. "I won't spill it out before Mum."

"Thank you, Teesta," I said, unwittingly confirming her suspicion.

"You remind me of Mrs Hore whom Dad had brought here two years ago," said Teesta with a broad grin. "She claimed she was an Ikebana artist and we had a jolly good time with her till she . . . here comes your hostess, Mrs Mitra."

I sprang to my feet and offered my hand as Mrs Basak, fresh from her bath, entered the room, exuding a faint flowery perfume. She greeted me in a soft whisper: "Glad to meet you, Mrs Mitra. Please make yourself comfortable." She barely touched the tips of my fingers and retreated two steps backward to sit daintily on a sofa across from me. I was so overwhelmed by Mrs Basak's beauty and her sweet, intoxicating perfume that I gaped openly at her face, ignoring her daughter's whisper, "Steady yourself, Mrs Mitra!" She was a tall, slender woman, probably in her mid-thirties, with a perfectly oval face, an ivory complexion, curly blonde shoulder-length hair, clear green eyes and a small, sensuous mouth with rosy, luscious lips. The memsahib wore an apricot-coloured pheran, the loose caftan-like apparel worn by Kashmiri women, embroidered lavishly around the neckline, sleeves and hem. Her long, slender neck was bare but a pair of hooped earrings dangled from her small, conch-shaped ears. I trembled with a passion that I had never felt for any man or woman in my life and I felt an irresistible urge to hold her face between my palms and smother it with a flurry of kisses. Surprisingly, this overwhelming emotion swept away my nagging fear of being caught by Mrs Basak and I found myself exchanging pleasantries with her in a warm, friendly manner.

"I am so sorry to disturb you at this late hour, Mrs Basak," I said, my eyes still riveted on her exquisite face.

"I am indeed very happy to receive a guest in this lean season," said Mrs Basak. "We keep open house during the plucking seasons because that's the time when . . ." She broke off to frown at her daughter who had curled up on a sofa with her dogs, one on each side, her legs drawn up immodestly, revealing her fleshy thighs and the fringe of her pink lace panties. Teesta was apparently engrossed in her Archie comic but from her darting looks at me I knew she was more interested in my debut as a fake journalist than Archie's wild capers.

"Tee, would you please go upstairs and check up whether Sarla has done the guest room?" Mrs Basak's voice sounded gentle but very firm. Teesta stood up with a defiant toss of her mane. "Mum, why don't you say straight out that you want to be left alone with Mrs Mitra?" she said haughtily. "I don't like your oblique hints. They're so typically English." She rolled up her comic, slapped it on her thigh and stormed out of the room, her dogs faithfully tagging along with her.

"A very spirited girl," I observed as I noted Mrs Basak's face hardening. "She is good at heart, I can tell you." But Mrs Basak shook her head and sighed deeply. "I thought a reputable convent school like St Catherine's would at least teach a girl how to walk and sit properly."

"Girls will be girls, Mrs Basak," I said indulgently, adjusting my glasses which tended to slip down on the bridge of my nose. "Times have changed, you have to admit."

"Perhaps I should have sent her to Cheltenham like my elder daughter Varsha," said Mrs Basak, then, with a slight shrug, changed the subject before I could say something inane to console her.

"What paper do you write for, Mrs Mitra?" she asked.

"I am a freelance, Mrs Basak," I said. "There are a few Bengali dailies like the *Anandabazar*, *Aajkal* and *Bartoman* who occasionally ask me to write an article on the current trends in the Gariahata sari shops or interview a lady entrepreneur marketing a new cooking gadget."

"Quite interesting, is it?"

"Not really. You have to work hard to produce good copy but the payments are niggardly. In fact, I intend to break fresh ground with a small, informative children's book on tea."

"That's very interesting. Sometimes I feel that we are not doing enough for our children. Little wonder that they are becoming more and more addicted to TV and comics." The hint that her daughter was a case in point was implicit in her tone.

"You are absolutely right, Mrs Basak," I said and wanted to add, "Anything that drops from those rosy, eminently kissable lips couldn't be wrong, darling."

Mrs Basak lamented that she had sent a proposal to the State Government that they should introduce a course on "art appreciation" in the school curriculum but the thick-headed Writers' bureaucrats had tossed her papers from one desk to other for over two years before they shoved them under the carpet. This, I decided, was the right moment to show my appreciation of art. I looked up and pointed my finger unerringly at the wall behind her. "That's Aslam Huda, I suppose?"

"You are absolutely right," said Mrs Basak, turning her head to appreciate her favourite picture.

"I wonder whether it's a gelding or a stallion," I said.

Mrs Basak smiled broadly, revealing her fine, close-set teeth. "That's a good joke, Mrs Mitra," she said and daintily pushed back a curl from her cheek. "It's actually an abstract painting that brings out the quintessential horse as seen through the eyes of a master painter. The power, the sinews, the majestic gait, the bold symmetry, the speed . . . in fact Huda has caught the distilled essence of the horse in a few vigorous strokes."

"Marvellous! Saying so much in so few lines. Does Huda paint only horses, Mrs Basak?"

"Not at all, dear," said Mrs Basak in a slightly argumentative tone. "True, Huda's international recognition came from his horses, but he has since moved on to fresh pastures and the results are equally stunning. In fact, he is presently experimenting with cheap materials of everyday use, adding a new dimension to collage."

"Sounds quite interesting," I said, crossing my legs.

Mrs Basak was holding forth about Huda's "Yellow Phase" when Mr Basak, wrapped in a tasseled, red ochre dressing gown, entered the room, whistling softly. He plopped down beside his wife, evoking the illusion of a happy couple for my benefit. "How about a hot Tibetan dish for our guest, darling?" he said in a voice that seemed to have been specially cultivated for his memsahib.

"You have taken me unawares, Mrs Mitra," said Mrs Basak, "but I hope tomorrow we will be able to serve you a steaming bowl of thukpa and some delicious momos."

"Thank you, Mrs Basak. I love exotic dishes."

"So does Maxine," said Mr Basak. "I have noticed that intellectuals all over the world share this remarkable trait — I mean this love for exotic food."

Mrs Basak darted a sideways glance at her husband to assure herself that he was not joking, but Mr Basak looked damn serious.

"Don't taunt me like that, Mr Basak," I said, feigning modesty. "I am no intellectual; I am only a freelance trying to eke out a living."

Mr Basak affected a deep sigh which sounded like a snort. "I am so sorry, Mrs Mitra," he said shaking his head mournfully. "I almost forgot about your recent bereavement . . . that ghastly car accident on G.T. Road that snatched away such a young and promising horticulturist from your bosom."

Mrs Basak looked genuinely concerned. "I am really sorry, Mrs Mitra, I should have guessed from . . . from all those marks on your face."

I pulled out my hanky and gagged myself, lest I burst out laughing. Mr Basak had suddenly opened a new vista in my life for which I had not prepared myself. A horticulturist husband! God! I had never even heard the term before!

"Dr Mitra was a very brilliant scientist at the Indian Council for Agricultural Research," Mr Basak informed his wife. "He was, in fact, working on a high-yielding, seedless strain of papaya when that killer lorry struck him down."

"Please Mr Basak!" I groaned, covering my face with my hands. "I want to forget my past — at least for a few days."

Mr Basak nodded. "I quite understand, Mrs Mitra. It hurts me deep inside when I remember vividly how a charming little girl with a pigtail once bounced up to the dais to garland me on Founder's Day."

Mrs Basak looked positively maternal. "A Champaboti girl! Why, Gour, you should have told me."

Tea with all its paraphernalia was brought in by the young bearer and arranged on the centre table with some fanfare. Satisfied with my impeccable performance, I sipped tea from a bone china cup and tucked away quite a few cakes and pastries, ignoring Mr Basak's discreet signals to exercise restraint. I washed down the snacks with big gulps of tea which had a very nice flavour.

"Finest tea I have had so far," I admitted rather naively.

"It's the muscatel flavour that makes Darjeeling tea so special," said Mrs Basak proudly. "No other area in the world can produce this unique flavour."

"Take out your notebook, Mrs Mitra, and start jotting right away," said Mr Basak. "Max is an authority on Darjeeling tea."

"Enough time for teaing off," quipped Mrs Basak. "Mrs Mitra must take some rest before supper."

When I came down for dinner, Teesta was slouching at the far end of the long dining table. She grinned and held up her thumb to indicate that she appreciated the sloppy way I'd draped my sari. I wanted to sit by her side but Sarla, the tall maid, pushed me into a chair on Mr Basak's left, opposite Mrs Basak, probably in strict observance of the seating arrangement followed at Rose Valley during a formal dinner.

"Let's start," said Mr Basak from the head of the table.

The khansama, a small birdlike creature sporting a pointed beard and a skullcap, scurried in with the soup tray and placed a steaming bowl under my nose. I didn't like the look of this viscous stuff and suspected that it contained, among other ingredients, the sweat and semen of the cook and his helper. I stirred my soup with the spoon, licked a drop or two, squirmed and then pushing away my bowl looked up at the miniature paintings that adorned the walls of the dining room. Mr Basak hadn't told me anything about this group of paintings but I preferred them to Huda's abstract horse and those mysterious Tibetan thankhas, simply because they depicted familiar subjects in bright colours. The one right above Mrs Basak's head showed a bashful woman courting a fiercely moustached prince; in another painting, a lady in a flounced ghagra was enjoying a swing ride in a lush garden while her beau looked on with a condescending smile.

"Mrs Basak, could you tell me why all the girls in those paintings have such big fish eyes and the men such sword-like moustaches?" I enquired as I was feeling very sleepy and needed some small talk to keep myself awake.

"Hmm-hurrumph!" Mr Basak cleared his throat boisterously in acute embarrassment and Teesta giggled and held up her thumb a second time; Sarla and the khansama exchanged glances that said: "Definitely not out of the top drawer."

"Mrs Mitra has asked me an intelligent question and I don't understand why people should make unseemly noises and gestures over that," Mrs Basak said very severely, forcing her husband and daughter to hide their smirks behind their table napkins.

"I quite appreciate your inquisitiveness, Mrs Mitra," said Mrs Basak very sympathetically. "These are actually Pahadi paintings, Basholi school. They are characterized by fiercely-drawn profiles, a legacy of the Jain Kalpa-sutras in which we find such fish eyes and savage intensity. The influence of Mughal kalam is no doubt discernible in Basholi paintings, but they have a folk style which is quite sophisticated. You will notice . . ."

I woke up with a start as Teesta clapped and cried, "Mrs Mitra, you will scald your face in the soup!"

"That's not done, Tee," chided her mother. "It's not a football match and you don't have to clap and shout like a hooligan. Sarla, go and sit behind Mrs Mitra. Hold her if she tends to fall off her chair. Nazir Mian, remove her soup and serve her fish."

All these commands were obeyed promptly without any fuss. I apologized to Mrs Basak for my sleepiness and began prodding the fish cutlet with a genuine interest, but after two or three bites my head lolled sideways and Sarla dutifully held me, offering her arm to rest my head on.

"I think we should allow Mrs Mitra to leave the table," I heard Mr Basak's voice even as I closed my eyes. "She is tired and needs some rest."

"But she must have something before she goes to bed," insisted Mrs Basak like a doting mother. Praising Aslam Huda's abstract horse and making absurd queries about fish-eyed girls seemed to have endeared me to her so much that she completely ignored my atrocious table manners. "A girl her age shouldn't go to bed hungry," I heard her say.

"Hungry! All those cakes and pastries she gobbled with tea . . ." reminded Mr Basak.

"Shush! That's not how one should talk about a bereaved woman."

"But, Mum, you are treating her like a child!" cried Teesta shrilly. "That's ridiculous. Why not ask her if she really wants to eat?"

"You be quiet, will you?" hissed Mrs Basak. "Let me handle this. Sarla, give her a gentle shake and put little-little pieces of fish into her mouth and then feed her a few spoons of custard, achha?"

So, the strict and efficient Sarla shook me awake and fed me like a six-month-old baby. I obliged her by parting my lips whenever I felt the spoon prying at the corner of my mouth.

"Now wipe your mouth and get up, Mrs Mitra," whispered Sarla as she woke me up with a final, and rather rude, shake. I clumsily cleaned my mouth with the napkin and stood up, apologizing to everyone for my drowsiness.

"I don't think she will be able to climb the stairs on her own," observed Mrs Basak. "Sarla, get Bhairon to help you if you can't manage her alone. Good night, Mrs Mitra."

"Good night, everybody," I said and took a couple of steps before collapsing theatrically in Sarla's arms. She called for Bhairon, the old, limping bearer, and a little later I had the exhilarating experience of being lifted bodily in the air by two pairs of hands and propelled down the corridor and then up the stairs. The last few words I heard from a panting male voice before I passed out were: "Thank God, she is not as heavy as Mrs Hore. Remember how that lady also fainted over her pilau and had to be carried upstairs?"

*

"A virtuoso performance, I must say," complimented Mr Basak when I met him on the veranda the next morning. Seated in a cane chair amidst a virtual jungle of potted ferns, cacti and hanging orchids, Mr Basak was sipping tea and flicking through the pages of the *Statesman*. I laughed. "Thanks to Aslam Huda and my horticulturalist husband I just scraped through. Where's Mrs Basak?"

"Out for her morning walk. She may return at any moment. What's your overall assessment of my Bourbon wife?"

"Very succulent," I said, pouring myself a cup.

Mr Basak gave me an arch look. "You aren't a lesbo, are you?"

"I wasn't, but your delicious wife has changed my sexual preferences overnight."

"Good for her. Go ahead with my blessings." Mr Basak literally blessed me, touching the top of my head with his palm. "It may cure her frigidity. That's what that dubious Harley Street sexologist suggested when he failed to cure her. Really, I'll pay you a handsome fee for taking her to bed."

I frowned. "You have a very dirty mind, Mr Basak. I was of course joking."

Mr Basak shook his head dolefully. "A pity. Two years ago I brought Mrs Hore to Rose Valley and she looked so impressed by Max's charms that I suggested she should take her to bed. She gallantly agreed, but then things took a nasty turn and . . ."

"Who is this Mrs Hore?" I interrupted.

"Mrs Hore?" said Mr Basak with evident interest. "Ah, she was a dark, voluptuous woman with just one scar on her forehead. I had picked her up at the Calcutta Club and brought her here for a short vacation. She claimed she was the only Ikebana artist of the Sogetsu school in India. She'd learnt her art in Japan from Mrs Koka Fukushima, the supreme exponent of this particular type of Ikebana. Naturally, she got a red carpet reception here and gave, just like you, a virtuoso performance on her first evening. Poor thing! She messed up on her third morning here when, goaded by Max, she tried to demonstrate her delicate art with twigs, painted broomsticks and eggshells. Now, please note, Mrs Mitra, there is a lesson to be learnt from that overconfident lady. Keep a low profile and restrain your urge to overact."

"Noted. But your precocious daughter has already rumbled me. What about that?"

"Win her over," advised Mr Basak. "You have only to . . ." He left the sentence unfinished as Mrs Basak, escorted by her dogs, appeared on the garden path. The dogs were in high spirits after their constitutional and one of them came bounding up the stairs and offered me one of its front legs for a handshake.

"Lord Steyne always prefers our lady guests," observed Mr Basak with a chuckle. "Even Mrs Hore . . ."

"Would you please stop talking about that imposter?" I hissed under my breath; the very name of Mrs Hore made me slightly nervous. "That's a very grand name for a little pug-nosed doggie," I said to him as Mrs Basak approached the stairs. "What's the name of Lord Steyne's girlfriend?"

"Becky, of course. Have you read *Vanity Fair?*"

"No, but I once read a few issues of *Modesty Blaise*. I couldn't keep track of her interesting adventures as the supply was very erratic."

"A pity. I will request Mr Thackeray to send you all the back issues of *Vanity Fair* when I go to London next time."

"Good morning, Mrs Mitra," called a cheerful Mrs Basak. She was holding a little bunch of purple and yellow pansies in her hand and looked very fresh and delectable in her ankle-length wine-red gown which I later learnt to recognize as a baku, a dress mostly worn by Tibetan women. "Did I miss anything?" she said, smiling.

"Nothing very special, darling," said Mr Basak. "Mrs Mitra was just coaxing me to tell her the secrets of your wonderful complexion. Of course, I haven't divulged anything."

Mrs Basak giggled and playfully threw her bunch of pansies at her husband, scattering a few flowers on me as well. Was Mrs Basak really unaware of her husband's relationship with Lola Mudgal or was she an actress of a high calibre? I wondered. Nevertheless I joined with Mr Basak in teasing the memsahib, just to see her blush and pout. It made my morning.

This idyllic atmosphere full of bonhomie and playful banter was shattered fifteen minutes later when a sumptuous breakfast was spread before us and, like a bad omen, Teesta blew in in her crumpled nightie with blotches of rouge on her cheeks, looking like an overworked whore after a night of orgy. She plopped down into a chair, drew up her legs high enough to reveal her plump thighs and her birthmark, grabbed a piece of toast and crammed it into her mouth. A thoroughly shaken Mrs Basak stopped spreading honey on her brown bread and hissed through her clenched teeth: "How dare you come downstairs in such a state?"

"Why, Mum, I am hungry and I must have my share of breakfast!" cried an indignant Teesta.

"Not in that bedraggled nightie and that clownish make-up," retorted Mrs Basak. "And would you please sit properly like a decent girl?"

"Now that's not at all fair," protested Teesta shrilly. "I too have a right to air my crotch now and then just like Dad or any other guy. Am I right, Mrs Mitra?"

Caught in the crossfire, I didn't know what to say. I tried to send a signal to Teesta that she should calm down, but she simply ignored my winks and tossed her dishevelled mane defiantly.

"Tee, I won't have that kind of talk at my breakfast table," warned Mrs Basak. "You'd better take a tray to your room."

Teesta grimaced. "Oh Mama, don't behave like Sister Agatha. This isn't Devon where people have to consult their etiquette book before taking a pee by the roadside. This is Darj, India. For Chrissake, try to be humane, Mum, and let me enjoy my hard-earned vacation."

"Hard-earned? Really! You have faked a tummyache and duped the sisters to get your sick leave. I am going to report you to your Mother Superior."

"Come on, Mum, that's quite normal in our school. If you only knew the trouble those fucking nuns give us . . ."

Mrs Basak turned crimson and averted her face in disgust.

"Tee, dear, we have a guest among us," reminded Mr Basak gently, barely concealing his smirk.

"I bet Mrs Mitra is enjoying our talk, Dad," said Teesta with a big wink at me. "Please Mum, don't scowl like Sister Francesca."

I had a hunch that Teesta was deliberately trying to rattle her mother and her efforts in this direction met with immediate success. Mrs Basak suddenly pushed back her chair and stood up, declaring that she would rather have her breakfast in the kitchen with the servants than suffer vulgar speech and behaviour so early in the day. The explosive situation was defused by the timely intervention of Sarla who rushed in with a knee-length housecoat and wheedled her "didimoni" into wrapping it around her naked legs.

*

Around ten in the morning, Mrs Basak and I drove out of the bungalow in a black, chauffeur-driven Morris Minor which, I presumed, was reserved for the memsahib's joyrides in the countryside. In about fifteen minutes we were driving through the Rose Valley tea estate which stretched over five hundred acres. During our journey I was continuously distracted by Mrs Basak's intoxicating perfume, her golden locks and her glistening lips painted a light pink, and thus partly missed her interesting anecdotes on the origins of tea. She gave me thumb-nail sketches of some well-known British planters of yore, including Mr Mackenzie, the former owner of Rose Valley who had replaced all wooden structures with brick and iron and constructed the massive boundary walls as he had a premonition of dying a horrible death either in a big fire or a midnight assault on his bungalow by his disgruntled factory workers. Mrs Basak called all of them "characters" and described with relish their little idiosyncracies. There was one David Mottle who ate peas with a knife and wore brown shoes with a morning coat, none of which, I pointed out, seemed interesting enough to qualify him as a bona fide "character", but Mrs Basak gave me a withering look and said, "They aren't done in good society" and I nodded. There was nothing funny about Gower Johnson who was hacked to death by his own labourers, but there were others like Freddy Thompson who was a good bass and could sing "Auld Lang Syne" as well as the Welsh song "Dean Cadalan", though he was neither a Scot nor an Irishman. Among the minor celebrities were Jim Loney (gloomy on Sundays) and Clive Crowe who married a Khasia woman who amused her husband's friends in the Planter's Club by mimicking his Yorkshire accent: "Oop at the froont, loovey!" Even as I enjoyed these interesting anecdotes I toyed with the delightful, though far-fetched, possibility of a stray bumblebee appearing from nowhere and swooping down on Mrs Basak's nose, making her fling herself on my bosom in panic and in the process pressing her full, luscious lips on mine for ten golden seconds. My musings came to an abrupt halt as I heard Mrs Basak's rather impatient voice: "But you aren't taking any notes, Mrs Mitra! How will you write your book?"

"From memory, Mrs Basak," I assured her, heaving a sigh. "I have a good memory. I can still recite *Lucy Gray* from beginning to end."

"That's very remarkable, I must say. But, still, I can't approve of your technique. We shouldn't rely too much on our memories. Now, look to your right, Mrs Mitra. That's the clone nursery, the place where your story should logically begin."

I feigned interest in the drab bamboo and thatch shade housing thousands of polythene bags, each containing a tea sapling, and scribbled a few lines in my notebook. During our one-and-a-half-hour tour of Rose Valley, Mrs Basak told me everything she thought I should know about Darjeeling tea, the "champagne of teas" as she called it: its varieties — China Jat, China hybrid and Hybrid Darjeeling; special characteristics like "tip" which is actually an abundance of tiny hairs on the underside of the tea leaf and the bud; plucking seasons — the "first flush" beginning in March, the "second flush" in May and the "autumnal" in October; kinds of tea — Green, Orthodox and CTC. I filled several pages of my fat notebook and snapped it shut with some relief when Mrs Basak finally decided to get down from the car to show me the delicate art of plucking tea leaves.

"Your pluckers seem to be quite slow, Mrs Basak," I observed as we watched a row of women plucking tea leaves and dropping them in big bamboo baskets slung on their backs.

"Come and show us how to do it faster," invited a lithe young plucker with a broad smile, revealing a set of sparkling white teeth which could have easily earned her a slot in a Colgate ad. I took the challenge and tore off a fistful of leaves, causing Mrs Basak and the women to giggle in unison. "That's not the way to pluck tea leaves, didi," said the Colgate queen and demonstrated the right technique by deftly snipping off a stem with two leaves and a bud which was not actually a bud but a new unfurled leaf.

Only after I had returned to the bungalow, enlightened and thoroughly exhausted, did I discover that I had forgotten to take my Hotshot camera with me, but when I lamented this serious lapse in my work, Mrs Basak consoled me that the changing beauty of the terraced tea gardens at different hours of the day could be caught only in pastel or watercolour and she advised me to engage an illustrator for this job.

*

In the afternoon, the Basaks invited the Khannas, owners of the adjoining Lebong tea estate, for tea and tennis. Some deckchairs were set out in the garden and Mrs Basak made several trips to the kitchen to see that the cakes and pastries were ready and the momos, which had to be served with a florid, pungent sauce, were done strictly according to her Tibetan recipe. Mr Khanna was a big, thickset man in his late thirties, though his hair had prematurely greyed around the temples. He was in the habit of pumping his host's hand after cracking a trite little joke and roaring boisterously "Haw-haw-haw!" His wife was as round as a pumpkin, very cheerful, overdressed and easy-going. Teesta had a tough time taming the two unruly Khanna brats, Bunty and Kukku, who hurled stones at Becky and Lord Steyne, climbed the ornamental lampposts, uprooted some dahlias and marigolds, brought down a few orchid and fern baskets on the veranda, streaked in and out of the house screaming like banshees and called me "Ghoom witch" on account of my numerous scars. Mrs Khanna giggled indulgently even as she bawled out: "You goonda-bodmas-rascal! Ask apology to auntie quick-quick or I will make Bata shoes with your hides."

While Mr Basak and Mr Khanna sipped their gin and tonics, cracking jokes and pumping hands, I noticed Mrs Basak's anxious eyes darting back to her desecrated garden even as she tried to respond to Mrs Khanna's sensational story about the recent theft of fifty tea-chests from the warehouse at Lebong. "You can't even imagine how clever those thieves were, Mrs Basak," gushed Mrs Khanna, her saucer-shaped eyes bulging in horror. "They dug a long-long tunnel under the ware-house, you see, and employed little-little boys who came at night through the tunnel and took away one chest at a time. No one even noticed it till Mr Khanna went to the warehouse on his weekly round and discovered the footprints."

"How terrible!" said Mrs Basak and pressed her lips tight as she watched a helpless Teesta trying unsuccessfully to entice Bunty and Kukku from their orgy of destruction into a sane game of cricket.

"You dirty bodmas boy! What are you doing to my sari?" shrieked Mrs Khanna as Kukku, the younger one, rushed in like a torpedo and blew his nose into his mother's sari before dashing back to his brother. "Very very naughty boy," said Mrs Khanna indulgently. "I don't like his rowdiness at all, Mrs Basak, but Mrs Singh, his class teacher, says, 'Why worry, Mrs Khanna? He will mend when he grows up. It's all right for boys to be naughty.' Now, I was telling you about those clever burglars . . ."

Mrs Basak suddenly excused herself and rushed back to the house, probably to take an inventory of the damage already done to her garden and try to save it from further devastation. Unfortunately, Mrs Basak had already introduced me to Mrs Khanna as an up-and-coming journalist and Mrs Khanna now pressed me to visit Lebong and write a sensational story in a Calcutta newspaper. She complained that the local police were not showing any interest in catching the thieves. "Take as many snapshots as you want, Mrs Mitra, I won't object," she assured me. "Just imagine! Fifty chests of best quality Lebong tea smuggled out over seven nights!"

I suffered Mrs Khanna's repetitious lamentations for about ten minutes, then excused myself to fetch my shawl from the house. I felt I should help Mrs Basak to pacify the Khanna kids but I found that Sarla had already accomplished that difficult job by dragging them to the kitchen and setting them loose on a tray of chocolate eclairs.

After tea it was time for a friendly game of tennis. Mrs Basak changed into a white pleated skirt revealing her smooth, shapely legs. Mr Basak also looked very elegant and dashing in shorts and a T-shirt and Teesta, for once, donned sensible sportswear, earning an appreciative nod from her mother. Mrs Khanna was too fat for tennis and I opted to be the ball girl, enabling Mr Khanna to claim Mrs Basak as his partner. While the father-daughter pair played aggressive tennis, Mr Khanna looked quite relaxed and was happy to leave most of the shots to his fair partner. Rather than watching the ball, I ogled Mrs Basak's bouncing breasts (and speculated about their shape and size) as she chased the ball around and occasionally rushed to the net to chastise her husband and daughter with a punishing smash or volley. I made a point of shouting "Good shot!" whenever she earned a point, ignoring her opponents' mild protests that a partisan spirit was not expected from a ball girl. Mrs Basak's flushed, pink face soon gathered beads of perspiration like dew drops and a dark stain slowly appeared around her armpits which, I guessed, would be as clean and smooth as her cheeks. After each game I rushed to Mrs Basak to hand her a towel and a glass of cold water and she recognized my services with a smile and a "Thank you, dear". "Oh, dear, don't fuss over me like that, I am not playing at Wimbledon," she protested when I suggested that she should take a bite of banana or apple after each game to replenish her lost energy. Covertly, behind her back, I buried my nose in her towel and sniffed her sweet-sour body odour which was as intoxicating as her perfume.

The match was judiciously abandoned after each team had won a set. Having finished a trayful of eclairs, the Khanna brats had already fallen asleep on the veranda and Mrs Khanna looked somewhat bored without an audience. "One for the road, Mr Basak. Haw-haw-haw!" roared Mr Khanna and tossed off a double gin while his wife, helped by Sarla, carried the sleeping kids to their red Maruti Gypsy.

*

In the evening Teesta barged into my room with a pillow and a blanket and declared, "I am going to share your bed tonight. Any objection?"

"No, my dear," I said. "In fact I am not used to sleeping alone."

"Nor am I."

Teesta threw her blanket and pillow on my bed and flopped down into the chair, putting up her legs on the headboard to assume her favourite sitting posture. She wore a fluffy red-and-white kitty cardigan over her loose pyjamas.

"What type of dog is that?" I asked, pointing at her bosom.

"Mum says it's Yorkshire terrier, but I think it's a cross between a Bhutanese and a Pomeranian. I haven't disturbed you, Mrs Mitra, have I?"

"Not at all."

"May I call you Hem? I reckon you are almost my age."

"I am twenty-three, my dear," I lied, picking up my glasses from the side table.

Teesta grinned and wiggled her toes. "Come on, Hem, you can't fool me. Let's be chums and share our little secrets. You know, Mrs Hore got caught because she didn't take me into her confidence."

I cringed a little as I perceived the implicit threat in her friendly appeal. She noted my hesitation and promptly shifted herself to my side. "I won't betray you, darling, I promise," she said, throwing her pudgy arm across my shoulder. She looked very sincere and moreover she had already seen through me, so I felt I might as well confide my real identity to her and win her over to my side as Mr Basak had suggested in the morning. I started telling her about my football career and how it was interrupted by my disastrous marriage, but Teesta was actually interested only in my relationship with her dad. She insisted that I should disclose everything about my affair with Mr Basak. I told her that though her dad had initially taken a fancy to me, I had rejected his advances and now we were on friendly terms.

"The Basaks start skirt-chasing right from their cradle and stop only when they are thrown on the funeral pyre," observed Teesta with a malicious chuckle.

I nodded. "You are absolutely right. Wasn't Lord Hiren over sixty when he took Isobelle as his mistress?"

"Yeah. The old goat had one foot in the grave when he seduced that petite hussy who was young enough to be his granddaughter. Still, I can't help liking my Don Juanish dad because he is so smart and warm. When I was a child, he occasionally allowed me to slip into his bed in the early hours, after Mum had left the room, and play with his limp prick for a while." I was shocked to the core by Teesta's candid confession, though she sounded very casual, as if she was talking about a child playing with a spent cartridge.

"One morning while I was playing with his dick it suddenly grew very big and stiff and squirted a little sticky stuff on my palm and I cried, 'Dad, what's this gummy thing you are peeing on my hand?' and Dad said, 'Phlegm, darling. Sir John has caught a cold and has given his first little sneeze.' Whatever you say, I like Dad's openness. A good sport, isn't he?"

I nodded mechanically and wondered if she still had access to her Dad's crotch.

"But Mum is entirely a different type, I tell you," confided Teesta. "All you can expect from her are a few hackneyed English tablets like 'Keep a stiff upper lip', 'It's not done' and 'One must draw the line somewhere.' I don't remember her cuddling me like Dad. Pretty boring, isn't she? I can't really blame Dad for shacking up with Lola. You know, Mum and Dad don't even share the same bed any more."

"How sad!" My hunch that Mrs Basak was a superb actress was at last vindicated by Teesta's spectacular revelation.

"But the queerest thing about this couple is that they don't split up," observed Teesta. "I suspect that Dad still loves Mum but she won't allow him to enter her bedroom."

"But why does he live with Lola then?" I couldn't help asking. "And why does he pick up dark, ugly creatures like me and Mrs Hore if he loves your Mum?"

Teesta looked at the ceiling and struck a meditative posture. "I think it's in their blood, this unbridled passion for dark, sensual women. The Basaks will always marry respectable, fair-skinned women to flaunt them in Society, but carry on with darkies, preferably a woman with a blemished face. Even Lola is as black as coal."

"Really? I and many of my friends at Champaboti always thought that she was a pretty, fair-skinned woman."

"Not at all, my dear. That's why Lola gets only bit parts — the hero's long-suffering mother or his crooked aunt — though she is not that old. You have to know the origins of the Basaks to understand their morbid passion for dark, scarred women. Are you feeling sleepy, Hem?"

"Oh, no. Please carry on. I am really curious to know a little more about the Basaks."

The Basaks, originally known as Vishakhs, were one of those nomadic tribes of Rajasthan which, unable to earn a livelihood from their traditional occupations, joined the ranks of the thuggees, the much-dreaded Kali-worshipping bandits who waylaid merchants at night and looted them after strangling their victims with a cord. When Warren Hastings declared war against the thuggees and the East India Company started rounding up these notorious brigands, Gumru Vishakh saved his precious life by taking shelter with a group of Vanjaras, yet another nomadic Rajasthani tribe who kept moving from place to place in their caravans, earning their livelihood as ironmongers. The Vanjaras were a matriarchal tribe fond of bright, colourful, mirror-studded dresses, chunky silver ornaments, dogs, tobacco and virile, unattached men whom they used as studs to increase their numbers. As soon as all the fertile women in the tribe had conceived, the Vanjaras threw out the men from their caravans. They kept only the girls and abandoned the boys after they were old enough to beg or steal for a living.

For the Vanjaras Gumru Vishakh was just one such faceless stud who found the host community less hostile because the tribe had been reduced to a dozen women by the ravages of a cholera epidemic. Most of the Vanjara women were past their prime, but they volunteered to be impregnated to save the clan from extinction. In fact, the young Gumru was encouraged to stay with the tribe and offer his valuable services a second time after the women had delivered their first bunch of babies. While camping near Lucknow, the Vanjaras were temporarily engaged by Amjad Ali Shah, the then Nawab of Oudh, to produce thousands of nuts and bolts required to fix the great collapsible iron bridge his ancestor Sadat Ali Khan had earlier ordered from England to span the River Gomti. Gumru helped the Vanjaras in the smithy and dutifully impregnated all the women, but when the tribal chief gave him his marching orders, he eloped with a robust, pox-blighted woman of the tribe and settled near Faizabad as a blacksmith. Gumru was subsequently engaged by the Lucknow Residency to produce horse-shoes and garden implements, but it was the help he rendered to Sir Colin Campbell's army during the Mutiny, when he rescued some

English women, children and wounded soldiers from the beleaguered Residency, that changed Gumru's fortune. The East India Company, in recognition of his great service to "angrezlok", gave him the "patta" of five villages in Katwa, Burdwan, and also bestowed on him the title of "Rajah" along with a coat of arms showing a pair of hissing cobras guarding a glittering diamond.

Rajah Gumru soon built a massive fortress at Katwa and later a European-style mansion at Alipore, Calcutta. He got his passport to Calcutta society when, in January 1897, he was invited by Sir Alexander Mackenzie to attend a glittering ball at Belvedere, which became Calcutta's most talked about social event of the year because Lady Mackenzie had chosen this particular occasion to arrange Calcutta's first private display of electricity, lighting up her ballroom with five cut-glass electroliers and eighteen wall brackets. Eventually, Gumru made himself indispensable as Lady Anne Mason's most reliable partner at the whist table. In fact, it was her royal connections that helped Gumru earn his knighthood in 1905, whereupon he anglicized his name as Sir Gomer Basak. As the pox-blighted Vanjara woman was considered unsuitable for display in society, Sir Gomer promptly degraded her to the status of mistress and married Sally Hack, a buxom, freckle-faced brunette of twenty-three summers whose surveyor husband had been devoured by a hungry cheetah the previous year when he was camping in the jungle of Hazaribagh.

The precedent (of marrying a respectable, fair-skinned woman, preferably a Caucasian, and keeping a dark mistress, preferably with a blemished face) was assiduously followed by the later Basaks like a commandment. Thus, while Lord Hiren married Champaboti and dallied with Isobelle, both fair and respectable women, neither of them knew that in his crumbling palace at Katwa he was secretly keeping Moti, a dark woman of Vanjara extraction who was rumoured to have warmed the beds of three successive generations of Basaks, including Mr Gour Basak, the honourable MP of Katwa.

"Dad is attracted to you because you look so exotic, so Vanjara-like," said Teesta, after she had concluded this turbulent history.

"I think I should take the first bus to New Jalpaiguri tomorrow morning," I said. "I don't feel safe here any longer."

Teesta laughed and patted me. "Don't be frightened, Hem. Dad won't trouble you unless, of course, you give him the glad eye."

"After that ghastly story about your ancestors, I fear I will have a bad dream tonight," I said.

"Quite possibly, but I am here to drive away the ghosts," assured Teesta.

But, contrary to my apprehensions, I had a very sweet dream that night in which Mrs Basak appeared outside my window as a tennis-playing angel and beckoned me to follow her. I told her I had no racquet. "Take your football gear with you, my dear," whispered Mrs Basak in her dreamy voice. "On our way to the heavenly court, you can exchange it with a football-playing angel." That was very clever of Mrs Basak, I thought, and got out of my bed to put on my football gear. What a divine experience it was to float through the window like a patch of autumn cloud and follow Mrs Basak across the horizon with so many stars twinkling all around us like rubies and diamonds!

*

In the morning I learnt that, on receiving a midnight telephone call from his political boss, Mr Basak had left for Delhi to attend an emergency party meeting. Mrs Basak seemed sad and slightly distraught (or was it just another example of her superb acting?), but I thought she looked even more enchanting in her new role of the demure and slightly aggrieved wife of a busy politician.

"I think a midterm election is around the corner," observed Teesta who, for once, sat properly with her feet firmly planted on the carpet and a tea napkin spread primly on her lap.

"I don't like these midnight calls," pouted Mrs Basak. "They remind me of those horrible Emergency days." She poured tea for Teesta, showing that she could be an affectionate mother if only her daughter obeyed the dictates of decency and decorum.

"I don't like politics," I opined, shovelling a sizeable chunk of cheese omelette into my mouth. "Politicians are mostly crooks and liars."

"Which is one good reason why the Heggs never contested an election for a seat in the Lower House, though there had been several peers in my family," said Mrs Basak, stirring her tea. "In fact, my great grandfather, Lord Algernon Heggs' famous speech on the decline of English agriculture is still quoted whenever there is a debate on the subject."

"Sister Francesca says that the Heggs must have originated either in the Scottish Highlands or in the Yorkshire moors and later migrated to South England," observed Teesta quite innocently.

Mrs Basak's face hardened and her eyes blazed. "I don't want to make any uncharitable remarks about your Australian nun, Tee, but you can tell her that the Heggs have an undisputed southern origin. The South Hams of Devon, stretching from Totnes to Plymouth, was the region where my ancestors flourished. In fact, 'Heggs Cove' near Dartmouth figures in the Domesday Book, which anyone can consult in the old Norman church at Woolbridge. Incidentally, that church also preserves, among other historical relics, a mace and a scimitar that my ancestors once wielded to drive away the Normans."

"There you go again, dear Mama," said Teesta with remarkable nonchalance.

I had thought that Teesta had finally offered the olive branch when she had put down her feet and spread the napkin on her lap like a good girl, but now I could see that she had merely changed her tack and the battle between the two continued unabated.

"I don't want to brag about my family," said Mrs Basak assertively, "but I can say that besides those half a dozen peers there have been several Lord Lieutenants and Justices of Peace in my family and some of them were chosen as Masters of Hounds when foxhunting was *de rigueur* among the country elites." Mrs Basak proudly mentioned "Beaconsfield", her family's sprawling Elizabethan mansion with its walled parks, game preserves, a farm, estate cottages, lawns, gardens and some carefully contrived wilderness created by "Capability" Brown, the famous eighteenth-century landscape gardener. She also referred to her family's close relations with Baroness Trestleton of Mugbury and Sir Peter Gumsey, the third earl of Lupinsville.

"Poor Mum!" exclaimed Teesta with a hint of sarcasm. "With such an impeccable aristocratic background, you should have married Prince Charles rather than my poor dad."

"I am not going to discuss my personal life with you, Tee," snapped Mrs Basak.

"Oh Mum, don't be so serious. Can't you see it was just in fun?" said Teesta.

"Fun? What do you mean by fun?" Mrs Basak demanded haughtily. "I can't allow my family's good name to be traduced by a Basak with a Thug for an ancestor."

Teesta giggled unashamedly. "Come on, Mum, calm down. When Adam delved and Eve span who was then the gentleman? No one, of course. What did your people do for a living, Hem?"

"They were mostly cowherds," I said. "My father's people, the Ghosh-Dastidars, originally came from Gava, now in Bangladesh, which I've heard was famous for its dairy products."

"Quite a respectable clan," said Teesta. "The Heggs were of course a cut above us. They were originally tile-makers, weren't they, Mum?"

"Decorative slates," corrected Mrs Basak. "Heggs Slates were much in demand all over Devon and much beyond in medieval times. They still hang them artistically like fish scales on the upper storeys. The Heggs, of course, didn't stay long in this profession as they later joined the burghers of Totnes and eventually became landed aristocrats, acquiring Darlington Hall where Christopher Blackwell was a regular visitor."

I feigned surprise and awe (by rounding my eyes and making suitable exclamations) at the swift and spectacular rise of the Heggs from humble tile-makers to nobility, though I could hardly follow Mrs Basak's narrative with so many foreign names and places cluttering her family history. Somehow it reminded me of my mother trying to impress us with her illustrious father, the Government-approved tube-well contractor, who "moved in the best Society of his time". Having fully restored the prestige and honour of the mighty Heggs, Mrs Basak now stood up, flashing a victorious smile at both of us. "Sorry, dears, I have letters to write," she mumbled and vanished into the house without giving her daughter a chance to pose yet another disturbing question about her forebears.

"I am not at all convinced," said Teesta, drawing up her legs to assume her favourite posture. "I never was. Whatever she might say, I am quite sure that Mum doesn't have an aristocratic background. Sister Francesca says the name 'Heggs' must be derived from haggis, the staple diet of the Scots. She says the Devonians love singing 'Widdecombe Fair' but I have never heard Mum humming that song. She is definitely a Scot because it's only those penny-pinching Scots who emigrate to the farthest corners of the earth to hook rich husbands. I am sure no sensible upper-class English woman would do that."

I was appalled by Teesta's low opinion of her mother and felt duty bound to rescue Mrs Basak's honour. "I beg to differ, Teesta," I said very firmly, though I knew almost nothing about England and its regional oddities. "Mrs Basak looks every inch an aristocrat and her impeccable behaviour also testifies to her high birth and good upbringing."

"You will certainly change your views if you get to know her a little more intimately."

"I wish to do that at the earliest opportunity."

"Best of luck, but be careful. She can be mean, if she wants to. Just like a true Scot."

Mrs Basak was very sweet to me during lunch. She looked very relaxed as Teesta had retired to her room with some kebabs and bread sticks, declaring that she hadn't come home to worsen her upset tummy with gallons of thukpa and tasteless boiled chicken. I would have been happy to join Teesta, but my surging love for Mrs Basak glued me to the chair. I casually scooped up a spoonful of thukpa and wistfully watched Mrs Basak's rosy lips parting sensually to tuck in a piece of boiled chicken. She chewed her meat so daintily that whatever little doubt I had about her aristocratic origins vanished and I was quite convinced that her ill-dressed daughter had spouted her venom out of sheer jealousy because she knew that with her plump figure and plain looks she would never achieve her mother's high stature.

It was drizzling outside and the sky was overcast, threatening a downpour at any moment. Mrs Basak lamented that she wouldn't be able to take me to the factory that day to show me the tea-processing techniques which, she assured me, were "quite fascinating". "Sarla tells me that the Darjeeling bandh is over," she said, "so we can go to Tiger Hill tomorrow morning to see the sunrise over Kanchenjunga."

"Thank you, Mrs Basak. Since Mr Basak isn't here, I am afraid I will have to depend on you for whatever little sightseeing I can squeeze in between my visits to the tea garden."

"I'd love to show you around, Mrs Mitra. If the weather holds we can even drive up to Kurseong and Kalimpong to visit a few orchidariums and some old Tibetan monasteries."

"That would be really wonderful, Mrs Basak."

"If you aren't too busy after lunch, we might perhaps retire to the library for a little chat," suggested Mrs Basak.

"I am absolutely free, Mrs Basak," I said, thrilled by her invitation.

*

I had feared that Mrs Basak would unleash a virulent diatribe against her wayward daughter and trot out some more invincible proofs of her Devon origin, but she was in a lighter mood and asked Sarla to bring her some port. With a smart flick of her lighter she lit a Classic kingsize from a packet left behind by her husband and exhaled the smoke with a gentle twist of her lips, just like her husband. "I generally avoid smoking and drinking in front of the children," she confided, resting her feet on a pouffe. "They can appreciate hard rock but not a mum who smokes and drinks in public. Don't you think that's very funny, Mrs Mitra?"

I nodded. "We are custom-bound, Mrs Basak. In our society people don't like women who smoke or drink."

Sarla brought in a decanter and two goblets. She poured the dark red wine in one glass and looked at her mistress. "No Sarla, I don't think Mrs Mitra would like to drink," said Mrs Basak. "Now pull the curtains and open the windows just a little. It's rather stuffy in here."

The semicircular library was lined with glass-fronted bookcases containing thick, awe-inspiring volumes the likes of which one confronts in a lawyer's chamber. Some journals, including a few back issues of *Parliament News*, lay on the long rectangular table. Sarla pulled back the heavy velvet curtains, revealing a vegetable patch dominated by cabbage, lettuce and spinach, the three abominable greens which presented themselves at Mrs Basak's dining table with unfailing regularity. It was still raining and the masses of grey clouds hanging low in the sky shut off the view. Mrs Basak looked reflectively into her drink, took a gentle sip and then gazed at my face, as if she was trying to read something there. My heart started pounding; was it possible that Mrs Basak had at last discovered my strong feelings about her?

"I need your help, Mrs Mitra," she said when Sarla had left the room after placing a beautifully carved bamboo ashtray before her.

"I am at your service, Mrs Basak."

Instead of broaching her subject directly, Mrs Basak told me about her life in Calcutta which, I learnt, was occupied by three main activities: playing golf in the morning, running her art gallery – Maxine's – during the day and attending the Calcutta Ladies' Club in the evening. That famous club, established by Lady Moyra in 1859, was going through a bad patch ever since Mr Thapar, the chairman of Footania Fast Food Industries, which owned the five-storey building adjoining the club's modest two-storey structure, had started sending feelers to the club's president, Mrs Jeejaboy, about buying the club. Footania needed the prime land to construct a highrise building for their future expansion and diversification programmes and they had already offered twenty lakh rupees, but Mrs Jeejaboy had made it quite clear that the prestigious club was not for sale. I interrupted Mrs Basak to tell her that the Marwari and the Gujarati businessmen were buying up a large number of old, dilapidated buildings all over Calcutta and constructing highrise apartment buildings in their place. It was a racket, no doubt, but big money was changing hands and the Calcutta Corporation was doing nothing to stop the illegal transactions.

"But have you ever thought about doing an article about this, about how they are spoiling Calcutta's skyline and its environment?" asked Mrs Basak.

"Oh yes," I said. "In fact I have been toying with the idea for quite some time but couldn't do a piece for want of evidence."

"I will provide you with all the necessary details about Footania's takeover bid," Mrs Basak assured me. "The world should know how a prestigious institution, one hundred and thirty years old, is being threatened by a jumped-up junk-food seller who once ran a grimy take-home tandoori food joint near Dharmotolla crossing. The worst part of it is that some club members are secretly helping Mr Thapar."

"Do I smell a scandal, Mrs Basak?"

Mrs Basak nodded and explained that after constant pressure from some very influential circles, the club had admitted about two dozen young members during the past two years without checking their backgrounds and antecedents, allowing them to jump the long waiting list. Notable among these lucky entrants was one Miss Rekha Jhajoria, a non-resident Indian living in London, who visited Calcutta every year in the winter like a migratory bird and tried her best to influence the members, particularly her young friends, in favour of Mr Thapar. This, coupled with the fact that the junk-food baron's offers to buy up the club always coincided with Miss Jhajoria's homecoming, naturally gave rise to a suspicion among the members that Miss Jhajoria was in league with Mr Thapar. As the vice-president of the club, Mrs Basak was of course doing everything possible to thwart Miss Jhajoria's evil plans, but she felt a little help from the fourth estate could make her job easier. What apparently troubled Mrs Basak most was that Miss Jhajoria was fast emerging as a contender for the president's chair which would fall vacant next year on the expiry of Mrs Jeejaboy's five-year term. To kill two birds with one stone, Mrs Basak wanted me to write an article which would expose the Thapar-Jhajoria nexus and what it portended for the club, projecting Mrs Basak as the most suitable candidate for the president's post. She lamented that none of the English papers she had approached had showed any interest in her story, so she thought she might, as a last resort, try her luck with a Bengali newspaper if only she could find a friendly journalist. I assured her that I would write a venomous piece that would crush her rival and pave the way for her victory in next year's election. Mrs Basak thanked me profusely and then said, "I suppose you have to observe certain journalistic conventions and there is also that bogey of libel, so I think it wouldn't be proper to use Miss Jhajoria's name in your article. I can however give you a thumbnail sketch of Miss Jhajoria so that everyone will recognize who you are talking about. She is a tall, plump, loud and preposterous Marwari girl with a flat in Belsize Park, London."

"That will come in handy for my article, Mrs Basak," I said, suppressing a yawn. Mrs Basak took the hint and smiled. "Sorry to detain you so long, Mrs Mitra. I know I mustn't press you, but do you think you can finish your article within a couple of days?"

Suddenly, the name of Mrs Hore leaped to my mind. Attempting a demonstration of Sogetsu-style Ikebana had proved fatal for her and now writing an article for Mrs Basak could be my Waterloo. I realized that I had foolishly walked into a trap set by Mr Basak to punish me for my refusal to accept his dirty offer. "But you don't understand Bengali, Mrs Basak, do you?" I asked, just to make sure that she wouldn't demand a rough draft of the article by the evening.

"I am really ashamed not to have learnt your beautiful language, Mrs Mitra," said Mrs Basak. "But Gour will be back by Saturday and he will translate the piece for me."

I realized that with Mrs Basak breathing down my neck, it would be too risky to enjoy Rose Valley's lavish hospitality for even another day, so I decided that early next morning I would sneak out of the house, leaving behind a chit for Mrs Basak.

"I will start writing my article tonight," I assured her and stood up.

"Not tonight," said Mrs Basak. "Tonight you must go to bed very early as we have to start for Tiger Hill at three tomorrow morning."

*

I had thought Tiger Hill would be deserted because of the Gorkhaland agitation and the chilly weather, but when we arrived there a crowd of around two hundred, including a fair sprinkling of foreigners, was milling around, waiting to catch the spectacular sunrise over Kanchenjunga on film. As the three-storeyed glass watchtower was closed, some of the tourists had perched on boulders or branches of trees to have a better view of the spectacle.

"Can you climb trees, Mrs Basak?" I asked, looking around for a suitable perch.

"No need to risk our limbs, Mrs Mitra," said Mrs Basak, slightly alarmed. "People are mad. If I knew the tower would be locked up, I would have brought two folding chairs for us. Let's sit on the grass and wait for sunrise."

But minutes rolled into an hour and still there was no indication of the sun making any serious effort to heave itself up over the horizon. All I could see in the eastern sky was a frozen sea of grey clouds through which a few inches of Kanchenjunga peeped out just to assure us that it was not a figment of our imagination. A dirty, snot-nosed Nepali boy with a dirtier kettle and a few earthen tumblers was trying to sell his tea among the tourists but very few patronized him. Mrs Basak too tried to shoo him away, but he came back to us after an unsuccessful round and begged us to drink his brew and get refreshed before the great spectacle unfolded before our eyes.

"I think we shall have to oblige this persevering urchin," said Mrs Basak sulkily. She took a two-rupee coin from her purse and dropped it on the outstretched palm of the teaboy who gave a little grin of triumph as he poured a dark brown concoction into two tumblers and carefully set them on the ground before us.

"Don't touch it!" warned Mrs Basak as I reached for my tumbler. "It's dirty and unhygienically prepared and I'm sure it will give you belly cramps." She picked up a twig from the ground and used it as a lever to flick the small tumblers down the hillside, demonstrating her good aim and wrist power.

"When will the sun come up, Mrs Basak?" I asked, suppressing a big yawn. Mrs Basak consulted her watch. "Fifteen to twenty minutes, I reckon. Please note, there is already a subtle change in the colour of the clouds from grey to mauve."

I tried to follow Mrs Basak's intent gaze, anticipating sudden bursts of colour, if not divine music emanating from the distant peak, but nothing whatsoever happened. I yawned and felt I'd better make small talk to kill time.

"Why do they call this place Tiger Hill, Mrs Basak?"

"I don't know, dear," said Mrs Basak with the hint of a frown. "All I know is that the hill is 2591 metres high. I am not sure if tigers once inhabited the mountain slopes, but now, thanks to unbridled poaching, wildlife in this region has dwindled to a few Indian civets, Himalayan flying squirrels and barking deer. But let's not disturb the other tourists who have come from every corner of the globe to watch Nature's most spectacular drama."

I started dozing. A little later I heard Mrs Basak saying, more to herself than me, "Perhaps I should have allowed you that tea."

"I am quite alert, Mrs Basak," I assured her.

But half an hour later, when Nature's big drama finally unfolded before a spellbound audience, I was dozing peacefully with my head buried in my chest. Mrs Basak woke me up with a mild shake. I rubbed my eyes, saw a glimpse of the spectacle and clapped ecstatically, shouting "Good show!" as I felt that even God needed a little encouragement now and then to put on His show tirelessly every morning. Some foreign tourists who were frenziedly clicking away around us shushed me and an American wondered aloud why the "goddamn authorities" couldn't keep Tiger Hill free of screaming banshees. I turned my head and shouted, "You shithead! Who do you think you are? I will do what I like. Tiger Hill isn't your father's estate." And I clapped again to show that I meant it.

"Oh no!" hissed a shocked Mrs Basak. "Please, Mrs Mitra, don't behave like a rowdy football fan." But amidst the flurry of shush-shushings and loud protests from all sides, I distinctly heard someone clapping on my far left, probably to express solidarity with me. I turned my head and spotted Khusi, our hefty Champaboti goalkeeper, who was sharing a boulder with a thin, quiet-looking young man and a chubby little boy.

"Khusi!" I cried, overjoyed at seeing an old schoolmate after so long. "Never thought we would meet again."

"Ditto!" shouted back Khusi, ignoring her husband's pleadings to keep quiet.

"Please keep quiet, Mrs Mitra," implored Mrs Basak. "This is not the moment to revive old friendships."

"Meet you later, Khusi," I shouted. "We shouldn't disturb the tourists."

"But we are going back by the 11.30 bus, Hem," shouted Khusi. "Someday I will come to the Maidan to see you and Tama."

"Do come," I said and ducked my head, panic-stricken. What if Khusi started blabbing about the good old days at Champaboti and that violent charity match with Chetla? Thank God, we were separated from each other by at least four boulders and a hundred heads and she was leaving Darjeeling in a few hours.

"Is she in sports?" asked Mrs Basak in a whisper, even as she watched the sunrise through her binoculars.

"Yes. A prized member of our school basketball team. She could net a ball from 25 yards."

"I may be wrong but her exuberance smacks of a more popular game. Here, Mrs Mitra, look at this glorious scene through the binoculars."

Ten minutes later, we threaded our way through the crowd towards our car. I was about to get in when I felt a tug at my leather jacket, and turning round I found a beaming Khusi with her husband and child in tow. "Meet my hubby Barnik, Hem," said Khusi. "I've told him so much about our dream team that he begged me to introduce him to you."

"Glad to meet you, Barnik," I mumbled and joined my palms for a traditional greeting. The meek and slightly nervous young man, wearing an ill-fitting tweed coat and a muffler round his neck, returned my "namaskar" with a smile and made a deferential bow to Mrs Basak who stood aloof near the bonnet and looked at us with a slightly puzzled expression.

"That's Mrs Basak, a good friend of mine," I said. "Sorry, Khusi, we have to rush to keep an appointment."

But Khusi couldn't be shaken off so easily; she was keen to revive our old friendship and show off to her hubby what glorious days she had spent at Champaboti.

"Where's your hubby, Hem? I heard he is in a mental . . ."

"Died in a car crash recently," I blurted out. "You can see all these scars on my face."

"How sad! But surely that one just above your upper lip must be from that charity match with Chetla?" Khusi turned to her husband with an ear-to-ear grin. "I told you about that famous match, didn't I?"

Barnik nodded and smiled.

"Let's forget that minor incident," I said as sweat broke out on my forehead even in that chilly weather. Desperate to divert Khusi from soccer, I pinched her son's cheek and cooed, "What a cute little boy you have got, Khusi! What's his name?"

"Tublu," said Khusi and prodded her thumb-sucking son who had been watching me with some curiosity. "Tublu, make a pranam to your auntie." The child squirmed and hid his face in a fold of his mother's sari.

"Shy boy . . . Sushil Mallik was of course the villain of the piece in that match. Remember?"

"The famous Mohan Bagan striker?" said Barnik with evident curiosity.

"Yes, who else?" pouted Khusi. "The rogue. It was his bad refereeing that . . ."

"Khusi, I am so sorry . . . we have to rush. Mrs Basak is waiting for me." I turned to beckon Mrs Basak's driver who was standing at a respectable distance, picking his teeth. "Narbahadur, let's start. We are already late . . . Mrs Basak, may I introduce you to my good friend Khusi?"

"But I am afraid I don't know much about soccer, Mrs Mitra," said Mrs Basak icily without budging an inch from her position near the bonnet.

"Why, Hem, doesn't your memsahib friend enjoy football?" whispered Khusi, but it was such a loud whisper that one could hear it from a distance of fifty yards.

"She is at present slightly allergic to soccer, but I am sure she will soon succumb to its divine charms," I assured my friend even as I met Mrs Basak's scorching look, realizing that the game was up and all I could do now was to put on a brave face.

After another five minutes of tittle-tattle during which Khusi declared how proud she was to see that at least two of her former teammates hadn't hung up their jerseys, we parted and I climbed into the car, anticipating an explosion from Mrs Basak. The presence of Narbahadur, however, protected me, for the time being, from her wrath.

During the return journey to Darjeeling Mrs Basak sat as stiff as a ramrod with her fingers locked on her lap, her eyes fixed on the road. When we reached Ladenla Road Mrs Basak got out of the car and declared that she would have her breakfast at Keventer's and I could join her if I wished. I meekly followed her to the open-air restaurant and sat at one of those green tables with an umbrella planted at the middle. No one had so far divulged to me exactly what she had done to Mrs Hore but it must have been something quite terrible to make the servants still talk about that ill-fated lady in hushed tones. Maybe after a last treat at Keventer's (in the time-honoured tradition of offering a good meal to a convict awaiting execution) she would take me straight to the police station and hand me over to the inspector with an inventory of charges against me. Or was Mrs Basak turning over in her mind some harsher and more humiliating English punishment for me?

Mrs Basak ordered bacon, eggs and coffee for herself and for me a plate of vegetable sandwiches and a milkshake, making it amply clear that she was no longer obliged to show me the courtesy due to a genuine guest. Fifteen uneasy minutes passed, the food arrived but Mrs

Basak still maintained her stony silence. I coughed to clear my throat and said, "I am extremely sorry, Mrs Basak . . . I told a couple of silly lies . . ."

Mrs Basak didn't respond.

"I can explain everything if you . . ." I ventured.

"You needn't take the trouble," snapped Mrs Basak even as she peppered her bacon.

"Surely, playing football isn't an unpardonable sin?"

"But impersonating a bereaved journalist is," said Mrs Basak curtly.

"It was actually Mr Basak's idea."

"I didn't ask for an explanation."

A real tough nut, Mrs Basak. There was nothing I could say to break the ice. "Shall I now drive you to the Mall, ma'am?" asked Narbahadur as we came out of Keventer's.

"Yes, of course," I said. "Let's do some shopping and then visit a few curio shops."

"We won't do any shopping today, Narbahadur," said Mrs Basak very firmly. "Drive straight to Rose Valley."

*

The moment I reached the bungalow, I rushed to Teesta's room and told her about what had happened on Tiger Hill. "I must get out of this house at once before she calls the police or does something more awful," I said, breathless, but Teesta clasped my hands and trilled merrily, "She has queered the pitch for you, darling, hasn't she? But don't worry, we will fight back if she takes any vindictive measures. You aren't really afraid of Mum, are you?"

"Not at all, but I feel I am now *persona non grata* in Rose Valley and I shouldn't stay here any longer. You know, I wanted to explain everything but your mother flatly refused to hear my side of the story."

"That's the stiff upper lip, my dear. Let her stew in her own juice. You must not leave this place till Dad returns."

"But suppose she turns hostile? How long can I hold out against her?"

"At least three days, I reckon. That's the period after which my parole from St Catherine's prison expires. If Dad doesn't turn up by that time to set things right, we will leave this shitty place together, but before we go we must teach Mean Max a good lesson. A star footballer like you shouldn't chicken out at the slightest hint of trouble. Right?" She stretched out her arm with an impish smile.

"All right, I will stay," I said and clasped her hand firmly in solidarity.

The hazards of being an unwelcome guest at Rose Valley didn't manifest themselves till I came downstairs to lunch and found that the table was laid for me alone and my meal was drastically reduced to rice, a thin dal and a mixed vegetable dish consisting of cabbage, carrots and potatoes, the mere sight of which churned my stomach. Sarla stood grimly in a corner of the dining room, probably keeping an eye on the cutlery.

"Is that all, Sarla?" I asked, unable to believe my own eyes. "No fish, no meat!"

"Accept whatever you receive by the grace of God, Mrs Mitra," intoned Sarla stoically.

"Why don't you say 'by the grace of my memsa'b'?" I taunted. "Mr Basak brought me here with the promise of royal treatment and now in his absence you people are forcing me to eat this rubbish as if I am a cow or a constipated old hag."

"Some of our guests didn't even get this three-course meal, Mrs Mitra," Sarla reminded me.

"I am not Mrs Hore, mind you," I pointed out even as I reached for the plate of rice. "You can't flush me out of this house with veg meals. If I want to stay, I stay. Now bring me some good pickles if you don't want me to create a big scene."

"You shouldn't have accepted that stuff," said Teesta when I told her about my spartan meal. "Wait till midnight and then we will raid the larder and have a grand buffet. If we can get into the wine cellar we will take out a bottle of champagne."

"Do you also drink wine and liquor like your mum?" I asked in surprise.

"Only champagne, my dear."

In the evening I waved away the bowl of milk and chapatis Sarla brought me in my room, and to express solidarity Teesta also refused to go downstairs for supper. She sent Lord Steyne and Becky down in her place and they came back after some time, smacking their lips and wagging their tails. Teesta picked up Lord Steyne and brought her nose close to the dog's muzzle and declared, "Wow! Mean Max must be guzzling Murgh-masallam tonight for a change!" I promptly picked up Becky and sniffed her mouth. "Delicious!" I exclaimed. "Smells like butter chicken. I hope we get some of this heavenly stuff in the kitchen."

But, alas, our midnight raid didn't even yield a loaf of bread, let alone butter chicken and champagne. The larder was locked, so was the cellar. After a thorough search of the kitchen shelves we came back with a few half-rotten apples, a carrot, a few soggy Britannia biscuits and a lump of sugar. "Mean Max somehow anticipated our plan and has locked everything up," grumbled Teesta as she sulkily dug her teeth into the apple.

"Is this a Scottish technique?" I asked, chewing my carrot with the lump of sugar. "I mean this starving of unwelcome guests?"

"I don't think so. Even Scots are more humane. I think she is really a Jew though her nose doesn't show it."

"Maybe she has shortened it by plastic surgery."

"Quite possible. But we won't take it lying down. I know where our next meal will come from. In the morning we will go to the factory."

"But I don't want to know another thing about tea."

Teesta grinned. "You won't have to, darling. Mr Ghosh, our manager, will, of course, give us an illuminating lecture on tea but we will just grin and bear it and then we will get our breakfast in the canteen. I am quite sure that Mr Ghosh will arrange some good snacks in our honour."

*

Mr Ghosh, the jovial, paunchy manager of Rose Valley, was happy to receive a young journalist writing on tea. He adjusted his braces and promptly took us on a tour of the factory. We had to suffer an hour-long lecture on the various stages of tea processing before Mr Ghosh rounded off his educative tour by presenting me with a pound of best quality Rose Valley Orange Pekoe tea, specially packed in silver foil, along with his famous "three beauty tips for the ladies": "1. Use strained tea leaves mixed with lemon juice to prevent falling of hair and making it glossy. 2. Steam your face over a bowl of very hot, freshly made tea after adding thin strips of mint leaves to brighten your skin. 3. After a tiring day, bathe your feet in a mixture of cold tea, lime juice and salt to get them into shape." Mr Ghosh then shook hands with us and rushed back to his office to receive a trunk call he was expecting from a Calcutta auction house.

"I'll get Dad to sack this uncivilized creature," declared a crestfallen Teesta.

"I think we should try to bribe Nazir Mian," I suggested, as we set out on our mile-long trek to Rose Valley.

"The idea! Why didn't you drop it before we started out on this futile expedition for breakfast?"

*

When I returned to my room I discovered that in my absence it had been stripped clean of its furniture, carpet, mattress, paintings, even the flower vase, leaving behind the iron cot and just enough bedding to keep me from freezing alive in my sleep. I consulted Teesta immediately and we decided to retaliate by making use of one of Mr Ghosh's beauty tips, the third one. I filled a bucket at the tap and asked Arjun, the young bearer, for lime and salt, but he brought only salt as Sarla wouldn't allow me any lime without her mistress' permission. Undaunted, I emptied the entire packet of Orange Pekoe in the bucket, mixed in some salt and then, sitting regally on my bare cot, dipped my aching feet in the bucket. To our great satisfaction, the abuse of Rose Valley's prime tea created the desired sensation among the servants; they tiptoed up to my door and peeped inside, exchanging ominous glances amongst themselves as if we had committed a sacrilege. Teesta took this opportunity to offer Nazir Mian a bribe of ten rupees to smuggle a tandoori chicken and some plain chapatis into our room, but the god-fearing Muslim cook pinched his earlobes and swore that he couldn't do such "namak haram" while "eating Maxine Memsahib's salt". Finally, it was the old gardener Vrindaban who took pity on us and produced some carrots and tomatoes for our lunch. As we chewed them desolately high-pitched music accompanied by the agonized screams of a female singer assailed us from downstairs. I wondered aloud if it was some Gaelic funeral song.

"It's worse; it's Italian opera." Teesta chucked her half-chewed carrot through the window and said, "I suspect she has Sicilian blood running in her veins. Have you ever seen a more vengeful mother?"

I shook my head and wondered if my mother had some evil Portuguese blood running in her veins.

"But we will give her a fitting reply," said Teesta. "Come with me."

I followed Teesta to her room which, thank God, had not yet been stripped of its furnishings. Teesta had nevertheless managed to give it a ravaged look with her dresses, books and cassettes thrown pell-mell all over the carpet. The walls of the room were plastered with lifesize posters of her favourite rock stars — Tina Turner, Usha Uthup and the most impressive of all, a bald, black woman in a shimmering, star-spangled leotard flailing her heavily chained arms.

"That's Cindy Torrence, the ultimate in hard rock," informed Teesta as she noted my keen interest in this dazzling female in bondage gear. "Cindy's Afro-Caribbean numbers would be a fitting rejoinder to that sickly *Tosca*. Would you like "Hey Hey Hannibal" or "Hoko-poko Tee-dum?""

"Tee-dum sounds better."

"You are perfectly right. Two girls in my dormitory have already confessed that their periods have been advanced by three days after absorbing a powerful blast of that soulful number." Teesta promptly picked up a cassette from the floor, slipped it into her cassette player and turned up the volume. I was impressed by Miss Torrence's formidable lung power and was overwhelmed by the eerie music and the blood-curdling animal cries in the background that powerfully evoked the atmosphere of an African jungle teeming with lions, hyenas and other blood-thirsty beasts chasing one another in the dark.

"Come, let's dance," invited Teesta and she started gyrating, kicking an odd book or a discarded skirt out of her way. I joined her, though with an empty stomach I hardly felt any enthusiasm for dancing.

After about ten minutes, Teesta stopped dancing all of a sudden, clutched her abdomen, and dashed towards the bathroom.

"It's those devilish carrots stirring up mischief," she reported when she came back five minutes later. "Tomatoes settle without any fuss, but those obnoxious carrots. . ."

"They grind and somersault," I said, in the sure knowledge that in about five minutes I would have to follow Teesta's trail.

"Let's stop the music, stretch out and read something soulful," suggested Teesta.

"Good idea. Do you have any comics?"

"Plenty. What's your favourite? *Archie* or *Tintin*?"

"I am not that selective. I read whatever I get."

"In that case I will introduce you to *Judge Dredd*. Terrific! It's the latest craze in our school though Sister Agatha isn't yet ready to roll out the red carpet for Hon'ble Judge Dredd because she thinks he's full of blood and gore. But you can't help spilling a little blood now and then when Mega City One is teeming with lousy crooks and there is only one poor Dredd to sort them out."

"That sounds quite reasonable."

"Our dorm think-tank has decided to hold a theological debate to beat the priggish nuns on their own turf. We have, in fact, persuaded a very scholastic girl from the twelfth grade to write an article entitled 'Is Judge Dredd a true Christian?' in the next issue of our school rag. The answer is of course 'yes', but Luke and Matthew have to be quoted copiously to absolve poor Dredd from the charge of being a trigger-happy random killer. Isn't that clever?"

"Very."

Teesta shoved a much-thumbed copy of *Judge Dredd* towards me and picked up an *Archie* for herself. But before I had turned the first page I had to fling Dredd on her bosom and sprint to the loo.

"Be quick!" shouted Teesta at my back. "My turn will come in another three minutes."

After Teesta's fifth trip, and my third, we decided to flutter the white flag as we felt too weak and dehydrated to continue our battle with Mean Max. We sent feelers to Mrs Basak through Sarla and the latter came back within ten minutes to inform us that Mrs Basak was ready to lift her food embargo provided we accepted her terms uncon-ditionally. She took out a crumpled chit from her blouse and read out, like a royal decree, Mrs Basak's humiliating terms. Teesta would be invited downstairs for a regular Rose Valley supper and a breakfast in the morning if she left for St Catherine's the next day by the ten o'clock bus, and I would get my ordinary dal-chapati-vegetable meal (to be served in my room) at night and a packed breakfast of two cucumber sandwiches and an apple if I left Rose Valley by six next morning.

"This is highly discriminatory and totally unacceptable to us!" cried Teesta, aghast. "This is not South Africa, Sarla. Tell your memsa'b that Hem must have meat and dessert and a good breakfast too like a respectable guest."

Sarla went downstairs to convey our demand to her mistress and came back with a slightly modified menu in which the vegetable dish was replaced by egg curry.

"Shall I accept it?" I asked Teesta.

"Yes." She whispered in my ear that she would pinch some meat and other delicacies from the table when she went downstairs for supper.

There was no mention of tea in the treaty, but in the afternoon Sarla brought us two cups of tea and two soggy Lily biscuits. We took a sip and groaned. "No muscatel flavour!" I exclaimed.

"The horrible CTC stuff they use in those pavement tea stalls," confirmed Teesta, wrinkling her nose. "That's like a true Scot. Even after we have surrendered and accepted her humiliating conditions, she is punishing us for washing our feet with Orange Pekoe."

I had dozed off after my spartan meal, but Teesta shook me awake after a while. "I have brought you meat, darling," she said, beaming. I sprang to my feet. "Meat! Where?"

"There! Look."

As if on cue, Becky and Lord Steyne entered the room with two juicy pieces of curried mutton in their jaws, their small, buttony eyes glittering and their bushy tails hoisted like two flagpoles.

"Oh, God! No, Teesta, I can't snatch meat from a dog's mouth."

"Don't be squeamish, darling. During the Second World War people even devoured human flesh," Teesta reminded me. "They are nice clean dogs and hunger is such a great leveller. Believe me, I tried to fill up my socks with some biryani but Sarla caught me in the act and I had to abandon the idea. I finally tossed two big chunks of meat at the dogs and drove them out of the room. Now, who will you kiss first? I suggest Lord Steyne because he is the less possessive of the two."

So, I picked up Lord Steyne on my lap and somehow managed to dig my teeth into a portion of the meat sticking out of his mouth. We had a sort of tug of war with each of us stubbornly holding on to his/her end of the meat between our clenched teeth. For the first time in my life I had direct contact with canine teeth and for a while I feared Lord Steyne would snap at me but, fortunately, he didn't lose his cool and I finally managed to wrench the piece free from his jaws. Becky, however, was a tough customer and wouldn't surrender her meat so easily, so Teesta had to forcibly prise open her jaws and retrieve the piece for me. The loss of her prize possession affected Becky so much that she started whimpering like a baby. So, after I had chewed off the meat, I presented her with the bone and allowed her to lick my face a little.

Before we went to bed we helped each other to pack. "We had such a jolly good time together, Hem," said Teesta, hugging and kissing me. "I wish I could have you as my classmate." She promised to meet me at the Maidan whenever she had a chance to visit Calcutta. We decided to say our goodbyes right then because my time of departure, fixed by Mrs Basak, was six sharp when Teesta would be in deep slumber. I could see tears glistening in her big eyes and knew she would miss me for a while. I wished I could also bring a few drops to her mother's eyes, but all I could see there after I fell from her grace was a greenish fire that threatened to set me ablaze.

At five thirty the next morning, I stood on the veranda clutching my box, waiting for my breakfast and transport. With no one around to bid me even a perfunctory farewell, I felt the sting of humiliation. Ten long minutes passed before Sarla appeared with my breakfast. It was wrapped in tissue paper and secured neatly by a rubber band.

"Here's your breakfast, Mrs Mitra," said Sarla as she handed me the packet. "I am glad to inform you that on memsa'b's orders we have replaced the apple with an omelette."

"Many thanks for your memsahib's parting gesture, Sarla," I said, brightening a little. "Now, please go inside and call your mistress. I would like to thank her personally for her wonderful English hospitality before getting into the car."

"But memsa'b told me that she won't come out to see you off," said Sarla. "And I have also been instructed to tell you that a tea van is coming from the factory to take you to the railway station. Please go to the gate and wait for it."

Transporting me in an open van like a tea chest! There is a limit to one's tolerance. In an outburst of fury, I tore open the wrapper, gobbled down my sandwiches and my omelette and shouted for water. Slightly alarmed, Sarla darted back into the house and returned quickly with a plastic tumbler of water. I drank it in one big gulp and then slumped into a wicker chair under a dangling orchid basket.

"I have decided to cancel my journey, Sarla," I declared. "I won't budge an inch from here unless I am provided with proper transport and Mrs Basak comes out and apologizes to me for her atrocious behaviour."

"You are asking for the moon, Mrs Mitra," said the unperturbable maid. "Memsa'b doesn't change her plans."

"We shall see."

Mrs Basak must have been keeping a watch on me from behind the curtains, for she now came out on the veranda and said firmly, "Please, don't create any more scenes, Mrs Mitra. You have got your breakfast and eaten it too. Now you should go. I am sure you will have a comfortable journey on the tea van and enjoy the fresh morning air and a lot of sweet bird chatter on your way. Goodbye, Mrs Mitra."

"Wait a moment, Mrs Basak," I said even as she turned on her heels with a swish of her long colourful skirt, exuding a whiff of her intoxicating perfume.

"Well?" she said, half-turning, a slight frown masking her alarm.

I walked up to her and smacked a kiss on her right cheek. Mrs Basak was certainly not prepared for this daring assault on her person and didn't jerk her head back until I had accomplished my stupendous feat. "Thank you very much for your lavish hospitality and all the kindness you have shown me, Mrs Basak," I said, beaming at my stunned hostess. Then I picked up my box, descended the stairs and headed for the gate, whistling softly. With that parting kiss the bitterness of the last two days became a thing of the past and as I skipped along the gravelled path, I repeated just one line in my mind again and again like a holy mantra: *"I have kissed her!"*

Five

I reached Calcutta just in time to attend our club's kit distribution ceremony and pick up my unlucky number thirteen jersey that no one else would accept. The kit distribution was celebrated with some fanfare, complete with speechmaking. Sushil Bhowmik, the famous Mohan Bagan striker, came to grace the occasion along with his pregnant wife who looked very sweet and graceful in her maternity suit. Tama and I wanted to hug and kiss our former Champaboti coach, but she was so big with the child that we couldn't reach her cheeks and ended up kissing her outstretched palms. Mrs Bhowmik was glad that, unlike so many girls she had coached, we had not given up the game. I felt a little embarrassed when she asked me about my two new scars and I had to update her about my disastrous marriage and the rest which made her gloomy for a while. She confided to us that the little footballer inside her could already respond to Mr Bhowmik's whistle. "The way she (she was quite sure that it would be a 'she') kicks clearly shows she is going to be a left-footer," she gushed with motherly pride. "We quarrel a lot about her position. Mr Bhowmik thinks that she should be groomed as a striker, but I want her to be a sweeper which, I think, is a pivotal position for retreating defence manoeuvres." We learnt from Mrs Bhowmik that her husband had come to our kit distribution ceremony in the dual capacity of chief guest and features editor of the sports magazine *Khela*. We were not surprised by this news as Mr Bhowmik seemed to prefer dual roles wherever he went. Even in that disastrous exhibition match with Chetla, he had played the dual role of chief guest and referee.

Mr Bhowmik had however improved a lot at speechmaking and he was able to speak coherently for about ten minutes. "The days of primitive, barefoot soccer are over," he declared, caressing the kit bags arranged on the table before him. "We shouldn't forget that we owe booted football to the late S. Rahim — peace and blessings of Allah be upon him." Mr Bhowmik then went on to narrate how the pitiable condition of the wretched Indian players running barefoot on the cold wet ground of Helsinki during the 1952 Olympics (in which Yugoslavia beat India by ten goals) so touched Rahim, the then manager of the Indian team, that he launched a crusade to modernize and update Indian football. Overwhelmed by the sad memory of those barefoot footballers of yore, Mr Bhowmik started sniffing and took out his big red handkerchief to wipe away his tears. The girls took the cue and dabbed at their eyes with identical pink lace hankies which they had received as gifts with their two Belle bras.

"It's much better than that incoherent speech he made last time, isn't it?" said Mrs Bhowmik.

Tama and I assured her that it was the best we had heard on the subject.

"I won't be surprised if he quotes from Tagore or Wordsworth to conclude his speech," whispered Mrs Bhowmik.

Mrs Bhowmik was wrong. After narrating at length how Rahim had introduced booted football and position play in India and helped us to finish among the big four in the 1956 Olympics at Melbourne, Mr Bhowmik rounded off his speech with a ditty:

> Fitness comes first
> Skill comes second
> Courage is a must
> Victory is round the bend.

"Original!" exclaimed Mrs Bhowmik excitedly.

"And very instructive too," nodded Tama. "It sums up the basic qualities we require to win a match."

After his speech Mr Bhowmik distributed the kit — a pair of boots, two pairs of socks, two jerseys, one blazer, a tracksuit and a kit bag — with prolonged handshakes, enabling his dutiful wife to take a few snaps of the memorable occasion for the pages of *Khela*. Mrs Mookerjee dampened our jubilant spirits when she demanded our signatures at the bottom of a cyclostyled receipt on the back of which there were detailed instructions on kit maintenance and a veiled threat that misuse of any item could lead to its immediate seizure by the club without warning. Finally, Mrs Chaudhury stood up, flashed her meaningless smile and sprung a big surprise on her audience by declaring me the winner of the newly instituted "Triple Star" award in recognition of my outstanding services to the club. I knew I was now in the good books of the club authorities for helping them to squeeze that big donation out of Mr Basak, and Mrs Mookerjee had particularly praised my courage and fortitude when I reported back to her how I had fended off Mr Basak's advances and yet received royal treatment at Rose Valley (withholding, of course, the unsavoury details of my expulsion), but I never expected to be honoured publicly. I felt very nervous and awkward as I stood up before my teammates and accepted from Mrs Chaudhury a football and a small bronze plaque, the latter engraved with three stars at the top, the club's name in the middle and the club's motto — "Football for health and discipline" — at the bottom. Everyone cheered and clapped and Mr Bhowmik, now free from his onerous duty as chief guest, crouched on the ground and asked me to hold up my trophy and grin for the camera.

*

Fitted out in our new boots and jerseys, we resumed practice with great enthusiasm. Miss Nag took advantage of our upbeat mood to brush up our passing techniques — the flick pass, the chip pass and the volley pass — with her eye-catching freeze-defreeze-reconstruction drill. But while Miss Nag ably demonstrated how in a tight situation a player should flick the ball with the outside of her foot through a wide angle, I could only think of Mrs Basak's sweet face, her rosy lips, heady fragrance and most of all that momentous kiss on the veranda, the sheer memory of which made my heart gallop like a racehorse. Miss Nag pulled me up several times for fumbling the ball and reminded me that such sloppiness was not expected of a "Triple Star", but with love occupying so much of my mind I couldn't care less about the flick pass. Annoyed at my petit-bourgeois sluggishness, Miss Nag ordered me to do a fast lap round the field.

But, in the evening, when I returned to Paromita's cottage there was no one to stop me fantasizing about Mrs Basak. Curled up in a chair on the veranda, I lapsed into erotic reveries of the wildest variety. In one of my favourite daydreams I became a peeping Jane crouching behind Mrs Basak's bathroom door, my eye glued to the keyhole. Mrs Basak sat on a low stool, naked above the waist, bathing her magnificient, alabaster-white breasts, one at a time, in a silver bowl filled with rose water. I gasped as I watched her gently rubbing the wet sponge around her pink nipples, making them swell up into two luscious plums. My mouth fell wide open in surprise when she gently lifted one of her twin assets on her palm like a pet dove and kissed it indulgently, murmuring encouraging words to her darling pet. While my feverish brain worked out these steamy details, I involuntarily rubbed my thighs together and pinched my nipples to bring myself much-needed relief.

Driven by my unbridled passion for Mrs Basak, one night I desperately buried my nose in Paromita's hair, but instead of sweet cologne, I got a whiff of the familiar Hena brand coconut hair oil which reminded me of my mother and all those colony aunts who patronized this obnoxious brand. Slowly, I slid down the mattress, pressing my nose close to her body, hunting for something sweet and exciting, but my Gandhian friend had nothing to titillate me. I smelt medicated, antiseptic Boroplus (which I used only when I nicked my finger) on her cheeks, glycerine on her lips and Johnson's baby powder around her armpits. I was quite sure that if I ventured further and buried my nose between her breasts, all I could expect was a faint smell of holy basil or even holier sandalwood. In utter frustration I thrust my hand inside her blouse and squeezed one of her tits which turned out to be quite big and round. Paromita stopped snoring and woke up with a muffled groan, pushing my hand away from her bosom. She blinked her eyes and cried, "Hemprova! This is unbelievable! What were you doing inside my blouse?"

"I am on a fact-finding mission, darling," I said sweetly, planting a kiss on her cheek. "My interest is purely academic. Isn't it odd that even your best friend hasn't the faintest idea about your marvellous boobs . . . I mean their size, shape and weight."

"Stop this midnight drivel, you rascal!" bawled Paromita. "Ever since you returned from your district tour, I have noticed that you are under some evil spell. From tomorrow we shall sleep on separate mats."

"Impossible!" I cried. "If I sleep alone I will start having those horrible dreams again."

"In that case, before we go to bed, I will tie up your hands with a thick coir rope."

"I don't mind, but give an honest reply to my question: Don't you ever feel any sexual urges?"

"No, I don't," said Paromita, affecting a beatific smile she had probably perfected over the years to chasten unenlightened souls like me. "I follow strictly the true path of Brahmacharya: good thinking, good reading, good work, vegetarian meals and plenty of meditation. That's how a celibate keeps her senses under control."

I was going to pooh-pooh her Brahmacharya but checked my flippancy to assume a respectful demeanour as I noted her intimidating look.

"Look Hemprova, if you really want to share my bed, you'll have to cleanse your soul of lust and other base instincts," warned Paromita. "I suggest that you start reading the *Gita* every morning."

"But I read it when I was convalescing!" I protested, horrified.

"Once is not enough," reminded Paromita sternly. "A tainted soul like yours needs several readings to get rid of the ingrained sensuality."

"And do I also need to work that abominable charkha?" I asked, gritting my teeth.

"Yes, if you are sincere and want quick results."

Since Mrs Basak was as inaccessible as the moon and Miss Nag was threatening to dump me in the reserves if I didn't shake off my petit-bourgeois sloth pretty quick, I decided, willy-nilly, to try Paromita's strict Gandhian regimen. To my amazement, I soon discovered that it worked. Of course, I couldn't completely erase Mrs Basak from my mind, but as Lord Krishna's harangue to Arjuna on the eve of the Kurukshetra war entered my tainted soul, I stopped fantasizing about her divine breasts and revived my interest in football. Miss Nag was happy to see me regain my proletarian spirit and graciously selected me with two other girls to demonstrate to my comrades the intricacies of the volley pass.

*

"It's about time you visited your big baby, Hemprova," Paromita reminded me one Sunday morning after she had shaken me up with a shout: "Wake up, you sleepyhead, if you don't want to miss your lunch." It was only seven thirty but even on a Sunday Paromita wouldn't allow me to sleep beyond that hour.

"I don't feel like meeting Dr Nandy," I said, rubbing my eyes. "He will start talking about yet another experimental treatment and that will upset me."

"Still, you owe Babu a visit every month," pointed out Paromita. "Being a mother, you can't simply forget your child like that."

"What reminds you of Babu this morning?" I asked as I sat up and coiled my dishevelled hair into an elo khonpa, a loose bun, at the nape of my neck.

"I don't know," said Paromita. "As usual I was trying to have a little chat with my Inner Voice and suddenly the bearded face of that poor creature loomed up in my mind. I felt as if he was waiting for us. Remind me to buy some toffees and chocolates for him on the way."

"Up, up, up . . . down, down, down . . . cut, cut!" The gruff, commanding voice we heard from Babu's room gave us a near fright. I feared that his roommate, the self-styled traffic constable, might have gone berserk and was playing some cruel trick on poor Babu. After we had thumped on the door several times, the voice suddenly fell silent and a little later the door was flung open. The bearded man with the peaked cap knotted his bushy brows and regarded us with suspicion and hostility even as he moved aside just a little to let us in. Babu sat on the dirty floor, clutching a slate, his big eyes contemplating a mysterious, incomplete "A" which he had been scrawling, following his roommate's military commands. Suddenly, I felt a surge of maternal love for my bearded helpless baby and I squatted down to hug him tight against my bosom and shed some tears on his head just like a doting mother visiting her only son after a long gap. Babu however didn't reciprocate my strong feelings; he solemnly pointed at the slate and said, "Ma A."

"Yes, darling, it's an A," I said. "And such a beautiful A you have drawn! Let's write a few more letters together, achha?" I held his hand and guided his pencil-clutching fingers over the slate to scrawl the next few letters of the alphabet, ignoring his roommate's fierce grunts and hostile looks. After we had progressed to "E", Babu's self-appointed teacher suddenly swooped down on us, snatching the slate from my hand, then he assumed the severe expression of a tyrant teacher and beckoned Babu to his side. But Babu clung to my neck and refused to budge. Paromita apprehended trouble and promptly distributed her goodies between the two, pacifying the enraged teacher instantaneously. Both of them gobbled their chocolates in the twinkling of an eye and then Babu's guru briefly reverted to his original role of traffic constable and showed his gratitude to Paromita with a smart military salute.

"I don't think these poor creatures get anything more than rice and dal to eat," observed Paromita. "Next time, we shall bring a loaf of bread and some sweets for them."

*

"There will be no further regression," said Dr Nandy when we met him in his chamber after the visiting hours. "Dr Vrugle was perfectly right in suggesting therapeutic dramatics. They worked like a miracle."

"Thank you so much, Dr Nandy," I said, feeling greatly relieved at this long-awaited news.

"You should rather thank Sophocles, Mrs Mitra," said the psychiatrist. "I am glad to report that your husband has now attained the mental age of a three-year-old and, hopefully, from now on he will have an accelerated growth rate."

"How long before he acquires his full vocabulary and returns to his typist's job at the Writers'?" I asked eagerly.

Dr Nandy coughed and patted his goatee. "I am afraid, Mrs Mitra, he will take several years to achieve that stage. We shall keep him under observation for another month or so and in the meantime help him learn the alphabet and to count up to ten. Thereafter, you will have to arrange for his re-education, preferably in a school for the mentally retarded. I'd suggest Dinobandhu Shikshayatan, which has a good reputation and an experienced faculty. The fees they charge are no doubt a bit on the high side but in these matters one should always go for the best."

I told Dr Nandy that I needed at least a couple of months to arrange for the money and till that time would he please keep Babu in his charge and, if possible, teach him a few more things like word formation and simple arithmetic? Dr Nandy grumbled he was a psychiatrist, not a kindergarten teacher, but when Paromita pointed out that Babu's roommate was doing most of the teaching, he agreed to accommodate Babu for a while longer.

We were walking down the corridor towards the main entrance when Dr Nandy's attendant came running, shouting, "Mrs Mitra, Dr Nandy calls you!"

I rushed back to the doctor's chamber, wondering whether he had suddenly changed his mind and would ask me to take Babu home right then.

"I forgot to give you this, Mrs Mitra," said Dr Nandy as he handed me a small brown envelope. "Someone from your husband's office came to see him a fortnight ago and left this envelope with me because he couldn't contact you at your Baghbazar address." Dr Nandy's impassive face didn't register any particular feeling but his eyes told me that he was annoyed at being used as a custodian of undelivered letters. "You should have given me your new address, Mrs Mitra," he chided me. "That's not like a responsible mother."

"I am extremely sorry, Dr Nandy." I picked up a ballpoint pen from his penstand and scribbled Paromita's address on a slip of paper.

Outside Dr Nandy's chamber, I tore open the envelope and took out a slip of paper on which Babu's boss had scribbled in a spidery handwriting the following missive:

Mrs Mitra,

Meet me in my office urgently if you are interested in doing a three-month stint in my office as a peon on a daily wage basis. I am sorry I can't at present offer you anything better.

Tapan Ghatak
Deputy Director (AH)

Six

I joined the Directorate of Animal Husbandry in the middle of December when the Writers' was in the grip of what the Secretariat people called "December fever" as the babus and the bureaucrats had taken leave *en masse* to enjoy their hard-earned vacations in Digha, Puri or Darjeeling. Mrs Bose, Mr Ghatak's plump and fussily-dressed Personal Assistant, dismissed these popular, overcrowded holiday resorts with a wave of her hand and informed me that that year the discerning tourists were actually gravitating to Dalhousie, and luckily she had already enjoyed her vacation there in November before the tourists started arriving in big numbers.

Mrs Bose had graciously offered me a stool in a corner of her cubicle, but most of the time I preferred to stand by the window and watch the endless traffic down below on Dalhousie Square, my ears pricked for Mr Ghatak's buzzers. The first one came around ten when Mr Ghatak had cleared the backlog of the previous day's work. Most of his files were very bulky because of the thick reports attached to them and I had to make two or three trips to Mr Ghatak's room to clear his "out" tray and dump the files on Mrs Bose's table. The latter promptly put a big smudgy rubber stamp on the margin of each file, scribbled the diary numbers and the date in the blank spaces, made entries in her diary-cum-despatch register and shoved the files back to me. I lugged one load along the corridor and up the stairs to a bigger cubicle occupied by Mr Giriraj, the private secretary of our Director, and came back to carry the other to Mr Mazumder, the section officer of the Animal Husbandry section. When I had first visited Mr Mazumder a few months before in connection with Babu's provident fund, he had been courteous enough to offer me tea and singaras, but now every time I approached him with some files he frowned at me and pressed his hand protectively over his heart as if I was a witch or a bad omen. Even the typist girl who had usurped Babu's job looked positively hostile and sometimes made a face at me when I entered the room. I was intrigued by the AH Section's unprovoked hostility towards me and complained to Mrs Bose. She explained that both Mr Mazumder and Miss Kar hated me because I was the courier of those bulky files which often portended trouble for them. Mr Mazumder feared the files because some of them contained detailed instructions from Mr Ghatak, like "Put up a self-contained note covering all the aspects marked 'A', 'B', 'C' & 'D' on the receipt for taking orders of Director(AH)" and this compelled Mr Mazumder to write a lengthy note running to five or six pages with innumerable references and cross references in the margins. The inexperienced, work-shy typist detested the files because they threatened to generate lengthy drafts, with numerous additions or alterations done by Mr Ghatak in his spidery handwriting, and to make matters worse those terrible drafts sometimes had a couple of tables (in eight columns) attached to them as well, making the typist quite hysterical. The only person who seemed to be totally unaffected by my intrusion into Mr Mazumder's fiefdom was Mr Bakshi who sat, Buddha-like, at his table near the window with his arms and legs crossed, contemplating the shining dome of the GPO.

Mr Ghatak's second buzzer at eleven was to summon Mrs Bose for dictation. She took great trouble to get ready for her first appearance before her boss. She painted her lips afresh, peered critically at her dark, round face in a small, egg-shaped mirror, powdered her proud little nose, drew a comb lightly through her long lustrous hair, reset a few hairpins and finally practised a discreet pout to look slightly grumpy. "Do I now look all right, girl?" she would ask me, tugging at her sari wherever the creases looked hard and unyielding.

"Perfectly all right, Mrs Bose," I would assure her. "You look very sweet."

"Be serious, Hem. One has to be very professional in my job, you know. Look carefully at my back and if you find an unseemly crease smooth it out. I hope my bra straps aren't visible."

I would assure her that everything was tip top. But Mrs Bose would take another full minute to decide whether she should cover her navel or keep it exposed. Mostly she decided to cover it partly with her sari. Finally, as she picked up her notebook and HB pencil, she would caution me, "Call me 'Ma'am' and not 'Mrs Bose' when you serve me tea in Mr Ghatak's room. Remember about the sugar. One spoon for him, two for me."

Around half past eleven I brought "half set" tea from the canteen, poured it in Mrs Bose's cubicle and carried the tray to Mr Ghatak's room. He would be in the midst of a long dictation on such unfamiliar and mystifying subjects as "Progeny testing programme" or "Buffalo development through frozen semen technology". I always found Mrs Bose in a very professional mood, taking her dictation with that lovely pout she had perfected in her cubicle. The most surprising aspect of her professionalism was that she would not talk to me in Mr Ghatak's presence. I had to say, "Here is your tea, ma'am" and then would get a gentle nod of recognition. I thought this was also very professional.

Outside Mr Ghatak's room, Mrs Bose could afford to be informal and chatty with a lowly peon. The Ghoses, the Boses and the Mitras comprised the creamy layer of the Kayastha sub-caste, Mrs Bose proudly pointed out, so she had no qualms about sharing my lunch and allowing me to share hers, though I found her cooking rather bland for my taste. After lunch, Mrs Bose popped in a vitamin tablet and a mint-flavoured lozenge, the latter to freshen her breath, and then she would prattle about her son's multifarious achievements at St Matthew's or about her wonderful vacation in the salubrious atmosphere of Dalhousie.

Mr Ghatak's third buzzer came around three to clear the files typed out by Mrs Bose before lunch. I made two more trips to Mr Giriraj and Mr Mazumder and usually found the latter dozing, his feet up on the table and his head lolling on his shoulder. I took great care not to wake the irritable old man from his siesta and noted that Mr Bakshi had already vanished. Miss Kar was still at her table, but she would normally be chatting and knitting with her typist friend from another section, their heads bobbing up and down and shaking from side to side in unison as if they were puppets on the same string. This time Miss Kar would either ignore me or give me a dirty look from the corner of her eyes and continue her chitchat.

The fourth and last buzzer prompted Mrs Bose to rearrange her sari and her hair in a way that made her look like a spoilt ten-year-old girl woken up in the middle of the night. She removed the pins, tousled her hair with meticulous care, smudged a little lipstick on her cheeks and practised in her mirror a rare smile which was half-somnolent and half-melancholic.

"End-of-the-day look," explained Mrs Bose, exposing her belly button fully. "Girl, stop grinning and help me to crease my sari. If you were in my position you would know how one feels taking dictation at this late hour. Do I look scandalous enough to shock that beanpole?"

"You look ravishing, Mrs Bose."

"Thank you. Don't forget to call me 'Ma'am' when you hand me the cup and saucer."

I had special permission from Mr Ghatak to leave office early for my football practice, so I slipped out of the Writers' around four thirty and dashed to catch a tram for the Maidan.

*

At the beginning of January, Mrs Bose and I had no work to do for a whole week as Mr Ghatak had gone to Denmark to attend an international conference on Oestrus Synchronization. Mrs Bose confided to me that Mr Ghatak would take advantage of his trip to visit some Danish farmers and persuade them to sell us a dozen handpicked heifers of the famous Fin Glen breed for crossbreeding purposes. To make best use of this unscheduled break from office work, Mrs Bose invited her two cronies, Mrs Kayal from the library and Mrs Maiti from the Housekeeping section, to invade the College Street and Gariahata sari shops and snap up some silk and tussor saris from the bargain sales. "Hold the fort for a couple of hours, Hem," said Mrs Bose as she trotted off with her friends, leaving me in the company of her old, lugubrious Remington. I sat in Mrs Bose's chair, rolled a sheet of paper into the typewriter and after ten minutes of careful key-tapping managed to print my name and address in a hopeless jumble of capital and small letters. Not my job, I decided, and returned to the window to watch the endless traffic on Dalhousie Square. But for a sprinkling of scruffy hawkers selling peanuts, ballpoint pens and guidebooks, the people crossing the square generally looked well-dressed, busy and purposeful, though the few sari-clad women I could see had a tired, listless appearance. A little colour was added to this dismal and unchanging scene when a tourist bus disgorged about two dozen foreign tourists and they started clicking away at everything they thought interesting around them, including the Writers'. My eyes were instantly riveted on a pretty but rather dumb-looking blonde encased in black harem pants and a tight blue top that seemed rather inadequate accommodation for her ample breasts. She was apparently attached to a bearded young man who wore a pair of sawn-off jeans, a wide-brimmed hat and a brown jersey with the legend "BOSS" printed on his bosom.

A small, sari-clad guide herded the tourists along the pavement, probably to visit St John's church and the Calcutta High Court, and soon they were out of sight. But that dumb-looking blonde had already done her job by stirring up my raw passion for Mrs Basak which I had so successfully (or so I thought) buried inside me with Lord Krishna's holy sermons. My heart began to beat faster as I remembered that having celebrated Christmas and New Year in Rose Valley with her family, Mrs Basak had by now returned to Calcutta. It seemed almost unbelievable that a divine beauty like Mrs Basak could live in this dirty city which was as ugly and scarred as my face and as stinking as my sweaty armpits (which I had learnt to use on the crowded bus as a potential antidote to bottom-pinchers who slunk away the moment I turned and brushed my armpit lightly against their noses). Mrs Basak, however, belonged to a different world where appreciation of Aslam Huda's abstract horses, Italian opera and the glorious sunrise over Kanchenjunga superseded the daily toil and clamour for bread. But how would I fit into her rarefied world? She had thrown me out of her house and before me Mrs Hore must have received the same treatment. As far as I could see, the only upshot of my misadventure would be that in future Mrs Basak would subject her female guests to a thorough cross-examination before she gave her durwan the nod to open the gate. Still, I couldn't reconcile myself to the heart-rending fact that Mrs Basak had vanished forever from my life. Suddenly, it occurred to me that if opposite poles could attract each other, why shouldn't this simple magnetic law be applicable to our relationship? There could be no doubt that we occupied the two extreme and opposite points on the Beauty Scale and therefore we ought to attract each other, given the right magnetic field which, alas, Rose Valley had failed to create.

I was still not convinced of my magnetic theory when I picked up the bulky, dog-eared telephone directory from the rack and started hunting for Mrs Basak's number. I finally located "Maxine's" and dialled the number, holding my breath as the ring came loud and clear from the other side. I could almost hear the wild fluttering of my heart as Mrs Basak's familiar voice floated in: "Mrs Basak here."

"It's Mrs Mitra," I said, and then paused, expecting her to bang the receiver down. But Mrs Basak responded icily: "I see."

"Can I meet you for a few minutes, Mrs Basak?" I said in a soft, pleading tone.

"Sorry, Mrs Mitra," came the expected reply. "I am awfully busy these days arranging an exhibition of Tanjore paintings."

"I know you are a very busy woman, Mrs Basak, but do spare me a few minutes."

"But I don't see how I can . . ."

"Ple-ase, Mrs Basak. . . I won't have any peace of mind till you allow me to apologize personally for my boorish behaviour. My guilt constantly gnaws away at me. . . It's so terrible!"

Mrs Basak sighed. "I don't feel there is any necessity to meet for that particular ritual. You may send a letter of apology if that helps you to restore your peace of mind."

"But I have something . . . something very important to tell you, Mrs Basak," I said desperately.

"I am listening, Mrs Mitra," said Mrs Basak, probably through clenched teeth.

"But it's very personal, Mrs Basak," I blurted out. "I can't write it in a letter or even talk about it on the phone. *I must meet you.*"

"But I told you, Mrs Mitra, I am terribly busy these days. . ."

"Please Mrs Basak!" I begged and since I couldn't think of any better way to coax her to change her mind, I deliberately sniffed and sighed into the mouthpiece. There was a longish pause and then I heard Mrs Basak's sigh: "OK, I think I can manage just about ten minutes for you, Mrs Mitra. Could you meet me at Flurys at five thirty sharp?"

"Thank you very much, Mrs Basak. Isn't that the café on Lindsay Street opposite the Globe cinema?"

"Yes. Upstairs."

I reached Flurys before time, but Mrs Basak arrived on the dot like a pukka memsahib. She nodded at me from the door and strolled towards my table, making a slight detour on her way to avoid a teenage couple sipping cold coffee through straws from the same glass, their heads joined over the table like an arch. Mrs Basak wore a sober tweed jacket over her long flowing skirt and I noticed that she had changed her hairstyle from seductive curls to a more conventional, slightly wavy pattern to assume a workaday look. Even her lips were drawn a light pink, without gloss, to play down their ripeness and sensuality. My only consolation was that she still exuded her distinctive flowery fragrance. I had no idea how I should open the conversation and felt much relieved when the fat waiter, smartly decked out in a green uniform and flared turban, appeared with the menu just as Mrs Basak took her seat across from me. She ordered coffee and a bowl of roasted cashew nuts, pushed back a strand of her hair which had strayed over her eyes and said, "Well, Mrs Mitra?" reminding me that I didn't have all the time in the world to justify my frantic call.

"I can't forgive myself when I think. . ."

"I think we have already talked enough on that subject, haven't we?" cut in Mrs Basak. "Excuse me for a minute." She rose from her chair and strode towards the ladies' room, leaving me in a quandary. She was playing it so cool that an elaborate apology or a bout of self-flagellation wouldn't work as they often did in my own society. It wasn't going to be easy to worm my way into her good books again. Unable to decide what I should say to Mrs Basak when she returned from the toilet, I stared gloomily at a colourful fresco depicting a floridly dressed rajah going out for shikar on an elephant, followed by his long retinue of lackeys and bearers decked out in their colourful best.

The coffee arrived and so did Mrs Basak. She took a sip, popped in a couple of cashew nuts and said, "I am sorry, Mrs Mitra, but I have to rush. . ." She dabbed at her mouth with her lace hanky, took another sip and then looked at my face. "Well, Mrs Mitra, you said you have something very important to tell me."

"Mrs Basak!" I blurted out. "I have come to seek your friendship."

Mrs Basak looked slightly alarmed and straightened up. "But I am afraid, Mrs Mitra, I can't afford a new friendship." She paused to stare hard at her cup and then raised her head to meet my beseeching look with a sad, condescending smile. "I am so sorry, Mrs Mitra. . . I have my art gallery and the club which keep me awfully busy throughout the day and the best part of the evening as well."

"I know you are a very busy woman, Mrs Basak, but if you could spare just half an hour for me once in a while. . ."

"Moreover, we are not of the same age group and we come from quite different backgrounds and cultures," said Mrs Basak as if I had not spoken.

"I am a single woman, Mrs Basak, and feel very lonely sometimes," I moaned.

Mrs Basak sighed. "I feel sorry for you, Mrs Mitra, but I think you ought to seek friendship within your own fraternity. We are *so* different. . . I don't think we will make a good pair."

"But opposite poles do attract each other, Mrs Basak, don't they?"

Mrs Basak smiled wryly. "Yes, but we are not magnets, Mrs Mitra. We are human beings and we observe certain rules and time-honoured customs for entering into a relationship. I hope I have made my point amply clear." She opened her bag, took out a twenty-rupee note and pushed it under her plate, indicating that the interview was over.

"Mrs Basak!" I cried and grabbed her hand. The arching heads of the teenage couple jerked back and turned forty-five degrees to shoot cold stares of disapproval at me. Mrs Basak retrieved her hand from my grasp and stood up. "Let's not make a scene, Mrs Mitra," she hissed. "I have to rush."

I realized that even if I prostrated myself before her and shed a gallon of tears, she wouldn't change her mind. Teesta was right; she was either a Scot or a Jew, if not a Sicilian.

"If you want a lift. . ."

I shook my head and pressed my hanky to my eyes to absorb the tears that stung my eyes.

"I am sorry, Mrs Mitra," said Mrs Basak softly. A decorous pause and then I heard her receding footsteps.

*

A week later, on the eve of our trip to Lucknow to participate in the prestigious Hazrat Mahal Cup matches, Mrs Mookerjee was giving her standard speech about the "adequate arrangements" the club had made for our accommodation. As usual, she advised us to carry candles, matchboxes, mosquito nets, pocket knives and a few other essential items. I suddenly jumped up and proposed, "Madam, why don't you take us to Delhi after the matches for some sightseeing?"

All the girls supported my suggestion in one voice.

Mrs Mookerjee exchanged a quick, meaningful glance with Mrs Chaudhury and cleared her throat. "Well, we shall consider this proposal . . . ahem, I mean, if our financial position permits. . ."

"Delhi chalo!" shouted my comrades. "We want to see the Red Fort and Kutub Minar."

"It's only four hundred and ninety-six kilometres from Lucknow," pointed out Damba, who seemed to have consulted her *Bradshaw* in advance. The treasurer and the secretary moved their heads closer, conferred in a whisper and then Mrs Chaudhury declared that the club would be happy to take us to Delhi, provided we won the Hazrat Mahal cup. A hard bargain, no doubt, but we accepted the deal as we were now quite confident of our invincibility. After two months of rigorous practice, Miss Nag had proudly declared that Rani Jhansi was now battle-fit and would storm the enemy's citadel like the Bolsheviks stormed the Winter Palace.

My comrades would have been shocked if they knew what really prompted me to suggest the Delhi trip. No, I had no wish to visit the Red Fort and Kutub Minar. Once we reached Delhi, I would invent some excuse to slip out of the hotel and go straight to Mr Basak's house to tell him that I had changed my mind and would very much like to join his harem. That's how I would take my sweet revenge on Mrs Basak, and God willing, I might even throw her out of Rose Valley and become his legitimate wife.

Watch out Mean Max!

Seven

Lucknow, the city of Nawabs and the present capital of Uttar Pradesh, appeared as congested and dirty as Calcutta. Outside the picturesque Charbagh railway station, we walked past a line of lepers and deformed beggars and climbed into some rickety rickshaws, pressing our hankies to our noses as the stench of urine overwhelmed us. One had only to turn one's head to see at least a dozen men pissing on the station buildings, treating them as public urinals.

The club had booked a few double rooms for us at the Hotel Avadh on Gautam Buddha Marg, formerly LaTouche Road, where, ironically, most of the shops dealt in firearms and ammunition. From the road our three-storey pink hotel with its ornate facade looked pretty and cosy, but once inside we discovered that the rooms were very small and stuffy and the furnishings worn out and wobbly. To make matters worse, the club treated us like cattle, herding four girls into one double room. Even Miss Nag grumbled that her proletarian team needed a little more breathing space, but Mrs Mookerjee made it quite clear that she could take additional rooms if only we agreed to forgo our enhanced daily allowance of ten rupees which the club had promised us during the matches. When we protested at this bania meanness, Mrs Chaudhury prudently threw a sop to us: she declared that the club would pay a tenner for each goal scored or saved in the ensuing matches. Mrs Mookerjee was visibly shocked by Mrs Chaudhury's largesse and muttered about the club's financial constraints, but the latter, for once, held her ground.

"A happy team is a better team, Mrs Mookerjee," she pointed out with a winning smile and we clapped and danced a jig around her even as we realized that our basic demand for better accommodation had been neatly shoved under the carpet.

Mrs Mookerjee must have carefully preserved her old lists from our ill-fated district tour, for I found myself once again in the company of weepy Leena, romantic Namita and three-question Utpala. In the middle of the night, Namita snatched my pillow, Utpala groaned and spluttered something incoherent (she was probably rehearsing a new set of questions in her dream), and weepy Leena gurgled like a child and kicked me on the shin when I tried to get my share of the blanket. Our cup was full when, in the morning, one of the hotel guests, a beanpole with a lantern jaw and protruding, yellowish eyes, tried to get fresh with our beauty queen Reba. Fortunately, Damba was around and she floored the rascal with a left hook and a karate chop. Humiliated by such rough treatment from a member of the weaker sex, the man sprang to his feet like a jack-in-the-box and threatened to fetch a gun from the nearest shop and shoot all the "shameless, leg-showing strumpets". The noise attracted a few more girls who came out brandishing their pocket knives, ready to castrate the lousy creature then and there. The manager rushed in to intervene, and when he learnt what had happened, he politely asked the man to leave the hotel before he called the police. Fifteen minutes later, the bellboy pasted a warning on the landing: "BEAWARE OF LADY FOOTBALLERS!" – with an arrow showing the wing we occupied.

*

For the Hazrat Mahal Cup matches, the twelve contesting teams, drawn from all over India, were divided into four leagues. Luckily, we were in League C with two mediocre teams from Delhi and Tamilnadu and that assured us of a safe berth in the semi-finals.

Lucknow was once famous for its poets, musicians and nautch girls but the Lucknowites were not traditionally soccer enthusiasts. It was therefore very heartening to see that even during the quarter-finals a modest crowd of about two thousand gathered at the K.D. Singh Babu stadium to patronize women's football. No doubt, some of them had come, as usual, to ogle our bare legs and bouncing boobs, but they had paid for their tickets and that made everyone, particularly Mrs Mookerjee, very happy.

Thanks to Miss Nag's revolutionary coaching and Mrs Chaudhury's capitalist incentive scheme, we trounced Tamilnadu in the quarter-finals and Maharashtra in the semis. The incentive scheme, however, posed unforeseen problems. Miss Nag noted with concern that more and more players were transgressing their own boundaries to take fancy long shots at our opponents' goal in the hope of earning a tenner, and Mrs Mookerjee's hand shook visibly when she had to disburse Rs 120 among the players after we defeated Tamilnadu by twelve goals.

Flushed with our bonus money, we marched to Aminabad bazaar to drive a hard bargain with the petty shopkeepers who lured us with their saris and kurta-kameez ensembles with their elaborate chikan embroidery, the hallmark of Lucknow craftsmanship. One evening, while exploring the intriguing mazes of Aminabad, we stumbled into Garbar Jhala, a cluster of tiny stalls tucked away from the main road where one could buy a dazzling array of imitation jewellery. The customers were exclusively women, while the shopkeepers were mostly Muslim youths with delicate features and kohl-lined eyes who seemed to enjoy our haggling and playful banter. We bought psychedelic glass bangles, teardrop glass-bead necklaces, anklets strung with tiny jingling bells, silver toe-rings and bottles of Lucknow's famous rose attar perfume.

Apart from trips to the enchanting world of Aminabad, the only other activity we enjoyed was what the locals called "ganjing" — a leisurely stroll along the city's most fashionable boulevard, Hazratganj, with some window shopping and gourmandizing (there was such a wide variety of delectable fare available on the pavements!) thrown in. One evening, we ventured as far as the towering Sahu cinema to see an Amitabh Bachhan starrer, but we had to retreat when we discovered to our horror that there was not a single woman in the queue and the males, some of them quite drunk and rowdy, started whistling and making obscene gestures as we approached the ticket counter.

*

On the day of the final match between our team and Kairali, a Kerala club, the stadium was jam-packed and the police had to wield their lathis to drive away the huge crowd gathered outside the main gate. The unprecedented rush had, however, nothing to do with soccer; the crowd had snapped up the tickets in order to catch a glimpse of Miss Priya Tiwari, an up and coming film actress, who had come all the way from Bombay to attend a relative's marriage in her home town and had decided on the spur of the moment to grace the occasion along with the rotund, Gandhi-capped state minister of sports and culture. The presence of the VIPs ensured wide TV and newspaper coverage and all the concomitant fanfare associated with a Government function. As the honourable minister took his seat in the VIP pavilion, flanked by the film actress on one side and his bodyguard on the other, a paramilitary band played "Sare jahan se achha" to instil the spirit of national integrity among the jubilant crowd who kept chanting in chorus "Priya! Priya! Kisko chumma diya?" (Priya! Whom have you kissed?)

From the very beginning of the match I had a hunch that our team was playing for a goalless draw, in order to clinch the victory in the tie-breaker. We actually played a cautious 4—4—2 game, confining ourselves to our backyard, our four midfielders seldom venturing forward to create any moves and our two ace wingers, Tama and Damba, looking quite ineffective. This was definitely not the way those intrepid Bolsheviks had stormed the Winter Palace, though Ira assured us that according to the latest game plan she had worked out with Miss Nag, we would change gear in the second half and play total football to overwhelm our rivals just when they started showing signs of fatigue. I was however not convinced by Miss Nag's strategy as I watched the Kerala team making dangerous forays into our citadel, swapping their positions with a swiftness that Miss Nag's set plays and eye-catching freeze-defreeze-reconstruction exercises had not prepared us to cope with. Under constant pressure, our defence crumbled and the inevitable goal came just before the lemon-break. It was a brilliant move originating with Kairali's right winger. Her floated cross was intercepted by their ace striker Prema on the left; she slipped the ball inside the six yard box for Majitha, another star player, to nod in from close.

There was panic and bitter recriminations in our camp during the interval. Mrs Chaudhury struck her head with her fist and threatened to resign if we lost the match and Mrs Mookerjee shook Miss Nag, howling, "You! You are solely responsible for this debacle. Wasting precious time on your balletic exercises and teaching no real technique to beat those girls!" Miss Nag, in her turn, shouted at Ira: "Who the hell told you to play 4—4—2? Why don't you flare out into 4—3—3 or even 4—2—4? Attack! Build up moves . . . create space for the wingers to shoot in." Ira meekly pointed out that Kairali were playing a very difficult game, changing their tactics all the while and giving us no scope to make a move on goal. "How could *they* create so much space in your box, may I ask?" retorted Miss Nag. "And how many times have I told you that zonal defence is the only way to cope with opponents switching their positions constantly in front of goal?"

The brainstorming session had its desired effect; we geared up to an attacking game in the second half, throwing caution to the wind. I held my breath as I saw Binita, one of our ace forwards, execute a lovely swerving shot from the edge of the box that beat Kairali's goalkeeper and hit the crossbar. A few minutes later I almost chewed my fingers when Damba diverted a free kick from outside the box to Tama whose prompt half-volley hit the left-hand post. The post intervened a third time, blocking a header from Binita, but this time Ira was on hand to take the rebound and even though there seemed enough time for Kairali's defence to regroup, she was able to place the shot right into the net with a nicety.

We leaped with joy, punched the air and hugged each other. Mrs Mookerjee, Mrs Chaudhury and Miss Nag danced a jig on the sideline and the paramilitary band played "Sare jahan se achha" a second time to remind everyone about national integration. But with the equalizer our team lost its enthusiasm for further attack and settled for a tie-breaker, the bane of women's football. We delayed our clearances and hit the ball out at the slightest sign of danger. Enraged by our dilatory tactics, the spectators unleashed a barrage of boos and catcalls.

"We should try to score," I said to Ira when she passed back to me for the umpteenth time.

"We can't, because Kairali also want a tie-breaker," said Ira.

"Let's try a trick."

"What trick?"

"Let's try the leapfrog," I suggested.

"What's that? Don't think I have ever heard of it."

I explained. We had learnt it from Mrs Bhowmik but had never made use of it because of its inherent risks. "I think I can pull it off with Tama," I said. "You just pass the word."

She did so during the next two throw-ins and our players imperceptibly changed positions. After yet another throw-in, one of our forwards tapped the ball back to a half-back who pushed it further back to a full back, creating the impression that we were determined to keep the ball in our own half till the referee whistled for the tie-breaker. This tempted the opposing forwards and half-backs to make a last-ditch attempt to snatch the ball away from us and score. When I noticed that as many as eight Kairali players had crossed the halfway line, I took the ball from a full back and sprinted forward, with Tama giving me cover, overlapping our own forwards and throwing the opposing team completely off-balance. There was no one to stop us except the two full backs who looked panicky as we stormed into Kairali's penalty area. We had little problem dodging one and got past the other with a couple of quick, short flick passes. The goalkeeper left her post and lunged towards me, trying to grab the ball from my feet, but I swerved sharply and tapped the ball neatly into the net. Thirty thousand people stood up and clapped, forgetting Miss Tiwari's pretty face for a while, and I leaped in the air and hugged Tama in an ecstasy I had never felt before. This was undoubtedly the happiest and most glorious moment of my miserable, scar-ridden life and I wept as my teammates hugged me and kissed me and tossed me in the air. Mrs Chaudhury and Mrs Mookerjee danced another jig on the touchline and Miss Nag, for once, forgot her Marxist vocabulary as she succumbed to the general exuberance sweeping our camp, shouting hoarsely, "We have won! We are on the top!" The paramilitary band dutifully played "Sare jahan se achha" a third time to remind the jolly crowd about national integration.

Before we received the prestigious Hazrat Mahal Cup and took our lap of honour around the stadium, we were subjected to a pompous ministerial speech that dwelt mostly on communal harmony and national integration. On our way back to the hotel, Mrs Mookerjee made history by announcing a bonus of Rs 100 for each player, and Mrs Chaudhury declared that the club would honour its promise to take us to Delhi for sightseeing.

*

My friends were very much surprised, if not vexed, when I dropped out of the sightseeing trip on the pretext that I had to visit an old and ailing aunt in Karol Bagh. I couldn't fool Tama who dragged me to a corner of the lobby and whispered, "What's the matter, Hem? You've never mentioned this far-flung aunt before."

"I am here to settle a score with an old enemy, Tama," I said. "I'll tell you all about it later."

I waited till the girls, dressed up in all their finery, trooped onto the Panicker Travels' tourist bus and vanished down the road, and then I turned the lock in my room and waded through a debris of discarded blouses, bras and petticoats to plant myself in front of the mirror. I knew my scars were enough to arouse Mr Basak's perverted passion, but I felt I should still tart myself up a bit and wear something attractive to gain his immediate attention.

One hour later, as I came downstairs in my pink, chikan-embroidered kurta-kameez outfit and heavy make-up, Mrs Bhanot, the sedate, matronly receptionist of Lakshmi Hotel (which was located in Paharganj, opposite New Delhi railway station, and was a cut above Hotel

Avadh in terms of space and other amenities) shot me a censorious glance to show her displeasure.

"May I use your phone, Mrs Bhanot?" I asked throatily, fluttering my mascara-ed eyes just to give her the creeps.

"Yes, you can," she responded gruffly and then asked me archly, "Are you going to a marriage party?"

"Oh no, I am going to meet a good friend of mine. But first I must give him a ring. Please hand me the directory."

I had no difficulty finding Mr Basak's number, but it took me a dozen attempts to get someone on the line. "Both sahib and memsahib gone out in the early morning," said a male voice, probably a servant's.

"Memsahib! Which memsahib?" I shouted, wondering if that bit-part actress, Lola Mudgal, had started calling herself "Mrs Basak".

"The one who comes here this time every year," the servant shouted back.

"Is she Indian or foreign?" I demanded, wondering if Mr Basak had recruited for his harem an itinerant mistress who visited him every year in winter like a migratory bird.

"She is a pukka memsahib," confirmed the servant. "Hundred percent phoren."

"Where did they go? Darjeeling or Calcutta?"

"No, no, they not gone that far. They are here attending some old car race." From further queries I gathered that for over a decade Mrs Basak had been joining her husband every year to participate in this race. I also learnt that the Basaks could be met at the India Gate lawns around five in the afternoon, on their return from the race. Very intriguing, I thought, and even as my hopes of seducing Mr Basak were dashed, I was curious to find out if the Basaks had won a prize.

"That's the Statesman Vintage Car Rally," explained Mrs Bhanot when I asked her why an MP should stoop so low as to join a car race in a battered jalopy. "They have been holding this childish race tamasha every winter, though God knows why. Is your friend an MP?"

I nodded. Mrs Bhanot's round eyes became rounder and she promptly arranged her facial lines to express cordiality and bonhomie. Espresso coffee and mutton cutlets arrived from the kitchen within five minutes and instructions were given to the cook, ignoring my feeble protests, to serve me tandoori chicken and stuffed naan for lunch. After such lavish hospitality I hadn't the heart to turn down Mrs Bhanot's request to help her get a gas connection from the MP quota for her newly married daughter. Mrs Bhanot even arranged for an auto-rickshaw to take me to India Gate and back in the afternoon.

*

I reached the picturesque India Gate lawns just a few minutes before the first vintage car heaved into view. A sizeable crowd had already gathered around an open platform on which sat the Air Chief Marshal's statuesque wife and a few office bearers of the Vintage Car Club of India. Even as a couple of volunteers arranged the various trophies — twenty-three, I counted — on a long, narrow table, someone rushed in with two flower vases and placed one at each end of the table. While waiting for Mr Basak's car I eavesdropped on two bantering vintage car buffs just to get the hang of it.

"I saw Mr Sahni crooning lullabies to his red and black Studebaker on the Sohna hill climb," reported a dapper senior citizen with a fine waxed moustache.

"I don't think Mr Chaudhury's 1927 Hispano Suiza will make it," observed his companion, a handsome middle-aged man in tweeds and a white baseball cap. "The old lady was spluttering near DLF Qutub and her fan belt groaned."

Obviously, these two gents knew most of the participants and had just returned from Sohna. I pricked up my ears in the hope of picking up some news about Mr Basak's performance, but the two car buffs soon engrossed themselves in making an inventory of the day's mishaps: the lousy, overspiced food served to the participants at the Sohna Tourist Complex; the theft of a valuable brass cap from a 1938 Chrysler Royal and a horn from a 1930 Mercedes Benz; and worst of all, the total lack of police bandobast on the entire route.

Then the bulk of the vintage cars chugged in, one after another, wheezing and groaning and spluttering amidst joyous shouts and applause. The old beauties had been spruced up, freshly painted and dressed for the occasion with silver streamers tied around their bodies. One car had a placard declaring "I am still faithful to my owner." The festive mood of the crowd was given a boost by the Air Force band which played "Rosy Polka," "Bella Figura" and "The Gladiator". Quite a treat for me after a surfeit of "Sare jahan se achha!"

The Basaks, dressed in period costume, created quite a flutter among the crowd as they arrived in their 1936 Bentley, smiling and waving at their friends and admirers. In his maroon, high-necked sherwani studded with shining silver buttons, gold chain and a flowing pink turban Mr Basak affected a princely air while Mrs Basak, rigged out in silk and brocade and weighed down by chunky gold and diamond jewellery (which must have been a Basak heirloom), looked very coy, graceful and extremely Indian. The crowd clapped and cheered lustily and some wag shouted, "Make way for the Maharaja and the Maharani, folks."

As I watched Mrs Basak in her new incarnation, affecting all the graces and airs of a vintage Indian princess, I realized once and for all that I was hopelessly in love with her and nothing on earth would alter this irrevocable truth. And when she alighted from her chariot and greeted her lady admirers, I felt an irresistible urge to sidle up to her and whisper in her ear: "You look great, Maharani!" and, if possible, plant yet another kiss on her fair cheek. But, on second thoughts, I checked myself, knowing that my presence would only embarrass her before her admirers. I couldn't, however, resist the temptation of hanging around for a while to find out if the Basaks had won one of those twenty-three shining trophies.

I had to wait for another half hour till the last car drove in, then a VCCI official stood before the microphone with a sheet of paper and started announcing the names of the winners. The lucky ones mounted the podium, one by one, to receive their trophies from the Air Chief Marshal's wife amidst thunderous clapping, hold them up with a broad grin for the cameras and then return to their friends and admirers for garlands and backpats. I felt a spasm of joy when the Basaks were declared winners of the Four Square King trophy which was reserved for the most elegant couple in period costume participating in the rally. On the spur of the moment, I snatched away a garland from the hands of one Mr Suri who had received the Foden trophy a few minutes before for his 1932 Chevrolet and made a dash towards the platform, elbowing and pushing everyone roughly out of my way. "Mrs Basak!" I cried as I scrambled onto the platform, shocking the chief guest and the VCCI volunteers, and threw the marigold garland around her neck. "You look great, Mrs Basak! You look like a real Maharani!" I gasped and beamed. Mrs Basak looked horrified and she squinted her eyes as though she wanted to confirm that I was not actually an apparition that had just emerged from the gathering shadows of the nearby jamun trees. "Thank you, Mrs Mitra," she said with a wooden smile. "But we must not inconvenience others." And with that slight reprimand for my unbridled enthusiasm, she came down from the stage with her trophy and embraced a stout middle-aged lady who promptly whisked her away to her other admirers.

After this humiliating encounter I tried to slink away, but Mr Basak, who had been chatting with an elderly man near the dais, grabbed my arm. "Mr Deb, you must meet Mrs Mitra," said Mr Basak with a devilish grin. "She is a real vintage car buff like you. Came all the way from Cal to cheer us on. Just imagine!"

Mr Deb, a great big hunk with a raspy voice, grabbed my hand and shook it vigorously. "Glad to meet you, Mrs Mitra," he said with a broad smile. "We vintage car buffs are a rare breed, aren't we?"

I looked daggers at Mr Basak and then turned my head to nod at Mr Deb.

"You remind me of Mrs Plover who used to come all the way from Dorking to follow the rally in her cute baby Austin," said Mr Deb, peering at my face affectionately through his gold-rimmed spectacles. "What do you think about this year's entries, Mrs Mitra?"

"Splendid, every one of them," I said and again looked at Mr Basak for help, but he seemed to be enjoying my discomfiture and did nothing to rescue me.

"Of course they were splendid, Mrs Mitra," persisted Mr Deb, "but, as a vintage car buff, don't you think pre-1930 Fords and Chryslers have dominated today's rally? There was the odd Lagonda or the Hispano Suiza, but still. . ."

"Mr Basak!" I cried in desperation. "I must rush to catch my train. Excuse me, Mr Deb. . ."

"I will take just a minute, Mr Deb, if you don't mind. . ." said Mr Basak and followed me out of the crowd.

"Now, what are you doing here, my dear?" said Mr Basak as we walked towards India Gate. I told him about our matches at Lucknow and lied that I had actually come to see India Gate along with my teammates and had stayed on to watch the vintage car rally about which I had heard so much in Calcutta.

"Did you meet Max?" he asked.

"Oh yes. I garlanded her and exchanged a few pleasantries."

"Really? I thought she was quite furious about your. . . of course, it was entirely my fault."

"Never mind, Mr Basak. We have already patched up our little differences," I assured him. "Now I must catch my train."

Mr Basak looked at his watch and smiled. "But there isn't a train for Calcutta before ten, my dear."

"I have to do some shopping too, Mr Basak," I said stubbornly.

"Well, in that case I won't hold you up. I just wanted to tell you that my offer is still open."

I felt a sneaking pride that Mr Basak still nurtured his perverted passion for me. I however feigned complete innocence and asked, "What offer, Mr Basak?"

"The one you refused in the car on our way to Darj."

"Oh, that one! But I turned it down then and there, didn't I?"

"You did, but in case you change your mind. . . Look, Hem, I am prepared to wait."

"I will remember that, Mr Basak," I said, careful not to annoy him, as I remembered how he had chafed and fumed at me when I had summarily turned down his filthy proposal. Mr Basak smiled and squeezed my hand. "That's a sensible girl. There's an empty bench over there. Let's go and sit down and have a little chat before Mr Deb buttonholes me again. I am curious to know exactly what happened between you two to make Max write such a long and nasty letter to me about your stay at Rose Valley."

"You have to excuse me, Mr Basak. Maybe another time. . ." I said sweetly. I had no intention of reminiscing about my bitter-sweet memories of Rose Valley to anyone, least of all Mr Basak. "I have to get back to the hotel and accompany my friends to Chandni Chowk for some shopping before we board the train," I explained and looked around frantically for the auto-rickshaw Mrs Bhanot had requisitioned for me. "Jugnu! Bring the vehicle double-quick," I shouted as I saw the black and yellow three-wheeler parked under a tree.

"So, you have your own transport, huh?" said Mr Basak, rolling his eyes in mock awe.

"It's better than some of those battered jalopies you people rode in," I quipped. "Bye Mr Basak." And without waiting for Jugnu to turn up, I ran towards the auto-rickshaw.

*

"Did you meet your MP friend? Did you tell him about my daughter's gas problem? How much time will he take to get her the connection?" Mrs Bhanot let fly her volley of three questions, just like Utpala, the moment I stepped into the lobby. In the sudden upsurge of my reawakened passion for Mrs Basak, I had completely forgotten Mrs Bhanot's request and had to invent a sensational story to save my skin.

"My MP friend and his English wife met with a serious accident near Sohna," I said, assuming a sad and solemn expression. "Their car fell into a ditch. Multiple fracture, I think."

"Oh no!" cried Mrs Bhanot, throwing up her arms in utter frustration.

"I am extremely sorry, Mrs Bhanot. You'll have to catch another MP for that gas connection."

Mrs Bhanot gave me a look that made the tandoori chicken somersault in my belly. "Maybe next time I'm here . . ." I mumbled and scurried towards the staircase.

Eight

A week after Mr Ghatak's return from Denmark, the Directorate of Animal Husbandry hosted an international conference on Animal Disease Surveillance which increased our work enormously. In the morning, as I dumped a record number of ten files on Mr Mazumder's table, he groaned and declared that he wouldn't survive the stress and strain of the conference. And in the afternoon, when I handed him a chit from Mr Ghatak demanding copies of a dozen old reports for reference purposes, Mr Mazumder went berserk and started shouting and gesticulating at Mr Bakshi and, for once, the contemplative assistant reluctantly uncrossed his arms and legs and stood up with a heavy grunt to harness himself to what he malevolently called "Mr Ghatak's funeral work". Miss Kar, the typist, looked panicky and I took this opportunity to settle a score with her by telling Mr Mazumder that some more typing work would soon be allocated to his section.

On the morning of the conference, Mr Ghatak sent me along with another two peons to the Committee Room to arrange the chairs, hang a welcome banner above the dais, pin some optimistic charts and diagrams on a display board at the entrance and fetch the electrician to change the fused bulbs and start the air-conditioner. In the midst of all these hectic activities, Mrs Bose (who looked very seductive in her soft, terry voile sari draped in air hostess style) flew in to deliver some red and green bunting produced by her talented son with an artistry which, Mrs Bose asserted, could only be expected of St Matthew's super-bright kids. She was very fussy about the proper display of her son's artwork and I had to climb the ladder several times, hitching up my sari far above my ankles, forsaking my modesty, to satisfy her artistic demands. And then, just when I thought that I had done my job and could sit back and relax, Mrs Bose suddenly remembered that the cyclostyled copies of Mr Ghatak's paper on livestock diseases had to be collected from the machine operator and put together for distribution among the participants. I could have complained of fatigue but considering the urgency of the work, I rushed to the cyclostyling room and carted back an enormous bundle of papers to Mrs Bose's cubicle. The latter promptly started sorting out the papers and then gave a shriek as she discovered that she had forgotten to number the stencils! There was hardly an hour left to prepare the sets and only Mr Ghatak knew the correct order. Mrs Bose dashed out of the room, ignoring her hourly toilet, and returned after five minutes with a slightly nervous Mr Ghatak who looked very uncomfortable in his grey suit and big paisley tie that hung like a pendulum from his scrawny neck.

"Nothing to be panicky about," assured Mr Ghatak when he realized our problem. "There is still enough time to set things right. Mrs Mitra, please rush to Mr Mazumder and get two extra hands from the section. Quick!"

I sprinted to the AH section and conveyed Mr Ghatak's order; Mr Mazumder asked Mr Bakshi and Miss Kar to help Mrs Bose out, but neither of them would budge from their chair. Miss Kar complained of exhaustion and Mr Bakshi grumbled that he had already "eaten a kilo of dust" to ferret out those old reports for Mr Ghatak and his aching back badly needed a rest. Moreover, he pointed out, he was an assistant and as per the work allocation set out in the Manual of Office Procedure, he couldn't be compelled to do jobs meant for class IV staff. A desperate Mr Mazumder finally joined his palms and begged Miss Kar to save his honour, calling her "my sweet mother", an "asset of AH section" and a few more pleasing epithets whereupon Miss Kar condescended to accompany me to Mrs Bose's cubicle with a long face, cursing Mr Mazumder, Mr Ghatak and Mrs Bose all the way.

Mr Ghatak promptly lined up Mrs Bose, Miss Kar and me along the table and handed Mrs Bose a sheet of paper on which he had scribbled the correct order of the livestock diseases. "There is no possibility of confusion about the tables and the charts as they have already been numbered," he explained. "Now buckle down to the job and bring me the sets in the Committee Room within half hour so that we can distribute them before tea break." Mr Ghatak looked at his watch, adjusted his tie and dashed out of the cubicle.

We started preparing the sets in earnest but I soon discovered to my horror that even after Mr Ghatak's intervention matters were no better. According to Mr Ghatak's scenario, Mrs Bose was supposed to pull out Bovine Tuberculosis and Contagious Bovine Pleuropneumonia along with three charts and pass them on to Miss Kar who was to add

Swine Fever, Canine Rabies and Pullorum Disease along with five charts and three tables and pass on the whole bunch to me to attach Rinderpest, Foot and Mouth Disease plus two charts, arrange the Introduction and Conclusion and complete the set for stapling. But after about ten minutes Miss Kar complained that she was getting too many Bovine Tuberculosis and very few Bovine Pleuropneumonia from Mrs Bose and I, in my turn, pointed out that I was getting half my ration of Swine Fever and too many Canine Rabies from Miss Kar.

"Stop grumbling, you girls!" chided Mrs Bose. "Catch whatever disease you can and make sure that the bunch doesn't look too thin or too fat. We actually only need two good sets, one for Mr Ghatak and the other for the chairman, in case the old fogey doesn't start dozing within fifteen minutes of the inaugural speech and decides to wade through this nauseating material. The other delegates will simply stuff it in their bags and forget it. Just make sure that the Intro and the Conclusion are where they should be. Now girls, buckle down."

Reassured by our team leader, we worked at a brisk pace and the sets piled up pretty fast. The last few sets had to be prepared entirely from Bovine Pleuropneumonia, Swine Fever and a bar chart showing the success of the state rinderpest eradication programme. Then Miss Kar and I started stapling the sets in a competitive spirit. I spotted a few pages turned upside down and tried to set them right, but Mrs Bose chided me, "Hem, you'd better leave that job to Miss Kar and help me arrange my sari before I rush to the conference room and distribute Mr Ghatak's paper." I obeyed Mrs Bose and started my usual work on her sari while Mrs Bose, mirror in hand, powdered her nose, painted her lips and practised a gentle nod and a little fluttering of her eyelashes to accompany her professional smile.

"Foreign delegates are mostly flirtatious by nature," she confided to us, removing a clip to allow a strand of her hair to slip over her face. Then she picked up the bundle of Mr Ghatak's paper, perfect ones on top, and dashed out of her cubicle.

Mrs Bose returned after fifteen minutes with a victorious smile. "Relax, girls," she chirped. "Everything is OK. Mr Ghatak and the chairman have got the good copies and the delegates are fanning themselves with the bad ones as the air-conditioner isn't working properly. You know, a fat Russian delegate even tried to slip his sweaty hand round my midriff."

"How scandalous!" gasped Miss Kar in horror and covered her own midriff as if it was in danger of being pawed by a foreign delegate.

"I think he was enchanted by my air-hostess-style draping and my professional smile. Now, girls, let's go out for a breath of fresh air and a light refreshment. I feel famished after such hard labour."

We went to the back of the Writers' Building where one could get an incredible variety of eatables – fruit chaat, jhalmoori, ghugni cooked with minced meat, sweet and sour bhelpuri and a host of delicious homemade sweets like monohara, shar-bhaja, ladikeni, all brought by the vendors on the morning trains from places as far away as Krishnanagar, Behrampur and Nabadwip. Each of us took a plate of ghugni and a couple langchas and then went to our favourite tea vendor who had made his reputation in this food carnival with his aromatic tea.

Back in Mrs Bose's cubicle, we stumbled on a furious Mr Ghatak who was crouching on the floor, frenziedly rummaging through the papers we had thrown in the waste-paper basket.

"Mrs Bose!" cried Mr Ghatak. "You have landed me in trouble. Give me at least five correct sets at once. This is scandalous . . . the delegates from Canada and Sri Lanka have returned their copies to the chairman, demanding complete sets, and some of the foreign delegates are smirking and showing their copies to one another. God! How could you women mess up the whole thing when I showed you how to put the papers together?"

"We are not machines, sir," retorted Mrs Bose. "We are fallible human beings and we have done our best within the very limited time you allowed us." She rolled her eyes menacingly and took something out of her handbag. I trembled at the frightening possibility of Mrs Bose committing suicide by sucking cyanide, but it turned out to be her favourite vitamin tablet which she popped in for a bit of extra energy to grapple with Mr Ghatak. Miss Kar showed her solidarity with Mrs Bose with a big snort, but as a beneficiary of Mr Ghatak's generosity I felt it prudent not to undermine his authority any further.

"For God's sake, don't talk back and waste my time!" growled Mr Ghatak. "Give me at least two good copies or the axe is going to fall on all of you." But Mrs Bose was made of sterner stuff and she protested haughtily: "How could you expect me to distinguish bovine something from bovine another thing when all I studied in my college were art and literature? You tear a Tagore poem into bits and I'll put the pieces together in a jiffy, but this . . ."

"Damn you!" shouted Mr Ghatak in a fit of rage and stormed out, snatching the stapler from the table, probably to assemble a few good sets from the defective copies.

"Phoo!" sniggered Mrs Bose. "I am going to meet the secretary of the Action Committee right now to report Mr Ghatak's misbehaviour. A gherao or sit-in strike has to be organized if we are victimized. Comrades, come along, there's no time to waste." Mrs Bose grabbed Miss Kar's hand and dashed off in the opposite direction from Mr Ghatak. I was eager to follow them but Miss Kar pointed out that, being a daily wage peon, I was not entitled to approach the Action Committee.

*

I got the sack around five, just after the conference was over. Mrs Bose was transferred out of the Directorate for "gross indiscipline and insubordination" and Miss Kar received a severe warning for "dereliction of duty". My termination order, signed by the Deputy Secretary (Admn), merely stated that my services were no longer required by the AH Division and I could collect my wages for the five days I had worked that month in the first week of the next month. I went to see Mr Ghatak and tried to argue that I had only obeyed Mrs Bose, my team leader, and that I was a helpless woman with a sick husband to care for.

"I too am quite helpless, Mrs Mitra," said Mr Ghatak, loosening his tie. "The situation got out of hand when some foreign delegates started making barbed comments about Indian efficiency. It made the chairman so furious that he summoned the Deputy Secretary in charge of the Administration into the Committee Room and ordered him to sack those responsible forthwith. But the Administration people couldn't touch Mrs Bose and Miss Kar as they are regular employees and are protected by the Action Committee, so you had to be the proverbial scapegoat. I am extremely sorry, Mrs Mitra."

"It would have been much better if you hadn't offered me this post at all," I said bitterly as I turned at the door.

"Wait a bit, Mrs Mitra," said Mr Ghatak, raising his arm. "I will give you something." He took out a big book from his bottom drawer and gave it an affectionate pat. "This is a standard work on Animal Quarantine, Mrs Mitra. Take it to Mr Das of Imperial Book Depot on College Street. I am sure he will give you three hundred rupees, if not more."

"Thank you, sir," I said and accepted the tome without the slightest hesitation. At least this would fetch me a month's wage, I thought.

*

I tried to make light of my dismissal, but Paromita was perturbed, probably fearing that I could lapse into my depressive fits again. She often found me slouching in a deckchair on the veranda, brooding about my bleak future.

What next? Huddled in my chair, I considered this disturbing question as I watched a pair of sparrows flitting in and out of their little nest built in a fork of the old mahogany tree near the boundary wall. I wished I were a brainless sparrow burdened with the minimal responsibilities of gorging myself on worms, laying eggs, hatching them and occasionally collecting twigs and grass for my little nest. But, as an earth-bound female, I could only mull over this disturbing question again and again: "what next?" Of course, there was Mr Basak's offer, but the very idea of entering into a purely physical relationship revolted me. Ah, if only Mrs Basak had accepted me as a friend, life could have been so pleasant and enjoyable with or without a job! Why, I wouldn't even mind working in her house as a scullery maid if that allowed me to see her sweet face every day and catch an occasional whiff of her heady fragrance.

Suddenly, it dawned on me that as the vice-president of the Calcutta Ladies Club and the owner of a prestigious art gallery, Mrs Basak must be well-known to Calcutta's top brass and she could surely help me get a small job in an office or a department store. She might have a hundred and one reasons to refuse me her friendship, but helping out a woman in distress was something quite different, particularly when that woman had, by fair means or foul, enjoyed her lavish hospitality for a couple of days. Thrilled by this idea, I sprang to my feet and darted into the room to snatch my purse from the shelf and dash to the nearest telephone booth.

It must have been the good karma of my previous seven births that the line was neither engaged nor dead and Mrs Basak herself picked up the phone.

"Mrs Basak here." The voice was so soft and sweet that I felt a lump in my throat.

"It's Mrs Mitra," I mumbled.

"Oh!" Her voice suddenly turned cold and slightly apprehensive. "But Mrs Mitra, I think I have already made my position crystal clear."

"Rest easy, Mrs Basak," I said. "I am not seeking your friendship this time. I need your help. I have recently lost my job at the Writers' and I badly need a new one. I have liabilities, Mrs Basak, and I don't know how. . ." I left the sentence unfinished and thought of affecting a sniffle, but withheld it as I remembered how she had ignored my tears at Flurys.

"I am sorry, Mrs Mitra," said Mrs Basak without the slightest hint of any emotion or concern. "I am afraid I don't have any connections in the job market."

"Any job will do, Mrs Basak," I pleaded. "I don't mind working in your club or gallery as an attendant or in some similar humble position."

"I am afraid there is no such position vacant at the moment."

"Ple-ase Mrs Basak! I am tired of job-hunting. If you don't do something for me, I will . . . I fear I will have no alternative but to throw myself in the Ganges or in front of a train."

There was a longish pause and I was afraid that Mrs Basak had gently put down the receiver on the table and walked away to attend a visitor.

"What are your qualifications?" she asked finally.

"MABF."

"Sounds quite impressive. Is it an American degree?"

"No, purely Indian. It stands for 'Matric Appeared But Failed'."

"Ah, that makes it a little more difficult. Are you *really* prepared to work for a low wage?"

"Anything above a hundred rupees."

"Have you a phone number?"

"No, but I have an address." I told her my address and repeated it for her so that she could note it down.

"I will get in touch with you if I find something."

"You will try, Mrs Basak, won't you?"

"Yes, I will."

"Thank you very much, Mrs Basak. You are such a good and kind-hearted lady. I can't blame myself enough when I think of my boorish behaviour at Rose Valley and . . ."

But I couldn't finish my sentence as Mrs Basak had gently replaced the receiver.

Nine

Ten days later, I received a small chit from Mrs Basak asking me to present myself before Brigadier Botball, the manager of a newly-opened organization called "Anyjob", for the post of receptionist. I tarted myself up for the interview, burying my scars under a layer of foundation, covering cream, face powder and blush-on and then practised a captivating smile à la Mrs Bose before my cracked mirror. After all, what does a receptionist do other than look good, smile a lot and answer the phone?

"How do I look?" I asked Paromita as I pirouetted on my heels, spreading the pallav of my sari with my hand like a sail, emulating those fabulous models advertising Garden saris on the TV.

"Ghastly enough to seduce a middle-aged widower," quipped my cynical friend.

Brigadier Botball (I later learnt that he was actually a discharged subaltern who had narrowly escaped court-martial for disobedience by pleading insanity) was neither middle-aged nor a widower, but he looked quite impressed by my appearance when I met him in his small cubbyhole office in a dilapidated building off Rashbehari Avenue. The brigadier himself reminded me of a slightly improved version of a scarecrow, capable of frightening not only winged creatures but also women and children from a distance of fifty yards. He had a head that looked like a tapering coconut shell with two small depressions for eyes set almost on his temples and a flat rudimentary nose that left no one in doubt about his true origin.

"How long have you known Mrs Basak?" asked Botball, fixing his sharp little eyes on my face.

"About two and a half years, sir," I lied.

"Brigadier," corrected my prospective employer. "A pukka memsahib, Mrs Basak. She hired us a few days ago to clean up her garden which was cluttered with some old Victorian statuary. Thirty poisonous snakes came out of the cracks and crevices and my boys had a field day catching those vipers alive and then selling them to the Halfkine Institute for a handsome price."

"Sounds fascinating. What are the other jobs that Anyjob do, Brigadier?"

"We do literally any job, jobs that other people shy away from. What's your first name, Mrs Mitra?"

"Hemprova. They call me Hem."

"Here we will call you Captain Hem. That's the lowest rank in our hierarchy from which you will be promoted depending on your performance and capability. You have to observe some basic rules here, Captain Hem." Brigadier narrowed his marble eyes and gave me a sharp look. I flinched a little under his cold, calculating glare, but decided to brave it and even managed to put on a smile. The brigadier raised his index finger authoritatively. "First rule or command as I call it: Don't discuss office matters outside this building, not even with your best friend. Is that clear, Captain Hem?"

I nodded.

"Command number two: Don't show inquisitiveness about anything you haven't been told about. Right?"

"Right, Brigadier."

"Fine. Now, a word about your personal appearance. In a military set-up like ours, you have to talk and look like a disciplined soldier. We don't appreciate make-up and perfume here. You'll have to cut your hair short and wear khaki like the other captains. Are you mentally prepared for this transformation?"

"Absolutely, Brigadier." I knew I had to grab this job at any cost, if only to show Mrs Basak that I was serious.

"You are in, Captain Hem," said the brigadier. "Reporting time for all officers below the rank of colonel is eight sharp."

I stood up and executed a salute.

*

Brigadier Botball commanded an army of two score and ten youths whose rank varied from captain to colonel, depending on the nature and importance of the jobs they handled. Those who were entrusted with routine jobs like reading newspapers for the blind and the convalescent, queueing up at the Corporation office or the electric office to pay bills, or destroying pigeons in office buildings had to be content with a captaincy. A more intelligent batch of half a dozen young men who had established a good rapport with the Income Tax officials, the Writers' bureaucrats, the excise inspectors and the like and were capable of offering specialized services to the brigadier's select clientele enjoyed the superior rank of major or lieutenant colonel. The prestigious rank of colonel was bestowed on only two brooding, criminal-looking creatures whose prime duty was to evict recalcitrant tenants from old houses put up for sale. This was a very delicate and risky business which the brigadier had given the code name "Operation Thunderbolt". The high-ranking duo raked in big money for the organization and they enjoyed a few privileges, one of which was that, unlike the lowly captains and the lieutenants, they were not subjected to any roll call or the half-hour morning drill.

But we who held the lower ranks had to assemble on the vacant lot adjoining Anyjob's headquarters at eight sharp and arrange ourselves in three lines for the drill. The brigadier, impressively turned out in his army uniform with a couple of medals dangling from his chest, first called the roll and then drilled us vigorously, barking his commands in an awe-inspiring staccato: "Left-right left-right left-right . . . 'bout turn! quick march! left-right left-right left-right. . ." After fifteen minutes' strenuous work-out, he ordered, "At ease!" and took out a cigarette holder and a silver cigarette case from his pocket to enjoy his first puff of the day. After drill, we were served tea and biscuits and then the captains and lieutenants fanned out to their scheduled jobs and I slipped behind the reception desk to attend to phone calls from our clients and keep a note of the jobs on a sheet of paper which I later passed on to the brigadier for the next day's duty roster. Whenever a distressed landlord rang up, I had strict instructions to put the call through to the brigadier, for such calls generally resulted in "Operation Thunderbolt" and therefore necessitated a meeting behind closed doors with the two colonels. Only after Colonel Ghoton and Colonel Phatik had set out on their sensitive mission, would the brigadier emerge from his office, looking quite relaxed, to chat with me for a while and then croon "Munney-munney-munney, sweeter than hunney" which, I presumed, was the unofficial anthem of Anyjob.

I was not supposed to discuss my work outside the four walls of my office, but the moment I got a clear picture of Anyjob's clandestine operations, I decided to talk to Mrs Basak in the hope that she herself would ask me to quit this risky job.

"I am happy that you have got a good job at last," said Mrs Basak cheerfully when I rang her from a telephone booth.

"But it's not a very good job, Mrs Basak," I said. "In fact I am thinking of. . ."

"Oh no! You know how difficult it is to get a job these days, don't you, Mrs Mitra?"

"Of course I know that, Mrs Basak. But. . ."

"No buts, please. Promise me, you will hold down this job."

Obviously, Mrs Basak had come to the conclusion that I was a grumbling ninny and needed to be dealt with with a firm hand. I also realized that my fragile connection with her could be snapped if I quit my job.

"There is no ideal job in this world, Mrs Mitra," pointed out Mrs Basak, sensing my reservations from my silence. "Don't leave your present job till you get a better one."

"I won't," I mumbled even as I felt that I was behaving like a slave.

"That's the spirit, Mrs Mitra." Mrs Basak had never sounded so encouraging. "How is your boss, the brigadier?"

"A strict disciplinarian," I said cautiously. "Keeps everyone on a tight leash."

"He has to. We need people like Brigadier Botball in this country to set things right. What about your colleagues?"

"They are very nice and chivalrous."

"Lucky you! Women often complain of harassment and misbehaviour from their male colleagues."

We continued in this vein for another five minutes or so during which I managed to extract a vague promise from Mrs Basak to have tea with me at Flurys "one of these days".

*

Paromita was happy as a lark when I brought home my first month's pay of five hundred rupees. "It's far better than that lousy daily wage job at the Writers', no?" she chirped as I handed her three hundred-rupee notes for my keep.

"A hundred times," I said, without batting an eyelid, for I knew that if I gave her as much as a hint about Botball's Operation Thunderbolt, she wouldn't allow me to continue with Anyjob. "Brigadier Botball is an ideal employer," I gushed. "Very strict and paternal. The boys working under him regard me as a sister."

"Really? That sounds almost too good to be true."

To celebrate my appointment at Anyjob, I took my teammates to my favourite restaurant behind the Elite cinema. I had invited Miss Nag to join us and she set a good example of proletarian hunger by wolfing down two plates of korma and a dozen paranthas in just about fifteen minutes. "Be aware of the forces of revisionism and deconstruction, comrades," she warned us when we came out of the restaurant, belching and toothpicking. We exchanged glances amongst ourselves, wondering what this new Marxist jargon meant. It was Ira, our clever and knowledgeable captain, who finally figured out what Miss Nag was trying to hint at. "We are fully aware of the Bengal State team's evil machinations to lure away our star players, Miss Nag," she said confidently. "But I can assure you that none of us will succumb to their temptations after our great victory at Lucknow."

Miss Nag frowned. "I think you girls should sometimes forget these petty local issues and look beyond your noses. Don't you read the papers?"

"Sports and film pages," confessed an honest Damba.

"I also read the comic strips, Miss Nag," I said to show my greater familiarity with newspapers.

"You should at least look at the headlines on the first page," said Miss Nag. "Do you know that all over Europe the revisionist forces have joined hands with the CIA to subvert the communist regimes and bring back the rotten capitalist system?"

We gasped in horrified surprise, suppressing our belches. No doubt it was a great blow to Miss Nag and it could cause a serious setback for the world revolution, though I couldn't quite figure out how this great catastrophe in Europe would affect Rani Jhansi's chances in the next year's Hazrat Mahal Cup matches. Weepy Leena started sniffing and Utpala said, "Three questions, Miss Nag. First, what will be the status of the Manifesto after this great upheaval in Europe?"

"The status and importance of the Manifesto will remain the same," assured Miss Nag. "On second thoughts, I feel it's better that you girls don't read the depressing news churned out by the dirty bourgeois press with such devilish glee. I am going to join an anti-revisionist rally on Sunday to burn the effigy of that monster Gorbachev."

*

At the end of my second month with Anyjob, I was upgraded to the rank of major as a reward for successfully handling a police raid on our premises when the brigadier was not in his office. Apparently, the police inspector had come on a complaint and wanted to check up our credentials. " 'Service With a Smile' is our motto, inspector," I said with a captivating smile which I had honed to perfection for our clients. I also showed him my daily work sheet on which I had noted down all the ordinary and innocuous calls that provided the necessary cover for the more lucrative Operation Thunderbolt. The inspector rang up some of our clients at random and when all of them confirmed that they had actually requisitioned our services to do some petty jobs, he looked slightly baffled. "Tell Botball to meet me tomorrow morning at the police station along with his registration certificate and all other necessary papers to establish his bona fides," the inspector instructed me before he left the office. The brigadier visited the police station the next morning, not with any document but with a bottle of rum and some hard cash. He came back trilling his favourite ditty "Munney-munney-munney, sweeter than hunney" and conferred on me the rank of major in an impromptu investiture held in our backyard.

"From tomorrow," declared the brigadier, after pinning a small bronze epaulette on my shoulder, "Major Hem will conduct the morning drill." Overwhelmed by this great honour, I clicked my heels and saluted the brigadier and then waved at my junior officers who greeted the announcement with vigorous applause.

The doors and windows of the neighbouring houses were flung open and men, women and children crowded the verandas and balconies as I drilled my troop in the morning, shouting commands at the top of my voice: "Left-right left-right left-right . . . 'bout turn! quick march! . . . left-right left-right left-right . . ." After the troop had marched up and down the compound a dozen times, I bawled, "At ease!" and, emulating the brigadier, I utilized the little break to pop in a piece of chocolate I had saved from the previous day. Then I carried out an inspection of my troop's uniforms and boots.

"Captain Paltan!" I shouted indignantly even as I sucked on my unfinished Cadbury's. "Your boots are dirty and your trousers look crumpled. I would like to know what you do with your generous kit allowance."

"Sorry, major. It's my wife who neglects. . ."

"That's no excuse. You are personally responsible for the proper maintenance of your uniform. This is my first warning."

"Excellent!" commented the brigadier when I reported to him this minor breach of discipline in the ranks. "That's how I kept my boys in the 29th Kumaon regiment smart and battle-fit. General Bagrodia used to tell us that the morale of an army can be judged from the shine on its boots and the creases of its uniforms. Keep it up, Major Hem."

I kept it up and became very popular in the bargain. It had never entered my head that my dark complexion and my ugly scars could arouse any other emotion than hate and perverted passion, but here in Botball's army my handicaps proved to be real assets. No one ever dared to ask me about my background, but their deferential treatment told me that they considered me a tough woman with adequate experience of the underworld to justify my superior status in the Botballian hierarchy. When a captain attached to Colonel Ghoton's special task force bowed and touched my feet before setting out on an important mission, I cringed and chided the boy, thinking that it was a crude joke, but I soon found out to my horror that it was not so. The well-known tradition of the much-dreaded Thugs who worshipped Kali before they fanned out for loot and murder had, in a mysterious way, percolated down to this day among Botball's army and I merely served as a living image of the dark, blood-thirsty goddess endowed with ominous powers.

"I have no right to tamper with my army's religious sentiments, Major," said the brigadier with a hideous grin when I reported the disturbing phenomenon. "There is, however, nothing to be alarmed about. Some of the subalterns in our 29th Kumaon regiment worshipped General Bagrodia as Lord Hanuman and they claimed that they received a shot of extra energy and enthusiasm whenever they touched the general's feet. That's how faith works, Major Hem."

Soon, the mother-worshipping captains started offering me small gifts which, I knew, had been purloined from the evicted tenants before they were thrown out on the road along with their boxes and bedding.

"Of course you can't refuse them, Major," said the brigadier when I objected to being the recipient of these second-hand gifts. "A successful army collects its booty and everyone should get their share. That's a time-honoured tradition from the days when Alexander invaded India. Don't you realize, Major Hem, that by refusing to accept your share you will undermine the morale of your subordinates?"

After this solemn lecture, I started accepting gifts from my subordinates, but instead of hoarding my share of the booty, I distributed it among my teammates. My popularity soared as I gave away combs, hairclips, nailcutters, rolls of ribbon, chocolates, cheese and pickles. In reply to Utpala's three incisive questions about the origin of these gifts,

I hinted slyly that I had no dearth of admirers at Anyjob, but sometimes I needed a little more ingenuity to explain my largesse. There was, for instance, the talking parrot. I claimed it had escaped from an aviary and, attracted by my red blouse, had perched on my shoulder, but I really knew that it belonged to a superannuated prostitute from Sonagachi who had been thrown out of her tenement for non-payment of rent. Ira, our captain, was very happy to receive this special gift and she fondly reminisced about her aunt's talking mynah which lost its excellent vocabulary after it had been mauled by a neighbourhood tom. I was however not amused when a thick-headed captain presented me an exquisitely carved leg from an antique rosewood table. This wasn't something I could offer to my teammates, so I lugged it home and handed it to Paromita, saying that I had bought it from a furniture shop for five rupees just because it caught my fancy. Surprisingly, Paromita liked my gift and kept it behind the door to use it as a weapon against burglars, though I couldn't see why a sensible thief would take the trouble to burgle our mud hut just to pick up a few enamel pots and pans.

I could have gladly borne my occupational hazards if only Mrs Basak had kept her promise to meet me at Flurys. Whenever I contacted her by phone to press for a rendezvous, she found some excuse to postpone it till the next week or some future date which, of course, never arrived. "Extremely sorry, Mrs Mitra," she would say, "but I am awfully busy fixing up this long-awaited exhibition of Mr Roy Chaudhury's watercolours," or "You have to excuse me, Mrs Mitra, I am dashing to Bangalore today to attend Aslam Huda's exhibition of graphics. Maybe we could meet some time after the tenth of this month." I felt so depressed and infuriated by Mrs Basak's transparent excuses that I prayed to almighty God that her gallery be gutted by fire so that she could spare a few minutes for me.

As my craving for Mrs Basak's company became irresistible, one Friday evening I told her that I would resign my job if she didn't agree to meet me.

"You sound rather agitated, Mrs Mitra," said Mrs Basak with a hint of irritation. "Well, let me check my week's engagements. . . Would Sunday at five thirty suit you?"

"Absolutely!" I cried excitedly. "What shall I wear for the occasion, Mrs Basak? I have bought several good saris in the past two months. Tanchoi, organdie, ethnic with temple motifs . . . you name it."

"I am glad to know about your latest acquisitions, Mrs Mitra. Since you have asked me . . . well, wear anything that's not too loud and gaudy."

"I think I shall wear my paper silk. I know you will appreciate its tender-banana-leaf colour."

*

But, alas, my long-awaited meeting with Mrs Basak had to be postponed once again as my Nioti, Destiny, played yet another dirty trick on me. On Saturday afternoon, just before the office closed, a squad from the Lalbazar police headquarters raided our premises. Brigadier Botball and the two captains who were present in the office demonstrated their excellent military training by breaking a window and vaulting over the boundary wall to vanish into the crowded local fish market. I tried to follow the same route but the agile policeman chasing me grabbed my flying hair and dragged me back to the burly, paan-chewing inspector who was rifling through my papers in the hope of picking up some incriminating evidence.

"She is the moll of the gang, sir," my captor informed him.

"I know absolutely nothing about Botball's activities, inspector," I said, trying to wrench my arm free from the policeman's iron grip. "I only worked here as a receptionist."

"Is she already in our books?" asked the inspector, darting a withering glance in my direction.

"I am sure she is from Ninni's pickpocket gang."

"Stop talking rubbish!" I bawled. "I never belonged to any pickpocket gang."

"You will sing a different song when they start grilling you at Lalbazar," the inspector assured me. "Rambhaj, handcuff her before she tries to escape again."

"This is highly objectionable!" I protested as the policeman clamped the handcuffs round my wrists. "You are treating me like a murderer!"

But the inspector ignored my protests and squirted a jet of red spittle on the wall. "Clever Botball!" he mused, scratching his groin with his dirty long nails. "Opening a brand new shop every six months, huh?"

"And filling his coffers pretty fast, sir," joined in Rambhaj.

Two hefty policemen emerged from Botball's office with some files and papers. "Nothing incriminating here, sir," reported one of them sulkily. "He has taken away all his important papers, including his blueprints for Operation Thunderbolt."

"Sisterfucker!" hissed the inspector and spat fiercely. "Now shove this woman into the van and get going."

Rambhaj gave me a prod in the ribs with his baton and pushed me towards the Black Maria. I lurched across the courtyard with downcast eyes as I didn't want to see those curious faces in the windows and the balconies whom I had once mesmerized with my impressive morning drills.

Ten

At Lalbazar the police inspector grilled me for over an hour about Botball (alias Kalibabu alias Dulu Mian) and his notorious gang. During my interrogation it was revealed that, under half a dozen assumed names, Botball had been involved in all sorts of illegal trades and practices, from the printing of fake educational certificates and the manufacture of spurious drugs to unauthorized property transactions and smuggling stolen idols out of the country to sell to art collectors and private galleries in Europe and America. He had been arrested twice, first for violating the Foreign Exchange Regulations Act, and then for selling a piece of prime land in central Calcutta, owned by a non-resident Indian, to a Marwari businessman. But surprisingly, on each occasion, Botball had been bailed out by his rich and influential friends who appeared in the court under assumed names and fake credentials. I didn't require the brains of an Einstein to figure out that the sudden raid on Anyjob and my arrest was a well-enacted drama perpetrated by the police to oblige a rival criminal gang on whose area Botball had unwittingly trespassed. The police took its weekly hafta from both the gangs and occasionally swooped on one to please the other, after, of course, taking some money from the latter. It was, however, beyond my comprehension how a respectable lady like Mrs Basak could send me to Botball without caring to check on his antecedents.

After I had signed my statement and given the addresses of Mrs Basak and Paromita so that they could be informed about my arrest, the inspector handed me over to a swarthy, foul-mouthed policewoman, instructing her to shove me into the undertrials' cell for the night. My irascible escort dragged me along a dimly-lit corridor and then across a cobbled courtyard where two drunken policemen were entertaining each other with some bawdy jokes, down another dark corridor and finally through a hatch-like opening in a massive grilled gate that separated the female ward from the male. I had to hand over my khaki outfit and my personal belongings at the Warden's office and change into a dirty, blue-bordered sari blotched with a few red stains which gave me a queasy feeling. I was eventually frogmarched to the women's cell where a squat, suspicious-looking warder frisked me thoroughly before she formally accepted me from my escort, along with a receipt, like a consignment of contraband goods. Through the grilled, heavily padlocked entrance I could see a long strip of veranda connecting a row of five or six rooms.

"Look, I am a bhadrolok's daughter," I said as the attendant opened the padlock with a click. "Don't throw me among hardened criminals."

"Bhadrolok's daughter, achha?" mimicked the attendant and rolled her eyes, feigning great surprise as if she had never heard a bigger joke in her life. "Sati-Savitri, hun? I will put you up with a few angels like you. Come on, sweetie." She grabbed my arm and dragged me up the veranda to the third room, opened another padlock and pushed me into a dingy, rectangular cell with a small barred window near the ceiling that presented a forbidding view of the prison's high wall fortified by iron spikes. The cell stank of piss and raw phenyl and its four walls were streaked with red paan-spittle. A naked electric bulb dangling precariously from a loose wire provided the illumination and the old Usha fan whirling sluggishly on the ceiling produced more noise than air. For company, I had two other criminals — a swarthy, pockmarked Amazon and a thin, suspicious-looking creature — who were playing cards on a string cot. I stood stiff and helpless in the middle of the room, wondering if I should exchange pleasantries with my room-mates. The older woman solved my problem by asking, rather nonchalantly: "Husband basher?"

"No, I am not a criminal."

"Baby strangler?" asked the thin woman.

I didn't respond.

"May be a child-lifter," observed the pock-marked Amazon.

"You have no business to talk about me like that," I fumed.

The women exchanged a quick, meaningful glance and then the older woman smiled. "Sorry, darling, we only want to help you."

"I don't need anyone's help," I snapped and strode to the vacant cot to stretch out and take stock of my situation. But I felt so tired that I fell asleep as soon as I closed my eyes.

I was awakened by a loud gong. "Mealtime" announced the hefty woman and gathered her cards. The door was thrown open and we came out of the room to squat on the veranda in a line along with a dozen women prisoners from the other cells. The warder stood at one end of the veranda and organized the feeding with military precision.

"Sal-pata!" she ordered. A three-foot dwarf who looked like a circus clown in his oversize khaki shorts and Gandhi cap, rushed in with a bundle of dried sal leaves (a few of which stitched together with toothpicks served as a plate) and scurried along the length of the veranda, dropping one of his disposable dishes before each one of us. Before he had reached the last woman in the line, the commander shouted, "Khichuri!" and a burly man, panting and puffing like a steam engine, chugged in with a bucket and a ladle and slapped two scoops of thick rice-and-dal porridge on each leaf, synchronizing the movements of his huge belly, shining bald dome and the serving hand in one perfect sweeping motion. Occasionally, he struck the ladle heavily on the rim of his bucket to dislodge the lumps that clung to it and admonished those little Olivers (I was one) who wanted more than the sanctioned quota of two scoops. After kichudi came laabda, a hodge-podge of half-rotten cabbage, potato, spinach, gourd and other garbage that the greengrocers generally throw away for the stray cattle in the bazaars.

Meal over, we were again herded back into our cells and the doors were locked up for the night. From the mealtime chitchat among the convicts I gathered that Uma, the thin, suspicious-looking woman, was a drug-peddler and that the pock-marked Amazon Khemi was working for a gang of burglars. The latter was in the habit of infiltrating rich men's homes as a housemaid and then helping her gang to rob the house at the earliest opportunity.

I thought that these two veteran criminals, who had already served a couple of terms (they even grumbled about the alarming decline in the quality of prison diet over the past few years), would allow me to rest in peace, particularly after my brusque responses to their evil insinuations about my crime, but I was wrong.

"Come on, dear," coaxed Uma. "Don't be so grouchy. Let's be friends and share our little secrets like true sisters."

"I can see the burden of your sin crushing you, sweetie," said Khemi, fixing her small, luminous eyes on my face.

"Spill out your story and get a big load off your chest," chimed in Uma.

"I was caught while eloping with a minor," I blurted out, just to stop these two nosey-parkers bothering me.

But they were not satisfied with such a cursory admission of my guilt and pestered me for further details. When I refused to oblige them, Khemi tried a different tack.

"Our scriptures say that in Hell all fallen women are forced to hug a thorny cotton silk tree till they bleed to death," the burglars' friend reminded me with appropriate gestures of horror.

"And what do the scriptures prescribe for those unfaithful servants who rob their masters' houses?" quipped Uma.

Khemi frowned. "I didn't rob anybody's house and I will prove that in court."

"It seems we are in the same boat," observed Uma. "Those little plastic packets of brown sugar were actually planted in my room."

Khemi quoted knowledgeably from the holy *Bhagavat* and Uma cited her neighbours' evidence to absolve themselves completely of their criminal charges. The two "wrongly confined" women then challenged me to prove my innocence and when I refused to do so, they sighed deeply, shook their heads dolefully, and after a brief, incisive analysis of my crime, concluded that in the eyes of God lust and lechery were the greatest sins that a woman could perpetrate against humanity. Compared to that, opening a latch for someone in the middle of the night to rob a filthy rich man of his ill-gotten money or selling drugs to spoilt brats were innocent pranks for which the scriptures hadn't pre-scribed any harsh punishment.

"But don't feel depressed, girl," Khemi consoled me as she noted the puzzled expression on my face. "There is still time."

"Are you sure?" Uma wondered, rolling her eyes with utmost concern.

"Yes," assured her companion. "We can still chant Lord Krishna's one hundred and eight names over her just before she dozes off. It takes a long time to whittle away the sin, little by little, with Krishna's holy names but that's all we can do to save a poor sinner from that painful ordeal in Hell."

I told them brusquely to mind their own business and assured them that I was not at all worried about hugging that thorny cotton-silk tree in Hell, because so many fallen women had preceded me to that place and rubbed their bodies against that famous tree that its bark must have by now become quite smooth.

"There! I can hear it!" whispered Khemi ominously, shaking her head in distress. "Deep in her heart the sin-bird flutters its wings!"

Uma nodded gloomily. "Her face shows it. Why do you think God marked her face with so many scars?"

"Leave me alone, will you?" I shouted.

"Chee-chee!" Khemi clucked disapprovingly. "We are only trying to help you, girl. But if you show us your red eyes. . ." She broke off on a discreet signal from her friend.

"She is only a child," cooed Uma. "She needs careful handling."

It seemed that these self-appointed guardians of my tainted soul wouldn't allow me to have a good night's rest, so I finally told them that I wouldn't mind a chant if that was all that they wanted to do to save my soul.

"Lord Krishna has at last heard my prayer," said Khemi with a sigh of relief and exchanged a meaningful wink with the drug peddler.

An hour later, we got our grub — kichudi and laabda served with military precision — and returned to our cell.

"Now, lie down and close your eyes," commanded Khemi, her eyes blazing with a religious fervour which I thought rather weird. I obeyed her all the same, wondering what bizarre rituals she would perpetrate on me to purify my soul. My saviour sat at the foot of my cot while Uma took her position near my head. The former started chanting Lord Krishna's one hundred and eight names — Govinda, Gopala, Keshava, Butter-thief, Lord of the cowherds and the rest — in a mellifluous voice, with Uma joining in occasionally, though the latter had neither a singing voice nor a familiarity with Krishna's lesser-known names. Religious fanatics, these two, I thought, and closed my eyes.

I had started dozing under the spell of Krishna's unending names when Khemi thrust her paw inside my sari and started feeling me up. I gave a shriek and opened my eyes, but the lights had already been switched off and I couldn't see a thing. "Relax!" hissed the Krishna-lover gruffly, pinning down my flailing legs with her powerful knees while Uma promptly tied my hands with her bra. "Hey, she is flat like the Maidan!" she reported after a cursory investigation inside my blouse.

"That makes my job a little more difficult," grumbled the Krishna-lover. "Now, let me investigate her sin from my end."

"You dirty shitheads!" I screamed. "Investigate your own sins between your legs. Take your hands off or I will kill you."

"You are straining your vocal cords, girl," said the Krishna-lover very sweetly as she drove her hand forcibly between my clamped thighs and prized them open with a powerful twist of her clenched fist. I shouted for help but Uma soon gagged me with her stinking, sweat-starched blouse and then both of them joined hands to strip me and tie up my legs with my own sari.

137

"Now my sweet sinner, relax and see how I rub off your sin little by little," whispered Khemi hoarsely and mounted me, almost crushing me with her weight. Her prickly pubes, which she rubbed vigorously against mine, felt like a quality scrubber that one uses to remove tough dirt from the kitchen floor.

"Strictly speaking, you are not entitled to the divine ecstasy at this early stage of penance," informed my molester in between her fierce groans and grunts. "But I will offer you a wee bit of it just to show what joy Lord Krishna shares with his six million cowmaids, each one a paragon of virtue, a sin-free soul."

My sinful soul prevented me from enjoying the divine ecstasy, but my tormentor had no such handicap and she enjoyed her violent love-making for over an hour, bruising my legs, lips and breasts with her teeth and claws. Fortunately, though her friend tried to encourage her to do her bit to save me from that thorny silk-cotton tree in Hell, the drug peddler didn't show any inclination to rape me.

I woke up late in the morning aching all over and with a mild fever, and demanded immediate punishment of my molester when the warder came to take us out for our morning ablutions. The squat, thickset woman first tried to laugh away the incident as a sort of jolly good ragging, but when I showed her the bruises on my breasts and thighs, she roared, "You rundi-kutti-haramzadi! How dare you hump my girls right under my nose? I will sew up your purse with twine." She roughed up Khemi, punching and kicking her at random and abusing her in the filthiest language I had ever heard from a woman's mouth. To my great surprise, the satiated Krishna-lover took the pummelling with a stoical calm and wiped the blood oozing from her ruptured lips with the back of her palm as if it was a trickle of water or spittle. When I begged the warder to stop battering the woman, the rogue smirked and shot me a wistful look which gave me the creeps.

*

Later, around eleven, I was ferried to the Alipore court and presented before the magistrate. In the visitors' gallery I spotted Paromita and Mrs Basak, the latter looking very solemn and dignified in a soft, powder-blue, cotton jersey dress, cloche hat and sunglasses. My heart started thumping as she raised her hand and smiled and I felt like dashing to her seat to clasp her hand between my palms and tell her how much I loved her and now that I had suffered so much in jail to respect her sentiments, wouldn't she accept me as a friend? She probably recognized my wild look and turned her face towards Paromita who, in her sepulchral white cotton, looked very grim and didn't respond to whatever Mrs Basak was trying to tell her.

It took no more than fifteen minutes for Mrs Basak's brash young lawyer to establish beyond doubt that I was a minor (a fake horoscope produced by the lawyer proved beyond doubt that I was only fifteen) unwittingly dragged into Botball's trap and then complete the necessary formalities to get me released on a bail of Rs 2000. I came out of the dock, threw my arms around Paromita's neck and cried on her shoulder. I had expected a few soothing words and anxious queries from my Gandhian friend but I found her very cold and totally unaffected by my tears. She just handed me her hanky, extricated herself from my clasp and said in a bitter tone: "I would have been much happier if I had rescued you from a brothel rather than a prison for serving a notorious criminal like Botball." I was stunned by Paromita's harsh words and looked beseechingly at Mrs Basak for sympathy.

"Of course it's entirely my fault, Miss Sen," she said apologetically. "I should have checked up first, but I had no reason to suspect that an apparently innocuous organization like Anyjob could be involved in criminal activities."

"We shouldn't blame Mrs Basak," I said to protect the memsahib from Paromita's fusillade. "She was only trying to help me."

Paromita gave me a nasty look. "I have no doubt about that. After all, she is your best friend, isn't she?"

I was puzzled by Paromita's response. Why was she so hard on Mrs Basak?

"Of course, Hem is a good friend of mine," said Mrs Basak emphatically, her lips pressed tight in consternation. "And I intend to help her in future."

I was thrilled by Mrs Basak's brave declaration and stole a glance at her face to find out if she really meant it. Mrs Basak sensed my doubts and took my hand. "Did they treat you well, Hem?" she asked softly, pressing my hand just a little. I took the hint and nodded. "Yes, Mrs Basak. They were very good and kind to me. The food was tolerably good and the bed was quite comfortable."

"Liar!" cried Paromita haughtily. "I can spot a battered woman from a mile because I handle them day and night." She pressed her palm to my forehead and cried, "Why, Hemprova, you are running a temperature!"

"I will take you to a doctor, Hem," said Mrs Basak. "Come with me."

"Thank you for the offer, Mrs Basak, but she doesn't really need any medicine," snapped Paromita and grabbed my other hand firmly. "All she needs is some rest."

I gave Mrs Basak a pleading look, but she let go of my hand. She obviously didn't relish the idea of taking on Paromita in a tug of war. But outside the court building, Mrs Basak offered us a lift in her car. Paromita looked at her watch, then at the glaring sun and finally at my wilted face before she condescended to accept the offer. Having won her battle with Mrs Basak over my possession, Paromita could now afford to be a little less hostile, if not condescending, towards her opponent. I stole another glance at Mrs Basak's face to gauge her feelings but she looked inscrutable behind her Ray-Ban sunglasses.

"I will feel greatly relieved if, from now on, you stick to your football and gardening," said Paromita, interlocking her fingers with mine to demonstrate to Mrs Basak her great anxiety about my future.

"But, Miss Sen, it wouldn't be proper to deny Hem an opportunity to earn a living," argued Mrs Basak, as she swerved her red Maruti to the left to avoid colliding with a stray bull.

"I know her from my school days, Mrs Basak," pointed out Paromita, "and I am absolutely convinced that she will never do anything worthwhile in her life beyond playing football."

I felt very depressed by Paromita's low estimation of my capabilities, but I preferred to keep mum and cast a furtive glance at Mrs Basak for support.

"I beg to differ, Miss Sen," said Mrs Basak, taking up the cudgels on my behalf. "I am quite sure that Hem is capable of proving her real worth in a job situation, if only we give her the right opportunity. In any case, how long could she play football? Another ten or twelve years at the most. And then? No, Miss Sen, I feel we should think about her future in a more constructive manner."

"I think Mrs Basak is right. I can certainly. . ." I shut up as I met Paromita's glare.

"Perhaps you are not aware, Mrs Basak, that I have tried to rehabilitate *your* good friend by giving her a suitable vocational training in my own organization. But patience is an alien concept to her, so. . ."

"I think she would enjoy a job involving travel and public relations," interjected Mrs Basak.

"You are absolutely right, Mrs Basak!" I trilled, ignoring Paromita's intimidating glare. "I do enjoy going places and talking to people of all sorts."

"And getting into all sorts of scrapes," said Paromita. "Well, Mrs Basak, I have no objection if your friend can land herself a good job involving lots of travel and public relations. But I wonder if a scarface non-matriculate could really get such a position."

"Of course, she would have to undergo plastic surgery to get back her looks before we think of a decent job for her," observed Mrs Basak.

"But do you really want cosmetic surgery, Hemprova?" asked Paromita sternly.

"Well, I am not that keen, but since some people seem to be biased against my face. . ."

"Enough!" cried Paromita indignantly. "Go for skin surgery and acquire the looks of Hema Malini. But a clean face isn't enough to get you a good job, do you understand that? What about certificates and testimonials? Are you prepared to go to night school and finish your School Final?"

I groaned at the mere mention of night school.

"I have thought of an alternative, Miss Sen," said Mrs Basak, "Why don't we send her to Mrs Blistop's finishing school where she can learn a bit of everything, from flower arrangement to book-keeping, even ballroom dancing?"

"That's the type of education I really need . . . a bit of everything," I observed.

"No one asked you," snarled Paromita. "Well, Mrs Basak, to be frank, I have very serious reservations about the type of education Mrs Blistop imparts. Everyone knows that behind the facade of that finishing school she actually drills those girls in the art of flirtation and obnoxious Victorian techniques of husband-catching."

"Maybe you are right, Miss Sen," conceded Mrs Basak with a flicker of a smile. "But it's also a fact that Mrs Blistop's certificate has helped many a Calcutta girl to find a job that they wouldn't have got even with a college degree. And may I inform you, Miss Sen, that along with what you call 'Victorian husband-catching techniques', Mrs Blistop also teaches manners and etiquette and a few other genteel arts which could open new vistas for Hem."

"New vistas for Hem!" sniggered Paromita. "Really! She is already insufferable and a few weeks at Mrs Blistop's would only make her swollen-headed. I bet she will never get 'finished'. She will skip her classes and goof around."

"That's not true!" I cried shrilly. "At Champaboti I used to attend classes regularly and get very good marks too."

"Till you joined the football team," reminded Paromita. "Have you ever heard of anyone getting a duck in each and every subject, Mrs Basak?"

"I don't believe it! Hem can't be that dumb," said Mrs Basak.

"You are right, Mrs Basak," I said. "I failed deliberately to foil my mother's plan to marry me off to a Writers' clerk at the age of sixteen. The whole world knows that."

"But you couldn't avoid marriage, could you?" said Paromita.

"I think we shouldn't judge her by her past lapses," said Mrs Basak. "She is now a mature woman and she will be maturer still when she is finished at Mrs Blistop's."

"Mrs Basak is absolutely right," I said, ignoring Paromita's frown.

"I think we should allow Hem to have her say in this matter," observed Mrs Basak.

"I never stood in anyone's way, Mrs Basak," declared Paromita haughtily and released my hand from her clasp.

*

Paromita must have communed very deeply with her Inner Voice to thwart my plans, for the very morning I was to consult a renowned surgeon at Woodlands Nursing Home about my cosmetic surgery, I received an urgent note from Dr Nandy asking me to shift Babu from the hospital within three days as he was unable to accommodate him any longer due to a heavy influx of patients in the mental ward. I had borrowed six thousand rupees from Mrs Basak for the surgery, but Paromita now suggested that I should utilize the money on Babu's rehabilitation, after getting the necessary permission from Mrs Basak. Unfortunately, I couldn't contact her as she had gone to Bombay to attend Aslam Huda's much-publicized exhibition of Ganesh paintings.

"I hope your best friend won't mind this unexpected diversion of funds from beauty care to childcare," observed Paromita archly.

"She will understand," I assured her.

"She has to, for, if he isn't transferred to that school for the mentally retarded immediately, he may revert to his thumb-sucking babyhood."

*

Dinobandhu Shikshaytan impressed us by its outward appearance: high, spiked walls, a huge, cast-iron gate guarded by a uniformed durwan, and a line of ancient palm trees flanking the driveway which lent this fifty-year-old institution a touch of elegance and respectability. The young and wise-looking principal, Mr Saha, assured us that the school had an excellent faculty, good hostel facilities and a clean, well-managed canteen. He was, however, slightly doubtful whether a twenty-six-year-old kid would be able to adjust with classmates whose average age was eight and a half. We assured him that, as certified by Dr Nandy, Babu was, for all practical purposes, a child of three and a half years and was very well-behaved too. Mr Saha nodded. "Of course, Dr Nandy knows best. After all, this isn't the first time he has referred a patient to us for re-education."

To my great relief, Babu showed extraordinary adaptibility on his very first day by befriending his chubby, nine-year-old roommate Prasun, who didn't enjoy playing with his toys like a normal child and preferred to sit still on his cot in lotus posture, like a baby Buddha, watching his earthly possessions with a contemplative air. Prasun's little kingdom could boast of a Philips two-band transistor, a brand new Atlas cycle, bottles of Kisan jam and Bedecker pickles, several jars of dried fruits and a set of Pears Encyclopaedia.

"I think this boy comes from a rich family and has got enough for both of them," observed Paromita shrewdly, after a careful survey of Buddha's worldly goods. "Let's give him a proper training in sharing things with others." Not a bad idea, I thought, particularly when I was not in a position to maintain a steady supply of toys and other goodies to my kid. So, Paromita and I gave a vigorous demonstration of "give and take" for the benefit of Prasun, exchanging things between us with the rapidity of two deft conjurors. Prasun, however, thought that this was a new game he was being introduced to and he promptly dumped his clothes and his bottles of jam and pickles on Babu's cot and then smiled beatifically, anticipating that the latter would immediately return everything. But instead of reciprocating his friend's generous gesture, Babu greedily opened a bottle of jam and dug his fingers into it. It took some mild chidings and several more elaborate demonstrations to teach both of them the finer points of "give and take".

"I think they will become bosom friends within a few days," said Paromita as we left, after showering both of them with a flurry of kisses. When we looked back from the gate, we saw them standing at the window, their faces pressed tight against the grille, looking dolefully at us. We waved at them and they waved back cheerfully.

"I feel I have at last done my duty as a mother," I announced with a sense of relief and satisfaction.

"I appreciate your sentiment. Now, are you going to ask your friend for another loan to patch up your face?" asked Paromita.

"Oh, no. I think my face can wait till I earn enough to pay for my own surgery."

"That sounds great," said Paromita. "A respectful nod at self-reliance, huh? But I have a hunch that Mrs Blistop won't allow you to enter her hallowed portals before you acquire a presentable face."

Eleven

Mrs Blistop ran her famous (or infamous, as many an enlightened woman would vouch) "Calcutta Finishing School" from her modest, pink stucco house on Wood Street. From time to time, women activists demonstrated outside her gate demanding immediate closure of her "husband-catching academy", but Mrs Blistop accepted them as an occupational hazard, displaying the remarkable fortitude and resilience she must have added to her survival kit when her husband, Captain Blistop of 34 Bengal Lancers, back from the successful Burma campaign, succumbed to the feline charms of a nightclub dancer at Firpos and eloped with his tootsie to settle in Hong Kong, leaving his better half in the lurch. Any sensible Englishwoman stranded in an alien country would have rushed home to seek a sympathetic shoulder to cry on, pick up the pieces and in good time hook a widower to start her second innings on the marital crease. But Mrs Blistop shunned this predictable course and stayed put in Calcutta, claiming that she loved the city and its people, even though her detractors pointed out that the only thing she ever loved was money. It would, however, be a travesty if Mrs Blistop was dismissed as a mammon-worshipping Anglo-Saxon, for, long before she started her school to "groom young ladies in the social graces" and got it recognized by Madame Chaplussi's famous finishing school in the French Alps, Chateau Mont-Choisi (*"situation magnifique; climat de joie, education de la foi"*), Mrs Blistop had earned her reputation as a social reformer with her novel, though abortive, attempt to revolutionize begging in and around Park Street. Moved by the spectacle of those uncouth creatures whining on the pavements and thrusting their dirty, dented enamel bowls in an undignified manner, Mrs Blistop had taken a vow to introduce dignified, low-key begging à la Petticoat Lane with the active help and co-operation of a few sympathetic Corporation officials as well as the white community. A door-to-door campaign was launched to collect old coats, trousers and hats, and second-hand mandolins were bought in bulk from A. Godwin & Co. Fitted out in their dignity-inspiring English costume, the beggars, including a fair sprinkling of Anglo-Indians, stood in Mrs Blistop's courtyard to learn how to strum their small guitars, sing dolefully "Lead Kindly Light" and "Abide With Me" and hold out their saucepan hats with the plaintive appeal: "A coin for the po' singer, guv." In their turn, the guvnors were encouraged to flick coins stylishly, preferably with a good aim, as they sauntered by. Mrs Blistop's noble venture was an instant success and Park Street soon became one of the city's major tourist attractions, claiming a hundred-word entry in Miss Fowder's India Kit, which every tourist was supposed to carry in those days. But, alas, with the "sahiblogs" gone, Mrs Blistop's flock of dignified beggars found themselves grossly discriminated against by their scruffy, whining brethren whom the brown sahibs who had swiftly moved into this posh locality now patronized to show off their patriotic fervour. The classy Petticoat Lane beggars eventually discarded their tattered coats, battered hats and off-key mandolins to revert to their old, undignified ways, much to the chagrin of Mrs Blistop. But, as Tagore had told us in one of his beautiful lyrics, no work of great merit is totally lost even in this cruel world. Many a Calcuttan would raise their eyebrows in disbelief if they were told that the city's most popular musical choir which regaled them at those lavish marriage parties at the Grand or the Park Hotel with such heart-catching numbers as "Forever! Forever!", "Sweet Bride of Champadanga" and "Husband Beware!" had their humble beginnings with those discarded mandolins, bulk-bought, third hand, from the same A. Godwin & Co. where Mrs Blistop's unsung heroes had dumped them for a few rupees.

The only standard bearer of Mrs Blistop's great and almost forgotten campaign was the frail, half-blind John Goody (whose father had been a sexton in the Park Street cemetery) who could still be seen on some evenings playing "Lead Kindly Light" on his ancient mandolin under a lamppost in front of New Market or at the entrance of the New Empire cinema. John's daily rounds took him to Mrs Blistop's kitchen door where he got a generous helping of mulligatawny soup (which, Mrs Basak later told me, was one of the great legacies of the Raj), doled out by Mrs Blistop's cook-cum-housekeeper Malini with a long-handed ladle in perfect English style. The saucy, mini-skirted Eliot Road girls who knew every little scandal in and around Park Street swore that ten years ago when John had not been stricken with gout and Mrs Blistop hadn't her backaches, the former had been caught sneaking out of his mentor's house in the wee hours with a barely suppressed grin flickering across his sallow, stubbly face – a rare spectacle that couldn't be attributed merely to an inspired all-night recital of "Abide With Me" in Mrs Blistop's parlour.

Mrs Blistop had reached the biblical age of three score and ten a couple of years ago, but arrayed in her shimmering pink silk gown and pearls and aided by her clever make-up and sparkling dentures, she looked much younger, almost fiftyish, with a yen for the good things of life. Before she took in a fresh batch of girls, Mrs Blistop interviewed each one of them in her office for about two minutes to diagnose her shortcomings in carriage and deportment or any particular area which needed special attention, and dictated her instructions to her secretary, Mrs Ganguly. I was worried that my scarred face would invite her immediate censure, but, to my great amazement, Mrs Blistop didn't make any unkind remarks about my face during my five-minutes interview (three minutes extra for coming with Mrs Basak's hand-written note!). She, however, gently probed about my upbringing and my social status and looked slightly puzzled, if not annoyed, when I told her that my husband was studying in a school for the mentally retarded. "Since you are already married, may I ask, Mrs Mitra, how do you propose to utilize your education here?" she asked me in her soft, drawling voice.

"I want to get a decent, well-paid job in a hotel or a travel agency," I replied.

"Manners and etiquette – five lessons," dictated Mrs Blistop, frowning.

I realized belatedly that I had earned a negative point by forgetting to tag on "Ma'am" or some more suitable honorific to my sentence. "I also want to know as much as possible about art, architecture and Italian opera, ma'am," I said hopefully.

"I am glad to know about your lofty aspirations, Mrs Mitra," said Mrs Blistop. "You will find a Turner in our ballroom. We also invite Dr Dasgupta to deliver a couple of lectures on the basics of art and architecture, but I am afraid, my dear, you'll have to supplement your knowledge by visiting art galleries and reading some prescribed texts. Try to visit Mrs Basak's gallery as often as possible to acquaint yourself with the current trends in modern art."

I nodded, feeling very happy indeed at this suggestion. Now I would have a valid reason to visit Mrs Basak in her gallery.

"Now, would you mind walking a few paces before me, my dear?" said Mrs Blistop very sweetly.

I obeyed, affecting instinctively the military gait I had learnt so well in Botball's army.

"Intense book balance," dictated Mrs Blistop. "Do you know how to handle a knife and fork, Mrs Mitra?"

"We are rice-eaters, ma'am," I informed. "We don't need a knife and fork."

Mrs Blistop frowned. "Hygiene demands that even rice should be eaten with the help of a spoon." She turned to Mrs Ganguly. "Table manners, three sessions."

*

If the enrolment register of Mrs Blistop's school was any indication of Calcutta's pecking order, then real estate agents, building contractors and second-hand car dealers definitely occupied the topmost rung. In fact, all the twenty-five women who joined Mrs Blistop's eight-week crash course, except myself and three Anglo-Indian girls from Eliot Road, had fathers or husbands in one of the three aforementioned businesses. The meteoric rise of their fathers/husbands from the mean bustees and dingy tenements of North Calcutta to the respectable world of New Alipore and Golf Links necessitated a lot of socializing and, for some of them, finding educated and well-placed grooms as well, and Mrs Blistop's school was a godsend to this new rich class. These women needed to learn not only etiquette and the art of entertaining, they also had to be carefully guided about their foreign trips — what to wear, where to go and how to spend — for, during the scorching summer months, they flocked to the comparatively pleasant climes of London and Paris to splurge some of the money their husbands/fathers had accumulated in shady deals conducted from their nondescript, cubbyhole offices in Burrabazar or Gariahata.

Our day started with Mrs D'Souza's elocution class which we found very irksome because of her insistence on what she called "Oxford accent". We hated her intensely for her impeccable pronunciation and her well-known bias against the Bengalis. She firmly believed that we had acquired thick, sluggish tongues from our over-indulgence in milk-based sweets like rosogolla and sandesh and try as we might, the correct pronunciation of English was beyond our capacities. To rectify our "genetic handicap", Mrs D'Souza handed us detailed charts with queer notations and markings, demonstrated how to stress the first or the last syllable, harangued us endlessly about sibilants and aspirants and finally, when all the choice arrows of her quiver were exhausted without our showing any real improvement, she punished us with a tongue-twister ("She sells seashells on the seashore") for exercising our thick Bengali tongues. Soon, I got into the habit of skipping Mrs D'Souza's class and instead popping into Mrs Blistop's kitchen downstairs to chat up Malini and cadge a spoon of Branston pickle which, she proudly informed me, her mistress always imported from home as she didn't relish the fiery Indian variety. On one occasion, when I was gossiping with Malini, John Goody arrived for his daily quota of mulligatawny soup. "John, I will give you a whole rupee if you can sing any other song than those two you have already bored us with," I said, waving a dirty one-rupee note. To my great surprise, John struck up a new tune on his old mandolin and sang "Dear Little Buttercup", displaying such emotion that his voice faltered and his head shook a little too much. When he had finished his singing and bowed English style, holding out his battered hat, I took out another rupee, a shining new coin, from my purse, wrapped it up in the note and threw it into his hat, making his wrinkly face break into a smile.

After Mrs D'Souza's elocution classes, it was sheer fun to attend the delightful drills that the amiable and cheerful Mrs Pasha put us through to improve our carriage and deportment. These highly sophisticated exercises, which earned the school its bad name, were practised behind closed doors in an auditorium which had a small stage at one end and a dozen large mirrors fitted on the walls. Two notice boards, mounted at the entrance of the auditorium, attracted everyone's attention. One was for "Our Trumpets" which proudly announced the recent engagements/marriages of Mrs Blistop's former students with company executives, businessmen and army officers, while the other dished out nuggets of wisdom under the caption "Thought of the Week". The day I got my entry into Mrs Pasha's enchanting world, an obscure Latin quotation on feminine virtues was replaced by a new and more earthy one: "Young misses whut frowns an' pushes out dey chins an' says, 'Ah will' an' 'Ah woan' mos' gener'ly doan ketch husbands. Young misses should cas' down dey eyes an' say, 'well, suh, Ah mout' an' 'Jes' as you say, suh' " – Mammy's advice to Scarlett: *Gone With the Wind*.

Mrs Pasha lined us up on the stage and gave us a heavy leather-bound Bible for the Book Balance exercise for acquiring a sensual, graceful walk. Each one of us had to walk a distance of twenty yards across the stage with the Bible precariously perched on the head ("Why the Bible?" I had asked. "Just because you naughty girls won't dare to throw it to the ground and commit a little sin" came Mrs Pasha's cheerful reply), one leg crossing the other slightly in front, emulating fashion models on a catwalk. Mrs Pasha sat on a high stool in front of the stage and corrected our steps as we shuffled past her: "Try to balance your weight on your toes, Beena. . . Mrs Pal, please don't square your shoulders, the Bible isn't that heavy unless you are already weighed down by your sins. . . Hem, for God's sake, don't crouch like that; you aren't going to trap a ball in midflight. . . Seema, stop swinging your hips so blatantly – sensual doesn't mean soliciting. . ."

After half an hour of Book Balance, Mrs Pasha invited us, one by one, to sit before her on a stool and laugh sensually. "The idea is to make the world stop, look and listen to you," she explained. "An ideal feminine laugh should sound natural and yet it has the sweet, heart-warming jingle of a jaltaranga." We hee-heed and hoo-hooed for fifteen minutes under Mrs Pasha's guidance and then stood before the mirrors to practise our "expressions" (a euphemism for three different kinds of smiles, with particular emphasis on the pout) and add "personality and sparkle to our faces". Mrs Pasha stood behind us to watch our performance in the mirror and occasionally remind us of the basic theory of "Pout Power": "A pouting mouth expresses displeasure in a light way and captivates the beholder instantly, but if you overdo it, it can easily degenerate into a sulk which nobody likes." Besides prescribing Vitamin E tablets and regular rubbing of olive oil at the corners of our lips, Mrs Pasha also gave us a delightful exercise to acquire soft, kissable lips. This involved puckering up our mouths in an exaggerated kiss and then stretching the lips back into a wider-than-life toothy grin. The difficult art of dimple formation was also ably demonstrated by Mrs Pasha, but it seemed that only two girls among us were really endowed with the right kind of cheeks for practising this high art.

Throughout these absurd exercises in pouting and puckering, I kept my interest alive only by visualizing melodramatic situations in which Mrs Basak offered me her divine lips for demonstrating my superior kissing techniques. The urge to see her increased day by day and one afternoon, after my classes were over, I gathered enough courage to ring her gallery.

"Do you like the curriculum, Hem?" she asked me.

"Immensely," I said. "I find the classes very interesting. Next week we will start dancing."

"How exciting! I hear that ballroom dancing is back in fashion. Of course, the waltz is so mesmerizing."

"Mrs Blistop has advised me to visit galleries to get acquainted with the contemporary art scene."

"Really? How thoughtful of Mrs Blistop. But dear, I don't think you'd be interested in Mr Bagh's abstract paintings . . . splashes of cadmium and ochre and some obscure figures peeping out from the corners of the pictures. I'll certainly let you know when I put up something more intelligible."

I could see that Mrs Basak was trying her best to keep me at arm's length, so all I could say was: "That would be fine, Mrs. Basak."

"Keep in touch, Hem," cooed Mrs Basak and hung up.

*

After enjoying Mrs Pasha's tantalizing lessons on carriage and deport-ment, I felt extremely bored with Mrs Khaitan's monotonous lectures on etiquette and table manners which was supplemented by Miss Gupta's bi-weekly classes on culinary concepts and the intricacies of entertaining guests in house parties. Mrs Khaitan was a wafer-thin, grumpy fusspot with the infuriating habit of suppressing our little queries with a stern rebuff: "Don't rationalize; do as I tell you." She claimed that she corresponded regularly with a senior editor at *Debrett's* to keep herself abreast of all the subtle changes that were taking place in the realm of etiquette and table manners. To drill us in the latter, she would make us sit bolt upright, like real ladies, at a long, narrow table with a plate of banana laid before each one of us and she would watch us from her perch on the high stool, like a hawk watching its prey, as we struggled hard with our knives and forks to chop miniscule portions of the fruit and transfer them daintily and correctly into our mouths. And while enjoying our "dinner", we had to conduct a genteel discussion on any inconsequential feminine subject like a visit to a flower show or a hairdresser, avoiding carefully the hazards of choking, belching, chomping, dropping food on the table-cloth and gulping too much food at a time. We also had to learn the difficult and exacting business of hosting a dinner and allotting places at the table for each guest strictly according to his/her social status as well as his/her relationship with the hostess. While every one of us appreciated Mrs Khaitan's dictum that a hostess should sit at the head of the table with the principal male guest on her right, we felt she was unreasonable to place the two most important female guests on either side of one's husband. A prospective hostess among us had the temerity to ask if it would be moral to give her husband such free access to the female guests, but Mrs Khaitan snubbed her with her patent reply: "Don't rationalize; do as I tell you."

The much-needed respite from Mrs Khaitan's tyrannical table manners came with the dancing lessons, which were exhausting and yet so exhilarating. Mrs Blistop herself took the classes with the assistance of Mrs Gill, a slim, petite lady from Goldstar Dancing school. The ballroom was rather small and had just enough space to accommodate a dozen girls at a time, but the big wall mirrors reflecting our movements at every step, the brass chandeliers hanging from the ceiling and the faded Turner landscape depicting the English countryside lent the room the distinctive aura of a Zaminder's jalshaghar where nautch girls from Lucknow and Benares might have once regaled their select audience. Anyone who stood before the massive, gilt-framed Turner for more than thirty seconds would hear Mrs Blistop's nostalgic sigh and soft murmur: "Of course, dear, it was Turner who taught us how to notice the subtle colour gradations and the golden haze of the English sunset." Wrapped in her flashy gold and brocade gown, with several strands of pearls adorning her scrawny neck, Mrs Blistop sat erect like a ramrod at her grand old Broadwood piano and pounded away, keeping a watchful eye on our faltering steps. "Slow, quick, slow . . . no Reba, that won't do. Use your left foot." It was very heartening to learn that the film actress Keya Tarafdar of *Love and Destiny* fame and Millie Mookerjee, the celebrated hostess of TV chatshows, had learnt their first hesitant steps from Mrs Blistop in this mirror-studded dancing hall. I had no great ambition to break into film acting or TV shows, but I enjoyed my "shuffling 'n' jiving" all the same.

Mrs Basak rang me twice after our last phone call but I told the receptionist to inform her that I was too busy to respond. I derived a rare satisfaction from my little act of vengeance, though I couldn't help wondering what prompted her to ring me twice within a week.

On a sweltering Saturday afternoon, when I was doing shooting practice on the Maidan with another three girls, a red Maruti drew up near our playground and out came Mrs Basak in a short, thigh-hugging, maroon skirt and a sleeveless, white cotton top that revealed the length of her smooth, slender arms. She wore sunglasses and had braided her hair from the top of her head down to the nape of her neck in a style which I thought very chic and exotic. I had steeled myself to forgo the pleasure of Mrs Basak's company for some time, but she looked so ravishing and delectable in her tight, undivided skirt and sheer blouse that I succumbed to her fatal charms and meekly went up to her car.

"Why are you avoiding me these days, Hem?"

"I was — I was really very busy," I fumbled.

"Are you busy *now*?"

"Oh no, we are doing a bit of shooting practice. It's too hot and humid for any strenuous exercise."

Mrs Basak removed her glasses briefly to look at my sweaty face and then her eyes momentarily grazed my bare legs, making me tingle with desire. "You need a towel, Hem," she reminded me.

"I have got one in my kit bag."

"Bring it and wipe your face. I was going to see Mrs Walters, the oldest member of our club, and thought I should pick you up on the way. You can see some good prints of Company paintings and lots of art objects in her flat. If you are interested. . . "

"I am interested, Mrs Basak, but I have no proper dress with me."

"Doesn't matter. You aren't going to attend a party. If you have something to cover your legs. . ."

"I have my tracksuit. Just wait." And I sprinted back to the field to fetch my kitbag.

"Who's that blonde siren?" asked Damba as I wriggled my legs into my tracksuit in a jiffy and pulled the zipper.

"A Marilyn Monroe clone," I quipped.

*

Mrs Margaret Walters was the septuagenarian widow of Mr Frank Walters, an ICS officer who had lost his cushy job in the Home Department for sympathizing with the Indian revolutionaries during the 1942 Quit India movement. In recognition of his valuable services to the nation, the Indian Government had offered Frank several good positions, including a Governorship in a Christian-dominated, north-eastern hill state, but he refused each of them and spent the last ten years of his life indulging in his two great passions — playing golf at the Tollygunj club and collecting curios. Deterred by Frank's obduracy, the Indian Government patiently waited till his death and then be-stowed on him a state honour — the posthumous Padmashree — and offered the widow a modest pension and a two-bedroomed flat on Rowdon Street where she now lived with her ayah-cum-cook Amina and the numerous paintings and curios collected by her husband over three decades.

Before she pressed the bell, Mrs Basak had whispered that she would introduce me as an ace tennis player, as Mrs Walters had hated football ever since she had heard about the rowdy British soccer fans running amok all over Europe. But Mrs Basak had to change her introduction abruptly when I got my feet entangled in a loose strand of Mrs Walter's old Kashmiri carpet and fell flat on my face.

"A perfect Indian-style prostration by Calcutta's most versatile disco dancer," announced Mrs Basak theatrically, with an elaborate gesture of her arm.

"Oh no! She must have hurt herself!" cried the old lady, flapping her arms in distress.

"Not a bit, Mrs Walters," Mrs Basak assured her. "She is into break-dancing these days and loves to flaunt her acrobatic skills rather dramatically before a responsive audience. Get up, Miss Hem, you almost shocked my good friend by your impeccable demonstration."

I scrambled up to my feet and grinned, forgetting my pain in Mrs Basak's astonishing face-saving intro.

"There!" trilled Mrs Basak. "You see, Mrs Walters, she is grinning like a Cheshire cat. Headspins, dolphin flips, cartwheels . . . you just name it and Miss Hem will be only too glad to entertain you."

"Thank you, Miss Hem, but it gets on my old nerves. I was never good at the gym . . . What would you like to have, my dear?"

"G 'n' T, if you please."

"Amina!" shouted Mrs Walters.

"Yes, Amma!" responded a thin reedy voice from inside.

"Serve us gin and tonic and bring that packet of Slims Mrs Roderiguz presented to me yesterday. Ashtray too."

"Miss Hem is genuinely interested in paintings and curios, Mrs Walters," said Mrs Basak, looking fondly at my face.

"I am glad to hear that. Go and look around, child, and don't feel shy to ask questions. What's up in your gallery these days, darling?"

"An abstract show of three young Calcutta artists. Oils and acrylics."

"Acrylics! Can't adjust myself to that horrible medium. Sounds as bad as engine oil which, I hear, some artists are using these days, though God knows why."

I darted a pleading look at Mrs Basak to spare me the painful ordeal of moving around with my injured leg, but the memsahib seemed quite forgetful about my condition. So, gritting my teeth, I stood up and dragged my feet slowly around the sitting room, throwing a casual glance at the paintings. As movement became increasingly painful, I stood before Gainsborough's *Peasants Going to Market* and wondered why that woman on horseback was accompanying the menfolk to the bazaar (to buy some trinkets, perhaps?) and even tried to figure out which one was her husband. As the unfamiliar English setting failed to arouse any further interest in me, I moved along and was soon rewarded with some attractive Company watercolours depicting Indian life in minute detail. The one that fascinated me most was William Simpson's beautiful painting showing a royal procession, with some ornate facades in the background. The picture also showed a sprinkling of ordinary Rajasthani men and women in their colourful costumes going about their daily chores, unaffected by the royal fanfare. I suddenly remembered that I had seen a somewhat garbled version of this painting on the wall of Flurys. I was so much absorbed by the Simpson that I didn't notice when Mrs Basak had left her friend to stand behind me, nursing her gin.

"Are you hurt, Hem?" she whispered in my ear.

"Just a little," I whispered back in gratitude. "I will be all right in a day or two."

"Look at those Marwari bankers in their flowing robes and turbans," said Mrs Basak aloud. "In England Simpson is primarily appreciated for his works on the Crimean war, but I rather prefer these detailed studies he did when he was in India between 1859 and 1862."

"I think he is better than Daniell," observed Mrs Walters.

"Say something nice about those art objects on the shelves and the sideboard and then hobble back to your sofa," whispered Mrs Basak and went back to resume her chat with Mrs Walters. I made appropriate noises about Mrs Walters' wonderful collection of Bankura's terracotta horses, Purulia's chhau masks, Krishnanagar toys, painted playing cards and finally found something on the mantelpiece that really interested me: a slightly comic pair of wooden owls. "Fantastic!" I cried and picked up the pieces to turn them around and see what they had done on their backsides. Just plain wood!

"Those are Amina's presents," informed Mrs Walters. "She bought them for a song in a village fair."

"Marvellous!" I chirped and somehow managed to return to my sofa without limping.

"Have you heard from Barbara?" asked Mrs Basak, lighting up a Slim. She held her glass and the cigarette in the same hand which, I believed, was very classy. I also noticed that she didn't exhale through her nostrils like Mrs Walters. Teesta was definitely wrong about her mother; Mrs Basak was an aristocrat to her fingertips.

"She had yet another tiff with Philip Syms, that boorish news editor of the *Chichester Chronicle*," Mrs Walters informed her.

"Professional rivalry, I believe?" said Mrs Basak.

"You are right. It was over Barbara's exhaustively researched piece on a freak storm that lashed the Isle of Wight some time in the middle of March and cut off the island from the mainland for over thirty-six hours. Amina! Bring lemon cake and orange sherbet for Miss Hem."

"Yes, Amma!" responded the invisible ayah.

"How sad!" murmured Mrs Basak and took a sip of her pink gin.

"She followed it right from the Icelandic depression."

"A commendable feat, I must say, going that far to trace the origin."

"But that creep Syms couldn't appreciate Barbara's devastating thoroughness. He hacked the article to a hundred-word news piece and printed it on the sixth page."

"Looks like another blatant case of gender bias. Poor Barbara!"

"But she had the last laugh. Thanks to Syms' clumsy editing, the printed piece was marred by one malaprop and two confusing parentheses. Barbara promptly sent it to the *New Yorker* as a filler and they merrily published it under the caption 'There will always be an England' and sent her a cheque for a hundred dollars which was five times what that stingy Syms paid her."

"Clever Barbara!"

Mrs Walters' shy and overdressed maid made her second entry with a small tray, bowed respectfully and set down my refreshment on the table with a coy smile and a nervous, oblong stare at my face which almost tempted me to ask if she was rehearsing for matrimonial interviews. But I checked myself as Mrs Basak seemed very keen to discuss club matters with her friend and light banter at this stage might be considered a *faux pas*. It appeared that Miss Sil, a club member belonging to Mrs Basak's camp, had managed, after several unsuccessful attempts, to publish a letter, albeit in a truncated form, in the *Statesman* eulogizing the good work Mrs Basak & Co. were doing to uphold the club's great traditions and denouncing the vile machinations of one particular non-resident member (the name of Miss Rekha Jhajoria, Mrs Basak's arch-enemy, was omitted by the editor) who was secretly colluding with Calcutta's junkfood baron, Mr Thapar, the chairman of Footania Fast Food Industries, to offer the club to the latter on a platter. Apparently, Mrs Basak had been trying relentlessly to vilify her enemy publicly and I remembered how she had tried to requisition my services, when I had visited Rose Valley.

"Boggles my mind," said Mrs Walters, shaking her grey head dolefully. "Why should a pretty, well-educated girl like Rekha try to cut down our old banyan tree."

"Money, of course, Mrs Walters," said Mrs Basak with a malicious grin. "Mr Thapar must have enticed her with a carrot. I have even heard rumours that this fat Marwari girl is smuggling Indians into Britain via France and Germany."

"Oh no! She doesn't look so vile."

"Appearances are often deceptive, Mrs Walters."

While the two women discussed club politics, I struggled to eat my four-by-two-inch slice of lemon cake in the pukka English style learnt from Mrs Khaitan. Mrs Basak gave me an approving nod even as she continued her tirade against Miss Jhajoria and sought Mrs Walters' active participation in the club's activities to boost the morale of her group. I breathed a sigh of relief when Mrs Walters finally diverted the discussion to family matters by asking Mrs Basak about her daughters. Mrs Basak informed her that while Varsha was expected to finish her A levels at Cheltenham in September, her younger one was making life miserable for the poor nuns of St Catherine's. Sister Agatha had recently complained that Teesta had offended the school authorities by smoking a cigarette on the stage while acting in a school play, bursting crackers in the school chapel and smuggling *Judge Dredd* comics into her dormitory with the connivance of a charwoman. I wanted to laugh aloud but couldn't as Mrs Walters made sympathetic noises to console her friend and hoped that the naughty girl would mend, like her Barbara, around seventeen or thereabouts.

"But some girls never mend, Mrs Walters," said Mrs Basak with a meaningful wink to make it abundantly clear to her friend that her experience of unmendable girls was in no way limited to her own daughter.

After another five minutes of gupsup, Mrs Basak decided to leave as she had some appointment in the evening. I had braced myself for a severe dressing-down for my scandalous fall in Mrs Walters' sitting room, but she gave me a pleasant shock when, driving back from Mrs

Walters' house, she asked me, "Did you like my fib about your acrobatic accomplishments?"

"Splendid! I wouldn't have the wit to fabricate such a devastating introduction about myself."

Mrs Basak gave a mock frown. "You liar! You are a past master in this game. The way you cheated me at Rose Valley! Why, I thought you must be a pro."

I grinned and wondered if I should reach out and squeeze her bare arm, but I finally decided not to distract her from her driving. The traffic was quite dense on Park Street and Mrs Basak was constantly pressing the horn to wriggle through the gaps appearing momentarily in the jungle of trucks and delivery vans blocking her way. Before she dropped me at the Hazra crossing, Mrs Basak asked, "How is your Gandhian friend, Hem?"

"Fine," I said. "Busy as usual with her work for the battered women."

"A saintly woman, isn't she? Sacrificing her precious life for those helpless people."

"Yes. She saved my life."

"She told me everything about you. How is your husband now?"

"Fine. He is making good progress in his new school."

"I am glad to hear that." Mrs Basak opened the door of her car and I got out. I took a couple of steps towards the pavement and then turned to ask her a question that had suddenly leaped to my mind. "Mrs Basak, may I ask you a question?"

"Please do."

"Are we friends now?"

Mrs Basak smiled sweetly. "Of course we are friends, Hem. Have you any doubt about that?"

"No. Thank you, Mrs Basak."

"Call me Maxine, if it suits you."

"But I don't like that name. It sounds so alien, dry and inaccessible. I feel you deserve a sweet and soulful name. I think 'Radha' will suit you best. She was also fair and beautiful like you."

Mrs Basak blushed. "But I don't have the virtues of Lord Krishna's divine consort, my dear. Still, if you insist . . . but please keep it between us two."

"Thank you, Radha." I wondered what she would have thought if I had told her that I myself wanted to be her Krishna! A car had been insistently hooting behind Mrs Basak for parking space. "See you again, Hem," whispered Mrs Basak and drove away.

As I walked along the pavement, I dreamed about the day when I would have the right to hold her hand and declare my love for my Radha, to kiss her emerald green eyes, her rosy lips and her divine . . . My trance was broken by a little beggar girl who had been trailing me for some time with a plaintive whine: "Didi, O didi, give me a coin . . . haven't had anything to eat since morning." I turned my head and saw a five-year-old girl in a tattered frock, with a pair of big, dark eyes which had prematurely lost their natural lustre.

"How much do you expect, sweet girl?" I asked, beaming at her.

"Twenty-five paise!" cried the girl, exuding a rare smile.

"I will give you a whole rupee," I said and pressed a big coin in her dirty little palm.

Twelve

One morning I skipped Mrs Neena Verma's "Beauty Care" (I had no beauty, so I felt I could do a bunk) and went to Mrs Basak's gallery which was just ten minutes' leisurely walk from Mrs Blistop's school. I was itching to call her Radha, a name I had been chanting a hundred times every day like a mantra. Since Mrs Basak had now accepted me as her friend, I felt I should meet her more often and accompany her to some exhibitions and theatres to cement our relationship.

"Maxine's" was located in an old double-storey building on Little Russell Street, off Shakespeare Sarani. The ground floor was occupied by Hardayal & Sons, who dealt in carpets and tapestries, while Mrs Basak ran her gallery on the first. I gathered from the small noticeboard near the staircase that a solo exhibition of Mr Dhrubojyoti Khashnob-ish's acrylics with the ominous title "Nemesis" was on view. As I pushed open the glass door and stepped into the gallery I saw a tall, gaunt and very aristocratic-looking gentleman, with a thin waxed moustache and gold-rimmed specs, chatting with Mrs Basak. He must be the painter of the Nemesis series, I thought, and as Mrs Sahni later confirmed, my guesswork was correct.

I had expected a warm welcome from Mrs Basak, but she looked positively annoyed at my unexpected visit and responded to my broad grin with a frown. I had started walking towards her to explain that Mrs Blistop had suddenly fallen ill and the classes had been cancelled for the day, but Mrs Sahni, the quiet and efficient assistant, who sat at a small table near the entrance with a heap of booklets and brochures, beckoned me to her side and offered me a chair. "Have you an appointment with Mrs Basak?" she enquired.

"No, but she is a good friend of mine," I said. "In fact, we are on first-name terms."

Mrs Sahni looked surprised. She was a small, birdlike woman with a beaky nose which twitched involuntarily like a rabbit's. "I may be wrong, but it seems she doesn't want to meet you right now," she observed.

"But that can't be true," I said. "I think she is feigning annoyance because I am meeting her after a gap of one week." But even as I said this, I found Mrs Basak darting hostile glances at me.

"I think Mrs Basak looks very angry," whispered Mrs Sahni.

I could see that she was right, though I couldn't understand why she should resent my presence in her gallery, particularly after she had agreed to be my friend. I wondered if Mrs Basak was following some queer English convention that forbade her to entertain unartistic friends in her gallery, her sanctum sanctorum. To avoid meeting her gaze, I picked up the glossy two-page catalogue of the on-going exhibition from Mrs Sahni's table and, with her permission, ventured to find out what "Nemesis" was all about.

Mr Khashnobish seemed to be obsessed with crumbling mansions and demure, beautiful women draped in wide, red-bordered saris, with ominous crows and galloping horses in the background. From the short biographical note printed on the back flap, I learnt that Mr Khashnobish's ancestors were zaminders and the subject of his new series was, appropriately, the upper-class homes of North Calcutta where the early settlers were mostly zaminders or big banias who used to trade with the East India Company. "Nemesis" was a homage to this crumbling glory, each canvas uniformly priced at Rs 10,000 which I thought was quite ridiculous.

I had moved halfway around the gallery when Mrs Basak suddenly got up from her chair and demanded sharply, "Hem, may I know what business has brought you here when you should be in Mrs Blistop's school?"

I was so shaken by her brusqueness that I forgot my well-rehearsed line about Mrs Blistop's sudden illness and mumbled, "Well, you know, it was that — that utterly boring Beauty Care class which I thought I might as well skip because. . ."

"I won't accept your explanation," cut in Mrs Basak savagely like an impatient teacher pulling up an incorrigible shirker. "Go back to your class at once," she ordered, pointing at the door, her other hand poised on her hip, making it abundantly clear that, if necessary, she wouldn't even mind using force to throw me out of her gallery.

"What are you doing?" I cried, aghast. "I am not a slave; you can't expect me to slog away like a third-grade schoolgirl at this age!"

"Yes! You have to be a third grader to learn things you don't know," retorted Mrs Basak. "There is no short cut to success."

"I don't want to be a success. I only want to. . ."

"Go back at once!" bawled Mrs Basak.

"All right, I will go back," I said, retreating, "but there is no need to shout at me like that. That's not how one treats one's friend."

I trudged back to Mrs Blistop's just in time to join our first waltz session which, I discovered, was more exhilarating than the "quick, quick, slow" of the quickstep or the "one, two, three, hop" of the polka. Half my bitterness was washed away by the soft, lilting music and the other half by the very round and soft breasts of my partner, Mrs Pal, who pressed them so hard against mine that I had some difficulty in breathing. Waltzing in languorous harmony with Mrs Pal, I felt that this warm and cheerful woman could be much better company than that unpredictable memsahib blowing hot and cold all the while.

"You have a lovely bosom, Mrs Pal," I complimented my partner in a whisper. "Very firm and yet so soft. Do you bathe them regularly in rose water?"

Mrs Pal looked slightly puzzled but she was too clever to admit her ignorance about breast care. "Only in winter, my dear," she said, giggling. "In summer I give them a lemon bath."

Mrs Pal confided to me that the Deputy Minister, Civil Works, was so fascinated with her extraordinary boobs that he invited her husband to all the state functions just to have a peek down her cleavage. She soon bored me to death with the details of her husband's recent big deals in real estate at Howrah and elsewhere. That was when I decided to change partner.

"Mrs Basak is a tyrant," I complained to Paromita that night. "I skipped a class and went to her gallery for a chat and she started shouting, humiliating me before Mrs Sahni and an artist. She isn't my guardian, is she?"

"Of course she is," said Paromita, struggling to operate the old pedestal fan which wouldn't start without some coaxing. "You have taken hefty loans from her and it's only natural that she would want you to obey her."

"But I will pay back every single rupee I took from her," I said, even though I hadn't the slightest idea how I would accomplish that impossible feat.

"Now, don't drag me into this," said Paromita somewhat irritably as she adjusted the fan for maximum air flow. "I expect you to behave like a mature woman and not like a spoilt kid used to spoon-feeding. Right or wrong, it was *your* decision to borrow money from Mrs Basak and rush to Mrs Blistop's school, and now if the memsahib calls the shots you shouldn't complain."

"Many thanks for your sanctimonious lecture," I said, pulling a face. "I could talk to a rain tree on the Maidan and get a more sympathetic response."

Paromita chuckled. "Ah! I see! So you need my sympathy, hun? That's fine. Look Hemprova, there's no harm if you learn a little foxtrot and Ikebana as long as they really help you to get a good job."

"But I can't see when I will ever get a chance to dance outside Mrs Blistop's house."

"Despair not, my dear. Who knows? Your memsahib friend may invite you to a ball."

"No need to rub it in, Paromita," I said, frowning. "You will see, from now on I will keep my distance from that woman."

"Glad to hear that, darling," said Paromita. "But don't give up your dancing lessons. They will surely come in handy during the rainy season for negotiating Calcutta's pot-holed streets."

*

But the Calcutta weather refused to provide an opportunity for me to try my polka or quickstep as yet. We were already in the middle of May and the monsoon was long overdue, but the sky was as clean as a freshly shaven face, radiating stupendous heat which shimmered like the thousand fiery tongues of the mythical snake Kalia, licking up the sap from the earth and all its living creatures. On the road, one could see the tar simmering like syrup in a vat, and even a short, leisurely trip of fifty yards to the nearest market to buy a loaf of bread or a bar of soap brought out a gallon of sweat, making one limp, clammy and thoroughly exhausted. I prayed to Almighty God for a change of sex in my next birth so that I could at least sit bare-chested on the veranda and dry myself under the fan, unfettered by the shackles of womanhood – bra, blouse and petticoat – which seemed absolutely redundant in this muggy weather. The only beneficiaries of this heatwave were the vendors of green coconuts and pickled cucumbers who did a brisk business on the pavements, saving the scorched passers-by from imminent dehydration. All outdoor activities, particularly sports, came to a standstill as one look at the deserted Maidan would tell anyone.

Miss Nag, made of sterner stuff, would have drilled us till the first monsoon downpour, but this year she gave us an early break which everyone attributed to the massive upsurge of the forces of revisionism and deconstruction in Eastern Europe. Moved by Miss Nag's agony, we had suggested to her that we should make a waxwork of Gorbachev and stick pins in it, chanting "Ikir Mikir Chamchikir" to make the devil vomit blood and croak in his Kremlin office, but Miss Nag said that she couldn't sponsor such medieval mumbo-jumbo though she would be very happy indeed if the father of the abominable "Perestroika" was thrown into the Black Sea with a sack of Stalin's twenty-three volumes of speeches tied round his neck.

With the football season over and the heatwave continuing unabated, Mrs Blistop's air-conditioned school gained importance, more as a refuge from the scorching heat outside than for any genuine interest in the school curriculum. Miss Sarkar, a lively young graduate from the Calcutta Catering College, spoke volubly on the intricacies of entertaining guests and the fat wives and daughters of real estate agents and second-hand car dealers carefully noted down a few vital tips on blending western dishes with Indian ones, which could come in handy for a hostess entertaining a few sahibs along with her Indian guests. Since I felt no compulsion to entertain anyone other than myself, I sat with my fingers crossed, staring blankly at the Air India calendar fluttering on the wall, even as my waltz partner, Mrs Pal, raised her hand from the first row to get an important clarification which seemed to have been agitating the minds of all the future hostesses in the classroom: if fish was the main dish for a sit-down, hors d'oeuvres could be a starter, but if it was chicken or rice, then. . .?

"Prawn cocktail, of course," came the pat reply from the knowledgeable Miss Sarkar. Enough culinary concepts to call it a day, I decided, and held up my little finger to gain immediate permission for "bathroom" and then sneaked downstairs to nag Malini in the kitchen for a spoon of Branston pickle.

Mrs Das was explaining the delicate art of expressing different moods through flowers (flower for joy, flower for love, flower for friendship, flower for the grave) and I was on the verge of putting up my little finger, when the fat ayah puffed into the classroom to tell me that the receptionist was holding a telephone call for me. I knew it was Tama, for she had promised to buy my ticket for *Ma Ki Awaz*, the latest Chunky Pandey starrer which was destined to keep the tills ringing for some time. The tantalizing posters appearing on lampposts, walls and public urinals all over the city screamed: "Gun in hand, girl clinging to his bosom, daredevil Chunky is out on the streets to wreak vengeance for his mother's death!"

I had a mild shock when I heard Mrs Basak's gentle voice floating in from the other end: "Hem, how are you?"

"Fine, Mrs Basak," I said coolly.

"I am extremely sorry for my rude behaviour that day."

"It's all right, Mrs Basak. I am quite used to it."

"I thought we were now on first-name terms."

"So did I," I wanted to retort, "till that inauspicious morning when you suddenly started bawling at me and chucked me out of your home as though I was a stinking rat". But I found myself saying: "I hope Mr Khashnobish's 'Nemesis' is doing well."

"Fairly well, you can say. We have already sold six of his works." And then, after a little pause, she cooed, "Hem, are you interested in opera? Eve Queler's opera is in town and they are performing Giordano's *Fedora* at Kalamandir on Saturday evening. It would be very nice indeed if you could join me and my friend Mrs Gulmohar."

"Thank you for the invitation, Mrs Basak, but I don't understand anything about opera."

"I will guide you."

"OK," I said, before I could think up a reasonable excuse.

*

"There is nothing as enthralling and sublime as Italian opera," gushed the stout and cheerful Mrs Gulmohar (Gulu to her bosom friends) as she planted herself between Mrs Basak and me. This seating arrangement suited me perfectly as I had decided to play it cool with the temperamental memsahib.

"Of course, opera is the most exciting, challenging and comprehensive of all the arts," echoed Mrs Basak, more for my edification than her friend's.

"Maxine dear, do you remember the last opera we enjoyed together?" purred Mrs Gulmohar.

"Of course I do," said Mrs Basak, who had put on a very chic floral cotton dress for the occasion. "The Welsh National Opera's *Otello*, directed by Peter Stein. To be honest, Gulu, except for the final fugue and an occasional chorus, I didn't enjoy it much."

"Let's hope *Fedora* will be more satisfying," said her friend.

Just before the lights went out, I noticed Mrs Basak leaning back in her seat with her fingers interlocked on her bosom as if she was anticipating a deeply religious experience. But within a few minutes I discovered to my horror that opera consisted of a lead male singer braying like a donkey, a lead female singer screaming like a banshee and some minor characters wailing choruses like a pack of jackals howling in the night. Turning my head, I saw Mrs Basak in a rapturous mood and Mrs Gulmohar ditto, but on a closer look I found that the latter had cleverly plugged her ears with swabs of cotton wool. As I had no such contrivance at my disposal to cut off the infernal music, I suffered in silence. At the beginning of the second act I recognized a familiar piece of music and cried, "Why, that must be a waltz!" but there was such a spate of shush-shushings from the opera lovers around me that I decided to slip out of the hall to enjoy a breath of fresh air. I gently unplugged Mrs Gulmohar's ear and whispered. "Could you lend me a tenner, Mrs Gulmohar? I promise I won't tell your dear friend that you are cheating her." The blackmail worked like magic and Mrs Gulmohar promptly slipped a tenner into my palm without a word. I ducked my head and scurried up the aisle and was soon out of the auditorium, feeling light and free. I crossed Shakespeare Sarani and headed for the nearest icecream vendor who seemed to be waiting for me and was happy to sell me a bar of Cassata worth eight rupees which I licked very slowly to make it last for at least ten minutes. After finishing the icecream, I counted my change and went over to another vendor to buy fifty grams of salted peanuts and snubbed the slimy creature when he tried to cheat me by a few grams with a deft flick of his wrist on the weighing rod.

During the next half hour, I marched up and down the pavement, munching peanuts and doing a bit of extempore community service: 1. I drove away a stray bull strenuously trying to get at the sapling planted inside a brick enclosure (my contribution to the "Keep Calcutta Green" campaign); 2. I literally hauled up a street urchin who had come, with a tin of water, to squat on the pavement, and directed him to a public convenience across the road (my contribution to the "Keep Calcutta Clean" campaign); 3. I dropped a ten paise coin into the donation box held out by a group of school kids who were collecting money for Mother Teresa's latest shelter for the dying.

I slipped into the hall a few minutes after the interval and found that in my absence Mrs Basak and Mrs Gulmohar had swapped seats, thereby forcing me to occupy the vacant chair next to Mrs Basak's.

"You scamp, what have you been up to?" whispered Mrs Basak light-heartedly. "None of your business," I wanted to say, but I mumbled, "Bathroom". Mrs Basak didn't say anything, but a little later she gently held my hand in the dark, throwing me into a great confusion. Did she really miss me during my brief absence or was her warm gesture inspired by that horrible opera? Whatever it was, I was thrilled by the warmth and the softness of her touch and was so mesmerized by her heady perfume that I found it extremely difficult to keep my vow of not responding to her overtures any more. Slowly, I interlocked my fingers with hers and squeezed her palm a little. Since Mrs Basak didn't make any effort to withdraw her hand from my clasp, I cautiously felt the length of her long tapering fingers and her finely manicured nails and finally fiddled around a little with her solitaire diamond ring. Suddenly, *Fedora* became the most beautiful and enjoyable performance of my life and I prayed to God that it would last for another two hours, if not more. But, alas, the end came too soon. During the final, heart-wrenching scene when Fedora implored Loris to forgive her, drank a cup of poison and flung herself in his arms, writhing like a salted eel, Mrs Basak heaved a sigh of distress and retrieved her hand from my clasp to take out her hanky and press it briefly to her eyes.

"Ah, what a heart-rending performance!" sighed Mrs Gulmohar, who had unplugged her ears just in time to hear the final shrieks. Mrs Basak was still in her trance and merely nodded. As we came out of the auditorium, I heard people praising the tenor and the soprano's "effort-less rise to high D" and a bearded intellectual quoting Bernard Shaw to denounce the opera as a "cheap shocker". This, however, didn't dampen the high spirits of Mrs Basak who chortled like an excited five-year-old: "Just imagine! The Prince of Wales once sustained the mute role of Vladimir in a Bernhardt performance."

*

After this wonderful reunion with Mrs Basak, I felt I shouldn't waste any more time to declare my love for her. She had definitely given me a feeler in the darkened auditorium and now it was my turn to make further advances. I toyed with the idea of visiting her house at Alipore with a bouquet of red roses but decided that I should first get a clear signal from her before I presented my red roses. I felt I needed a go-between at this stage and Mrs Gulmohar's name naturally leaped to my mind. After I had discovered her ear-plugging technique, I knew she wouldn't dare to refuse me her valuable services as an intermediary.

Mrs Gulmohar lived in a modest, three-bedroomed flat in Dover Lane, just opposite a row of ugly Government quarters. It was my first visit to her house, so, following Calcutta's time-honoured custom, I took a packet of delicious Bhimnag sandesh and I was happy to note that Mrs Gulmohar appreciated my gesture and even murmured that the brash young generation seldom cared about such social niceties these days. To endear myself a little more to my prospective intermediary, I made it a point to praise lavishly every little item in her sitting room, from the Chola Nataraj displayed on a corner table to the mandatory family photograph on the TV cabinet. With her daughter happily married and well-settled in Bombay, her older son holding a commissioned rank in the Indian Navy, the younger one studying chemical engineering at an American university and her retired colonel husband engaged in the profitable business of mushroom cultivation, the Gulmohars appeared to me as the only happy family I had ever come across in my life.

"I am in love, Mrs Gulmohar," I declared after she had served me tea and some pineapple pastries. "I have been suppressing my feelings for quite some time, but I have at last decided to bare my heart to a sympathetic soul."

Mrs Gulmohar's eyes lit up. "Oh, dear, that's very good news indeed! Who is this lucky chap? Some Pele or Maradona from Mohan Bagan I suppose?"

"I love Maxine Basak," I said, beaming.

Mrs Gulmohar pouted. "Now, Hem, this is a bit too much for my old nerves. Don't tell me you have come all the way puffing and panting like a dying horse just to say you adore the memsahib. Of course, everyone loves dear Maxine. Such a lovely woman! Who's your Prince Charming? Ever since my right eye started dancing in the morning, I knew there has to be some good news for me."

I had great difficulty convincing the staid, middle-aged lady that my love for Mrs Basak was quite different from what she or Mrs Basak's other friends felt for her. "I want to kiss her mouth, her breasts . . . all over, you understand?" I explained. "And I want to make love to her too. Is that clear?"

Mrs Gulmohar's eyes widened and her mouth fell open in horror, revealing a gold-filled tooth, and her hands shook, spilling some tea on her beautiful, hand-embroidered tea napkin. She looked so stunned that I gave her a mild shake to bring her back to life.

"Lesbian!" she gasped, finding her voice at last. "Good heavens! I thought the disease had struck only the western countries and now, here in Calcutta, right before my eyes . . . oh God! I can't even imagine . . ."

"There is nothing western or unnatural about my love for Maxine Basak, Mrs Gulmohar," I said coolly, wiping my mouth with the napkin. "Love between women in its all manifestations has been beautifully portrayed in those immortal sculptures on Konark's Sun temple. They are a thousand years old and they haven't been imported from America or Europe."

Mrs Gulmohar frowned. "You have come well-prepared for a fight, haven't you? I thought you were a sane, normal creature with a sporting background, but now you appear to be something quite different! I don't even know why you have come here to spoil my day with your libidinous outpourings."

"I need your help, Mrs Gulmohar," I said. "You are her best friend."

"And that's one good reason why I won't help you," snapped Mrs Gulmohar. "Does she know that you harbour such dirty feelings about her?"

"It's not a dirty feeling, it's pure love," I protested, "and I have sufficient reasons to believe that she is willing to reciprocate. On that opera evening, after I came back from outside, she slipped her hand into mine, which clearly shows that . . ."

"You are a fool!" cried Mrs Gulmohar. "You are misinterpreting a simple friendly gesture. Why, she often holds my hand when we share something good and beautiful."

"Like Italian opera, hun?" I taunted.

Mrs Gulmohar grimaced. "Look, Hem, I know Maxine has a soft spot for you. She has sent you to Mrs Blistop for a proper grooming and she is keen to see you settled in life. But don't try to take advantage of her good nature. Remember, she comes from an aristocratic family of Devon, having very close connections with Baroness Trestleton of Mugbury and Sir Peter Gumsey, the third earl of Lupinsville. A highly accomplished English lady with an Oxford education and an impeccable background wouldn't give away her heart for a rogue like you."

"If I am a rogue, Gour Basak is a scoundrel!" I burst out, enraged by Mrs Gulmohar's vilification of my character.

"That's Maxine's greatest mistake in life — marrying that incorrigible skirtchaser," conceded Mrs Gulmohar with a sigh. She told me that Mr Basak had actually taken full advantage of the "hulla-gulla" associated with the Oxford and Cambridge boat race to woo the young and inexperienced Maxine Heggs. Of course, Mrs Heggs had her doubts about her daughter's choice, but poor Maxine had already absorbed so many of Mrs Calvery's "Out of Bound" romances in which starry-eyed Priscillas, Doreens and Rachels met their rich and ruggedly handsome heroes in far-flung Australian ranches, Brazilian cocoa-plantations and picturesque Indian palaces (the latter appeared particularly alluring because of their long retinue of turbaned servants who could be summoned with the snap of one's fingers!) that she couldn't help falling for Gour Basak's devilish charms hook, line and sinker and tied the nuptial knot after a brief courtship of just one and a half months.

"As they say, marry in haste, repent at leisure," said Mrs Gulmohar and shook her head mournfully. "It breaks my heart when I go to a party and find women ogling poor Maxine and whispering about Mr Basak's affair with that bit-part actress what's-her-name?"

"Lola Mudgal. I think Mrs Basak should get a divorce."

Mrs Gulmohar gave me a withering look. "No one has asked your opinion on this sensitive issue. Maxine is intelligent enough to make her own decisions."

"I only want to help her," I said.

"By offering your services as a lover, I suppose?"

"You are right," I said, grinning. "I assure you, Mrs Gulmohar, I will be a very caring companion."

"Try courting her," said Mrs Gulmohar with the hint of a challenge. "I won't stand in your way. If Maxine really finds solace in your arms, who am I to object? I only want to see my best friend happy and cheerful."

"So do I, Mrs Gulmohar," I said, beaming. "Since both of us are working for the same cause, you ought to help me."

Mrs Gulmohar offered me a puckish grin. "No one can help in love, my dear. You can meet her any number of times and no one will suspect you just because you wear a sari and have long hair, though I don't see any other outward signs of your femininity. Woo her morning and evening, send her flowers — yellow roses are in fashion these days, I hear. And best of luck."

I laughed. "Many thanks for your good advice, Mrs Gulmohar, but before I send her yellow roses I want to be sure that she is ready for such overtures. And that's why I need your help."

"What do you want me to do? Convey your disgusting proposal to Maxine? That's something you shouldn't expect from me."

"You won't have to act as my courier, delivering missives and all," I assured her. "You have to perform a more delicate job."

I explained that what I really wanted her to do was to suggest very subtly (and innocently) to Mrs Basak that I might possibly be in love with her and faithfully report back her reaction. Once I had an inkling of Mrs Basak's mind I could proceed on my own.

"And suppose she rejects your lesbian love straight away?" said Mrs Gulmohar archly.

"I will wait. True love always wins."

Mrs Gulmohar shrugged. "You are crazy. Well, I will sound out Maxine if that's all that you want me to do. But don't blab about your queer love to all and sundry and float a rumour to damage her good reputation in Calcutta society."

"Mum's the word," I assured her. "And thank you very much for your co-operation, Mrs Gulmohar. I hope you will relish my sweets."

*

"I am happy to report that Maxine is absolutely straight," Mrs Gulmohar said with evident glee when I met her a week later at Flurys. "I think she likes you for your little antics."

"Did she say *that*?"

"In clear and unambiguous terms, my dear. 'That charming rogue' — yes, that's what she said about you."

"Did you — did you really give her a hint that I might be in love with her?"

"Yes, of course. I told her that people could easily misconstrue this very unusual friendship between a young footballer and a highly ac-complished aristocratic lady as a lesbian affair. But Maxine laughed. 'Don't be crazy, Gulu,' she said. 'I am not a queer and I don't need to proclaim it from the housetops. Of course, I like Hem. She is so young and bubbly. But having *that* type of relationship with her . . . oh, no, you must be joking!' Which only shows that she is quite impervious to your perverted passion for her."

My groan could be heard from the other end of Chowringhee; my appetite for cheese sandwiches, which Mrs Gulmohar had so graciously ordered for me, vanished and even the tea tasted like quinine. I pushed away the cup and stood up. "Thank you, Mrs Gulmohar," I said. "I am so sorry, I wasted your valuable time."

"And I am sorry to disappoint you, my dear," said Mrs Gulmohar, barely suppressing a grin. "By the way, she was asking about you. She is awfully busy these days fixing up an exhibition of watercolours by one Mrs Beena Datta, otherwise she would have given you a ring."

"Tell her not to bother," I said, gritting my teeth. "I too am awfully busy these days learning the intricacies of male psychology and blind dating."

*

Two days later, while I was dozing in Mr Dasgupta's class on art and architecture, the ayah came to inform me that Mrs Basak was on the line. I jumped up and raced downstairs and then, as I remembered my talk with Mrs Gulmohar, I slowed down.

"Have you deserted me, Hem?" Mrs Basak's voice sounded sad and remorseful.

"Not at all, Radha. Fresh and interesting subjects are coming up every day and I am trying to absorb as much as possible."

"I am very glad to hear that. What are they teaching you now?"

"Art and architecture. Dr Dasgupta was telling us everything about columns. Doric, Ionic and three other types I just forgot."

"Tuscan, Corinthian and Composite," Mrs Basak reminded me with a soft, clinking laugh. "Dr Dasgupta is an authority on Indian architecture. I read his recent monograph on the terracotta temples of Bankura and Bishnupur. Why don't you drop in one of these days and have a look at Mrs Datta's flower studies? They are very soothing and quite fascinating, I assure you."

"Frankly speaking, Radha, I don't feel like going out in this muggy weather. It's very cool and comfortable here."

"Ah, the weather! It's really killing us, isn't it? Twenty years in India and still I find June so trying. But for this long-awaited exhibition of Mrs Datta, I would have fled to Darj." Mrs Basak paused a little and then said, "Hem, why don't you come and join Gulu and me on the golf course early tomorrow morning? A walk in the cool woods, with the birds twittering all around, will soothe your nerves and give you a little respite from this terrible heat."

"But I am a late riser, Radha. I don't get up before seven," I said, slightly intrigued by Mrs Basak's eagerness for my company when all she could offer me was a dollop of her bleached friendship.

"No problem," said Mrs Basak. "I will pick you up on my way to the golf course, achha?"

"Achha."

Thirteen

Situated behind Dum Dum airport, the Ladies Golf Club was a newly developed — underdeveloped, to be more correct — crow-infested nine-hole course where all golfing activities came to a standstill for a few minutes when a plane took off or landed with an ear-splitting roar. In those cataclysmic moments, even the cunning, ball-pinching crows stopped hopping around and looked up at the horizon with their beaks wide open, wondering if the end of the world was near. The clumps of trees and bushes planted along the borders of each hole would take at least another two or three years to provide any kind of shade and the pleasing bird chatter promised by Mrs Basak was simply non-existent unless you counted the solitary raucous cry of a bored crow. The bent grass sown all over the place showed much reluctance to grow and proliferate in spite of all the pampering it received from the sprinklers, and there were some big bald patches which stubbornly refused to sprout any vegetation.

To me, getting up at the crack of dawn and driving fifteen kilometres out of town just to hit a small ball with a number of queer-looking sticks seemed sheer madness. Mrs Basak noticed my puzzled look and briefly explained that the basic idea of golf was to hit those balls down the "fairway", avoiding all "hazards" (the hopping crows? the sprinklers? the sandpits?), into a hole, four and a half inches wide and four inches deep, dug into a bit of manicured lawn called a "green". I had started pestering Mrs Basak for a more thorough elucidation when the tyrannical starter looked at his watch and ordered the duo to tee off as two Japanese ladies were impatiently waiting their turns.

"We will explain everything about the game as we go along," Mrs Basak assured me as she took her stance for the drive. "Don't bother," I wanted to say, "because I am not remotely interested in this fancy game. And many thanks for wearing something sensible at last!" To my great delight, Mrs Basak had slipped into a pair of pink tights and a flimsy top which threw her tantalizing curves into sharp focus. As I stood behind her I could almost visualize the dimples on the top of her sumptuous derrière and had to summon great self-control to prevent myself from kneeling down behind her, throwing my arms around her legs and planting a dozen kisses on those heavenly orbs. While Mrs Basak fussed over her stance and grip and shifted her weight from one leg to the other before taking a swipe at the ball, I stole several penetrating glances at her bosom and concluded that she was endowed with a 38 bust shaped somewhat like a pair of avocados. After she had trotted away to chase her ball, I turned my attention to Mrs Gulmohar (who had encased her plump, matronly figure in a pair of golfing slacks and a blazer) to find out why she looked so unappetizing in my eyes. Now, here was a good, healthy specimen of Indian womanhood — fair-complexioned, well-endowed and virtuous to her fingertips. What was wrong with her and why shouldn't I feel attracted towards her? Nothing really, I concluded objectively. The patriotic slogan "Be Indian, buy Indian" also came to my mind. But, the moment Mrs Gulmohar bent forward to take her stance and her boulder-like buttocks stuck out, creating such a marvellous cleft, I had an irresistible temptation to roll a wad of cotton on my palm into a wick, place it in that valley, and strike a match, folding my palms together with a short prayer like we did on the Kalipuja night after lighting those little wicker lamps all around the house. I sighed deeply. No, even with my patriotic spirit soaring high, Mrs Gulmohar could only inspire holy ideas in my tainted soul.

While Mrs Basak and Mrs Gulmohar strode merrily from one hole to the next, talking shop and trying to improve their scores, I pushed the golf-cart along and handed out the clubs, mostly the wrong ones, drawing much flak from Mrs Gulmohar for not being able to distinguish between woods and irons or between a driver and a putter, though Mrs Basak assured her sulky partner that, being a sportswoman, I wouldn't take more than a couple of days to acquire the sterling qualities of a good caddie. I breathed a sign of relief when we finally dragged ourselves back to the club lounge, famished and thoroughly exhausted, collapsed into three cane chairs and ordered some sandwiches and orange juice. The young, athletic bearer who brought our food and drinks surreptitiously tried to brush his bulging crotch against Mrs Basak's bare arm as he bent forward to set down the tray on our table. I thwarted his evil design with a gentle tug at Mrs Basak's arm and then dipped my fingers in my glass and deftly sprinkled a little chilly orange juice on Mr Romeo's crotch with my fingertips. The dark, lantern-jawed bearer straightened up like a ramrod and threw me a murderous look before walking away.

"Thank you, my dear," said Mrs Basak, blushing, as she realized what I had just accomplished. "You have such wonderful reflexes." Mrs Gulmohar, however, was furious. "I am going to talk to the secretary right now," she fumed and heaved herself from her chair, but Mrs Basak pulled her down. "Gulu, don't! He is at least clean, quiet and prompt and that's what we expect from a good bearer. An old scruffy creature, with dirty nails and bad breath, moving at a snail's pace wouldn't be a good bargain."

"You are right, Mrs Basak," I said, sipping my well-earned orange juice with a contented air. "But I think in future you girls should carry pocket knives."

*

The next Sunday, Mrs Basak invited me, along with Mrs Gulmohar, to tea at her palatial mansion on Belvedere Road, Alipore, to celebrate my successful completion of Mrs Blistop's course. Dr Dasgupta, who had taught us art and architecture, had neatly divided Calcutta's old buildings into two distinct categories, baroque and neo-classical (the only exception being the Writers' Building which he dubbed Gothic), the former to be recognized by its ornate, undulating facades and the latter by the presence of any of the five types of columns and semicircular arches. According to this categorization, Basak House with its thick pillars and arches appeared to be a wonderful specimen of neo-classical architecture, but Mrs Basak explained that it was actually Bengal Baroque, an amalgam of different architectural styles ranging from classical to rococo with a few traditional Hindu or Mughal motifs thrown in as a minor concession to Indian sensibilities. At my request Mrs Basak took me on a tour of her house and I soon discovered that Basak House's dalliance with the classical spirit ended with the grand flight of steps and the towering Doric portico (with "AD 1863" carved into the pediment). The builder had given vent to his passion for baroque and rococo all over the elaborate stucco facade which was covered with fishes, urns, cherubs and angels, some of which were peeling off from the buff front. The eye-catching rooftop statuary included galloping horses, Aphrodites, Neptune blowing a conch shell, lions and several, barely-draped ladies in tantalizing postures.

"Shoddy and vulgar," sniggered Mrs Basak as she noted my growing curiosity about her house which, I reckoned, must have at least fifty rooms, if not more. "I have recently removed a Venus de Milo, two Apollos and a Queen Victoria from the garden with the help of Botball's boys and utilized the space to plant some roses. It's such a pity Gour won't allow me to clean up the front and the roof." Mrs Basak wistfully recalled her Devon house, Beaconsfield, which had looked more dignified and elegant because of its strict adherence to classical principles, with just a few later additions and alterations done in the nineteenth-century pseudo-gothic style. But, despite her contempt for its baroque follies, it seemed Mrs Basak had a sneaking pride for her house, for, even while climbing an ornamental staircase, she stopped to point her finger at the stone balustrade and said with an impish grin: "Look, there's a touch of gothic for you there, those ogees, I mean." She was however slightly apologetic about the faded specimens of Reynolds, Titian and Rubens staggering up the stairway. "One has to fill up so much open space," she murmured.

Most of the upper rooms were locked and part of the eastern wing was in such a state of disrepair that it could easily inspire a talented artist like Dhrubojyoti Khashnobish to embark on yet another series of acrylics with the ominous title "Nemesis". Mrs Basak confided to me that her husband was very keen to donate his ancestral house to a public trust as a charitable hospital, but Mrs Basak was stubbornly resisting; she would prefer to repair the building and throw it open for the general public in the good old tradition of some famous country houses in England, charging a nominal entry fee for its upkeep. Mrs Basak also told me that she occasionally earned a bit of money from the Tollygunj film studios by renting out her ballroom and the galleries as a set for period films.

The ballroom, with its enormous chandeliers hanging from braided brass chains, looked as big as the prayer hall at Champaboti, its floor made of diamond and lozenge patterned marble which (Mrs Basak informed me, not without a hint of pride) was carted all the way from Jaipur in Rajasthan. The huge ballroom could also serve as a museum of antique chairs as each of the fourteen exquisite specimens of carpentry and upholstery lining the walls represented a different style and age. Mrs Basak sat in her favourite English Chippendale with floral upholstery and struck a regal posture, holding up her chin, while I opted for a more comfortable settee with carvings on the back and legs.

"Queen of Alipore, huh?" I quipped.

Mrs Basak laughed heartily, allowing me a rare glimpse of her small, exquisite teeth, and I suddenly became aware that she was slightly tipsy. In fact, she was rather unsteady on her feet as she stood up and invited me to visit her picture gallery.

The collection consisted mainly of unintelligible modern paintings, with the redoubtable Huda dominating the show with his abstract horses and semi-cubist compositions. "Note the peculiar grandeur brought out by Huda through a dramatic play of light and shade," whispered Mrs Basak reverently as I stood before one of his paintings, just to please her. I soon moved away to a corner of the gallery set aside for family portraits and was instantly riveted by the muscular and fierce-looking Sir Gomer (looking very much like the Thug he actually was, despite his cravat and frock coat) flanked on either side by his smiling, sharp-featured benefactress and whist-partner Lady Anne Mason and his buxom, wide-eyed and slightly mournful wife Sally. Sir Gomer's pock-marked Vanjara wife, whom he had downgraded to a mistress after marrying Sally Hack, was conspicuous by her absence. I also couldn't ignore Sir Hiren, the dandified grandpa of the present Basak, who sported a fine waxed moustache, a well-cut, three-piece suit and a carved walking stick. But I avoided meeting the stern gaze of Champaboti, Sir Hiren's virtuous and philanthropic wife, as I feared that she would frown at me for sullying the good name of her school. "Why don't you hang a portrait of Isobelle by his side?" I asked Mrs Basak. "Sir Hiren definitely deserves more cheerful company than that sulky harridan."

"I would gladly commission a portrait if I could get a photograph of her," said Mrs Basak, smiling. "But the Basaks seem to be very secretive about their mistresses. I have flicked through a dozen old family albums, but there is no trace of Isobelle!"

"I can bring you a photograph of Lola Mudgal in case you need it for the future," I could have told her, but Mrs Basak looked so vulnerable and groggy that I hadn't the heart to hurt her. I couldn't however help asking her something which had been tormenting me ever since I caught a whiff of her sour, alcoholic breath in the ballroom: "Why do you drink, Radha?"

Mrs Basak turned her face and gave me a sharp look. "You aren't trying to assume the role of my guardian, are you?"

"No, but as a friend I certainly have a right to ask."

"All right. An Englishwoman needs a drink occasionally. A small glass of sherry in the morning, a good wine for lunch, some port after the meal, gin in the evening and . . ."

"Brandy in the afternoon," I filled in.

Mrs Basak glowered. "It's port, of course."

"You can't cheat me, Radha. I can smell it on your breath."

Mrs Basak grimaced. "Well, brandy then, if you insist . . ." She fumbled in her pocket, took out a packet of Slims and lit up rather clumsily after several attempts with her lighter. A couple of quick, lusty drags on her cigarette and Mrs Basak was ready to face me.

"A fortyish woman living all alone in a big house like this, with just a couple of servants, really needs something strong to drive away the blues. Do you understand that?"

"But brandy will certainly do you no good, Radha. You have your gallery, your club . . ."

"Gulu madam calling you, memsa'b," interrupted a short, wiry woman whose greasy, shoulder-length hair exuded a strong smell of coconut hair oil.

"Go tell her we coming double quick," said Mrs Basak in her best pidgin.

"Tea also ready, memsa'b," reminded the maid.

"Very good, Chinta."

"You want tikoji too, memsa'b? Hari saying you want tikoji every time."

Mrs Basak frowned. "Hari is a big ass. No teacosy in hot season, remember. Bring tea-things to sitting room in five minutes, achha?"

The maid nodded and left with a bow.

"They think it's a showpiece that has to be flaunted before the guests," said Mrs Basak, smiling, and then lowered her voice. "Not a word about liquor in front of Gulu, mind," she said, half-pleading, half-intimidating. I nodded.

We had our tea in Mrs Basak's huge, dimly-lit sitting room that boasted some heavy, Burma-teak furniture, each piece carved exquisitely and painstakingly in the late-nineteenth-century style. The floor was dotted with half a dozen huge copper urns nurturing aspidistras and a variety of other foliage plants, while the walls were adorned with massive gilt-framed pictures by Rubens (*The Return of Ulysses*), Raphael (*La Velata*), Titian (*Horseman and Fallen Warrior*), William Blake (*The Angels of Good and Evil*) and Van Gogh (*Sunflowers*).

"Once, we used to display some decorative pieces in this room — vases from Sèvres, goblets from Bohemia, figures from Dresden and ormolu clocks from Paris," Mrs Basak told us as she poured tea for us. "But I had to lock them up in a chest after a Toledo sword was stolen by a servant."

"Don't you sometimes feel like Miss Havisham, guarding the Basak treasures in this big old house?" asked Mrs Gulmohar very sympathetically.

"I rather enjoy my loneliness, Gulu," said Mrs Basak cheerfully, even as she suppressed a hiccough with a gulp of water.

"That's one great advantage of having a good, English public school education," I said, to please Mrs Basak. "It makes you absolutely self-reliant."

Mrs Basak shot me a sideways glance to make sure that I was not pulling her leg and then smiled indulgently at me. Mrs Gulmohar however gave me a frown and enquired when Varsha would finish her A levels.

"Next month." Mrs Basak then announced that she was planning to throw her yearly bash in mid-August to coincide with Varsha's homecoming.

"If we have a good monsoon and the weather cools down, you could have a barbecue sundowner in your garden," suggested Mrs Gulmohar. "It's the latest craze in town."

Inevitably, the two women started comparing notes on their children. Mrs Gulmohar prattled on about her naughty grandchildren, her son's brilliant results in chemical engineering in some American university whose name I couldn't quite catch and the lucrative order recently bagged by her husband for exporting mushrooms to South Korea and Singapore. Mrs Basak appeared a little preoccupied, though she tried hard to show her keen interest in the well-being of her dearest friend's family with timely nods and appropriate noises. Mrs Gulmohar's babble about her children, however, reminded me of my surrogate child Babu who, to my great delight, had recently sent me a postcard, saying: "Dear Ma, I can now add and subtract up to four digits and draw birds and horses. When I learn clay modelling next month, I will send you a good present. Prasun's father gave him a mouth organ which he allows me to play. We regularly exchange things as you and Paromita auntie showed us. Love, Babu."

Then Mrs Gulmohar and Mrs Basak started discussing club politics. I gathered that Miss Rekha Jhajoria was expected to arrive next month from London and queer the pitch for Mrs Basak. To me, far more interesting was the news that Footania Fast Food Industries, in collaboration with America's Lovejoy Foods Inc., was soon going to launch its prime chicken prodcut "Chicky Chick" in an attractive tetra pack. But my friends were not interested in Mr Thapar's masala chicken and they speculated gloomily about the junkfood baron's next move to buy up the club which always coincided with Miss Jhajoria's homecoming.

It was almost dark when Mrs Basak saw us off at the gate. Mrs Gulmohar graciously offered me a lift in her Fiat which I readily accepted, and then regretted as I realized that the real purpose of her magnanimous gesture was to have a word with me in private about my unrequited love for Mrs Basak. "I am happy that you are at last reconciled to a good, wholesome friendship with Maxine," she observed with a hint of sarcasm.

"I still love her," I declared haughtily, "and I am prepared to wait."

"But for how long?" teased Mrs Gulmohar. "Three . . . five . . . ten years? You will have to wait till the end of your life or hers. She is a woman of very high principles and she won't succumb to your charms however much you may try to win her heart with your little antics. Why don't you forget Maxine and write some love poems in her memory as some failed lovers do?"

I felt like jumping at her neck and strangling her, but I merely gritted my teeth and retorted, "Some jilted lovers take to the bottle and die a miserable death. Perhaps you would be happy if I met the same fate."

"Touch wood!" Mrs Gulmohar touched a box of tissues on her dashboard in absence of real wood and then touched my head. "Live a hundred years, sweet girl, and beget as many children."

*

My growing friendship with Mrs Basak redeemed, to some extent, my unrequited love for her. Perhaps it was my new persona (forged in the workshop of Mrs Blistop and embellished with a step hair-cut and a light, scar-screening make-up) or maybe it was my little antics, but whatever it was, Mrs Basak seemed genuinely fond of me, and on my part I tried my best to keep her in good humour. To Paromita's great surprise, I now woke up at five sharp and eagerly waited at the gate for Mrs Basak's car. I caddied for her with total devotion, handing her the right clubs, driving away the crows and searching for lost balls. Mrs Basak declared that I was definitely the best caddie she had ever had and she particularly appreciated my excellent golf etiquette as I never failed to congratulate her lustily whenever she birdied and complained about the unfavourable wind and unimaginative flag position when she bogeyed.

In the club lounge I played the Knight Errant with my usual panache and kept Mr Romeo at bay. When I saw him approaching our table, I plucked a hairpin, straightened it with my teeth and twirled it playfully between my fingers, fixing my gaze on his crotch.

"Hem, please, don't be so savage," implored Mrs Basak.

My daily rendezvous with Mrs Basak on the golf course came to an abrupt halt when the monsoon finally broke, lashing the city with torrential rain for six full days. On the second day of the deluge a strong gale blowing at ninety kilometres per hour tore through the city, razing over a dozen dilapidated old houses in Shyambazar, Entally and Behala and uprooting a large number of those haggard roadside trees that had miraculously survived the previous year's monsoon. Alarmed by the devastating storm, Mr Sen, Paromita's fat and solicitous father (who also happened to be her employer) rushed in with two servants to rescue us from the imminent danger of our being buried alive under the debris of our mud hut. He was horrified to see his daughter up a ladder, frantically trying to tie down one side of the thatched roof with a reef knot (learnt as a part of her Girl Guide training) and me moving pots and pans around the room to catch the raindrops that trickled through the numerous cracks and holes in the thatch. The brief exchange between the panicky father and the aggressively self-reliant daughter deserved to be included in a school text for the edification of those weak-minded girls who would normally be unable to cope with real-life adventures outside matrimony.

"Thank you for your concern about our safety, Mr Sen, but I don't think there's any real danger to our lives," said Paromita even as she tugged fiercely at the unyielding rope. "You see, Hem is moving the pots and I am fixing the roof."

"Don't be crazy, Mita!" cried her father in acute distress. "That roof has decided to take wings and you can't hold it back."

"Mr Sen is absolutely right, darling," I said. "Even if you manage to fix the roof, you can't stop it dripping. At this rate, we won't be able to cook our rice because all our pots and pans will be busy collecting rainwater."

"I know you are hankering for comfort and security," bawled Paromita, giving the rope a final tug. "Here, I have fixed it, but you may go with Mr Sen if you are so scared."

Mercifully, even as she chastised me for my cowardice, a strong gust of wind tore Paromita's reef knot with one big jerk and a part of the roof keeled over, compelling her to accept, willy-nilly, her father's invitation to accommodate ourselves in the servants' quarters at the back of Mr Sen's house on the understanding that she would be allowed to return to her ashram as soon as the rain stopped. It was a great relief to have a solid concrete roof over my head, but I had to exercise great restraint not to offend my Gandhian friend by any unseemly display of exuberance at the loss of our mud hut. In fact, Paromita snubbed me when I summoned a housemaid to bring ginger tea and some crisp papadoms, reminding me that we had only taken temporary shelter in Mr Sen's house and shouldn't behave like two pampered girls of the scrap baron.

Paromita made two valiant attempts to return to her ashram, first when next morning, Mrs Basak sent two big tarpaulins with a chit, begging Paromita to accept her humble gift and make our life a bit comfortable in this great deluge, and then again in the afternoon, when the general secretary of Swadhikar sent her an old tent and two sack-loads of wood-shavings, the latter to be spread on the mud floor to protect us from pneumonia. But God must have heard my silent prayers, for even as Paromita hunted for pegs and ropes to fix the tent and the tarpaulins inside our roofless hut, its four walls and the wooden beams which had miraculously withstood the raging storm so far, caved in with a dull crash. I wanted to dance a jig on the veranda but checked myself to attend Paromita who fainted with a heart-rending groan as she saw her ashram collapse like a house of cards right before her eyes. Paromita's mother, a plump, matronly woman who wore her martyred expression like a talisman, came to console her daughter, but Paromita was unable to reconcile herself to the unexpected termination of her strict ashramic life and I had much difficulty in persuading her to take a bite or two of the rich and delicious vegetarian dishes sent by her poor mum. However, as the rains continued unabated even after the fourth day, my Gandhian friend had to accept, willy-nilly, the parasitic life of a rich man's pampered guest and all she could do to flaunt her austere lifestyle before the maids and the bearers of the big house was to read the *Gita* for three hours in the morning, work her charkha for another couple of hours and refuse pilau, paesh and a few other delicacies which she declared unpalatable because of the ghee, sugar and costly dried fruits that had gone into them, though I relished these dishes precisely because of their rich ingredients and mouth-watering aroma.

But even while I enjoyed Mrs Sen's lavish hospitality, I felt restless. I had to restrict my movements to a narrow strip of veranda where I kept myself busy with my ball exercises, flicking my football a dozen times from toe to head and back to toe. Depressed by the monotony and boredom of my cramped existence, I finally took to amusing myself by pelting stones at the ugly green frogs who had sprouted overnight all over the waterlogged backyard, like weeds after the first monsoon shower.

After deluging the city for one full week, the rain god finally took pity on us. On the eighth day the rain petered out to a light drizzle and the masses of grey clouds parted occasionally to offer a glimpse of blue sky, buoying up my spirits. I borrowed a battered umbrella from a housemaid, hitched up my sari and ventured out on the road, wading through a stretch of ankle-deep water before I reached the main road. At the bus stop a sudden gust of wind caught my umbrella and blew it inside out. Obviously, this was not the right weather for socializing, but I had missed Mrs Basak's company so badly during my internment that I couldn't let one more day pass without seeing her sweet face.

I was quite surprised when Mrs Basak's durwan informed me that she had gone to her gallery. Was she mad? Who would come to buy her watercolours in this foul weather? But, apparently, Mrs Basak was no fool, because, half an hour later, when I reached her gallery, I found her with a natty, somnolent-looking Japanese couple who were smiling and nodding at whatever Mrs Basak was showing them. I had a fleeting desire to sit this cuddly little pair on my lap, one on each knee, tell them a nice little animal story from the *Panchatantra* and tuck them in bed for a good night's sleep. I was thrilled when Mrs Basak left her rich clients to greet me as if I too was one of her prospective buyers, though a look at my battered umbrella and sodden sari told a different tale.

"Hem!" cried Mrs Basak, with a very uncharacteristic and unmemsahiblike exuberance, as she offered me her hand. She wore a dazzling lengha-choli ensemble studded with fancy mirrorwork and a matching stonebead necklace. "Trying my ethnic wardrobe, though I am a bit too old for such a splash of colours," she chirped merrily. "How are you? How is your friend? Did you get those tarpaulins and were they any use?" Mrs Basak asked all these questions in one breath.

"We had to shift to Mr Sen's house, darling," I said, quite moved by her concern for us. "Our hut collapsed in the rains but Paromita says she will rebuild it very soon."

"How sad! God! You are thoroughly drenched." And like a doting mother she lightly touched my hair and then the pallav of my sari to confirm her diagnosis. "Wait! I will fetch you a towel from the bathroom."

"Don't fuss over me, Radha, I can look after myself," I assured her. "Please go and attend your clients. I hope you sell one of Mrs Datta's paintings to that rich couple."

Mrs Basak smiled wanly. "I doubt if the Hagomotos will buy any work, still . . . I think I'll be free within a few minutes." She trotted back to her clients and I went to the bathroom to dry myself. Mrs Basak had never shown me such warmth before, I thought, as I wiped my arms and face with her soft, pink towel. Could it be possible that our brief separation had finally opened her eyes and she had at last decided to accept me as a lover? "Mother Kali!" I prayed fervently. "If it's true I will definitely sacrifice a goat at your altar."

I came out of the bathroom and waited nervously at Mrs Sahni's table while Mrs Basak went about her routine with a fixed smile, spouting her well-rehearsed lines about "velvety pansies", "dour petunias", "elegant larkspurs" and "vibrant roses". In response, the somnolent couple nodded, smiled and whispered something soft and polite which I couldn't catch from my table.

Ten minutes later, Mrs Basak bade sayonara to the Hagomotos with a perfect little bow and came back to my table to slump into a cane chair opposite me with a dramatic gesture of helplessness.

"I've heard that the Japanese adore flowers," I teased her.

"So have I. Just imagine! All the while they were smiling and murmuring 'Itish nize . . . thatish bootifool' and Mrs Hagomoto made a gurgling sound like an overfed baby when she spotted a butterfly sitting on a flower and her husband responded with a chuckle and a string of Japanese exclamations." Mrs Basak shrugged. "But that's business, my dear . . . Forget it. I was really worried about you, Hem — I mean both of you. I even thought of bringing you to my house during the deluge but dropped the idea as I felt that your Gandhian friend mightn't like it."

There! Mother Kali had finally cast her benevolent look upon me. This was certainly not the uncharitable Mrs Basak who couldn't even spare me a few minutes for two whole months when I had been slogging in Botball's criminal den. "How sweet of you to think of me in my distress, Radha!" I exclaimed, fixing my eyes on her face.

"In fact, I was going to come and visit you this evening."

"Really?" I leaned forward and clasped Mrs Basak's hands. "I can't tell you how pleased I am to see you again, darling," I said, my heart fluttering wildly in anticipation.

"Same here . . . how about a cup of tea, darling?"

I followed her into a kitchenette at the back of the gallery and even volunteered to make the tea, but Mrs Basak wouldn't allow me that privilege.

While she busied herself with the paraphernalia of teamaking — taking out, from a shelf, a tin of Milkmaid, a packet of Britannia gingernut biscuits, two cups and saucers and finally lighting the gas and putting the kettle on — I kept darting sidelong glances at her face in the hope of seeing a blush or some other tell-tale sign betraying her nascent love for me.

"I am afraid I will have to offer you the abominable Orange Pekoe of Rose Valley," said Mrs Basak lightheartedly. "The tea you once washed your feet with."

"I wish I hadn't behaved so outrageously."

"Oh, no. I rather enjoyed that skirmish we had at Rose Valley. To be honest, I always had a sneaking admiration for your pluck and your trouble-making potential."

"You are joking, aren't you?"

In reply, Mrs Basak smiled, shook her head and shot me a sidelong glance that assured me that she really meant it. "I really enjoy your company, darling," she said, plucking a spoon from a groove on the shelf. "You are one in a thousand."

That was the moment I threw my arms around her waist from behind and pressed my cheek firmly between her shoulderblades, murmuring: "Radha, I love you!"

Mrs Basak's hands shook and the spoon fell into the sink with a clink and I felt her body stiffening. "Jesus!" she gasped in horror. "I thought only schoolgirls have such pashes — yes, that's exactly the term we used when a girl used to have a crush on a senior or a class teacher. Good Heavens! You are well past that age and now . . ."

"This is no pash, Radha," I declared, rubbing my cheeks desperately on the small of her back. "God is my witness, I fell in love with you the moment I saw you that first time at Rose Valley."

"Take your hands off me, Hem," said Mrs Basak quietly but firmly, suddenly withdrawing all the warmth and sweetness from her voice. "We must talk, Hem," she said. "Now I understand why Gulu was insinuating the other day about a possible relationship between us."

Stung by her uncharacteristic harshness, I released her from my clasp. Mrs Basak turned sharply, her eyes blazing. "Look Hem, as I told you just now, I do enjoy your company, but that does not mean that I am willing to enter into *that* kind of relationship with you. I am sorry, dear, but I am afraid I can't reciprocate your overtures."

"So you don't . . . you don't love me at all?" I screeched, choking with frustration and anger.

"No, not in the way you want me to love you."

"Thank you, Mrs Basak," I said. "And please forgive me for my atrocious behaviour. I think I should go now."

Mrs Basak tried to hold my hand and say something about the tea, but I roughly brushed her hand aside and stormed out of the kitchen and her gallery, forgetting to pick up my battered umbrella on the way.

As I strode along Little Russell Street, I had a morbid urge to throw myself in front of a speeding delivery van coming from the opposite direction, but I checked myself, thinking that I still had one crutch to support me in my dreary journey through this wretched life. Football.

"You look like a zombie," said Paromita when I returned to our dismal barrack, drenched to the bone. "What has happened to you? Struck by a thunderbolt or what?"

"I have had an abortion," I said gloomily and collapsed into a chair. "I am still bleeding."

Fourteen

I was drafting an application for the post of a salesgirl in Khazana, a newly opened boutique on Fern Road, when a housemaid came running, her eyes bulging and her mouth agape in astonishment, to inform me that a pukka memsahib had just entered through the gate and was trying to find out my whereabouts from the mali in her unintelligible Bengali. The news startled me so much that my hand shook uncontrollably and the nib of my pen stuck into the paper. After Mrs Basak's rebuff on that windy morning, I had stopped visiting her altogether and three long weeks had already passed without her showing any interest in reviving our old friendship. I, naturally, assumed that our brief and uneasy relationship had at last come to an end. And now this sudden and unexpected visit to my messy room! What did she want from me? Hadn't she already tortured me enough? I unstuck the nib from the paper and frowned at the housemaid. "Tell that woman to get lost," I said savagely. "I have no time to meet people who drop in without an apointment." And to demonstrate how busy I was, I resumed my writing at a brisk pace. The puzzled maid had barely left the room when I heard Mrs Basak's approaching footsteps on the veranda. I stiffened, clutching my pen like a sword. I must play it cool and behave like a mature, self-respecting woman of great determination, I cautioned myself.

"Ah, so you are here! What luck!" chirped Mrs Basak as she entered my room, after scraping her shoes on the door mat. I turned my head slowly like someone afflicted with spondylitis. "Oh, it's Mrs Basak," I said coldly with a casual air as if I couldn't care less. I, however, didn't fail to notice that she had put on a demure, round-necked navy blue blouse splashed with white dots and a long, floral skirt with soft folds.

"How are you, Mrs Basak?" I asked with a wooden smile.

"I am fine, darling," said Mrs Basak, ignoring my cold reception. "I hope I haven't disturbed you."

189

"Oh no, I was just doing a piece for a sports magazine on this new off-side rule they are introducing from next season."

"Really? That's fantastic! You must show me your article."

"I will send you a copy of the magazine," I said coolly. "Please be seated, Mrs Basak. There is a mora over there."

"Thank you, but I have actually come to take you to my club," said Mrs Basak and then took a quick look around my disorderly and barely furnished room. "You will have a glimpse of my rival, Miss Rekha Jhajoria, who arrived from London this week."

"But I am not a member, Mrs Basak," I pointed out, wondering why, all of a sudden, she was inviting me to her club.

"You will be my guest," said Mrs Basak.

"But what am I to do there?"

"Swell the audience for Miss Gordon-Green, an up-and-coming British novelist whom we have invited to read out a chapter from her book-in-progress. I am sure it's going to be a fascinating experience for all of us as Miss Gordon-Green isn't an ordinary writer of fiction; she is a post-modernist."

I was not the slightest bit interested in going to a novel-reading session, and stared hard at my incomplete application. "I am afraid I have a deadline to meet," I murmured.

"I am sure it can be extended by a few hours." Suddenly, Mrs Basak stepped forward and placed her hands on my shoulders, squeezing them a little. "Don't desert me, Hem," she whispered. "I need your company."

My carefully cultivated indifference gave way to an irresistible urge to take her in my arms and assure her with a gentle kiss that I needed her more than she needed me. But I merely touched her arm and said, "I will go with you, Radha."

*

Sandwiched between the towering, five-storey, glass-and-concrete structure of Footania Fast Food Industries and an ugly block of tenements, the sober, pink, two-storey building of the Calcutta Ladies Club on Free School Street looked like a damsel in distress, with no knight in shining armour in sight to rescue it from its present moribund state.

It was quite obvious that Mr Thapar, the chairman of Footania, who wanted to grab the prime site occupied by the club, didn't care two hoots for the club's glorious past, but those who did care could find much to praise and adore in its chequered history of one hundred and thirty years. Lady Canning had laid the foundation stone of the club in 1859 (the year Free School Street was illuminated with gas by the Oriental Gas Company), and Mrs Molly Muddlestone, the wife of Mr Edward Muddlestone, the then chief architect, Public Works, had designed the architectural plans for the building. Mrs Muddlestone had been much influenced in her work by the huge fifteenth-century gothic mansion of the Duke of Dogsworth, which she had seen in her native Motley-on-Trent. Undaunted by the shortage of available space, she had given vent to her gothic spirit by putting in as many as twelve slender, Corinthian pillars to support a small portico and enough high, pointed-arch windows and doors to earn her architectural extravaganza the epithet "Molly's Folly" among the snobbish members of the Bengal Club with whom CLC had always vied for honours and accolades. In fact, it was the Bengal Club's stubborn refusal to host a dinner for the ladies of a London theatrical group visiting Calcutta in the winter of 1858 that so infuriated Lady Moyra that she launched a vigorous campaign for funds to build an exclusive club for the memsahibs of Calcutta who found themselves restricted to the narrow confines of the lounges and the dining rooms of the male-dominated Calcutta clubs. The appeal for subscription, published simultaneously in the *Englishman*, Calcutta and the *Illustrated London News*, spelt out in clear, unambiguous terms that the club would provide a forum for the enlightened English ladies of Calcutta to meet in a congenial atmosphere and exchange news and views over a glass of sherry, read the latest books and journals from home, enjoy a game of cards or checkers and occasionally organize social and cultural activities to uphold the traditions and cultural heritage of the English people.

The laudable intentions of Lady Moyra, the first president of the club, were swept aside after her death in 1871 when the club turned into a happy hunting ground for spiritualists and the advocates of animal magnetism, homeopathy and other esoteric ideas. Under the influence of Madame Blavatsky and the Philadelphia spiritualists and later Mrs Annie Besant's Theosophical Society, the club held regular planchette sessions in its Blue Room and published the proceedings in *Eve's Own*, the first women's magazine of Calcutta, edited by Mrs Judith Hope who also happened to be the vice-president of the club.

The first salvo against the club was fired by Sister Nivedita (née Margaret Noble), a disciple of Swami Vivekananda, when the then club president, Mrs Blakey, unwittingly invited the great missionary lady to preside over a function held in the summer of 1891 to felicitate Miss Jeanette Van Tassel, the famous aeronaut, on her successful and widely publicized parachute jump from a balloon on the grounds of the Agri-Horticultural Society, Alipore. The Sister, while applauding Miss Van Tassel for her heroic act, didn't forget to castigate the club for its total indifference to the pressing problems of Indian women of the day — their lack of educational facilities, purdah, child marriage and the rest — and for its unhealthy obsession with planchette and other dubious spiritual practices. Two years later, it was the turn of a renowned educationalist, Miss Muller, BA (Cantab), to shock the memsahibs by her hard-hitting speech against "Shakespeare and the musical glasses" (which summed up a genteel woman's education since the days of *The Vicar of Wakefield*), advocating a more practical and plebeian education that included cooking, domestic economy, sick-nursing, washing and — horror of horrors — scrubbing of floors! Neither Sister Nivedita nor Miss Muller was able to break the insularity of the elitist, all-white club, but from 1895 it condescended to show its concern for the local women by making a small yearly donation to Mrs Pugh's Women's Friendly Society which worked for the rehabilitation of the prostitutes of European descent. In 1920, the club again drew a lot of flak from the local press when its members picketed the front gate of the Bengal Club to collect money for the subscription fund set up in London to help the family of the infamous General Dyer who had perpetrated the Jalianawalabagh massacre the previous year.

Like all other white-dominated institutions, the club went through a turbulent period in the wake of India's independence when the inevitable exodus of memsahibs necessitated several amendments to the club's constitution to admit the brown memsahibs. Every Calcutta woman possessing a college degree clamoured for membership to upgrade her social status. The membership was however restricted to five hundred, and the applicants were thoroughly screened to ensure that middle-class women from such undistinguished localities as Dum Dum and Tangra couldn't enter the club and spoil its elitist ambience with office gossip and kitchen talk. In fact, most of the present members could boast of a foreign degree or two, and half of them were non-resident Indians who lived in London or New York and sent their yearly subscription in pounds or dollars and in return received a glossy, four-page, monthly bulletin which mostly contained the achievements of individual members and the minutes of the last executive committee meeting. Those unfortunate members who couldn't afford a foreign address and had to sweat it out in Calcutta's muggy weather, came to the club in the evening to refresh themselves by playing cards, drinking subsidized gin and tonic and discussing the latest fashions or a more topical subject like Mr Thapar's takeover bid. In fact, it was Mr Thapar's insinuations that the club had degenerated to an addakhana, a gossiping place for middle-aged, menopausal women, that prompted the club's president, Mrs Jeejaboy, to admit about a dozen young and vociferous women like Miss Rekha Jhajoria, Miss Sanchita Babeja and Miss Labanya Chaki to give the club a youthful image, and also to organize talks and cultural activities to absolve it of the charge of being a cheap addakhana. Recently, the club had invited Mother Teresa with the laudable intention of making a donation of ten thousand for her leper home, after which she would surely say a few nice words praising the club and its multifarious activities. But as ill-luck would have it, just as her car turned into Free School Street, Mother spotted a dying beggar on the pavement and ordered her driver to stop the car. She picked up the dying man from the street and returned to her Nirmal Hriday, depriving the club of its one and only chance to get a Nobel Laureate to sanctify its premises.

Miss Marjorie Gordon-Green, the up-and-coming British novelist, was not yet a Nobel Laureate but she was definitely made of the same timbre, or at least that was the general impression I collected from the little gupsup the club members had had in the hall before they settled in their chairs, with Mrs Basak's supporters occupying the right side of the aisle and Miss Jhajoria's supporters the left. Mrs Basak introduced me to her friends as the "Maradona of women's football" but I only met contemptuous, if not hostile, glances from the brown memsahibs who had dressed up for the occasion in dazzling Kanchipuram and Mysore silk saris and all their finery. Mrs Gulmohar, the only sympathetic soul in this hostile crowd, sidled up to me and whispered in my left ear that I should have at least tarted myself up in a designer kurta-kameez outfit from Ms Som's boutique to earn a little respect and recognition from her fashion-conscious colleagues. Mrs Basak noted my predicament and whispered in my right ear that she would like to embellish her intro "just a bit" to elicit a better response from her colleagues, if I permitted her to do so. I nodded, for it was extremely humiliating to be cold-shouldered by those fat women flaunting their pearls and diamonds when, thanks to my unscrupulous mother-in-law, I hadn't even a thin gold chain around my bare neck. It was Mrs Basak's idea to bring me here and now let her manage as best as she could.

"By the way, Mrs Malhotra," I heard Mrs Basak saying to a flabby, double-chinned woman with a bird's-nest coiffure, "Miss Hem has received a very lucrative offer from Sheikh Rashid-bin-Hulbula, the king of Al-Niaz, to introduce football in his harem. In fact, the sheikh is reported to be very keen on starting an inter-harem football competition in his kingdom." This tantalizing revelation made the fatsos in Mrs Basak's camp turn their immaculately coiffured heads to watch me with some curiosity. A dark, rotund female with a kettle-shaped mug enquired how much the sheikh was going to pay for my services. "Miss Hem's salary and perks are yet to be settled, Mrs Patil," Mrs Basak informed her. "But we can safely assume that it will be around a million dirham per annum." She even hinted slyly that there was a distinct possibility of Miss Hem eventually filling the coveted fourth slot in Sheikh Hulbula's hierarchy of thirty wives as that particular slot had recently fallen vacant on the sudden and unexpected demise of Begum Zubeda in childbirth. This sensational news created quite a flutter among the members and they looked at my face very searchingly, probably to find out my selling point. I blushed a little and said with appropriate coyness: "Mrs Basak is slightly exaggerating. It's actually a package deal — this marriage-cum-coaching offer. There are five other girls in the field and all of us have to undergo the potato test before the sheikh makes his choice." Miss Sil, a thin, gaunt lady, famous for her numerous letters published in the *Statesman*, fished out a small notebook from her bag and requested me to elaborate a little on the potato test, but Mrs Basak rescued me, promising Miss Sil full information on the subject after the novel-reading session.

"I feel I should disassociate myself from both of you," grumbled Mrs Gulmohar as we took our seats in the third row. "What was the necessity of floating such a big lie?"

"Shush, Gulu! Not so loud," whispered Mrs Basak over my shoulder. "We must protect Hem from our cantankerous colleagues."

"I think you are spoiling her," pouted Mrs Gulmohar. "She has received her certificate from Mrs Blistop's school and now she should make some serious efforts to get a good job."

"I have decided to appoint her as my assistant," declared Mrs Basak in a whisper. "She will maintain personal contacts with my artists, commission new work and scout around for fresh talents."

"Fantastic!" I whispered excitedly. "That's the type of job which suits me best. I accept your offer, darling. I think I will need a card with my name printed in fancy italics."

"You will have that, my dear," said Mrs Basak indulgently.

"I can see your gallery closing down in six months," prophesied Mrs Gulmohar darkly.

"But Gulu, after that Botball episode I can't take any more risks with Hem," argued Mrs Basak.

"You are absolutely right, darling," I said. "These days Calcutta is teeming with criminals and a simple, innocent girl like me . . ."

"Simple and innocent!" snorted Mrs Gulmohar. "Those two words would drop out of the dictionary in shame if you attach them to your back."

I was going to protest vehemently against this deliberate vilification of my character but the members sitting around us hushed us as Mrs Jeejaboy, the pale, wafer-thin, grey-haired president of the club, ascended the dais with Miss Gordon-Green who, in marked contrast to her fragile, soft-spoken hostess, was tall, robust, mid-thirtyish and very brash. She had dressed herself down in a pair of baggies and a greenish T-shirt, with no make-up to hide her worry lines and the bags under her eyes. All the venerable presidents and distinguished members of the club, whose portraits adorned the four walls around us, frowned upon Miss Gordon-Green's shabby dress and unladylike behaviour as she stamped out her half-burnt cigarette under her platform heel, slapped the fat roll of manuscript on her thigh and planted herself before the lecturn.

"We have been hearing so much these days about post-modernist fiction," began Mrs Jeejaboy her introductory speech, taking a peep at the chit she held in her palm. "Today I am happy to introduce one of the most talented practitioners of this fascinating genre, Miss Marjorie Gordon-Green, who has been aptly commended by *The Times* as 'Britain's bold answer to Latin America's Marquez'." We learnt that Miss Gordon-Green's first novel *Sue Mummy!* was an indictment of Britain's progressively deteriorating National Health Service and it provided some delectable glimpses of the magical realism that pervaded her ambitious novel-in-progress entitled *Adam's Spittle*. Miss Gordon-Green had been to Girton, Cambridge, to obtain her degree in sociology and had done some seminal work on paranoids and paraplegics before turning to fiction writing. She had two children from her three unsuccessful marriages and . . .

"That will do, Mrs Jeejaboy," interrupted Miss Gordon-Green. "I will take about an hour and ten minutes to finish my first chapter, so let's get down to business." And before Mrs Jeejaboy had shuffled back to her chair, Miss Gordon-Green started reading her novel, Part I, Chapter 1, subsection (i), in a powerful and impassioned voice. With my very limited experience of novel-reading (four to be exact, out of which two were Miss Brinda Bagui's College Romances), *Adam's Spittle* seemed to me quite extraordinary because it propounded a startling new theory about the origin of races. In the novel, Adam was a chain-smoker with a nagging cough racking his chest. Enraged by his unceremonious expulsion from the Garden of Eden, Adam turned his face upward, coughed uproariously and shot a big lump of spittle towards Heaven to besmear his unforgiving Creator. Alarmed by Adam's devastating missile, God promptly sent out Gabriel to divert the spittle from its perilous course. Hit by the angel's trident, Adam's · spittle was split into four blobs of different colours − the black, infected by nicotine and tar, the yellow, the brown, tinged with congealed mucus, and the white, pure and untainted − each blob carrying the seeds of life for the black, brown, yellow and the white races respectively. The first chapter of Miss Gordon-Green's fascinating novel narrated, with great precision and extraordinary vocabulary, the tantalizing journey of the fragmented spittle through the stratosphere.

"Where do you think that white gob will ultimately land, Mrs Basak?" asked Mrs Malhotra, turning her face from the first row.

"Hampstead Heath, I guess," said Mrs Basak knowledgeably.

"It has to be Hampstead Heath, my dear," nodded Mrs Gulmohar. "All big events happen there. In fact, Ronnie and I bought those Chinese lanterns you see in my home from near that very place on an Easter Monday for just five quid."

"I don't see why that spittle shouldn't land in Golders Green," said Miss Jahjoria, the fair and buxom rival of Mrs Basak, across the aisle. "That's the place where Ravi proposed to me on bended knees."

Mrs Basak curled her lips to show her contempt for Miss Jhajoria and her utter ignorance about London's important venues where great things were supposed to occur.

"Could anybody tell me where the black portion is going to land?" I asked a bit loudly as no one seemed concerned about this important fragment of the spittle.

"Silence please!" cried Professor Sen, the most erudite member of the club, from the front row. She had been exclaiming "Magico Realismo!" at regular intervals of five minutes or so and that evidently pleased Miss Gordon-Green, for, whenever Prof. Sen exclaimed those magic words, she smiled, nodded indulgently and then raised the pitch of her booming voice by a few decibels. Chastened by Prof. Sen, the members leaned back, shuffled their feet and coughed, behaving like a pack of restless schoolgirls. When the minor disturbances failed to distract the unperturbable novelist, the ladies started dozing. Soon, I could hear the drone of collective snoring from all sides. Mrs Basak looked straight ahead, but I could see that her interest in *Adam's Spittle* was flagging and she was struggling hard to keep her eyes open. Mrs Gulmohar plugged her ears and closed her eyes for an undisturbed catnap, fixing a synthetic smile on her face like a mask to show her continuing appreciation of post-modernism. I was planning to black-mail her for a tenner and slip out of the building to have a lick of ice-cream when the lights suddenly went out. I thought that this would bring Miss Gordon-Green's novel-reading to an abrupt and desirable end, but my expectations were dashed when the novelist asked Mrs Jeejaboy to arrange for a couple of candles and when they were fetched by a bearer, Miss Gordon-Green resumed her reading.

I was about to pluck the swab of cotton from Mrs Gulmohar's ear when Mrs Basak leaned back in her seat and gently laid her golden head on my shoulder, upsetting my plan. "If you don't mind . . ." she mumbled.

I was slightly confused by her unexpected and very intimate gesture. "It's all right, Radha," I said, thinking why should I deny my shoulder to a good friend even if she wasn't in love with me? But, as the sweet smell of cologne from Mrs Basak's hair entered my nostrils, I felt the old stirrings of desire which made my heart race in wild anticipation. I longed to bury my nose in her carefully tousled hair and slowly work my way up to her slender throat and then to her rosy lips. But I checked myself, fearing yet another snub from Mrs Basak, and reasoned with myself that after my open declaration of love in her gallery, the ball was now in her court and therefore I should not make any overtures. Mrs Basak however made no further advances and I closed my eyes even as Miss Gordon-Green narrated in her impeccable prose the tantalizing journey of the fragmented spittle through the stratosphere, refracting sunrays into their myriad colours.

I had just started dozing when I felt Mrs Basak's arm going around my shoulders and her long tapering fingers gently feeling my collarbones and then the border of my voile blouse. I thought it very intriguing that, after proclaiming her heterosexuality from the rooftops on that rain-soaked morning, she was now teasing me without the slightest provocation from my side. Maybe she was merely examining the cut of my blouse, I tried to convince myself even as other daring and forbidden thoughts surged up in my mind. My heart quickened as I considered the wonderful possibilities that lay before me, if Mrs Basak's hesitant fingers condescended to dip further and explore around a bit, even though I had so little to offer for her investigations. I held my breath for a few tense seconds as her fingers, answering my fervent prayers, slid further downward, grazing my left breast, to explore my bare midriff. The torment became unbearable when she spread her palm wide and pressed it lightly on my flat tummy, her little finger tentatively probing my belly button. I placed my hand upon hers and whispered, "Radha, please, don't torture me like this."

"Don't you like my touch, darling?" asked Mrs Basak huskily.

"Of course, I do, but since you aren't in love with me you'd better stop tormenting me." In reply, Mrs Basak nibbled my earlobe and whispered, "I do love you, Hem. I can't cheat myself any longer. You are *so* irresistible, darling . . . you feel so much like an athletic young boy." Overwhelmed by her earth-shaking avowal of love at last, I flung my right arm around her neck and kissed her eyes and her cheeks lightly, murmuring, "I love you, Radha. You are *so* delicious!"

"Like a mango?" quipped Mrs Basak even as she nudged my nose with hers.

"You are a heavenly feast, darling," I rejoined, tracing the length of her warm, moist lips with my fingers. "I want to devour you, every bit."

Without further ado, Mrs Basak cupped my left breast through my blouse and started probing around my nipple with her thumb. I promptly reciprocated by exploring the outlines of her breasts which, I reckoned, weighed over a kilo each and appeared to be rather longish.

"Radha, are we really lesbians?" I asked her rather naively.

"I hate that word," said Mrs Basak ruefully even as she managed to undo two hooks of my blouse and slip her hand inside my bra to feel my breasts. "There must be a less forbidding term to express our slightly unnatural yearnings."

"Friendly gropings?"

"That sounds better."

We continued our friendly gropings for a while and then, just as I started unbuttoning Mrs Basak's dress from the neck downward, Prof.

Sen, disturbed by the collective snoring, cried, "Silence please!" The members (except Mrs Gulmohar, with her ears plugged and beatific smile intact) woke up from their slumber and started yawning and throat-clearing, making us freeze in the midst of our intense petting session.

"Let's go out for a breath of fresh air," I suggested to Mrs Basak in a whisper which sounded so hoarse that a few lately awakened members shushed me sanctimoniously. Mrs Basak pinched my arm, slid out of her seat and scurried along the aisle towards a side door which was barely visible in the candlelight. I followed her with the agility of a monkey, reaching the door almost at the same time. Out on the veranda, I threw myself on her bosom and chanted: "I love you – I love you – I love you!"

"Hush!" hissed Mrs Basak. "Let's go upstairs before the lights come on."

We rushed down the veranda, scrambled up the dark stairs and stumbled along a gallery lit up by strips of moonlight that filtered through the venetian blinds. Mrs Basak stopped before a door, took out a key from her bag and slid it into the keyhole. "This is my office," she informed me and then she did an unladylike thing: she took a step backward, hitched up her long skirt above her knees and kicked the door which opened with a loud creak. "After the rains, this damn thing won't budge an inch without a good kick," she grumbled as we entered the dark room which smelt faintly of lime and fresh paint. "Don't move till I open the window," warned Mrs Basak. In the pitch dark I heard the rustle of her skirt as she moved across the room and, a little later, a creak as she threw open one of Molly's little, pointed gothic windows, allowing in a patch of moonlight that made at least half of the room dimly visible. Mrs Basak's office was small but well-furnished with a mahogany table, a couple of chairs, a filing cabinet and, most important of all, a small, brand new settee with flowery upholstery.

We flew to this settee and locked ourselves in a fierce embrace. I held Mrs Basak's face between my palms and smothered it with a flurry of soft kisses, whispering sweet nothings. "Ummm!" responded Mrs Basak in ecstasy and threw back her head, her lips parted in anticipation of a lingering kiss. I rubbed my cheeks against hers, cat-like, buried my nose in her fragrant hair, nibbled her earlobes playfully and finally sealed her mouth with a passionate, searing kiss which lasted for about five minutes and left both of us breathless and quivering with desire. The couch being too narrow to accommodate both of us, I persuaded

Mrs Basak to lie back on it and I knelt down beside her on the carpet for better access to her recumbent body.

"Darling, does every woman in your country grow such a long, exotic variety?" I asked as I fumbled with her buttons. Mrs Basak giggled and stroked my cheek. "No, my dear. They come in all shapes and sizes. If I had a choice I would have opted for the wide and flat type, with a gentle convexity . . . something like the lid of a soup tureen."

While sucking one of Mrs Basak's fat, plum-like nipples, I had my orgasm, a quiet but powerful one that almost brought tears to my eyes. "Lucky you!" Mrs Basak congratulated me, as she made her little discovery from my sudden stillness and quick breathing.

"What about you, darling?" I inquired.

"You have pipped me at the post."

"I am *so* sorry. Let me help you." But as I slid my hand towards her crotch with a missionary zeal, I discovered that Mrs Basak's fist was already clamped tight between her legs. "I am already on the job," she assured me. "It'll be a great help if you continue doing what you have been doing."

"Will you tell me when you come?"

"I will make an announcement," Mrs Basak assured me.

Five long minutes passed while I sucked her nipples with the ardour of a newborn baby, but no announcement came from Mrs Basak.

"Radha darling, are you sure you are following the right technique?" I enquired anxiously.

"Yes, my love."

But I still had my doubts. How could a woman take so long to come on her own if she was serious about her orgasm?

"May I know how many fingers you have employed?" I asked.

"Three."

"God! Withdraw one at once or you will hurt yourself."

"Now, Hem, you are pushing me too far!" protested Mrs Basak. "It's *my* body and I ought to know how it works."

"I am sorry, darling."

"Keep quiet, will you? I need absolute silence to get my act together."

"I perfectly understand, darling." I kept my mouth shut and prayed fervently to God to favour Mrs Basak with a very pleasurable climax within the next thirty seconds. But it took another five minutes or so before Maxine's breath quickened, her muscles tensed up and finally her back arched.

"Radha darling!" I cried excitedly. "Are you really *there*?"

Mrs Basak smiled and raised her two forked fingers to give me the victory sign. I grabbed her hand and hungrily licked her wet fingers, but as I was not quite satisfied with her meagre offering, I dived between her legs for her honeypot.

*

"Where have you been?" demanded Mrs Gulmohar when we slipped back into our seats.

"We went out for a stroll on Park Street," said Mrs Basak coolly. "You were asleep, Gulu, otherwise . . ." She stopped short as Miss Gordon-Green finished her reading just at that moment and invited questions from the audience. Miss Jhajoria wanted to know the particular brand of cigarette Adam patronized and got snubbed by the novelist for asking an irrelevant question. Miss Sil then solicited Miss Gordon-Green's opinion on contemporary British fiction.

"Insular, anaemic and consistently third rate," came the pat reply, which made many a mouth gape in horror as if their lives depended on the sound health of British fiction. Finally, Prof. Sen consulted her notebook and asked how the novelist would explain the creation of the Red Indians. "Very pertinent question," said the novelist and hastily scribbled something on the margin of her manuscript. "I think it would be perfectly reasonable if Adam coughs up a speck of blood too, along with his normal quota of phlegm and tar. As we all know, chain-smokers with a dry lung condition occasionally spit blood. Thank you very much for pointing out this minor flaw in my book."

"Very educative," said Mrs Gulmohar, unplugging her ears discreetly, as we filed out of the hall.

"Yes, but it's very unEnglish, I must say," observed Mrs Basak, her green eyes still sparkling in the afterglow of her hard-earned orgasm. "By the way, did any of us hear where that white blob finally landed?"

"A spooky place called Teigh in Rutland," said Mrs Malhotra gloomily.

"Just imagine! That bloody spittle couldn't find a nice spot anywhere in London!" exclaimed Miss Jhajoria indignantly. I was going to ask about the black segment, but Miss Sil sidled up to me and whispered excitedly in my ear: "Miss Hem, we must correspond!"

"About what, Miss Sil?" I asked, quite baffled.

"About your experiences as a coach and, hopefully, as a Begum too in the sheikh's harem."

"On *that*? Of course, I will keep you posted, Miss Sil."

"Now, will you please tell me something about the potato test?"

"Another day, Miss Sil. I am too tired to talk about such sensitive matters right now."

"I quite understand, Miss Hem. I hope we can meet again in the near future. These days I don't find many interesting items to write about."

I fell back two steps to attach myself, temporarily, to Miss Babeja who was telling her bosom friend, Miss Jhajoria, that after *Winnie the Pooh* she hadn't been able to find any British fiction worth reading. Miss Jhajoria told her friend that recently, while waiting in her dentist's anteroom at Finchley Park, she came across yet another landmark in British fiction: *The Wind in the Willows*. Miss Babeja seemed impressed by the brief outline of the story dished out by her friend and I too thought it quite interesting, though I couldn't help suspecting that a book in which Mr Mole, Mr Rat and Mr Badger repossessed Toad Hall from the wicked weasels must be an animal story for children. I had edged forward to enquire from Miss Jhajoria whether this masterpiece of English literature was available as a comic, but Mrs Basak grabbed my arm and dragged me back to her side. "Don't mix with those bad girls, achha?" she chided me softly, like a doting mother chiding her wayward daughter. I nodded and meekly trotted alongside her towards the gate, clasping her hand. Both Mrs Basak and Mrs Gulmohar offered me a lift but I accepted Mrs Basak's offer and received a dirty look from the latter that clearly said, "How dare you!"

"I don't like the way your Gulu looks at me," I said peevishly when we were out on the road. "Someday I am going to give her a piece of my mind."

"Don't. Gulu is a nice woman. I think she is a bit annoyed because she thinks I am spoiling you."

"I bet she is jealous of our friendship."

"One can't rule out that possibility. After all, she has been my closest friend for over a decade now."

"She has enjoyed your company too long, hasn't she? Now it's my turn to monopolize you." To show how I intended to monopolize her, I snuggled close to her body and clamped my thigh possessively on hers.

Mrs Basak drew up her car in a by-lane near my house. We kissed, exploring each other's mouth with our tongues.

"Do you really love me, Radha?" I asked as she fondled my breasts.

"Do you still have any doubts, darling?"

"Oh no. I only wonder why you took so much time to reciprocate. Maybe I should have given you a clear signal when we met that first time at Rose Valley."

"But there was no necessity of that, my dear. You are so transparent that even a cat can see what you are thinking at a particular moment with a casual glance at your face. Why, even on that evening of your arrival at Rose Valley, I noticed that you were watching me greedily as if I was a delicious bun just taken out of the oven!"

"God! I never suspected *that*. Of course, I kissed you deliberately on the veranda before you threw me out. I think that was a give-away."

"Ah, yes. That only confirmed my suspicions. The way you broke down at Flurys, when I refused you my friendship, made me really scared."

"And you tried to avoid me on one flimsy pretext or other. I thought you were deliberately keeping me at arm's length because I am so ugly and can't appreciate art and Italian opera."

Mrs Basak playfully nibbled my earlobe and whispered, "Oh no! That's not at all true. To be honest, Hem, I was attracted by your raw vitality and feline charm right from the beginning, but I tried to avoid you like the plague because I knew you would be big trouble and I was afraid you'd bring chaos to my quiet and peaceful life. Frankly speaking, I wasn't mentally prepared to have a torrid affair with a girl my daughter's age."

"That sounds very funny indeed . . . denying oneself the pleasure of loving and being loved. Ah! If only I'd known what was brewing inside my very propah memsahib! Why, I even thought you were a cruel and cold-hearted woman!"

"But I do have a streak of cruelty in my character and you know that," confessed Mrs Basak with a sigh which broke my heart. I flung my arms around her neck and assured her: "I love your little cruelties, darling. They are *so* feminine."

We could have continued talking in this vein till morning but for the sudden appearance of the beat constable who tapped his thick, oily stick on the pavement and asked very brusquely why the red Maruti bearing number WBB 8563 was parked on the wrong side of the street. I gave her a parting kiss and tumbled out of the car, smoothing my crumpled sari with my palms to assume a normal look.

Next morning, while we were having tea on the veranda, Paromita neatly picked out three long, golden hairs from my head. I feared she would throw a tantrum, but she merely dropped the hairs on my lap and said quietly, "I can now see why that memsahib was so keen to give you those hefty loans."

"Do you want to throw me out of the house?" I demanded, bristling at her insinuation. Having won Mrs Basak's heart, I no more cared what this dowdy, spoilsport Gandhian thought about me.

"Who am I to throw you out?" said Paromita. "This is Mr Sen's house and you are free to live here as long as he permits you. But, from tonight, we shall have separate beds."

"That's fine for me!" I cried. "I myself was going to suggest such an arrangement because I can't stand the horrible smell of your coconut hair oil any longer."

"Not surprising, after your recent discovery of cologne and French perfume," said Paromita scathingly. I gave her a scorching look and she returned it with a glacial stare.

A week later, when I got Mrs Basak's beautiful card inviting me to her much-awaited dinner party, I deliberately kept it on the table so that Paromita could see it morning and evening and recognize my enhanced status in Calcutta society.

Perhaps I could have spared my Gandhian friend this ennobling experience because, as it turned out, the yearly bash at Basak House didn't really add any feather to my cap.

Fifteen

Like Utpala, my inquisitive teammate, I wanted to pose three, nay four, incisive questions to any young girl going to a Calcutta party in a posh area like New Alipore or Golf Links: "1. Are you a rich, beautiful and famous woman like Keya Tarafdar of *Honeymoon* fame? 2. Are you conversant with such classy and fashionable subjects as art, haute couture, haute cuisine and the English monarchy? 3. Can you buy, borrow or steal Ms Bhavna Som's latest designer kurta-kameez ensemble ('The emphasis is on subtle glitter and sunset elegance, using basic cuts') in crepe, organza or tussore, embroidered in shades of gold, bronze and pewter, and a few accessories as well, like block-heels, oxidized bangles, big hooped earrings, Alice bands (Scrunchies are out, please note) and, of course, a packet of bubblegum, the last item being a universally understood symbol of teenage revolt. 4. Do you spend your summer vacations in London and Paris every year?" If your response to each of these four vital questions is in the negative, I am afraid you are going to cut a sorry figure, just as I did on that pleasant September evening at Basak House.

And yet, I couldn't blame my fair hostess for my miserable odd-girl-out condition. She had received me personally at the gate, like all the other guests, when I got down from my hired taxi (taken from the other end of Belvedere Road just to show that I didn't come in a bus) and escorted me to her capacious sitting room where about a dozen sedate matrons from her club were anxiously discussing something in hushed tones. I thought it was either Mr Thapar's latest offer or a recent death of a veteran club member, but Mrs Basak whispered to me that her venerable colleagues were actually discussing the serious crack that had been found in the upraised leg of Eros in Piccadilly Circus! Unable to participate in this highbrow discussion, I turned my attention to my hostess's dress. I had half-expected to see her in a low-necked cocktail dress revealing her cleavage, but Mrs Basak had decided to present herself as the quintessential upper-class Bengali woman in a gorgeous, pure Dhakai silk sari with elegant zari work on the border which produced a rich crackle and rustling sound as she bustled around, smiling and greeting her guests. "How do I look in my sari, Hem?" she asked as she noted my interest in her unusual attire.

"You look fantastic, Radha," I whispered. "You really look like a zaminder-ginni and I like your diamonds too. Are they from Bowbazar?"

Maxine blushed. "No, dear, they are American. Bailey, Banks and Biddle, though I prefer Elizabeth Duke. Gour has recently been to the States with a Parliamentary delegation." She beckoned to her elder daughter who had just popped her head into the room. "Varsha, come and meet my friend Hem," called Mrs Basak. "Here is one of the best footballers we have in Calcutta."

"Glad to meet you, Miss Maradona," whispered Varsha with a measured smile and an intonation which was half-drawl, half-stutter. She had the same oval face, small sensual mouth and finely cut nose as her mother, but her eyes and her hair were black, the latter cropped and spiked to give her the desired punkish look. She wore an ornate, gold-embroidered bolero with a white-lined kameez, defying Miss Som's dictum on Calcutta's teenage fashion. "See you later, Miss Maradona," whispered Varsha throatily and strode away to meet a very pale, handsome young man in tuxedo who had just appeared at the door. All eyes in the room were momentarily riveted on the young pair and Mrs Basak nodded in response to her friends' meaningful winks to indicate that Cupid's devastating arrow might have really done its job. She also informed us that Robin Roy, Rob Roy to his friends, was at Christchurch and since Varsha was planning to be at Somerville, the couple could be expected to see each other quite a lot during the next couple of years. Mrs Basak was about to divulge Rob Roy's rather complicated family connections with the royal house of Coochbehar when a bearer approached her to announce the arrival of half a dozen artists and she rushed out of the room, throwing a valuable piece of advice in my direction over her shoulder: "Circulate, darling!" That was when I left the sitting room to ruminate behind a massive Doric pillar and frame my four soul-searching questions for the future party-going girl.

"Do you know Dippy?" asked a small, frumpy woman swathed clumsily in a gaudy, temple-print sari. Apparently, she had been hovering on the fringe of a small group of women on my left without being able to make any dent in the charmed circle.

"Dippy? No, I don't think I have heard the name. Who is he anyway?"

"My husband, Dipten Ghosh," said the woman without any rancour. "Exports cotton garments to Youkay and Youessay. It's he who smuggled in the Campari they are serving here. You know, Mr Basak is a bosom friend of Dippy." She waved at a bearer who was strutting around like a peacock in his white tunic, flared pink turban and red cummerbund.

"What's that you are serving, Abdul?"

"My name is Mohan, ma'am," said the bearer with dignity and a hint of a frown.

"It hardly makes any difference, dear, though I prefer Abdul. Isn't that Campari?"

"Yes, ma'am, with orange." He reluctantly lowered his tray and Mrs Ghosh picked up a glass, muttering, "Thank you." She threw a I-told-you look at me and took a not-so-gentle sip with a slurping sound. "They advertise it as the spirit of Italy. Hee-hee!" She laughed raucously, probably to attract the attention of her target group centred around a highly articulate young lady who held her half a dozen goggle-eyed teenage admirers in thrall with a blow-by-blow account of the latest movie she had seen on video which was about a naughty ghost going berserk in a New York supermarket.

"I don't think Miss Kunju will have anything more interesting in her repertoire to regale her audience with," observed Mrs Ghosh as she finished her drink with a gulp. "After all, she hasn't been to Youkay this summer. Let's try that group over there. Have you heard Leena Lahiri's latest album?"

I shook my head, feeling slightly vexed in the queer company of this oddball who didn't even have the courtesy to ask me who I was.

"The finest Rabindrasangeet singer we have in Calcutta these days," informed Mrs Ghosh. "Of course, she went to Santiniketan for her musical training. She was recently invited by the NRIs of Youkay to perform at Wembley stadium. Isn't that very exciting?"

With no better option on hand to kill time, I accompanied Mrs Ghosh to attach ourselves to a slightly bigger group, the core of which was a svelte, stunning beauty arrayed in a see-through, pastel chiffon sari and backless choli. Miss Lahiri was reeling off in a high-pitched, south-of-Park-Street stutter (definitely a notch below Varsha's imported variety) her recent forays into London's haute couture which afforded her some rare glimpses of Vivienne Westwood's bondage trousers, David and Elizabeth Emanuel's "The Empire State

Collection", Katherine Hamnett's funky cross dressing and Murray Arbeid's spectacular evening clothes.

"Isn't she fascinating?" exclaimed Mrs Ghosh, her mouth gaping in surprise.

"Very," I said, then gave Mrs Ghosh the slip. I walked down the majestic wide stairs, passing on my way a bevy of artists, led by Mrs Basak, among whom I spotted the tall, gaunt figure of Mr Khashnobish, the celebrated painter of the "Nemesis" series. Mrs Basak smiled and waved at me and I waved back though I knew it was only a meaningless exchange of gestures that promised me nothing. I strolled to the other end of the garden, exploring on my way the newly-laid bed of roses, an arbour, a cave lighted by small, hidden bulbs, and a rockery. I enjoyed a ride on a swing hung from a lower branch of a tall litchi tree, but the deserted garden soon bored me and I ambled back, stopping briefly by the lily pond to look at a tableau of clay figures set up on the banks, showing a muscular fisherman casting his net and, facing him, on the opposite bank, a bespectacled, dhoti-clad Bengali baboo perched on a low stool, holding a fishing rod in one hand while his eyes were focused on an open book lying on his lap. This was obviously Mrs Basak's idea, I thought, a gentle dig at the Bengali's well-known passion for fish and poetry.

"Where have you been, Hem? I was searching for you frantically," said Mrs Basak as she caught me at the foot of the stairs.

"But why were you searching for me, Radha?" I asked, slightly piqued. "You aren't going to introduce me to your artist friends, are you?"

"No, my dear, I think I am in trouble. Have a look at my sari. I'm afraid it's going to fall down around my feet in a heap within the next five minutes."

I gave a tentative tug at her sari and smiled. "I don't think there is any real danger of your performing a striptease before your honourable guests, but I will be happy to undress you to find out the flaws in your draping as soon as you are free."

"You rogue! Just wait . . ." Mrs Basak darted away to greet an English couple who had just tumbled out of their Jag. They were one of the most singularly mismatched couples I had ever seen: a beefy, boisterous and elegantly dressed husband completely dwarfing his mousy, washed-out blonde wife who couldn't find anything better in her wardrobe than a nondescript, lemon yellow gown.

Mrs Basak returned after ten minutes of animated talk with her compatriots. "That was David and Cynthia," she told me. "David is now the president of the UK Expatriates' Association. He has a strong lobby at Westminister and he is expected to get an OBE next year. Helps us a lot to get duty-free booze and other stuff from home."

"Is he the one who helped you to get your Campari?"

"Oh yes, and Scotch too. It was very kind of him as I am not a member of the Association, being an Indian by marriage."

"Just now one Mrs Ghosh claimed that her husband Dippy had smuggled in the liquor for you."

Mrs Basak looked horrified. "Good Heavens! But I am quite sure that I didn't send her an invitation this year! Last year she got drunk on Scotch, danced Bhangra in my sitting room and then threw up on Mrs Malhotra's lap. I must ask a bearer to keep an eye on her."

"It looks a bit like a hen party," I observed as I saw a fresh batch of women, with a resplendent Miss Jhajoria in the lead, coming up the stairs.

"That's why I had to invite some boys from the Goldstar Dancing School to partner the unattached ladies. Now . . . I must rush to receive Miss Jhajoria and her cronies or she might spread some canard about my lack of hospitality. Wait for me in the sitting room, achha?"

Willy-nilly, I returned to the sitting room, only to find Mrs Basak's colleagues speculating animatedly about the chances of Queen Elizabeth abdicating her throne in favour of Prince Charles in her next Christmas speech. The main participants in this interesting debate were Mrs Mahadevan, a dark, short, squint-eyed lady with a garland of mogra coiled around her thick braid, and Mrs Walters, the oldest member of the club, who seemed to know almost everything about the English monarchy. While Mrs Mahadevan strongly believed that the Queen wouldn't be so selfish as to retain her throne till poor Charles became old and gouty, Mrs Walters pointed out that the Queen appeared to be keen to break the impeccable record of her great great grandmother Queen Victoria's reign of sixty-four years. The debate was interrupted by the squeals and giggles of Miss Jhajoria and her young friends as they entered the room with Mrs Basak. All eyes were riveted on Miss Jhajoria's dazzling Patola sari which, every woman in the room knew, cost a cool fifty thousand rupees or thereabouts. It had bold, grid-based patterns juxtaposed with intricate geometrical, floral and figurative motives woven in the double ikat technique. "Don't you think it's rather vulgar, spending a fortune on a six-yard sari?" whispered Mrs Basak in my ear as she saw her rival stealing the show in her own sitting room. "Yes," I nodded even as I craned my neck to have a good look at Miss Jhajoria's outfit.

"I think I should change into a Jamdani or Bangalore silk," said Mrs Basak petulantly.

I turned my head. "Don't. You look very elegant and dignified in Dhakai."

"Are you sure?"

"Absolutely, though I feel you can look more gorgeous if you opt for a different style of draping. I think, 'Maharani' would suit you best."

Mrs Basak beamed. "That's the sort of advice one expects from one's dearest friend. Darling, let's rush to my bedroom and finish the job before the last batch of guests turn up." Mrs Basak virtually dragged me upstairs and darted across the dancing hall where, under the glittering chandeliers, a dozen lithe John Travoltas and Patrick Swayzes, hired from the Goldstar Dancing School, were gyrating to tunes from *Dirty Dancing* played by a dapper little musician on his univox from a podium erected at the far end of the hall.

Mrs Basak's bedroom wasn't as exotic as I had expected it to be, though the room could boast a finely carved fourposter with tiger-paw legs, an antique flower stand with an engraved glass flower holder on a mirror base, and some chintz curtains. The squat, heavy chest of drawers along the wall was an eyesore and the drab watercolour on the wall — Piccadilly in the rain — by the omnipresent Huda only made the room look gloomier.

"Do you like my bedroom?" asked Mrs Basak matter-of-factly as she started taking out her sari clips and the safety pins from her shoulder and waist to unwrap herself. "Immensely," I said, gathering her sari in measured folds. I couldn't help laughing as I discovered that she had actually fastened the sari around her waist with a belt!

"Twenty years in India and still you need a belt to hold your sari in place. Chee-chee!"

Mrs Basak grinned sheepishly. "You won't believe me, but I took some sari-draping lessons at the Handloom House when I came to India and Gulu also tried to teach me the intricacies from time to time, but it's such a complicated job . . ."

"There is no complication at all. You just watch me doing it."

"Wait a sec, Hem." Mrs Basak darted to a small cabinet beside her bed to take out her bottle and a small glass.

"Can't you forgo your brandy even for one evening?" I said, frowning.

"I need to fortify myself, darling," cooed Mrs Basak and poured herself a big shot. "People make me jittery." She drained her glass and scuttled back to me, sprightly and cheerful. "Now the Maharani drape." She looked at me with awe and curiosity as I fastened the sari tightly around her waist and then went about my task with a professional air, squatting and crouching before her, tucking in a fold here, smoothing one there, arranging her front pleats meticulously and pinning up the loose ends carefully with safety pins, some of which I held between my teeth for easy retrieval. Mrs Basak had to hold my shoulders to steady herself as I turned her roughly like a marionette to adjust and readjust her pallav several times before I was satisfied with the characteristic "V" shape that she had to flaunt from the front and back to assume the maharani look. "Now, go and look at yourself in the mirror," I said at last, slapping her on the bottom.

"Marvellous!" she exclaimed as she stood before her dressing table.

"What will you give me for my labours?" I asked.

"Anything that doesn't require me to undress or redo my face and hair."

"Clever girl!" I knelt before her and gently kissed her lower abdomen.

"You twit! Can't you even land a kiss properly?"

"I only kissed your womb, darling," I said, grinning.

"God! What's so special about my womb?"

"Well, it bore you two lovely girls. Aren't you proud of them?"

"Oh, that . . . of course I am proud of them. You know, Tee has stopped tormenting me. It's such a great relief."

"Really? I am so happy to hear that. Is she here?"

"Yes, but she is below party age, so I told her to keep to her room, though I know she will sneak downstairs with her two friends after a while."

"And where is Mr Basak, our host?"

Mrs Basak shrugged. "No idea. He arrived from Delhi this morning but I haven't been able to talk to him for more than five minutes. I guess he is now holed up somewhere with his politician buddies to enjoy a bottle of Scotch and probably hatch a dirty plot to do in his opponents."

"That's very selfish of him. He could have shared your burden of playing host to so many people."

"He says he can't cope with so many women."

"Ah, that sounds like Krishna shunning his six million cowmaids, doesn't it?"

"Thanks for that apt comparison, my dear. Maybe he is taking a breather."

"I don't think so." I was tempted to tell her about Mr Basak's affair with Lola Mudgal and also about his proposal to me, but I didn't want to spoil this beautiful evening. "Radha darling, you must have another child," I said ecstatically, planting two more kisses on that vague part of her anatomy which I had identified as her womb.

Mrs Basak feigned horror. "Are you crazy? I am almost forty, and for your information, I don't share a bed with Gour."

"A pity. Maybe you should break that rule for a few nights."

There was an urgent knock on the door; Mrs Basak padded across the room and turned the knob. A bearer announced that Aslam Huda had just arrived from Bombay and was waiting for Mrs Basak in an ante room.

"Huda!" cried Mrs Basak. "So Huda has made it! God, I thought he wouldn't." She turned to face me, her eyes glowing. "Hem, darling, you'll have to excuse me," she said. "I must rush to meet Huda. He's so sentimental that if I don't fuss over him, he will throw a tantrum." Mrs Basak dashed out of the room, leaving me distraught and wondering what devastating spell those abstract horses and semi-cubist compositions had cast on her that made her so crazy about the septuagenarian artist. Full of jealousy and impotent rage, I decided there was no point in hanging around a moment longer. I slipped out of the room and strode along the gallery, seething with rage and indignation, but half-way down the passage I bumped into Mr Basak, who had just emerged from a dark corridor at the end of which, I guessed, was a men's toilet.

"Well?" said Mr Basak with a hideous grin. "Where are you rushing to, my dear?"

"Let me pass, Mr Basak," I said coldly, scowling. "I have business downstairs."

"Chasing old Max, eh?" leered Mr Basak. He looked strikingly handsome in his embroidered silk kurta worn with a Nehru jacket. The devil exuded a mild attar scent.

"I think you are drunk, Mr Basak," I replied. "I have more important business than chasing your wife."

"I am sure you have. Someone told me just now that the dining room is being thrown open in about five minutes. But you are angry . . . what's the matter, darling?"

"None of your business, Mr Basak, and don't darling me. Let me pass."

"Oh sure." Mr Basak stepped aside with a mock bow as if I was Empress Nurjehan.

"Thanks," I said primly and trotted off.

"When you have simmered down a bit and can spare me a few minutes, I'd like to have a word or two with you in private," said Mr Basak at my back.

"Another time," I replied, without turning my head, as I hurried towards the stairs.

While cutting across the sitting room, I noticed a slow but unmistakable drift towards the dining room which, I discovered, was located very inconveniently in the western wing, at the far end of a long corridor. No harm if I tucked in a couple of fish fries and a few spoonfuls of pilau before I left Basak House, I decided and joined the traffic.

The dining hall turned out to be disproportionately small for a big mansion with two sprawling wings consisting of fifty odd rooms. The lack of space and the exigencies of a buffet automatically imposed severe discipline on the diners who had to queue up for the choice dishes. I picked up my plate, spoon and paper napkin from one end of the long table and joined a queue at the other end for a helping of smoked hilsa which exuded such an irresistible aroma.

Having finished my hilsa, I was thinking of joining the queue for sweet and sour prawns when someone rushed into the dining hall to announce that Miss Keya Tarafdar, the much-acclaimed heroine of *Honeymoon*, had just arrived. This news created such a big sensation among the diners that the long queues for hilsas and prawns broke up and there was a mad scramble for the door in which Ms Som's Kurta brigade easily outstripped the sari-clad women by a clear margin of two and a half feet. Unable to resist the temptation of catching a glimpse of the famous film star, I too joined the race and found myself jostling a tipsy Mrs Ghosh who brandished a half-chewed drumstick and threatened to break it on my head if I didn't allow her to pass through the door first. But I elbowed her to one side to clear my passage and, once I was outside the hall, I hitched up my sari and sprinted to catch up with the Kurta brigade before they reached the far end of the long corridor. And then, just as I thought that I had assured myself of a ringside seat for an uninterrupted view of Miss Tarafdar, someone from the left grabbed my arm with an iron grip. Enraged by this obstruction, I turned sharply and raised my hand to slash at the offending arm, but I checked myself just in time as Miss Sil, striving hard to look elegant in her tussore silk sari, cried, "Miss Hem! Please spare me a minute! I have been trying to find you for quite some time . . ."

"Look Miss Sil, I can't spare you even a second right now," I said curtly. "I have an important message for Mrs Basak. Please let go of my hand."

"No use, Miss Hem," said Miss Sil with a hideous grin. "Miss Tarafdar has already been gheraoed by at least thirty admirers."

"You are lying!" I cried, aghast. "Everyone was in the dining room when she came. How come . . .?"

"Those boys from the Goldstar Dancing School and some of Miss Jhajoria's friends were already there when Miss Tarafdar arrived. But don't grieve, Miss Hem. *Honeymoon* is, after all, a third-rate masala film meant for goggle-eyed adolescents. In my eyes you are much more interesting than Miss Tarafdar."

Clever Miss Sil! I smiled and dabbed at my mouth with a paper napkin that I found mysteriously clinging to my palm. "Well, Miss Sil, I think I can spare a couple of minutes for you. I have to rush home because I am expecting a call from Sheikh Hulbula around midnight."

Miss Sil dragged me to a corner and fished out a notebook and a stub of pencil from her bag. "May I presume that you have already passed the potato test, Miss Hem?"

"Yes, by Allah's grace."

"Would you please explain how this test is conducted?" Miss Sil's big protruding eyes shone like searchlights and I had to step back to avoid her bad breath.

"I had to compete with six other girls, Miss Sil. Each one of us was given a baby potato, a kitchen knife, a cooking pan, fifty grams of butter and a small packet of spices, and then we were asked to peel the potato and cook it. It's a very difficult, time-honoured, Arab test for selecting a housemaid or a wife."

"But cooking potato isn't a difficult job, Miss Hem!"

"There's a catch, Miss Sil. You have to be very careful at every step. For instance, if you peel the skin too thick, you lose marks because it shows you are a spendthrift. You can also lose marks if you peel it too thin because that shows you are a miser."

"How fascinating!" Miss Sil's hand moved fast on her notebook as she took down the essential details of the potato test.

"Not for nothing did I practise potato-peeling for six months, Miss Sil."

"Congratulations on your stupendous success, Miss Hem! By the way, was there an interview after the test?"

"Of course there was an interview, but it was a cakewalk for me."

"I am happy to note that beauty isn't the only consideration for the sheikh."

"You are right, Miss Sil. I beat the other three girls who passed the potato test with me by a quirk of fate. There was a bearded mullah on the interview board who took about ten seconds to read the sacred words 'La Ilaha' in my scars and exclaimed, 'Inshallah! We must take this boygirl because she is absolutely halal.'"

"Fascinating! Miss Hem, we must correspond."

"Any day, Miss Sil. The sheikh has promised to send his private jet to fly me to Al-Niaz. I am quite confident that inter-harem football competitions will soon replace camel racing as the chief national sport in the sheikh's kingdom."

Miss Sil pressed my hand with evident emotion. I looked at my watch. "I must rush, Miss Sil. The midnight call from the sheikh . . . I told you." And I dashed for the sitting room with the faint hope of catching a glimpse of the film star.

But when I finally reached Mrs Basak's sitting room, Miss Tarafdar was already surrounded by at least fifty heads, arranged roughly in three concentric circles, which I had no chance of penetrating unless I threw a grenade. All I could hear by pricking up my ears was Miss Tarafdar's excited babble about how she had lost one of her favourite Gucci shoes on the Digha beach while shooting a song and dance sequence for her debut film *Love and Destiny* and how she had wept for her beloved shoe, forcing everyone in the unit, from the director to the clapper-boy, to hunt for it on the beach all night with torches and hurricane lanterns.

"She is interesting, isn't she?" someone whispered in my ear.

I turned my head and glared as I saw Mrs Ghosh chewing her drumstick behind me. "I think she is very immature and childish," I said cuttingly. "And please stop rubbing that messy bone on my neck."

"Sorry, my dear. I have almost finished it but I can't chuck it out because there isn't a window within reach." She gave her drumstick a final lick and held it up in front of my nose. "My dear, could you do me a favour and throw this bone in a corner of the garden? I simply can't detach myself from Miss Tarafdar. She is *so* irresistible."

Since I was eager to detach myself from Mrs Ghosh and leave Basak House as early as possible, I agreed to wrap her drumstick in my paper napkin and take it outside.

Five minutes later, I stood behind one of those huge Doric pillars, wondering if I would be able to pitch the bone with enough force to take it right over the boundary wall to the other side. No harm in trying, I thought, particularly when no one was around to judge my performance. I hitched up my sari above my knees, backed a few steps, took a short run and threw the bone with some force. Unfortunately, it hit the top of the wall and fell back into the garden.

"That was a fine throw, my dear," applauded a familiar male voice behind me, "but you'll have to improve your technique if you want to participate in an international bone-throwing competition."

I whipped around and saw Mr Basak emerging from the shadows with an ingratiating smile. "I never thought the Basaks would be the sort who snoop on their guests," I said, frowning.

"I plead not guilty," said Mr Basak, his smile intact. "I had come up the stairs from the other side of the portico, after seeing off my politician friends, and just happened to catch you in the act. By the way, Hem, you have very fine legs."

"You will find some finer legs inside," I retorted.

"What's the matter, dear? You are still boiling like a vat of coconut oil. Haven't they provided you with some food?"

There was no point in venting my ire on Mr Basak, I thought, and simmered down a bit. "I have had some hilsa, thank you," I said. "I am feeling bored here and I want to go home. Could you please ask someone to call a taxi for me?"

"I will send my chauffeur with the car, my dear," said Mr Basak, his voice suddenly becoming soft and intimate. "But before you go, I'd like to tell you that I have decided to revise the terms of my offer."

"I am not interested in your dirty offer, Mr Basak, as I have told you umpteen times."

"Still, there's no harm in knowing your worth — in my eyes, of course. Instead of a two-bedroomed flat and two thousand rupees a month, you are now entitled to a three-bedroomed flat, a monthly allowance of three thousand and a cook-cum-housemaid."

"Thanks for that tempting offer, Mr Basak, but I want to keep my independent status."

"I won't fetter you, I promise. I've already told you that you can keep a lover in my absence."

"That only makes your proposal more bizarre and thoroughly detestable. I am not a commodity, Mr Basak, to be bought and sold."

Mr Basak frowned. "That sounds like hackneyed dialogue from a third-rate Bengali weepy. Let me tell you an unpalatable truth, Hem: lust can be a stronger and more enduring bond than love."

"You are a vile creature, Mr Basak."

" 'Man is vile and vile is he who calls him vile for that.' That's Dostoevsky, I believe."

"But I am not vile, Mr Basak. No self-respecting woman would ever join your harem, I can tell you. Money isn't everything; there are things like dignity, self-respect, morality . . ."

Mr Basak shrugged in exasperation, then his eyes narrowed and his jaws hardened. "I will force nothing on you, my dear," he said with a wooden smile. "But how about a bit of shuffling and jiving before we part, maybe forever? Max told me that you have learnt dancing at Mrs Blistop's. Assuming, of course, that you don't consider dancing with me an immoral act."

"I am not a nun, Mr Basak," I said haughtily. "But I can't give you more than ten minutes."

"I am honoured," said the devil, grinning.

*

The simultaneous presence of two celebrities at the party had polarized the guests, with the younger section, led by Miss Jhajoria, monopolizing the film actress in the sitting room, and the older and artistically inclined group, led by Mrs Basak, gheraoing Aslam Huda in an ante room which had been cleared of its heavy teak furniture and spread with an extra Mirzapuri carpet to create more space and a laid-back ambience preferred by the great artist. Those who were neither young nor artistically inclined gathered around Mrs Walters who, sitting majestically on a couch in a room opposite to Huda's, was conducting a quiz on British Royalty.

Mr Basak obviously had other things in mind when he proposed that dance, for as soon as we approached the staircase, he looked around to make sure that the coast was clear and then dragged me under the staircase for a stolen kiss. I struggled to wrench myself free, but he was adamant and pressed his mouth hard on mine, making me gasp for breath. "Mr Basak, I am going to scream!" I threatened as he released me. "Hush!" said Mr Basak and tried to kiss me again, but this time I foiled his attempt by keeping my lips firmly sealed.

"From the way you have resisted my little advances, I am now pretty sure that you have been laying my wife for some time," said Mr Basak with a sly smile.

"You have a dirty mind, Mr Basak," I snarled.

"Well, Hem, we now know each other a bit, don't we?" jeered Mr Basak. "Not that I mind your intimate relationship with old Max, because ours is an open marriage. Still, I'd have been happy if you had the guts to own up to the fact. To an ordinary hetero like me, a close friendship between a soccer fiend and a pukka memsahib hooked on art and Italian opera is suspect. Do you understand that?"

I knew Mr Basak was trying to provoke me into a confession but I refused to take the bait. "You are free to draw your own conclusions, Mr Basak," I said, trying to look unflappable. "And let me tell you something I have so far avoided telling you: *I hate you!*"

"Hi Dad!" cried Varsha from the landing. "Where did you vanish to? There are guys up here who want to talk to you."

"This is your mum's bash, darling," said Mr Basak. "You know very well that I can't stand art talk and club politics. Thank God, Hem is keeping me company. Why don't you ask your dear mum to do some hosting?"

"But she is holed up in that room with Huda," said Varsha sulkily. "Miss Maradona, would you mind lending me Dad for a few minutes?"

I smiled. "Not at all, my dear. I am afraid I have already bored Mr Basak to death with my soccer talk."

Mr Basak looked daggers at me and then reminded me of my promise to dance with him, before he reluctantly followed his daughter upstairs.

Free at last! But before leaving Basak House I couldn't resist the temptation of taking a peep at Huda to find out what made him so irresistible in the eyes of a beautiful woman like Mrs Basak.

Huda was a tall, gaunt, bearded man in his late sixties or early seventies who appeared to be striving hard to nurture his public image of a reckless bohemian. He was dressed in acid-washed jeans and a dirty but colourful (and collarless) designer shirt worn under a coarse denim jacket studded with numerous brass buttons. Surrounded by his wide-eyed devotees, the Indian Picasso sat cross-legged on the soft Mirzapuri carpet, leaning his back against the wall, and talked slowly with a drawl, occasionally flashing an impish smile which his admirers recognized as enigmatic. Mrs Basak sat at his feet like a good disciple, her legs daintily tucked under her in the perfect Indian style, her eager, shining face tilted up as if she was expecting a halo to appear around her guru's head at any moment. Huda was holding forth about his recent attempts to bring art to the doorsteps of ordinary people living in far-flung villages and small towns — the farmers, factory workers, clerks, hospitalized patients, even the prostitutes. His revolutionary concept appeared to be that rather than people going to selected galleries to appreciate art, it should be the artists who go to the people in their homes and workplaces and create art before their eyes with easily identifiable objects of everyday use. Huda had just returned from a coastal village in Andhra Pradesh where he had entertained over fifty thousand fishermen and women by creating artworks from local materials, in this case ten thousand sardines, five thousand tuna, three thousand mackerels and two dozen live cats. "I still smell fishy, ha! ha!" guffawed Huda with an impish (or enigmatic) grin. "Here, sniff it." He offered his hallowed palm to his female admirers amongst whom Mrs Basak's position was undoubtedly at the top as she got the first chance to sniff it. I envied Huda for his absolute, god-like power over his admirers and wondered if Mrs Basak would sniff my hand so eagerly even if I sprayed it with the world's finest perfume. Someone begged Huda to talk about his famous "chilli art" which was widely publicized in India and abroad. "That was in Warangal," said Huda with a gentle shake of his mane and a comical twitch of his bushy brows. "I saw women drying fat, luscious red chillies on their dungwashed courtyards and requested them to allow me to use the stuff just for a few hours. It was my most ambitious and certainly the most dangerous venture to date with edible art. I sneezed for a whole week and had to be hospitalized in Hyderabad." There was a spate of "ahs" and "oohs" from the women devotees to register their horror as well as deep sympathy for the great artist. Mrs Basak clasped Huda's hands and her face registered the anguish of a true shishya at the suffering of her beloved guru.

Mrs Ghosh gently tapped on my shoulder and whispered, "One wonders, dear, if Mrs Basak is having an intimate relationship with . . ."

"Please, Mrs Ghosh!" I groaned and felt a very strong urge to slap Mrs Basak and give her a good shake as well. "I will teach that bitch a good lesson before I allow her to touch me again," I vowed as I strode briskly towards the door, ignoring Miss Tarafdar and her fans in the sitting room.

I had reached the foot of the stairs when a bearer came running with a chit from Mr Basak. It said: "You promised me a bop, remember? I am waiting for you." My initial impulse was to crumple the chit in my fist and throw it in the face of the dumb-looking bearer, but I contained my anger as a nasty idea crossed my mind. If Mrs Basak could flirt openly with Huda, why shouldn't I do the same with Mr Basak? Tit for tat! That would be the proper way to teach my unfaithful lover a good lesson. "Tell Mr Basak, I'll be there in five minutes," I told the bearer and retraced my steps to the house.

Thanks to Miss Tarafdar's magnetic appeal, the dance floor was empty except for a few middle-aged couples moving sluggishly to tunes from *My Fair Lady*. I found Mr Basak slouching in an English Regency chair, nursing his drink. He brightened up as he saw me enter the room and beckoned me to a spindle-back Louis VI chair near him. "If you hadn't turned up within the next ten minutes, I would have gone to bed," he said petulantly and took a quick sip. "I feel like a stranger in my own house. I hardly know any of these people."

"You ought to stay a few months every year in your ancestral house to familiarize yourself with Calcutta society," I advised him like a good old aunt.

Mr Basak grimaced. "I can't stay in Calcutta for more than twenty-four hours at a time. It stinks."

"And what about those of us who haven't been fortunate enough to find a better place? Do we also stink?"

"I will answer that question when I have had a good chance to sniff you." Mr Basak tossed off the remaining portion of his drink and rose from his throne. "What's your favourite dance, my dear? Foxtrot, tango . . . just name it."

"Waltz," I said.

"Waltz it will be, darling."

"We have had enough of your rock and pop, Mr Gonzales," he shouted to the univox player. "Play a Chopin waltz for us."

"As you wish, suh," said the dapper little musician and twiddled with his knobs for a while before he found the right keys. The few dancing couples looked momentarily puzzled and fumbled for a while before they adjusted their steps to the three-beat waltz rhythm.

Mr Basak danced very elegantly, but I faltered and trampled his feet a couple of times.

"You seem rather tense, Hem," reminded Mr Basak. "Learn to relax a bit . . . how about a tot of gin?"

"I don't drink, Mr Basak," I said sanctimoniously.

"Break the rule on this pleasant evening. For *my* sake."

I was not taken in by this charming rogue, but I thought, "Why not break the rule for once?" If I really wanted to flirt with Mr Basak, a spot of booze would certainly make my job easier. I stopped a bearer to pick up a glass of gin and tonic, gulped a mouthful and squirmed involuntarily as the sweet and slightly pungent liquor passed my throat.

"Bravo! You have created history tonight, dear," teased Mr Basak.

"You are a devil, Mr Basak," I said even as I took my second sip which tasted slightly better.

"You are glowing, my dear," chortled Mr Basak with delight. "Now we can swing to the heavenly music of Chopin."

The combined effect of liquor, the lilting music and the sweet attar scent exuded by Mr Basak's warm body momentarily transported me to a dreamland where everything was smooth, soft and wonderful. I could feel the envious stares of several thirty-plus ladies as they sailed past me with their podgy, middle-aged partners and I felt I was on the top of the world. I only prayed that Mrs Basak would see me in this intimate posture with her husband and feel the same stab of jealousy as I had felt when I saw her clasping Huda's gnarled hands.

"You have enormous potential, Hem" said Mr Basak sotto voce as he pressed his body a little tighter against mine.

"What about your Max? Hasn't she any potential?" I teased.

Mr Basak smiled. "That's for you to certify, my dear. I haven't slept with her for over a decade."

"You are mistaken about my relationship with your wife, Mr Basak. I am just one of her close friends, like Mrs Gulmohar," I pointed out without rancour. "I think Huda is more competent to certify your wife's potential."

Mr Basak grimaced. "I won't be surprised if that hoary painter starts feeling up his lady admirers, including Max, as a prelude to his next art movement, using pubic hair and menstrual blood as his natural mediums. I hope the old girl has put on a sensible pair of knickers under her voluminous sari to stave off Huda's artistic advances."

"Your Max is well-fortified, Mr Basak," I assured him and then promptly changed the subject as I realized what I had said.

Mr Basak suddenly assumed a serious expression as if he was going to talk about a pending bill in Parliament. He stopped a bearer to pick up a Scotch, gulped down the drink like cough syrup and returned the glass to the tray in one smooth sweeping motion of his arm. To emulate his grand style, I too picked up a glass of Campari, knocked back the liquor and hiccoughed, attracting a big frown from the tall dark bearer who looked like King Tut risen from his coffin.

"Lola has ditched me," said Mr Basak abruptly, without any prelude.

"Am I supposed to convey this good news to your dear wife?"

"Hush!" said Mr Basak as yet another mismatched couple careered past us like an overloaded galleon without a rudder. Mr Basak tried to smile but I could see the hurt in his eyes. "If you need a shoulder to cry on I can offer mine," I said, grinning.

"Is that all you have to say?"

"I now realize why you had to hike up my price."

"I will stomach that barb without protest, but it's a fact that only you can replace Lola and you know that," said Mr Basak very solemnly as though it was a question of replacing an old, inefficient manager in his tea garden with a go-ahead young substitute. But the liquor had already broken my protective shell and I found myself giggling irrepressibly.

"Why don't you make up with Lola, Mr Basak?" I suggested gleefully. "Buy her diamonds or take her to Youkay or Youessay for a vacation."

Mr Basak gave me a dark look and then grabbed another drink, downed it and returned the empty glass in a flash. I took the cue and picked up a pink gin which I managed to gulp down without hiccoughing, eliciting an approving nod from King Tut. Mr Basak smiled. "Vying with me, huh? Fine. Look Hem, Lola won't come back to me. She has already shacked up with a fourth-rate film director doing one of those trashy, Government-sponsored serials on national integration in which Lola has been offered, for the first time, the role of a heroine."

I tried my best not to laugh aloud at Mr Basak's misfortune but couldn't restrain myself altogether. "How sad!" I trilled and swayed a little.

"I need you, Hem," whispered Mr Basak even as he tried to steady me on my legs.

"So does your wife . . . at least I thought so till I saw her with Huda," I said, giggling, lowering my guard at last under the exhilarating influence of liquor. "Why don't you two toss a coin and decide my fate, Mr Basak?"

"God! You are drunk!" exclaimed Mr Basak. "Someone should have told you not to mix your drinks. Steady yourself, Hem."

"I am quite steady, Mr Basak," I assured him even as I leaned my head heavily against his chest and closed my eyes. "I just need a little rest, Mr Basak," I mumbled. Mr Basak held me protectively around my shoulders and slowly dragged me out of the hall on to the gallery where I felt slightly better as a mild, refreshing breeze touched my hot cheeks. So much was my dependence on Mr Basak and his supporting arms that I didn't complain when he gently cupped my breast with his hand. As we lurched along the gallery I heard tell-tale creaks and squeals emanating from behind the closed doors.

"At this hour my house is like a cheap brothel without a madam to control the traffic," grumbled Mr Basak as he tried several doors on the way without any success. A door on our left was suddenly flung open with a loud creak and out came a lithe Goldstar boy tucking in his shirt tail while his plump and rumpled companion peeped out from behind the door.

"Hi!" drawled the satiated gigolo. "Could you guys tell us if there's a bathroom within a mile or so?"

"I think the pond will be nearer and more convenient for you," snapped Mr Basak and moved on, lugging me along like a sack of potatoes. Halfway down the gallery he turned a corner and stood by a door which seemed to me familiar. Mr Basak squeezed my breast and kicked the door open as if he needed that squeeze to summon the extra strength required for activating his leg muscles.

"God! This is Maxine's bedroom!" I cried. "I can't sleep here."

"Don't worry," said Mr Basak as he pushed me inside. "With Huda around, Max won't return to her room tonight." Mr Basak closed the door and turned the key. He lifted me in his arms, staggered forward a couple of steps and then dumped my body on the bed which felt so soft and cosy that I sprawled out, uttering an involuntary "aah!" and closed my eyes. I felt Mr Basak's hand pulling off the slippers from my feet and then gently massaging my calves. It felt so good that I dozed off within a minute.

I woke up after a while with a pleasurable sensation radiating from the region of my crotch and discovered that Mr Basak's head was firmly planted between my legs, his mouth working on me with a fervour that reminded me of the hyperactive Hoover I had seen Malini plying in the parlour of Mrs Blistop. As I clutched his head and writhed with agonized moans, Mr Basak slithered up my body like a snake, panting a little from his arduous labours, and without further ado entered me with great aplomb. In spite of my hatred for his mercenary attitude towards me, I found myself aiding and abetting Mr Basak in his virtuoso performance which was accompanied with some fierce grunts, and muffled paeans to my "excellent vaginal climate". I enjoyed two and a half skimming-type orgasms in about four and a half minutes before Mr Basak gritted his teeth, clenched his fists and showed other horrifying signs of an epileptic fit as he collapsed on my bosom, gasping and panting. He was even unable to disengage himself from my body, so I pushed him over and out of sheer curiosity, stole a peek at his long, slender prick.

We woke to the sound of an urgent and continuous rapping on the door. "Oh shit!" growled Mr Basak as he tumbled out of the bed, snatching the bedsheet to wrap it around his loins.

"Sorry to disturb you, Gour," said a very cool and composed Mrs Basak as she slipped past her husband into the room. "I didn't mean to interrupt you two," she murmured, darting a murderous, sidelong glance at my naked body which I was frantically trying to cover with two pillows. "I have to put my jewellery back in my box before I go for my morning bath."

Sixteen

I had always been aware of the cruel streak in Mrs Basak ever since she had thrown me out of Rose Valley and I knew for sure that she would punish me for sleeping with her non-resident husband, but it never crossed my mind that this punishment could have anything to do with the handsome loans I had taken from her on IOUs on two different occasions. Therefore the legal notice served by Mrs Basak's solicitors, Chaudhury and Chukerverty, asking me to repay the staggering sum of Rs 11500 within thirty days or face prosecution in a court of law came like a bolt from the blue. Paromita had broken off all communication with me after she had stumbled on that indelible proof (in the shape of three blonde hairs on my person) of my intimate relationship with Mrs Basak, but now my stunned expression thawed her a little and she asked me casually if I had again been thrown out of the team by Miss Nag for my unMarxist behaviour on the field. In response I handed her the notice without a word and cupped my chin in my palm, fixing my gaze on my wet petticoat fluttering on a line on the veranda. To suit my black mood, the sky had stayed overcast since morning and it was now drizzling. From the corner of my eye I saw Paromita's brows developing deep furrows as she read the notice a second time.

"Well, what are you going to do now?" she asked finally.

"I will send a polite reply pointing out that I am an unemployed woman and I need at least one year to earn, beg or steal that huge sum."

"That will cut no ice with her, my dear. The memsahib means business or she wouldn't have sent you this frightening notice under Section 80 of the Civil Code of Procedure. If you fail to repay the money within the stipulated time, she can throw you in prison for three months."

"How terrible!" I groaned.

"You must have done something quite awful to invite her wrath," said Paromita, eyeing me with suspicion.

"Nothing of that sort," I lied. "She just saw me dancing with her husband and . . ."

"Liar!" cut in Paromita savagely. "She must have caught you *in flagrante*. Go and apologize to her forthwith if you don't want to be jugged."

But the daunting prospect of facing the infuriated memsahib within three days of that shameful incident made me quite nervous. "Don't you think I should first dash off an apologetic letter to soften her heart?" I said tentatively. But Paromita turned down my suggestion with an impatient jerk of her head. "You don't have much time for sweet correspondence, Hemprova. You must act fast."

I nodded gloomily and looked at the overcast sky which promised a heavy downpour at any moment.

*

It was still drizzling when I folded up my umbrella, gave it a good shake to dislodge the water collected in its numerous folds and peeped inside the gallery. Mrs Basak was showing some landscapes to an elderly, elegant lady whose face seemed familiar though I couldn't place her immediately. The memsahib looked very hip in her trendy, long denim skirt topped with a cropped blouse and from the way she smiled and gesticulated, I had no doubt that she was in a buoyant mood. Thank God, I had come at the right time, I thought, and pushed open the glass door. Mrs Sahni beckoned me to her table and whispered, "That's Lady Ranu, Calcutta's top socialite and a great connoisseur of art."

"Really? I think I have seen her inaugurating a flower show or something like that. Looks very aristocratic, doesn't she?"

"Very."

"Your boss seems to be in a cheerful mood on this rainy day, no?"

Mrs Sahni winked mischievously. "That's a professional smile. We can't sulk in front of our customers, can we?"

I was going to nod in agreement but my neck stiffened as I met Mrs Basak's glare. It was full of venom and hostility. I smiled sheepishly but that only deepened her furrows and tightened her lips. Lady Ranu obviously noted this rapid change of mood in Mrs Basak and hastened to complete her tour of the gallery. As the great lady made a quick exit, I braced myself for an angry outburst and a volley of choice English abuse, but Mrs Basak did nothing of that sort. She moved to the window, turned her back on me and said in a dry, rasping voice, "Mrs Sahni, would you please ask Mrs Mitra to leave my gallery at once?"

"This is not at all fair, Radha," I protested. "Calling me Mrs Mitra when we had agreed to be on first-name terms! Let me explain what actually happened on that evening and you will understand . . ."

"Mrs Sahni, would you be kind enough to point out to Mrs Mitra that I don't relish strangers addressing me by some fancy Indian name?"

Mrs Sahni rolled her eyes and made an eloquent gesture to indicate that she was totally baffled.

"Your boss is completely off her rocker, Mrs Sahni!" I cried and waved the notice in the air. "Have you ever heard of one friend serving another a threatening notice like this one through a lawyer? Her head needs to be examined, Mrs Sahni. And please ask your boss, if I am really a stranger, why did she take the trouble of inviting me to her party? I can show you the invitation card she sent me."

Mrs Sahni joined her palms together and begged me to leave the place "for pity's sake".

"Mrs Sahni, I have neither the time nor the patience to enter into an elaborate and fruitless argument about the propriety of my action," said Mrs Basak, raising her voice to an intimidating pitch. "If the defendant has anything to say against the notice, let her go and talk to my solicitor. Now, Mrs Sahni, please come and help me take an inventory of those oils languishing in our storeroom." Mrs Basak whipped around with a defiant toss of her head, cut across the room and vanished behind the curtains, reminding me of those jatra theatre heroines who never failed to draw thunderous ovations from their captive audience with a memorable line and a dramatic exit.

"Give her time, Mrs Mitra," advised Mrs Sahni as she rose to follow her boss. "That's the best advice I can give you at the moment."

*

Mrs Gulmohar was entertaining a few guests in her sitting room and seemed reluctant to let me in. "I am sorry, Hem, but I can't help you," she said bluntly when I told her about Mrs Basak's terrible notice. "I couldn't attend Maxine's party because of a sudden attack of flu, but what I heard from her is shocking, to say the least. Chee-chee! Isn't it the height of ingratitude? Biting the very hand that fed you? No wonder we Indians don't get our due respect in London society with a few black sheep among us like you and Miss Jhajoria. Chee-chee!"

"But you haven't heard my side of the story, Mrs Gulmohar," I pleaded.

"I am not interested. I am glad that Maxine has at last put her foot down. It was Ronnie who warned me when I was expecting my first: 'Gulu, never spoil your children. If you do, they will give you trouble for the rest of your life.' How true! Maxine spoilt you thoroughly in spite of my repeated warnings. She even sent you to Mrs Blistop against my advice. Do you know why? To civilize you, to make you a lady. And now . . . chee-chee!"

A vision of my mother chee-cheeing me after she had discovered my scandalous affair with the barber leaped to my mind with such vividness that I turned tail before Mrs Gulmohar could heap some more chee-chees on me.

From the Dover Lane post office I bought an inland, picked up a discarded refill from a waste-paper basket and wrote a stinging letter to Mr Basak, cursing him squarely for my trouble and reminding him that the least he could do for me was to pay my debts and save me from the humiliation of a jail term. Only after I had licked the gum and stuck down the flap of the letter did I realize that I didn't have Mr Basak's Delhi address. I approached a silver-haired senior citizen who was painstakingly pasting a dozen big and small stamps on a fat parcel, and said, "Excuse me, sir, have you any idea where our MPs live in Delhi?" The gentleman slowly turned his head to peer at my face through his bifocals. "Sorry, my dear," he said in a phlegmy voice. "I have no idea about those rare birds. But, since Parliament is now in session, I suppose they are expected to attend the House occasionally to claim their allowances. Are you sending one of them an invitation to some function?"

"Oh, no. It's a personal letter."

"I see. Send it to the care of the Speaker, Parliament. I hope you remember the name of the honourable MP."

"Yes, thank you."

I dropped my inland in the red letterbox outside the post office, thanking in my mind the great man who had invented this wonderful system of carrying important messages from one place to another, separated by mountains, rivers and all other obstacles. Just imagine! I had spent only fifty paise from my pocket to write that lethal missive but when it would reach Mr Basak two or three days later, he would certainly be smitten by remorse and send me the cheque for Rs 11500 along with an elaborate apology. Whether I should accept his apology or not was something I wanted to mull over in my mind for a few days, but first I would rush to Mrs Basak's gallery and fling the cheque before my persecutor. "Mrs Basak," I would declare with great solemnity, "here's the cheque. Now you will have to invent some new trap to humble me."

But my faith in the postal system was rudely shattered when my inland came back a week later with a couple of smudgy post marks and an almost illegible scribble: "Incomplete address. Returned to sender."

*

"One should be very careful before signing IOUs, Mrs Mitra," pointed out Mr Chaudhury, the junior partner of Chaudhury and Chukerverty. Mr Chaudhury was a fair specimen of that vanishing tribe whom the puritans spitefully called "Ingo-Bongo", the anglicized, middle-class Bengali trying to show off his Englishness in his three-piece suit, tie and heavily accented English even while nurturing at heart his native passion for rosogolla and ilish mach and a great devotion to Ma Kali and Ma Durga. In fact, Mr Chaudhury sported three fat ugly rings studded with gems to ward off the evil effects of three malevolent stars, and under the glass sheet of his table he kept a calendar cut-out of Kalighat's awe-inspiring Kali who sanctified all his legal skulduggery, including the heinous act of frightening a poor godforsaken woman like me with a Section 80 notice. I tried to soften his heart with a sob story — my disastrous marriage, husband's sickness and the rest — but Kali worshippers seemed to be made of sterner stuff and while I whined on and on like a professional beggar, Mr Chaudhury diverted himself by exploring his ear with a paper cone fashioned out of a strip of manila envelope.

"Ours is an exacting profession, Mrs Mitra," said Mr Chaudhury at last, extracting an incredibly big chunk of earwax which he scraped on his ashtray with apparent satisfaction. "We have to think of our client's interest first."

"Naturally, sir, but you must also realize that your client is a cold-blooded memsahib with a bania mentality," I pointed out. "I can't possibly expect any mercy from her, but you are my compatriot and a Kali worshipper too. Saving a helpless sister in distress would definitely endear you to the goddess."

The godfearing Mr Chaudhury quivered a little and adjusted his tie, revealing in the process a string of holy rudraksha beads cleverly hidden by his tie knot.

"But I don't see how I can help you, Mrs Mitra. Do you have any assets to offer as collateral? House, property, jewellery . . . anything that can be valued above ten thousand?"

I shook my head. "I had some gold ornaments, sir, but they were taken away by my mother-in-law when she eloped with my uncle."

"I am sorry. Any savings like some sovereigns from the time of Queen Victoria buried under the image of Goddess Lakshmi by your pragmatic ancestors for a rainy day? Any family heirloom? Just try to remember."

"Nothing of that sort, sir. We are actually refugees. My father lost everything we had in East Bengal during the partition riots and came to Calcutta as a pauper."

"In that case I don't see how I can help you, Mrs Mitra," said Mr Chaudhury, picking up his paper cone for more mining of earwax. I looked pleadingly at his face but all I could see there was a silly, childish smile which was indicative of the successful excavation he was carrying on with his little shovel.

"Sir!"

Mr Chaudhury frowned. "I told you, Mrs Mitra . . ."

"You can at least persuade your client to allow me some extra time, say six months or so."

"Impossible!"

"Three months, then?"

"I cannot help you, but I shall talk to my client and let you know within a day or two."

And that vague promise was all I could extract from the Kali worshipper before I left his office.

As I threaded my way through the hawker-infested pavements of Rashbehari Avenue, I couldn't ignore the fact that Durga puja, the five-day festival that every Bengali, be she rich or poor, looks forward to for nine months of the year, was just round the corner. Thanks to the heavy influx of villagers from the neighbouring districts, the makeshift pavement stalls were doing a brisk business in cheap cotton saris, shirts, frocks and hosiery. But for an occasional light drizzle, the weather was now tolerably good for late October and in the evening a refreshing breeze blew in from nowhere, reminding everyone of the advent of autumn and its distinctive features — the glistening dew drops on the grass in the morning, the fragrant white and orange sheuli blossoms, khejurer gur, the aromatic jaggery made from the juice of date palm, and the harvesting of paddy — which are inextricably associated with the yearly Durga puja festival invoking the ten-armed goddess and her retinue of minor gods and goddesses with drumbeats and conch-blowings. The showcases of well-established sari shops flamboyantly displayed the latest designs while the pavement stalls employed urchins with lung power and a little ingenuity to hawk their wares and grab some of those floating customers hunting for bargains. A beanpole in a clown's outfit, complete with a conical hat, stood on an upturned drum in front of a stall and screamed at the top of his voice: "Grab the loot before the police catch you! Come on Miss, come on Mister! Thirty rupees for whatever you pick – sari, frock, babysuit, trousers, shirt . . . six lace hankies as gift for every three items you choose! Don't feel shy or you will repent later."

I averted my eyes from the dazzling saris and tried to cheer myself up with the new and encouraging development on the club front. After tottering on the brink of bankruptcy for over two years, Rani Jhansi had at last bagged the sponsorship of a new cosmetic manufacturing company called "Luckme" which, by its clever evocation of the original brand name Lakme, had already carved out a good market for its low-priced products in the districts. No one in our team knew the exact terms and conditions of the contract signed between Mrs Chaudhury and Mrs Pal of Luckme, but expectations ran high among the girls that at last we would have a regular, though modest, income from our labours on the field. Tama, Damba and a few other girls, who had been skipping our practice sessions off and on for quite some time to play hockey and volleyball with some college or office teams in the hope of landing themselves good jobs in a bank or the Railways, were now seriously considering if they should opt out of those secondary games and stick to football alone in view of the lucrative Luckme sponsorship.

Thank God, I wouldn't have to beg my pocket money from Paromita any longer and God willing I might be able to pay back Mrs Basak her entire loan from my own income – if only she allowed me sufficient time. Three months was too short to liquidate such a big debt, but once she agreed to allow me three months I could press her for further extensions of time with a little help from the Kali-worshipping Mr Chaudhury.

*

Two days later, I got a letter from Mr Chaudhury informing me that in view of my insolvency his client was prepared to offer me a suitable opportunity for paying back the money I had borrowed from her.

According to my creditor's proposal, I would be offered the job of Junior Accountant in the Calcutta Ladies Club on a monthly salary of seven hundred rupees from which two hundred would be recovered by my employer every month towards my loan repayment. I was stunned. Mrs Basak obviously wanted to humble me before her colleagues, those fat, vain women with whom I had mingled as an equal at that post-modernist novel-reading session. What would Miss Sil, who had been so eager to correspond with me, say when she discovered that I was just an ordinary clerk saddled with a big debt, eking out a miserable living at the mercy of Mrs Basak? And I could visualize Mrs Gulmohar gloating over my downfall: "Thank God, Maxine has at last decided to teach that rascal a good lesson!"

"I'd rather declare myself bankrupt and go to jail," I told Paromita clenching my fists.

"I think it's the best possible offer she could have made you," observed my Gandhian friend. "I must thank that pragmatic woman for hitting two birds with one stone — ensuring strict recovery of her money and at the same time helping you to rehabilitate."

"I don't need anybody's help to rehabilitate myself!" I cried haughtily. That particular word always incensed me. Was it not enough that I was playing football and trying my best to live the life of an honest citizen without debasing myself in a dirty profession like prostitution or indulging in petty crime?

But, unfortunately, my teammates not only shared Paromita's view, they seemed quite jubilant that I had cleverly grabbed a decent job by inconveniencing the memsahib with some unrepayable loans. "You shouldn't have any qualms about exploiting a bourgeois whenever you can," advised Miss Nag, who had temporarily stopped talking to me when she had heard that I had joined Mrs Blistop's highly reactionary school. "Don't forget, that club is the last bastion of the Raj in Calcutta," she reminded me viciously, "and as a proletarian it is your moral duty to deal it a mortal blow whenever a chance arises." Even Tama, my best friend in the team, thought the offer was not that bad. Once the debts were cleared, she argued, I'd be a free woman again, earning a modest monthly salary, which was something very few footballers could expect in these days of mass unemployment. I pointed out that I could be sacked as soon as I liquidated my debts, but Tama was not prepared to impute such meanness to Mrs Basak's character.

After struggling with myself for another forty-eight hours, I finally wrote back to Mr Chaudhury that I was ready to accept his client's offer.

Seventeen

The office of the Calcutta Ladies' Club was located in a small room on the ground floor near the entrance. This had once been the cloakroom where the memsahibs handed over their bonnets and umbrellas to an attendant and powdered their noses before going upstairs to the card room for a game of whist or checkers or to the Blue Room for a highly exciting session of planchette, or to the library to browse three-month-old issues of *The Illustrated London News, The Cornhill* and *Blackwoods magazine* to catch up with the latest trends in fashion and literature. The renovated office room was dark and damp and it exuded a musty smell, thanks to the voluminous club records, accumulated over a hundred years, dumped in some wooden almirahs lining the walls. The staff consisted of an office superintendent, an assistant, a junior accountant, a typist and a bearer. Minoti, the petite, chirpy typist and I sat at two small tables along the back wall, facing Mrs Brar, our office superintendent, like two obedient schoolgirls, while Mrs Abraham, the pale, haughty assistant who considered herself a cut above us all, was privileged to have her table set at a different angle, under a window, away from the direct gaze of Mrs Brar, to emphasize her superior and independent status. Everyone, including the obese, paan-chewing bearer Phoolmotia, called Mrs Brar "Toad" behind her back as she bore a striking resemblance to that lovable creature: she was plump and expressionless, wore thick bifocals and sat motionless for hours at a stretch with her shoulders hunched and her chin sunk into her neck as if she was waiting for a fly to dive into her slightly open mouth. Toad accepted me with the enthusiasm one shows while receiving a slightly inflated bill from the grocer. Minoti later confided to me that Mrs Brar had not even batted an eyelid when my predecessor, a commerce graduate experienced in accounts work, had been sacked by the club two weeks before because of a suspicion among the office bearers that she had been leaking vital information about the club's day-to-day financial transactions to Mr Thapar. In the circumstances, it was very surprising indeed that Mrs Basak and her colleagues had found me suitable for this sensitive post. As I had no experience in accounts work I had to approach Toad for guidance and she broke her silence briefly to explain to me in a few dull, uninspiring words that my job would be to enter the bills and vouchers in a fat, ruled register and submit it to her at the end of the day for her inspection and signature. Once a week I was also required to take the register upstairs to Mrs Jeejaboy, our president, for her signature. Compared to my duties, Minoti's seemed quite heavy as she had to type everyone's letters, including Mrs Abraham's. Minoti was however happy to have someone of her own age group to whom she could natter freely about her daily squabbles with her mother-in-law and her one-year-old son's mealtime antics.

To avoid Minoti's unending chatter I started taking refuge in the club's auditorium during the lunch hour and spent some happy hours there studying those gilt-framed portraits of former presidents and renowned members that adorned the walls. Later, I followed up their checkered careers from the numerous notes and journals left behind by these luminaries in the club library. There was Lady Bowels (1848–1890), the delicate, unearthly memsahib looking very uncomfortable in her voluminous flounced skirt, her small oval face framed by a large bonnet. No wonder she had made her mark as a clairvoyant and had an unabiding faith in magnetotherapy which, alas, could not save her from the killer dengu fever. There couldn't be a greater contrast in appearance and costume to Lady Bowels than Mrs Macready (1837–1910), the stout, formidable hunter in khaki shikar outfit complete with shola pith helmet, her shotgun cocked at a rakish angle and the dead panther sprawled before her feet. Next to the famous huntress beamed Lady Moony (1878–1940) who looked very Indian with her round face (and hence her nickname "Moony") and big saucer-shaped eyes. She kept up a regular correspondence with the Philadelphia spiritualists, particularly Mr Henry Foulke (whom Madame Blavatsky had chosen as her successor) and she was reported to have seen her mentor's astral body floating in her bedroom after her death. Alarmed by the sudden spurt of terrorist attacks on British officials in the wake of Lord Curzon's partition of Bengal in 1905 and the growing influence of the vernacular press on the Indian masses, Lady Moony, in one of her much-publicized planchette sessions, had asked the spirit of Lord Macaulay two vital questions: 1. whether British rule in India was really endangered? and

2. what was the future of English in India? From Lady Moony's interview in *Eve's Own* it was revealed that Lord Macaulay was evasive about the first query and very enigmatic about the second.

While the nineteenth century was dominated by the spiritualists, the twentieth certainly belonged to the real-life adventuresses. Mrs Hogg-Smith (1893–1961) joined her anthropologist husband in a hair-tingling adventure into the dense, unexplored jungles of Great Nicobar Islands in search of the primitive Gompen tribe who thrived mainly on crabs and coconuts but turned cannibals at full moons after performing their fagu-magu dance accompanied by drumbeats and communal drinking of Hadia wine. Mrs Hogg-Smith's *Nicobar Diary* was a real treat for the aspiring botanist. A sample: "After finishing our fruity breakfast with some bananas and a big luscious papaya. Jim and I set out for the day. We passed through a solid wall of mangrove pneumatophores and spiny leaves of Pandanas. Interiors revealed gigantic terminillia and fig trees covered with climbing bamboo canes and other epiphytes."

Lady Edna O'Donovan (1901–1984), the only Irish woman in this portrait gallery, became one of the most unpopular presidents in the club's long history, primarily because she had spent the best part of her five years' term fighting the much-maligned Ilbert Bill. Her combative spirit was reflected in her sharp, pointed chin and the fierce gleam of her small, luminous eyes, both faithfully caught by the renowned painter Suzanne Gailey whose famous portrait "Lady Willingdon Relishing a Mango" still adorned the main parlour of Raj Bhavan. And finally, there was the portrait of the notorious Mrs Trent (1921–?), a former vice-president of the club, who had married the nawab of Azimgunj, a small principality near Dacca, with the laudable intention of taking exhaustive notes on the nawab's harem in order to write a sensational memoir. Mrs Trent gave birth to three beautiful babies — two girls and a boy — in three consecutive years, got her talaq from the nawab and left India with her voluminous notes to write her magnum opus *Mango Days, Banana Nights*, which was published by Modd and Mead, London, and became a bestseller in the early fifties, selling over half a million copies. In fact, this was the only book among the numerous diaries and journals left behind by the versatile club celebrities that remained in circulation. Out of sheer curiosity, I too had flicked through Mrs Trent's seven-hundred-and-sixty-three-page tome but couldn't find much sensational material except a vivid and slightly nauseating description of her first delivery and a very sadistic account of her son's circumcision ceremony, which was celebrated by the nawab with all the pomp and show associated with a royal marriage, including fireworks and mujra dances by nautch girls brought from Lucknow.

During my frequent trips to the library to dig out information on the club celebs, I couldn't ignore the formidable presence of Professor Bishakha Sen, Triple MA (ancient history, anthropology and Sanskrit) poring over several thick volumes spread before her, taking meticulous notes and occasionally puffing away at her Goldflake. Prof. Sen's reputation as a scholar shot up a few notches after she had pointed out that serious flaw in Miss Gordon-Green's novel. Her latest work was a monograph about India's diplomatic relations with China in the wake of Hiuen Sang's visit to India during the reign of Chandragupta Maurya. I was told that Professor Sen was presently researching Indo-Roman trade and commerce at the beginning of the Christian era and I had no doubt that in due course she would join the portrait gallery beside Mrs Hicks (1905– 1979), the only other scholastic member who had published several heavily annotated translations of the *Upanishads*.

While Prof. Sen was neck-deep in Indo-Roman trade, her less illustrious colleagues were squabbling over petty issues, giving rise to some unpalatable rumours which reached us by courtesy of Phoolmotia, our bearer and trusted gazetteer. For instance, Mrs Mahadevan, the secretary in charge of food and beverages, had been trying for quite some time to introduce South Indian dishes, idli and dosa, in the club's breakfast menu, but Mrs Malhotra, the secretary Administration, had been resisting the move tooth and nail because she thought her favourite North Indian dish chhole-bature was much more delicious and popular among the members. This resulted in some sharp exchanges of notes between the two via Mrs Jeejaboy, each quoting exhaustively from cookbooks and newspaper articles to establish the superiority of her favourite dish. The long-drawn war between chhole-bature and idli-dosa was however pushed to the sidelines when a fierce battle between the supporters of ping pong (Miss Sarin and Miss Chaki) and billiards (Mrs Gulmohar and Mrs Patil) shook the club, forcing Mrs Jeejaboy to go on an unscheduled month-long vacation to her sister in Hong Kong. One would think that an aristocrat like Mrs Basak, who occupied the prestigious chair of vice-president and handled such a delicate portfolio as "Art and Culture", would keep herself above petty rivalries, but it seemed that she too had an axe to grind. Her recent refusal to allow Miss Babeja, a staunch supporter of Miss Jhajoria, to hold her first solo poster exhibition on the club premises had drawn much flak from the younger members, though Mrs Basak had tried to justify her action by pointing out that Miss Babeja's posters blatantly plagiarized the works of Toulouse-Lautrec and Ravi Varma. No one, of course, had the temerity to cross swords with Mrs Basak as she ran an art gallery, but Miss Jhajoria had a good opportunity to lambast her rival when the latter unwittingly invited Dr Jeeb Mehta, the propagator of off-beat medicines, for a talk and it turned out that he was only a quack with a bag of incredible remedies, like curing AIDS with the chanting of Rigveda!

It was obvious that the intermittent squabbles between the rival camps were merely warm-up exercises before the two heavyweights actually leaped into the ring and fought for the president's chair which Mrs Jeejaboy would vacate next year on completion of her five-year term. Phoolmotia gleefully compared it with the Kurukshetra war of Mahabharat and brought us tantalizing news from upstairs about the preparations going on in the rival camps. It appeared that while Mrs Basak was banking on the support of her senior colleagues like Mrs Walters, Mrs Gulmohar and Miss Sil, Miss Jhajoria was not depending entirely on the backing of her young friends and was desperately trying to make a dent in the rival camp by inviting a few older members to the Grand and the Great Eastern at weekends for lavish dinners. The success of Miss Jhajoria's clandestine dinner diplomacy could be judged by Mrs Mahadevan's sudden assumption of the dubious role of a fence sitter ("Aai-aai-o! I am only neutral!" she declared raucously when one of her senior colleagues accused her of duplicity), Mrs Patil's tacit support for ping pong and Miss Sil's sympathetic mutterings about the club's neglect of young talents.

Whatever Mrs Walters, Mrs Gulmohar and the other stalwarts in Mrs Basak's camp said about Miss Jhajoria and her unholy nexus with Mr Thapar, she impressed me from day one because she was tall, almost as tall as Mrs Basak, wheat-complexioned and very high-spirited. True, she was on the plump side and her face was as big and round as a water-melon, but she was so young and vivacious and I had discovered that our reading habits were more or less similar: comics, animal stories and an occasional romance. My urge to cultivate Miss Jhajoria was fuelled by the fact that Mrs Basak had of late started darting hostile glances at me whenever I came within fifty yards of her. I was tickled pink at the very idea of watching the haughty memsahib gnashing her teeth and trembling with rage and frustration as she saw me dallying with her arch enemy. But as a lowly clerk slogging in the club's dimlit office downstairs, my chances of befriending Miss Jhajoria seemed quite remote unless a miracle brought us together.

*

The miracle did occur, thanks to Mr Thapar and his not-wholly-unexpected call on Mrs Jeejaboy one drizzly November evening. Soon after he left, the president summoned all the office bearers to her room for an urgent closed-door meeting. We sent Phoolmotia upstairs to eavesdrop and she came back after fifteen minutes with the spectacular news that the junkfood baron had given the club a final offer of ten million rupees to hand over the historic building to Footania within three months and move to a new location near Dum Dum. The news created such a tremor in our office that even the imperturbable Toad's impassive face showed slight concern as she gulped air twice through her open mouth and Mrs Abraham, who considered herself immune to petty office gossip, turned her chair about fifteen degrees clockwise to take a long, thoughtful look at Phoolmotia's pockmarked face.

As Phoolmotia had rightly predicted, the closed-door meeting in Mrs Jeejaboy's room was soon followed by a General Body meeting to apprise the members of Mr Thapar's latest offer and take a firm decision about the club's future.

It was during this highly charged meeting that my services were requisitioned by Miss Jhajoria to note down her speech in toto as she suspected that while drawing up the minutes Mrs Jeejaboy's private secretary, Mrs Sengupta, might deliberately omit some vital points she would raise in the meeting.

The GB meeting was held in the club auditorium under the watchful eyes of our illustrious former presidents and other notables. About seventy members gathered in the hall, even though I had helped Minoti dispatch as many as four hundred and fifty-six notices, half of which, of course, went outside India. Just before Mrs Jeejaboy rose to deliver her opening speech, I whispered to Miss Jhajoria, "Ma'am, do I need to be angular?" Miss Jhajoria turned her face and frowned. "I think you are already very angular, Miss Hem." "I mean my handwriting, ma'am," I explained. "My letters tend to be big and round – like this." I wrote an 'a' on my note pad and held it up for her inspection. "But Mrs Jeejaboy doesn't like it, so I make it a little angular – like this." "I like the original," said Miss Jhajoria. "Stick to that."

Mrs Jeejaboy's address was clearly aimed at bringing together the two warring factions. To drive home her point, the president mentioned several controversies that had rocked the club in the past (e.g. homeopathy versus animal magnetism, celebrating Edward VI's coronation with fireworks or a solemn prayer at St Paul's, Queen Mary's coiffure for Delhi Durbar) and how these disputes had been amicably settled by the members by following the time-honoured "give-and-take" policy. "The old hag is spouting rubbish," hissed Miss Jhajoria under her breath. I was going to note it down but then dropped the idea as I felt that Miss Jhajoria wouldn't really like to include this uncharitable remark about the president in the minutes. I looked across the aisle at the enemy camp where Mrs Basak sat very still and tense, surrounded by her trusted lieutenants, Mrs Walters, Mrs Gulmohar and Mrs D'Sa, the last one being a newly inducted member who looked so pale and sick that I wondered if she had come straight from the labour room after a painful Caesarean. When Miss Jhajoria's turn came, she stood up, gathering her notes, amidst lusty shouts of "Three cheers for Rekha!" from her young supporters. My pen moved at a brisk pace as Miss Jhajoria began her speech: "Friends, every one of you will agree with me that we need a modern club with enough space for a swimming pool, tennis court and a well-laid garden, but we can't provide ourselves with any of these amenities here because of our cramped surroundings. Above all, we need a clean environment free from Calcutta's terrible noise and air pollution." Miss Jhajoria paused briefly and shot a sidelong glance at Miss Sil who sprang to her feet, clutching a sheet of paper, and said: "With the permission of the chair, may I substantiate Miss Jhajoria's statement regarding noise and air pollution in Calcutta with some statistics? The present noise level in Calcutta is seventy decibels against WHO's safe standard of forty-five, and the effluents polluting the atmosphere is over five hundred and eighty micrograms per cubic metre against ISI's tolerable limit of a hundred and fifty. No wonder sixty per cent of Calcutta's inhabitants are suffering from respiratory ailments."

"Thank you, Miss Sil, for your illuminating statistics," said Miss Jhajoria amidst shouts of "Hear! Hear!" from her supporters, ignoring the protests from her rival camp that Miss Sil was providing valuable assistance to Miss Jhajoria against all the rules. One could however see that Miss Sil owed this little service to Miss Jhajoria for all the good food and drink she had consumed, gratis, at the Grand and the Great Eastern.

"A rolling stone gathers no moss!" thundered Miss Jhajoria with a dramatic flourish of her massive arm and I noted down this oft-repeated wise saying — one of my favourites too — with great satisfaction. "We are stranded here in this spooky, dilapidated building on Free School Street designed by a crazy Englishwoman who had no idea about the real needs of modern women." Mrs Basak rose to say something in defence of Molly Muddlestone and her pseudo-gothic architecture but she was shouted down by Miss Jhajoria's supporters, a few of them even chanting "Molly's Folly!" in a chorus accompanied by table-thumpings. Mrs Jeejaboy vainly shouted "Order! Order!" and struck her gavel but the pandemonium continued for three full minutes. Alarmed by the hullabaloo, Mrs Jeejaboy judiciously declared a fifteen-minute tea-break.

"Have you noted down my speech *in toto*, Miss Hem?" asked Miss Jhajoria as the members queued up before the two snack counters set up on the adjoining veranda to serve chhole-bature from the Vape da Hotel and idli-vada from the Udipi Restaurant.

"Including the cheers and the clappings, ma'am," I assured her, even as I debated in my mind which queue I should join.

"Thank you, my dear," said Miss Jhajoria with evident satisfaction. "I think idli-vada will be more delicious. After all, Mrs Mahadevan is now in my camp."

"Is she? Then, I think, I should try idli-vada."

Mrs Basak and her supporters queued up for chhole-bature, confirming my suspicion that Mrs Malhotra had thrown in her lot with Mrs Basak. Miss Sil came to shake hands with Miss Jhajoria and exchanged a meaningful smile before joining the queue for idli-vada. It really pained me to see her ignoring me completely as if I didn't even exist! Who would believe that even a month ago she had begged me to correspond with her? Thank God, she didn't consider it necessary to warn Miss Jhajoria about my dubious appointment in Sheikh Hulbula's harem. While polishing off my half a dozen vadas with coconut chutney, I noticed the London-based Miss Jhajoria giving an involuntary shudder as the man at the counter nonchalantly dropped two white idlis on her plate and doused them with a ladleful of greenish sambar containing bits and pieces of turnip, radish and brinjal. I looked at the other counter and saw Mrs Basak and Mrs Gulmohar grimly struggling with their rubbery batures, avoiding the super-hot chhole as far as possible. Mrs Walters, however, looked so shocked by the fiery red gravy served on her plate that she was allowed, as a very special case, to cross over to the enemy camp and try the comparatively harmless idli-vada.

In the post-tea session Mrs Jeejaboy drew up a panel, taking an equal number of speakers from either side, and allowed five minutes to each. This resulted in a lot of bad, extempore speeches which were systematically heckled by the opposite camp. Mrs Jeejaboy struck her gavel frequently but when no one showed any respect for her authority, she crossed her fingers and leaned back in her chair, allowing the meeting to lapse into a free-for-all. Amidst the pandemonium one could hear Mrs Gulmohar making a fervent appeal to Miss Jhajoria to hold her supporters in leash and Miss Jhajoria retorting that India being a free and democratic country and the Constitution having provided all its citizens with freedom of speech as one of their fundamental rights, her venerable colleagues couldn't be restrained from airing their views on the issue. I faithfully recorded this altercation under the sub-heading "Miss Jhajoria's clever repartee to Mrs Gulmohar".

The hostilities between the rival camps reached boiling point during Professor Sen's very educative, though slightly digressive, speech on the origin of British club culture and its successful transplantation to Indian soil, when Miss Jhajoria threatened to stage a walk-out with her group unless the speechmaking was stopped forthwith and the main issue — acceptance of Mr Thapar's ten million offer and relocation of the club to a new site — was put to a vote. Mrs Jeejaboy succumbed to the pressure, ignoring the flurry of objections from Mrs Basak's camp, and requested the members to help her conduct the vote smoothly and peacefully. Miss Chaki promptly offered her services as Presiding Officer and Mrs Mahadevan, who had already proclaimed her neutrality, staked her claim to the dignified office of the Returning Officer. Phoolmotia had already lugged in the old wooden ballot box from the library and Miss Chaki had started distributing her ballot papers (a squarish piece of paper with a number inscribed at the top) among the members when Mrs Walters pointed out that as per Section 24 read with the preamble of the club's Constitution, issues relating to the club's dislocation or winding up had to be considered first by a five-member subcommittee representing all shades of opinion, before they were placed before the GB for a final decision. This unexpected revelation from the club's oldest member stunned the Jhajoria faction, though some of them were heard protesting that since this obsolete provision in the Constitution had never been invoked before, it should be scrapped. Mrs Jeejaboy, however, struck her gavel hard on the table and said, "I am afraid amendment of the Constitution is not on today's agenda. Now, ladies, would you please keep quiet and help me constitute the subcommittee?"

Names were immediately put forward by each side. Miss Jhajoria's name was suggested by Miss Chaki and seconded by Miss Babeja. Mrs Basak begged her supporters to spare her and suggested Mrs Gulmohar's name in her place as she had to fix up an important exhibition of watercolours in her gallery and she couldn't possibly give enough time to the Committee's deliberations, but she had to succumb to their pressure, provoking some derisive laughter from the opposite camp. The names of Professor Sen, the scholar extraordinary, and Miss Sil, the great correspondent, were proposed and duly seconded by the opposing camps. Finally, Mrs Jeejaboy herself suggested the name of Mrs Mahadevan in recognition of the latter's well-advertised neutrality, though the eagerness shown by the pro-Jhajorias to patronize her idli-vada left no one in doubt as to which side the fence-sitter would jump. Mrs Basak's supporters raised serious objections to Mrs Mahadevan's inclusion in the subcommittee but the sheer lung power of Miss Babeja & Co assured Mrs Mahadevan her precious berth and the elated lady joined her palms and thanked Lord Ayappa for giving her an opportunity to serve her dear club.

The newly-constituted five-member subcommittee was at least unanimous in rejecting Calcutta as a venue for its meetings and the members joined voices to demand that they should be allowed to go to a calm and quiet place outside Calcutta to deliberate dispassionately about Mr Thapar's offer. Mrs Jeejaboy reminded the subcommittee of the club's financial constraints but when Prof. Sen pointed out that the fate of Germany had to be decided at Versailles and not in Berlin, the president requested the members to select a suitable place within a hundred and fifty kilometres of Calcutta. That, of course, excluded Darjeeling and virtually narrowed the choice down to two seaside resorts — Digha and Bakkhali. The subcommittee unanimously agreed on Bakkhali as Digha was reputed to have an overcrowded beach with hordes of honey-mooners and weekend vacationers crowding the hotels throughout the year.

Mrs Mahadevan was going to propose a vote of thanks to the chair when Miss Jhajoria startled everyone by proposing to take along Miss Hem for secretarial assistance.

"Thank you, ma'am," I whispered, trying hard not to show my teeth in sheer ecstasy. But my "thank you" seemed a little premature when

Mrs Basak pointed out that since the five-member subcommittee would have only one item on its agenda, there would be no need for any secretarial help at Bakkhali. Mrs Gulmohar further explained that detailed records of the meetings would not in any case be required because all that the subcommittee was expected to produce was a one-line resolution with the members' signatures appended at the bottom.

"In that case I will take Miss Hem to Bakkhali at my own expense," declared Miss Jhajoria. "I need a companion-cum-secretary to write my private letters."

"But this will set a bad precedent, Miss Jhajoria," pointed out Mrs Jeejaboy. "Now, suppose every member of the subcommittee wants to take her private secretary along . . ."

"I may kindly be spared, ma'am," I said to end the controversy.

"Keep quiet, girl," chided Miss Babeja. "You are not supposed to open your mouth in a GB meeting."

"Sorry, ma'am."

"I am afraid I can't allow any member to bring a companion or secretary on this brief three-day outing," said Mrs Jeejaboy with an air of finality. "But Miss Hem may accompany the subcommittee for housekeeping and general supervision of the domestics and for rendering whatever little secretarial assistance the committee may require for its smooth functioning. Any objection?"

There was none.

Eighteen

I spent more than two hours on the wind-swept Bakkhali beach hunting for some good comics for Miss Jhajoria but all I could get in those small, makeshift beach stalls that sold mostly balloons, soft drinks and paan-cigarettes were a few back issues of *Chacha Chaudhury*. I knew an accomplished, England-returned lady of Miss Jhajoria's stature wouldn't like this kid's stuff, but what could I do? I couldn't produce *Spiderman* or *Tintin* out of thin air like a magician. Miss Jhajoria had also asked me to find out from the local post office if they had received any letters for her from London, but there was nothing in the post. This was certainly one of those days when everything went wrong for Miss Jhajoria from the start and I could very well appreciate her demand for some good comics to divert her mind from the unexpected setback she had suffered in the very first meeting of the subcommittee.

It seemed that treating Miss Sil to lavish candlelit dinners at the Grand and the Great Eastern and patronizing Mrs Mahadevan's idli-vada in the GB meeting hadn't had any lasting effect on the recipients of these favours. The subcommitte had left Calcutta in two cars, Miss Jhajoria in her shining black Contessa Classic and Mrs Basak in her red Maruti 1000. To flaunt their supreme confidence and nonchalance (or to find out the opposing camp's strategy) Mrs Basak had allowed her close ally and confidante Prof. Sen to travel with Miss Jhajoria, and the latter, not to be outsmarted by such subtle tactics, reciprocated magnanimously by sending Miss Sil in Mrs Basak's car. Miss Jhajoria kept Mrs Mahadevan by her side for a while, but the latter, to show her absolute neutrality, changed cars in mid-journey when we reached Kakdwip around twelve, after five hours' bumpy ride from Calcutta, with a brief stop over at Diamond Harbour for breakfast. In my humble position as housekeeper-cum-clerk I was not supposed to take sides or speculate on any individual member's tilt towards one camp or the other, but I could clearly see how Mrs Basak's company (or was it her

intoxicating perfume?) had affected Miss Sil's loyalty when Miss Jhajoria and the others invited her to have lunch with them in the Ma Tara
hotel and she excused herself, mumbling about her lack of appetite.
One could understand the pukka memsahib wrinkling her snobbish
English nose at the sight of the flyblown, grimy, wayside eatery and its
groin-scratching, pot-bellied manager, but Miss Sil, born and brought
up in the stinking Calcutta environment, refusing her staple midday
meal of macher jhol bhaat on a flimsy pretext was not only unthinkable,
it was preposterous in the extreme. The mystery was cleared up when
I had a chance to eavesdrop on a private conversation between Mrs
Basak and Miss Sil on the ferry boat that took us across the River
Hetania-Doania to Fraserganj. It transpired that Mrs Basak had already
won Miss Sil over to her side by promising to publish the former's
letters in a limited edition, with a foreword by the editor of a reputed
Calcutta daily. I felt I should warn Miss Jhajoria then and there
about this serious depredation in her ranks, but on second thoughts I
decided to keep quiet till we reached Bakkhali and settled in our new
quarters.

Notwithstanding the bitter rivalry between the two camps, the subcommittee was unanimous in approving of our cottage, The Sea Lion.
Entirely made of wood and standing on stilts, its entrance was accessible only by a ladder. It had four comfortably furnished rooms, two
on each side of the corridor that joined the front and the back verandas.
The kitchen was at the back, separated from the house by a short
covered walkway. Sitting on the front veranda, one could hear the
wind whistling among the pines or watch the waves rolling in and
breaking a hundred yards away. The prime attraction of the cottage
was, of course, its exclusive private beach where one could play beach
ball in a bikini (if only one dared) without being ogled by those loutish
youths scouring the seafront throughout the day for a glimpse of bare
female flesh. However, the general spirit of bonhomie inspired by the
pleasant surroundings took a jolt when Mahesh, the cook-cum-
caretaker of the cottage, prostrated himself before Mrs Basak's feet
with the instinctive knowledge that the memsahib was the leader of the
group. Quite used to such obsequiousness from her own servants at
Rose Valley, Mrs Basak accepted the pronam with a gracious smile and
a benedictory gesture which irked Miss Jhajoria enough to ask the
docile, middle-aged cook sharply what he was going to serve for our
evening meal. Puzzled by Miss Jhajoria's rudeness, Mahesh sprang to
his feet and replied with great solemnity: "Madam, tonight I can offer

you only a simple meal of rice and dal. For memsa'b I will have to cook English food — tomato soup and boiled potatoes."

"Thank you dearie," said Mrs Basak cheerfully. "I hope you can get some eggs tomorrow."

"Chicken and eggs will come tomorrow, memsa'b," assured Mahesh. "For breakfast you will like my chow mein, cabbage coming directly from my own garden. In the morning my wife Sukhi will also come from the village to clean up the place and help me in the kitchen, and my son Bhim is willing to wash your cars for only ten rupees . . ."

"We shall think about cars tomorrow," interposed Miss Jhajoria curtly to make it clear who was the real boss. "Now go and bring some tea and help us unpack. We want to hit the sack early."

Since there were only four rooms in the cottage, Miss Sil and Prof. Sen had to share one room as Mrs Mahadevan made it abundantly clear that she needed a lot of space to accommodate Lord Ayappa and his puja paraphernalia. As leaders of the two opposing camps the claims of Miss Jhajoria and Mrs Basak for separate rooms could not be disputed, though Miss Jhajoria wasn't happy to note that her opponent had grabbed the best room in the cottage, one with an unrestricted view of the sea, while Miss Jhajoria's opened out on a clump of straggling pines and a few bald sand dunes. No one bothered to inquire where I was going to doss down for the night, so I finally made my bed in the passage on a couch which Mrs Mahadevan had pushed out of her room to accommodate her deity. Listening to the wind howling in the pine forest and the roaring of the sea, I dozed off into a fitful sleep and woke up with a start in the wee hours as Mrs Mahadevan threw open her door and started singing her prayers to Lord Ayappa in a loud, unmusical voice.

In the morning Mahesh served a thoroughly Indianized version of chow mein with onions, chilli paste and a sprinkle of finely chopped coriander leaves and it was relished by everyone except Mrs Basak who pushed away her plate after trying one forkful of the hot, spicy stuff and demanded egg and toast. Refreshed by the finest Rose Valley Orange Pekoe (supplied by Mrs Basak) the subcommittee assembled on the veranda for its first session. I sat at a small round table, a little away from the distinguished members, to take notes. The convenor of the meeting, Prof. Sen, started the day's business by reading out the details of Mr Thapar's offer and then invited the individual members to put forward their arguments in favour or against the deal. Miss Jhajoria first presented her viewpoint, which turned out to be a forceful reiteration of her earlier speech, the main thrust of her argument being that the club, as envisaged by Lady Moyra, had long outlived its usefulness and a change of identity was absolutely essential if it wanted to serve the cause of a new generation of emancipated women in a free India. But this laudable task could not be accomplished as long as the club continued in its present site with all its colonial moorings intact. Even before Miss Jhajoria had finished her spirited speech, I noticed Miss Sil exchanging covert glances with Mrs Basak, and five minutes later she stunned both Miss Jhajoria and Prof. Sen as she reeled off her seemingly well-rehearsed counter arguments against the Thapar offer. Miss Jhajoria tried her best to stop Miss Sil with hard, intimidating glares but Miss Sil looked adamant and continued her impassioned speech, eulogizing the club's great heritage, its achievements and even its architecture. When the neutral Mrs Mahadevan also started nodding to Miss Sil's panegyric, indicating that she was no better than a weathercock, Miss Jhajoria had no other option but to excuse herself from the meeting on the pretext of a severe attack of migraine, and retire, asking me to see her in her room immediately.

"I bet Mrs Basak has bought off Miss Sil," said Miss Jhajoria as I entered her room. "I wonder if it's money or some other favour that prompted Miss Sil to betray me." I felt the temptation to divulge what I had overheard on the ferry boat, but I kept my mouth shut, reminding myself that small fry should not meddle in big affairs of state. Miss Jhajoria flung a hundred-rupee note at me and said, "Hem, get me some good comics; I need to relax my frayed nerves. And find out from the local post office if they have received any letters for me from London." As I came out of the cottage, Prof. Sen called to me from the veranda and gave me a tenner to bring her a packet of Goldflake and Mrs Mahadevan shouted that she wanted a packet of joss sticks.

*

As I had feared, Miss Jhajoria flared up at the sight of *Chacha Chaudhury* and shrieked, "You idiot! Am I a five-year-old that you bring me this trash?" She threw the bundle in my face and slammed her door shut before a bewildered Mahesh and his wife Sukhi. I wanted to hurl a few choice epithets at Miss Jhajoria but somehow choked back my anger and went out on the beach to soothe my frayed nerves. I walked along the shoreline, letting the waves break on my feet. My sari billowed in the strong sea breeze and my hair blew all over my face, but I felt much better and wondered whether the world was really three parts water and one part land as our geography teacher, Mrs Sudha Lahiri, had once tried to convince us. I had never believed it, but now, gazing at the vast expanse of the Bay of Bengal and the distant horizon merging with the sea, it appeared to be a distinct possibility. Maybe the world was also round – another myth I could never reconcile myself to.

After about an hour's aimless meandering by the sea, I finally settled myself down on a sand dune and watched a swarm of tiny, red, one-pincered crabs (Miss Sil later wrote a letter to the *Statesman* about this exotic species) scurrying in and out of their little holes in the sand. I tried to trap one with my hand but it was too fast for me. A little later, I found Miss Sil and Mrs Mahadevan coming down to the beach with towels flung over their shoulders. They hesitated a little when they reached the water's edge and squealed as the naughty waves lashed their feet and crept up their legs. And then, summoning courage, they hitched up their saris and waded into the sea, frolicking in the shallows like two little girls on vacation. I smiled indulgently at them and felt that they had been right in making mincemeat of that uncivilized Marwari girl who didn't know how to behave. But where was Mrs Basak, the leader of the pack? I half-expected her to emerge from the cottage at any moment in a sheer bikini and join her frolicking friends on the beach, but she appeared a few minutes later in sober khaki Bermudas and a wide-brimmed straw hat with the diminutive Sukhi trotting behind her, carrying her painting gear. A pang of jealousy shot through me as she waved at Miss Sil and Mrs Mahadevan and then blew them a kiss before walking off to the far end of the beach to set up her canvas on a folding aluminium easel. The well-engineered coup seemed to have stoked up her creative spirit and I could bet that whatever she was going to paint that morning would be in bright, vibrant colours.

After about an hour I tiptoed stealthily behind her to steal a peek at her work over her shoulder. Mrs Basak was wielding her brushes vigorously to paint in oils a deep blue sea (though it looked quite murky to my unartistic eyes) and had already drawn the outlines of two gliding seagulls and a solitary boat at the upper region of her canvas.

"That's going to be an excellent seascape, ma'am," I observed.

"Thanks," responded Mrs Basak primly without turning her head, as though she couldn't care less about such stray compliments coming from nonentities like me. I had, in fact, expected Mrs Basak to be slightly forgiving in her victory, but her curt monosyllabic response only convinced me that she hated me as much as, if not more than, Miss Jhajoria.

Returning to the cottage, I found Professor Sen on the veranda, poring over one of her tomes. I tried to slip by but she lifted her eyes from her book as she heard my footsteps and smiled, reaching for her Goldflake. Even the solemn scholar had a rare glint in her sombre eyes which I couldn't but attribute to the unexpected victory of her protégé in the first bout. "You look very happy today, Professor Sen," I said. "Have you made any progress in your research?"

"Yes, my dear," said Prof. Sen, lighting up. "I am now fairly convinced that throughout the first hundred years of the Christian era those intrepid seafaring people of the Sunderbans delta were the principal suppliers of honey and deerskins to the Roman *horreas*. Fascinating, isn't it . . . this ancient trade link between a hunter-gatherer tribe and a highly evolved western empire?"

I was going to say something polite and encouraging but stopped short as Miss Jhajoria burst in on us and grabbed my hand. "Where have you been?" she demanded petulantly. "Come to my room at once. I need you."

"Miss Jhajoria, please remember I am not your maidservant," I said sharply and freed my hand from her grip with a powerful jerk. "I have been deputed by Mrs Jeejaboy to supervise the domestics and provide secretarial assistance to the subcommittee. I am not an errand girl."

"Miss Hem has a point there," said Prof. Sen, blowing a thin trail of smoke through her nostrils. "She reminds me of a second-century Roman feminist satirized by Juvenal who told her dumbfounded husband: '*Ut faceres tu quod velles nec non ego possem/Indulgere mihi. Clames licet et mare caelo/Confundus! Homo sum!*' — We agreed long ago that you were to go your way and I mine. You may confound sea and sky with your bellowing, I am a human being after all."

Miss Jhajoria glowered at Prof. Sen and hissed, "No need to quote Latin to drive home your point, Prof. We know who's confounding whom, don't we? As they say, when an elephant gets stuck in the mud even a mouse gives it a kick." Miss Jhajoria darted back into her room before Prof. Sen had a chance to quote some more Latin for her edification.

My estrangement from Miss Jhajoria brought me unexpected dividends during lunch. My plate was continuously filled with pilau and curried chicken (the latter coming directly from Mahesh's poultry) as Miss Sil and Mrs Mahadevan ordered Mahesh to treat Miss Hem "as one of us", which made Miss Jhajoria curl her lips in disgust. I would have enjoyed my enhanced status a little more if only Mrs Basak had also risen to the occasion and reciprocated my morning overture with a few kind words, but the memsahib stubbornly avoided meeting my gaze and chatted merrily about her seascape while gorging herself on her special no-spice meal of tomato soup, boiled chicken, green salad and caramel custard. Mrs Mahadevan, who was also privileged to have her special vegetarian meal of rice and sambar, startled everyone, most of all Miss Jhajoria, when she threw off her mask of neutrality and proposed stridently that the subcommittee should sit immediately after lunch and wrap up the pending business, so that the next morning the members would be free to go on a sightseeing trip around Bakkhali and, if time and energy permitted, they could even opt for a little adventure by taking a boat to Jambodweep, a tiny island barely visible from the shore. Mrs Basak and Miss Sil wholeheartedly supported this wonderful proposal but Miss Jhajoria, sensing imminent danger, once again complained of her nagging migraine and left the table in a hurry, leaving behind a heap of untouched pilau and curried chicken which Sukhi promptly whisked away to the kitchen to devour with her husband.

"Miss Sil, could you please enlighten us from the Constitutional angle as to how a committee should proceed in a situation like this when an important meeting is being repeatedly adjourned due to the non-co-operation of a particular member?" asked Mrs Basak pointedly as she attacked her boiled chicken with some zest. Miss Sil licked the gravy off her thin, bony fingers, cleared her throat and adjusted her thick glasses to assume the seriousness of a constitutional expert. "I am afraid, Mrs Basak, there is nothing in our constitution to help us in a tricky situation like this," she stated with a quiet authority, "but, from the perusal of the minutes of some interrupted meetings during the reign of Lady Edna O'Donovan, I gathered that if there was a quorum, they generally took a decision without compelling the reluctant member to participate in the proceedings."

"Thank you, Miss Sil, for that nugget of information," said Mrs Basak with evident satisfaction. "I think I shall try a piece of curried chicken." She helped herself to a juicy drumstick which I had been eyeing greedily for some time. I had no doubt that she would soon throw a lavish party at the Grand to celebrate her victory over Miss Jhajoria.

After lunch, Mrs Basak, Mrs Mahadevan and Miss Sil left for the beach to bask in the warm sunshine and decide on their next move. I followed them at a respectable distance in the hope of overhearing a few snatches of their conversation, and was somewhat disappointed when I found them dispersing on the beach, each one taking a different route. Mrs Basak went back to her unfinished seascape to apply some more vigorous strokes on her canvas; Mrs Mahadevan dozed in a deck chair, shielding her head from the sun with a Malayalee magazine; Miss Sil, armed with her field glasses and notebook, ventured into the pine forest, probably to study the local flora and fauna. Even the sedentary Prof. Sen came out on the beach for a few minutes to appreciate Mrs Basak's work and then retreated to the cottage to resume her research on Indo-Roman trade.

The ladies, except for Miss Jhajoria, were in high spirits when they gathered on the veranda for tea. Mrs Basak gleefully told the company that she had added one more seagull to her original duo to bring out a pleasing harmony in her composition; Miss Sil claimed that she had spotted an albino crow in the pine forest; Prof. Sen divulged that the seafaring Sunderbanians, who had dominated Rome's honey and deer-skin trade for over one hundred years, had a serious setback in the beginning of the second century when the Egyptian traders stopped supplying papyri and started dumping enormous quantities of inferior quality honey and alligator skins at the port of Ostia. "Of course, I have to cross-check with Ptolemy's *Geographica* before I come to a definite conclusion," said Prof. Sen, blowing a perfect smoke ring in the air. Everyone expressed deep concern for Miss Jhajoria's health when Sukhi brought news that she wouldn't be able to join her colleagues for tea as she was still languishing in her bed with severe migraine and nausea.

That evening Mrs Mahadevan prayed fervently before the image of Lord Ayappa while her colleagues, including Mrs Basak, stood solemnly behind her, their palms joined together to seek the blessings of the benign god. I was particularly amused when Mrs Basak covered her head with her kerchief to emulate her Indian colleagues who had respectfully drawn the pallavs of their saris over their heads. My suspicion that this was a very special puja performed for the victory of Mrs Basak was confirmed when, at the conclusion of the ceremony, Mrs Mahadevan took a pinch of holy ash from Lord Ayappa's feet and smeared it on Mrs Basak's forehead with a chant. "The Lord never lets down a true devotee, Mrs Basak," she said. "But may I request you to stick to a vegetarian dish tonight to please the Lord?"

"No problem," said Mrs Basak and asked for the holy prosad.

Early the next morning Miss Jhajoria woke me up with a gentle push. I sat up on the couch and rubbed my eyes, fearing that it must be a fire or a theft that brought the high and mighty Miss Jhajoria to my bed at that ungodly hour, but the latter dispelled my fears as she clasped my hand between her palms and said, "Hem, will you please forgive me for my rude behaviour?"

"Oh Miss Jhajoria!" I cried, moved by her repentant tone. "I forgave you this evening when I found Mrs Mahadevan invoking the blessings of Lord Ayappa to beat you. I always side with the weak, Miss Jhajoria."

"But I am not weak, Hem," said Miss Jhajoria, her eyes glittering in the dark. "I am only keeping a low profile . . . and biding my time to strike the mortal blow. What do you know about your benefactress, Hem?" Miss Jhajoria asked me when we retired to her room after breakfast.

"A stone-hearted Devon aristocrat."

"Do you really believe that rubbish?" snorted Miss Jhajoria as she picked up her red lipstick from the dressing table and rubbed it casually on her lips. "I bet she was doing brisk business around King's Cross in fishnet tights, miniskirt and a feather boa before that desperate Basak picked her up from the kerb one evening."

"Oh, no!" I cried, horrified. "The Heggs are a very respectable family, having very close connections with Baroness Trestleton of Mugbury and Sir Peter Gumsey, the third earl of Lupinsville. Everyone knows this."

"I hope I shall be able to shatter these widely believed myths very soon . . . if our lousy postal system doesn't let me down."

I was about to ask her how the postman could possibly help her, but Miss Jhajoria flashed an enigmatic smile, flicking her tongue tentatively over her painted lips and said, "Now, please go and tell Miss Sil that I want to have a word with her in private."

"I don't think she will come." Now that I was on friendly terms with Miss Jhajoria, I had no qualms about telling her what I had heard on the ferryboat.

"I guessed as much," said Miss Jhajoria, her eyes glowing with a cold fury. "But I know how to tackle her. Tell her it's very, very important."

Miss Jhajoria didn't allow me to stay in her room when Miss Sil arrived, but I had no problem overhearing the heated exchanges between the two from behind the closed door.

"You have no business calling me separately for a private discussion, Miss Jhajoria," pointed out Miss Sil haughtily.

"You look very agitated, Miss Sil," said Miss Jhajoria with a remarkable restraint. "Please be seated. One occasionally turns to an old friend in a crisis, no? I need your help, Miss Sil."

"Sorry, I can't help you," said Miss Sil curtly.

"Even for old times' sake?"

"I can't compromise my ideals. You had misled me, but not for long. I now know where I stand."

"Of course you know where you stand, Miss Sil. I understand that Mrs Basak has promised to publish a collection of your letters at her own expense."

"Every writer has ambitions to see her work in print. I have no reason to refuse a good offer from a sympathetic colleague."

"Of course you haven't. But Miss Sil, your volte-face is more intriguing and damaging than Mrs Mahadevan's dubious neutrality."

"One has to change one's opinion on a subject when the objective situation demands such a change," said Miss Sil rather defensively.

"I haven't called you to lecture me on the philosophy of opportunism, Miss Sil," said Miss Jhajoria sharply. "I always thought that the Bengalis were trustworthy, but you have given a big jolt to my long-cherished trust and faith in your people. Miss Sil, you have behaved like a renegade, a scoundrel."

"Rekha!" shrieked Miss Sil. "You-you are going too far! I will sue you!"

"Forget those candlelit dinners at the Grand and the Great Eastern, Miss Sil," said Miss Jhajoria, ignoring the former's outbursts. "You have at least a duty to your compatriots, your own country. How could you stoop so low as to lick that white bitch's feet when you know so well what her country did to us during its two hundred and fifty years of misrule? How could you forget that they always shooed us away from their clubs and swimming pools with signs like 'Dogs and Indians not allowed'?"

Through the peephole I could see a perturbed Miss Sil cleaning her glasses with a shaky hand. "I don't think it's right, Rekha, that you should dredge up those bitter memories of the Raj. India is now independent and we can enter any place we choose, even the notorious Bengal Club and the Calcutta Club. Mrs Basak has married an Indian and adopted this country as her own. Why, Rekha, she is one of us."

Miss Jhajoria responded to Miss Sil's speech with a majestic display of her histrionic talent: she roared with laughter, holding her sides lest they split asunder. Miss Sil looked panicky and dashed to the bathroom to fetch a glass of water while Miss Jhajoria wiped her tears and shook her head. "*One of us*, hun?" she giggled even as she drained the glass. "Just go and ask that bitch to squat on a WC and shit like a true Indian woman and see how she throws a tantrum. Give her a glass of unfiltered tap water to drink, offer her telebhaja, pakora or golgappa from a pavement stall and see how she wrinkles her nose. The ghosts of bacteria, filth and stink and a perpetual dread of contamination by undesirable contacts with the brownies haunt her as they haunted her countrymen who flocked to our dirty land only to bleed it and fill up their coffers and then go back to their home-sweet-home to live a luxurious retired life, forgetting the blood they had shed and the corpses they had trodden."

"Please Miss Jhajoria!" begged Miss Sil, joining her palms together. "Let's try to forget that unpleasant chapter in our history. Let's not infuse bad blood into the subcommittee just because she happens to be an Englishwoman."

Miss Jhajoria produced an abridged version of her famous belly laugh. "Who are you and me to infuse bad blood, Miss Sil? It's already very much there, only you don't want to see it. Can't you see how that dubious Devon aristocrat is constantly trying to show off her superiority? Grabbing that east-facing room with the best view, eating soups and salads, avoiding the sea just because it's not as clean as Brighton and flaunting her artistic talents with that puerile, schoolgirlish seascape. None of us here is quite quite, Miss Sil, not even our learned pundit Prof. Sen who unfortunately patronizes Mrs Basak, probably because she is so absorbed in her research that she can't see through the hypocrisy of that woman. But what about you, Miss Sil? You are one of the best correspondents we have in India these days, and yet, can you vouch with your palm on your heart that she gives you the respect and consideration you really deserve? If this isn't apartheid, Miss Sil, I don't know what that word really means."

Miss Jhajoria's impassioned speech had its desired effect on Miss Sil. Her jaws hardened and her small grey eyes blazed. "Thank God, I have brought my correspondence with Professor Morton of Sussex University on the Bengal famine. Reading a few select passages from that incendiary material in the next meeting would definitely take the wind out of Mrs Basak's sails," she said with great determination and then in a sudden outburst of patriotic feelings, she grabbed Miss Jhajoria's hand and kissed it. Miss Jhajoria's face broke into a triumphant smile. "You are a true patriot, Miss Sil. No one can forget that historic battle in the

Statesman's letters column which held us spellbound for over three months."

"And I won the battle too!" trilled an excited Miss Sil, clenching her fist. "I proved conclusively that more than a million people died in that man-made famine due to the utter negligence and callousness of the then British administration."

"That's it! Utter negligence and callousness. We died because in their eyes we were just an expendable, sub-human species. We died like flies and ants because we were not quite quite. Miss Sil, if you haven't already handed over your valuable correspondence to Mrs Basak, I'd like to take it back to London and publish it in an expensive, leather-bound volume with gilt-lettering and a foreword by an Oxford don."

Miss Sil's thin, emaciated face glowed like a sixty-watt bulb and she looked very emotional. "Published in London! Why, that's what I have been dreaming of all these days! Rekha, you must forgive me for being misled by . . ."

"Don't mention it," said Miss Jhajoria, pressing Miss Sil's bony fingers reassuringly. "Now, go to your room and prepare yourself for our next session which I am going to attend."

*

In the meeting that morning, Miss Sil launched a frontal attack against the club, branding it a bastion of racialism, British imperialism and all sorts of anti-national activities. "The culture bred and propagated and still being perpetuated" (she gave a significant sidelong glance at Mrs Basak who looked stunned and petrified) "by the club is obnoxious and smacks of our servile past," argued Miss Sil with devastating effect.

"I think we are going off the track, Miss Sil," pointed out Prof. Sen.

"I am very much on the track, Prof," retorted Miss Sil emphatically. "I am absolutely convinced that as long as the club continues in that old colonial building reminiscent of those days of apartheid, inequity and racial prejudice, it cannot serve the real cause of the enlightened Indian woman."

"Before attacking the apartheid and inequity practised by my countrymen, Miss Sil, what about the apartheid you have been practising on your own people from time immemorial?" countered Mrs Basak spiritedly. "Why this discrimination against the girl child, lower castes and the dark-skinned? We didn't bring these prejudices with us, or did we? But, let's not digress from the main issue. If you have any solid argument in favour of the Footania offer . . ."

The heated arguments between the two continued for about an hour during which Miss Sil lambasted Mrs Basak and her country for the tyranny of the East India Company over the peasantry, Clive's treachery, Dalhousie's abominable Permanent Settlement Act, the unlawful annexation of Oudh, Jhansi and other princely states, the partition of Bengal in 1905, the Jalianwala massacre of 1919, the 1943 Bengal famine and the partition of India in 1947. Mrs Basak retaliated viciously by reminding everyone of the gruesome murder and mayhem perpetrated on the innocent men, women and children of her country by so-called patriots like Siraj-ud-daula and Nana Saheb during the Calcutta Black Hole incident and the mutiny of 1857. I sat at my small table, wide-eyed and agape, listening to this historic battle and filling up the yawning gaps in my knowledge of British Indian history. The acrimonious debate whetted the appetite of the participants and Mrs Mahadevan, who had already tilted towards Miss Jhajoria after Miss Sil's fiery speech, sent me to the kitchen to find out what Mahesh was going to serve for lunch.

"Prawns in coconut and mustard gravy for non-vegetarians, dosa and sambar for Mrs Mahadevan and tomato soup and boiled chicken for the memsahib as usual," reported Mahesh cheerfully.

"For a change why don't you serve curried prawns to Mrs Basak as well?" I suggested to eradicate the apartheid Mahesh had been perpetrating on us so blatantly all these days.

"O Miss Hem, that's not possible!" cried a visibly shocked Mahesh. "Ingrez people have very delicate stomachs. Just put one chilli in their soup and they start howling as if their mouths are on fire."

"Don't talk rot, Mahesh," I snapped. "They make all those noises just because they want to show off how superior they are. The days of the Raj are over. As a self-respecting cook of a free country you must exercise your right to serve spicy, Indian dishes to everyone who comes to our country." But the obstinate cook only scratched his head and said, "But Miss Hem, it's much easier to make soup and boil chicken than to prepare curries."

Unable to instil any patriotic spirit in Mahesh's servile character, I returned to the veranda just in time to hear Miss Jhajoria warning Mrs Basak that as long as she was firmly attached to her commode, skirt-blouse-hat, soup-salad-boiled chicken and all other trappings of the typical Anglomaniac, she shouldn't dare to call herself a true Indian however long she might be domiciled in this holy land of thirty-three crore gods and goddesses. Mrs Basak looked helpless and slightly nervous after this virulent attack on her personal life and it fell to Prof. Sen to bail her out with the argument that there were any number of Indian women who maintained the English lifestyle as it suited them and yet they were considered very loyal and patriotic Indians. By this time, everyone looked tired and famished and Mrs Mahadevan, having been informed that lunch was ready, adjourned the meeting till teatime.

*

"How did I fare, Hem?" asked Miss Jhajoria when I accompanied her to the beach for a leisurely stroll.

"I think Mrs Basak has started showing chinks," I said. "She is clearly on the defensive."

"You are absolutely right. I hope the afternoon post brings me my Brahmastra, the ultimate weapon which could settle this long-drawn battle in the twinkling of an eye." Miss Jhajoria snapped her fingers with such devastating effect that I feared she was going to eliminate Mrs Basak before nightfall. "Have you ordered a pistol, Miss Jhajoria?" I whispered in great alarm.

Miss Jhajoria grinned mischievously and patted my cheek reassuringly. "No my dear, the days of duels are over or I'd have asked you to be my second. Just wait and see."

"And suppose your Brahmastra doesn't arrive in time?"

"I will still beat her. Miss Sil hasn't yet taken out her famous correspondence with Professor Morton. I can tell you one great truth, Hem. If Mrs Basak wins this battle she'll have the edge over me in next year's presidential election and if she wins that too, the club will definitely end up in the hands of the pro-British sycophants like Mrs Gulmohar and Mrs Walters. I fear that once they get power they will purge all pro-Indian elements like me and Miss Babeja from the club and fill up the resulting vacancies with British expats, after amending the constitution. You can count on Mrs Basak to turn the clock back a hundred years and re-introduce apartheid, racial discrimination and what have you."

"Looks like a well-planned conspiracy, Miss Jhajoria," I observed.

"You have a good nose, Hem. You realize that a large-scale infiltration of these pro-British elements in our club could have sinister political implications."

"Miss Jhajoria, do you really think the Brits are trying to return, using these backdoor methods?"

"I will reserve my judgement on that particular point till I get the full dossier on that dubious Devon aristocrat from London."

"Your Brahmastra?"

"Ah, yes. Before I left Calcutta I contacted a private detective agency in London to check up on Mrs Basak's antecedents, including her connections with M16, and instructed them to send me a full report here. But keep your trap shut, Hem, till I give you the signal."

"Mum's the word, Miss Jhajoria. Now I can see why Mrs Basak has been trying to keep me at a distance all along."

"She has to observe the strict code of conduct imposed by her M16 bosses in London, my dear. Now, could you do a bit of snooping for me and find out what our Lady Muck is doing over there with her brushes and paints?"

"No problem, Miss Jhajoria." I approached Mrs Basak stealthily from behind and was puzzled to discover a radical change of atmosphere on the canvas. The clear blue sky had suddenly clouded over and the sea was taking on a darker hue as Mrs Basak frantically slapped on a mixture of grey and ash colours with her palette knife. Even the gliding, care-free seagull trio had been tampered with to denote fright and alarm and the dark speck representing the solitary boat had simply vanished from the canvas!

That ominous-looking seascape with the drowned boat should have conveyed Mrs Basak's dejected mood to her colleagues, but no one, not even Miss Jhajoria, was prepared to take Mrs Basak's painting seriously and therefore they had a shock when she returned from the beach at teatime and declared that she was going to resign from her vice-presidentship as well as her primary membership of the club. She asked Sukhi to serve tea in her room and begged her colleagues to excuse her as she had some important letters to write. Miss Sil, who had carefully arranged her famous correspondence on the Bengal famine like a pack of trump cards to demolish the evil Raj and its vile institutions, gasped and exchanged a meaningful wink with Miss Jhajoria. Prof. Sen, the only member who had stood by Mrs Basak through thick and thin, put down her tome and rushed to Mrs Basak's room, probably to persuade her to change her mind, but she returned after ten minutes, looking very sad and puzzled, and informed her colleagues that Mrs Basak was packing her boxes as she would drive back to Calcutta early next morning. To Mrs Mahadevan's anxious query if it would be safe to let

Mrs Basak drive a car in her present state of mind, Prof. Sen replied that Mrs Basak had accepted her defeat with good grace and fortitude like a well-bred English lady and she had requested her colleagues to draw up a resolution so that she could sign it before she left Bakkhali. Everyone appreciated Mrs Basak's parting gesture and Miss Sil lost no time in drafting a three-line resolution which I copied beautifully with an occasional flourish of italics. Within five minutes the momentous decision to accept Mr Thapar's ten million and relocate the club to a new site in the vicinity of Dum Dum was made, with all the members, including Mrs Basak, signing the damning resolution with a vengeance.

"I think we should open a bottle of champagne to celebrate this great occasion," proposed Miss Jhajoria and she revealed that she had brought a bottle of '82 Dom Perignon pink champagne in anticipation of her victory. Mrs Basak gallantly joined the revelries and raised her glass in a toast, wishing Miss Jhajoria good health and a long innings with the club and the latter responded with a gracious "thank you". Everyone keenly watched Mrs Basak's face for a trace of sadness, if not an unbidden tear, but there was nothing of that sort to betray her grief. The memsahib held up her head proudly, though I noted that she drank much less of the bubbly liquor than the others, probably to guard herself against runaway emotions.

The postman arrived just when, at Prof. Sen's request, the ladies had magnanimously raised their glasses a second time to drink a final toast to Mrs Basak's good health and her sterling services to the club.

"A letter from London, I suppose?" said Miss Jhajoria as she rose from her chair.

"It's a cable from London, madam," said the poker-faced, khaki-clad messenger as he delivered a small white envelope with the blotchy, almost indistinguishable mark of P&T at the top.

"Man, you could have saved some of my precious time and energy if you had delivered it this morning."

"But it came only half an hour ago, madam," said the messenger.

Miss Jhajoria flung a fiver at the postman, waved him away and then turned to her friends. "Just a personal message from Ravi," she said even as she shot a triumphant look at her vanquished adversary. Mrs Basak flinched a little as though she had a hunch that the cable boded evil for her. "I think I should go back to my room and finish my packing," she said and left the table with an alacrity that made everyone look at Miss Jhajoria for a revelation. "She needs some rest after a hectic day," said Miss Jhajoria with a beatific smile. "Hem, come to my room after an hour or so. I have an important letter to dictate."

*

From her recumbent position on the bed, Miss Jhajoria dictated a letter to her bosom friend Chitra Sood of East 43rd Street, New York, in which she gave a slightly embellished description of her spectacular victory over Mrs Basak and hinted that the latter's unexpected resignation had immensely brightened her prospects in next year's election. Could her dearest friend let her know the current price of a diamond set from Bailey, Banks and Biddle like the one her rival was flaunting so aggressively at Calcutta's cocktail parties? She would also need a copy of Karen Dinkly's *Braid Aid* as she was *so* tired of traditional Indian braids and would like to try some exotic styles, particularly the French and the Dutch. Nothing exciting was happening in India at the moment except that the much-awaited Gala of London deodorant sticks were at last available in Calcutta at a reasonable price of Rs 23, and Asha Virmani ("Remember our quiet, nail-chewing classmate who often got caught dozing on the backbenches by Sister Rebecca?") had written an illuminating article in *Bodycare* on hair removal ("Doesn't it sound queer, Chitra, that eighty per cent of those British women who remove body hair still reach for the razor — invincible Boots statistics, my dear! — when girls like you and me living in a backward place like Calcutta had so smoothly graduated from painful waxing to the more advanced techniques of bleaching and depilatory creams even before we passed out of Loreto?") And now that little query about her famous recipe for Muli Masala. How scandalous that coriander leaves and mango dust were not available in the Big Apple! Why, one could buy them all the year round in Mr Chopra's Subzi Bhandar in Southall. There were really no substitutes for those two essential ingredients, but if one had to cook Muli Masala without them, a sprig of fresh mint crushed with fifty grams of ginger, one green chilli and a few drops of tamarind juice would give the desired hot and sour taste, or almost. Two big kisses on Baby Chumki's two puffy cheeks and namaste to Anil bhaiya. Lots of Love. Rekha.

"So you have finally got your Brahmastra, Miss Jhajoria, haven't you?" I asked as she took the letter from my hand for signature.

Miss Jhajoria frowned. "Who told you that?"

"I guessed it from the way Mrs Basak suddenly left the table."

Miss Jhajoria smiled. "That's strange, isn't it? It shows that our sixth sense does really work sometimes. She could guess what I had in my hand."

"But is it really *that* bad?"

"It's worse."

"May I see it, Miss Jhajoria?"

"No. It's top secret material."

"Please, Miss Jhajoria! I have been looking for a chance to settle old scores with her."

"Really? All right, I will show you my Brahmastra, but only on an oath of secrecy. Now touch my head and swear."

I touched her head and swore in the name of goddess Kali, whereupon Miss Jhajoria took out the small envelope from under her pillow. My hands shook uncontrollably as I read the devastating message:

INTERIM REPORT ON MAXINE BASAK FOLLOWS STOP WORK- ING CLASS ORIGIN GRANDFATHER TYNESIDE MINEWORKER FATHER DITTO ANCESTRAL HOME SELBY SOUTH YORKSHIRE MAIDEN NAME FLORRIE HEGGS STOP FAMILY MOVED TO EAST LONDON SUBURB LOVINGDALE GARDENS IN MID- SIXTIES ON CLOSURE OF MINES CAUSED BY NORTHSEA OIL EXPLORATION AND FATHER FOUND EMPLOYMENT AS SHOP ASSISTANT IN COVENT GARDEN STOP FLORRIE DROPPED OUT OF SCHOOL AT SIXTEEN TO WORK IN A BLOOMSBURY BOOKSHOP AND LATER MOVED TO OXFORD WHERE SHE WORKED AS A PROSTITUTE FOR OVER TWO YEARS BEFORE HOOKING RICH INDIAN GENT BASAK STOP TRESTLETONS AND GUMSEYS DON'T FIGURE IN BURKE'S PEERAGE STOP FULL REPORT IN TWO WEEKS

HARRIET

ACE DETECTIVE AGENCY

"This is unbelievable!" I gasped. "All that crap about her aristocratic Devon background, her connections with the Trestletons and the Gumseys and what not! How could she cheat everyone in Calcutta all these years?"

"It's because we trust the Brits and their honesty a little too much," said Miss Jhajoria and snatched the cable from my trembling hands before I could have a second look at it. "But I can't blame her," said Miss Jhajoria. "Thanks to the addictive effects of those cheap Mills and Boon romances, every shopgirl or typist from Hackney dreams of marrying a handsome count or a Duke in Ruritania and living a luxurious life like Liz Taylor or Princess Di. Well, poor Florrie was no exception. She knew she had no future in her own country and therefore hooked that degenerate Basak pretty quick, obliterating her proletarian past in the process and assuming an aristocratic identity for she knew quite well that she would never be challenged in these parts where the Raj still holds sway."

But even as Miss Jhajoria charted the spectacular social climbing of Florrie Heggs, a disturbing thought crossed my mind: what if Miss Jhajoria leaked the scandal? The genteel, hidebound Calcutta society which had held Mrs Basak in high esteem all these years would suddenly start treating her like a leper. Mr Basak would definitely divorce her to save his political career, but what troubled me more was the fact that her two innocent daughters would have a hell of a time coping with their mother's horrid past. I was damn sure that no Indian boy from a respectable family would ever ask for their hands. "Your Brahmastra could completely wreck Mrs Basak's life, Miss Jhajoria," I said tentatively, just to find out her future plans. Miss Jhajoria grinned mischievously. "I am not a fool, Hem. Superpowers stockpile nuclear missiles mainly for their deterrent effect. Unless Florrie changes her mind and tries to queer the pitch for me she is safe. Do you get my point?"

"Yes," I nodded. "But shouldn't you drop a word of warning in her ear in case she is tempted to withdraw her resignation under pressure from Mrs Gulmohar and her other cronies."

"Not a bad idea. Will you be my emissary to convey the warning in as few words as possible?"

I nodded and rose from the chair, then asked her a question that had been nagging at me ever since she had harangued Miss Sil that morning.

"Why do you live in London, Miss Jhajoria," I asked, "particularly when you have such strong patriotic feelings?"

Miss Jhajoria stuck out her tongue and gave the little blob of gum she was chewing a contemplative look, then she smiled. "Business reasons, my dear. Moreover, I prefer London because that's the only place where you get Indian things in their pure and unadulterated state. Here in India I find that everything is either adulterated or of poor quality. In fact, if you want to get the best basmati rice, spices, clothes, dried fruits and many other Indian goods London is definitely the right place. For the latest designer saris you go to Wembley or Forest Gate, for gold and diamond jewellery you may visit Ram Prakash Sunderdass of

Southall, for laddus and best quality pista burfis you can always trust the Ambala Sweet Centre in Drummond Street and if you want to eat out in style there is Chutney Mary. Why, even an Amitabh Bachhan blockbuster comes to Ravi's East West Video Centre long before it is released in India. No wonder all decent and patriotic Indians now live in London and help the motherland from outside."

"Why, she actually wants to enjoy the best of both worlds!" I thought, and my respect for the patriotic non-resident Indians like Miss Jhajoria suddenly took a nosedive. I now realized that Mrs Basak, despite her snobbishness, her addiction to soup-salad diet and her English dress and manners, was much more Indian than Miss Jhajoria, for she was merrily slumming it in the stinking hell that was Calcutta and was not complaining about it either.

I slipped out of Miss Jhajoria's room and tapped softly on Mrs Basak's door. I must warn her about Miss Jhajoria's Brahmastra, I decided, even if she snaps at me for disturbing her so late in the evening. Mrs Basak didn't answer the door, so I pushed it open and discovered that she was not in her room, even though all the lights were on. I was gripped by a sudden fear that, unable to bear her humiliating defeat, Mrs Basak might have drowned herself in the sea but, on second thoughts, I assured myself that the cold-blooded memsahib wouldn't end her precious life so dramatically. Still, I felt an urgent need to locate Mrs Basak and apprise her of Miss Jhajoria's evil designs. I rushed out of the cottage and felt immense relief as I spotted the hazy outline of her slouching figure at the very place where she had spent those precious hours working on her ill-fated seascape. As I strode towards her, I noticed that she was draped in a pink nightie and was sitting in a careless, slatternly posture with her legs drawn up and planted apart, her shoulders hunched up and her dishevelled hair blowing about her face in the strong sea breeze. She had a cigarette jammed between her lips at a rakish angle and I suspected that she was drunk. From a distance the general impression was of a battered woman contemplating suicide. As I came nearer, I felt an irresistible urge to rush to her side, gather her in my arms and say a few soothing words to revive her spirit. "Mrs Basak!" I cried and started running towards her.

"Any more papers to sign, Miss Hem?" asked Mrs Basak matter-of-factly as she turned her face towards me with a frown.

"Oh no, I just want to talk to you."

"Not now, Miss Hem. I have done enough talking today. Would you please leave me alone?" Mrs Basak flicked away her half-burnt cigarette and picked up a quarter bottle of brandy from her lap. I could see that she had already finished more than half of the bottle. She unscrewed the cap and was going to take a slug but I grabbed her wrist firmly. "Florrie, don't!" I implored.

Mrs Basak was visibly shocked and I took this opportunity to snatch the bottle from her hand and chuck it into the sea.

"There's no Florrie here," hissed Mrs Basak, retrieving her hand from my clasp with a jerk. "I am Maxine Basak and may I remind you, Miss Hem, that as a junior clerk you are not supposed to behave so brashly with the vice-president of CLC."

I laughed aloud at Mrs Basak's heroic attempt to flaunt her aristocratic hauteur in her present situation. "Florrie, your game is up," I said. "That Cable Miss Jhajoria got this afternoon lets the cat out of the bag. I have come to warn you that . . ." But before I could finish, Mrs Basak slapped me on the face. Stung by the sharp pain, I instinctively drew back my arm and returned the slap, a bit more powerfully than I had intended.

"You bitch! How dare you . . .?" screamed Mrs Basak and pounced on me but after a brief struggle I overpowered her and pinned her down with my arms. "Now! I have got you at last!" I cried triumphantly.

"Get off my chest, you devil, or I'll . . ."

" ' . . . Send yet another Section 80 notice through my solicitor', hun?" I sneered. "But you won't get a chance, Florrie, because I am going to strangle you right now."

"You are mad!"

"I am quite sane, my dear," I assured her. "And I am now quite convinced that as long as you are alive, you will go on torturing and humiliating me and I want to put an end to it once and for all." I pressed my palms gently on her slender white neck and felt a familiar tinge of excitement coursing through my veins.

"Do it quick, if you must," dared Mrs Basak, her eyes looking straight into mine. "Maybe the Indian Government will give you a medal for eliminating an unpatriotic memsahib who stubbornly refuses to squat on a WC and relishes her boiled chicken and salad."

"I don't want a medal but I will kill you all the same," I declared.

"And how much will you get from Miss Jhajoria for this dirty job?"

"I am acting on my own," I assured her. "But enough of idle talk. I think I should molest you before I kill you."

"In the best Indian tradition, huh?" jeered Mrs Basak.

"I will follow the universal criminal code. First rape and then murder." I squeezed one of her breasts through her nightie and then lowered my face to kiss her, but Mrs Basak turned away her face resolutely. "You'd better go and fuck that Marwari girl," she spat out viciously, her eyes blazing. "She has bigger tits and a patriotic pussy."

"Aha! Spoken like a real Devon aristocrat! I wish Teesta were here." I held her face tightly between my palms and pressed my lips on hers, first tentatively and then savagely. Mrs Basak offered some resistance but finally parted her lips and as I kissed her passionately, she flung her arms around my neck and started crying.

Nineteen

The day after we returned from Bakkhali, Mrs Basak's servant Hari brought me a chit with a frightening message: "Come and kiss me goodbye, darling. I think I am dying." When I pressed him the servant merely told me that the memsahib was bed-ridden though he knew nothing about the exact nature of her illness. During our return journey from the coast Mrs Basak had hinted that she would soon install a WC in her bathroom in order to practise squatting like an Indian woman. I had thought that it was only a joke, but now I couldn't ignore the dreadful possibility that she might have slipped and broken her pelvis while trying to squat properly on her newly-installed WC. The mystery deepened further when I dashed to Basak House and met on the veranda a cheerful Chinta who giggled and gagged her mouth with her sari as I anxiously asked her if Mrs Basak's condition was really serious. I had to give her a good shake by the shoulders before she opened her mouth: "God knows what ghost has suddenly possessed our memsa'b, didi. Just imagine! Gobbling telebhajas from that dirty street corner shop which caters to rickshawalas and other riffraffs. I tried to remove them from her table but memsa'b was adamant. Go inside and see how she is writhing like a bloodied chicken."

I was shocked by the stupidity of Mrs Basak, who would normally think twice before she accepted a piece of curried chicken cooked hygenically in her own kitchen. Even I, with my salmonella-proof Calcutta stomach and a passion for hot and soury stuff, avoided those greasy harbingers of diarrhoea fried in cheap palm oil which the thrifty pavement shopkeepers recycled for several weeks till it looked dark and viscous like diesel. I dashed upstairs to Mrs Basak's room and found her writhing in pain, her red and green cotton sari in hopeless disarray, exposing her midriff and her small, shallow navel which, I thought, was rather unattractive in her otherwise faultless anatomy.

"If you are really so keen to commit suicide, there are a dozen less painful methods," I said even as I knelt beside her bed and clasped her hand. "It's no fun shitting oneself to death."

"Forgive me, darling," said Mrs Basak, trying to grin bravely through her pain. "I couldn't resist the temptation of those hot, crisp telebhajas. I wish I had the WC installed by now. It's *so* convenient in such a condition."

"You will never have your WC," I declared. "I will see to that."

"You are angry, my dear. Come, listen to the deep rumblings inside my belly and predict my next trip to the loo."

I couldn't help laughing as I pressed my ear to her abdomen to hear the tumult that signified an imminent storm. "I give you five minutes," I predicted confidently, but after two minutes Mrs Basak pushed my head off her belly and dashed to the bathroom in her petticoat, peeling off her sari on the way. I gathered it from the floor and went out to enquire of Chinta if she had already called the doctor. She assured me that Dr Hazra must be on his way. "Tell the plumber that Mrs Basak has changed her mind," I said. "She won't need that WC any more."

I returned to Mrs Basak's bedroom just in time to see her shuffling back from the bathroom, exhausted and thoroughly shaken by the ordeal.

"Radha, are you punishing me for all that bilge Miss Sil and Miss Jhajoria spouted about your lack of Indianness at Bakkhali?" I said as I helped her to tuck in her sari loosely around her waist.

"Oh no, I really want to reform myself," she said as she stretched out in her bed. "I do want to be a true Indian."

"Like Miss Jhajoria? In that case you have to take up residence in Belsize Park, London, for nine months of the year."

Mrs Basak smiled wanly. "I am serious, darling. Won't you help me?"

"Gladly. But you needn't sacrifice your life in the process. We are going to celebrate Calcutta's tercentenary next year and we will need you badly at that time."

"Why me of all persons, may I ask?"

"Calcutta hasn't anything beautiful to show off to the world on this great occasion except the Victoria Memorial and Maxine Basak."

Mrs Basak laughed and pinched my cheek in the true Indian style. "I have no objection to becoming a tercentenary fixture at a road crossing if that's how Calcutta wants to utilize me," she said. "But, darling, you have to save me from the crows and the stray dogs. I won't enjoy being defiled continuously by those creatures like the statues of Gandhi and Subhas Bose."

Our playful banter was cut short by the intrusion of Dr Hazra whose imposing bulk, stentorian voice and fat medicine bag seemed to aggravate the patient's condition. Mrs Basak started groaning and writhing and looked beseechingly at her family physician. "This is the eye of the storm, Dr Hazra," she moaned, drawing a neat circle round her navel with her finger.

"Hmm," nodded the grave physician. "May I know what we have been eating lately, Mrs Basak?"

"Mostly telebhajas from the pavement shops," I told him. Mrs Basak gave me a dark look and I stuck out my tongue. Dr Hazra noted this most unusual non-verbal exchange between the mistress of the house and her new housemaid with a frown and decided to put an end to our frivolity. "Mrs Basak, now please show me your tongue," he said authoritatively and then turned to me. "Girl, bring me a bowl of hot water. I have to give an injection."

*

Mrs Basak's passion for imbibing the true Indian spirit didn't subside even after that nasty bout of diarrhoea. She made me take her to Mahajati Sadan for an evening of Rabindrasangeet. Supported by an able orchestra consisting of tabla, tanpura, flute and harmonium, the renowned artists rendered Tagore's sweet, soulful lyrics beautifully and with finesse but, for someone like me reared on the vigorous foot-tapping music of Kishore Kumar and Asha Bhonsle, it was a bit slow and unexciting. Mrs Basak initially affected great enthusiasm for the long drawn-out, raag-based songs even though she hardly understood a word of Tagore's lyrics, but soon I caught her stifling a big yawn. Fortunately, we were not the only ones who couldn't appreciate Rabindrasangeet properly and after the first three or four songs, half the audience started dozing. It reminded me of Miss Gordon-Green's postmodernist novel-reading session at the CLC and our flight to Mrs Basak's room for a quickie. "Let's get out for a breath of fresh air," I whispered in Mrs Basak's ear, cupping her breast with my hand.

"Oh no, that will be too rude," whispered back Mrs Basak. "Maybe we aren't concentrating properly . . . why, I like that tabla immensely. Let's stay at least till the interval."

"In that case, I will have to divert myself with a bit of friendly groping," I declared.

269

"Don't be crazy, Hem. This is a public place and we should maintain some decorum. I wish I had brought my shawl."

"No need of cover, darling," I assured her. "It's almost dark here and most of our neighbours are snoring peacefully."

We leaned back in our chairs, ducked our heads and joined our lips for a slow, lingering kiss. We could have easily broken all the previous records for kissing in a public place but had to pull away when we heard a gentleman sitting behind us arguing with his female companion in a loud whisper: "No my dear, we mustn't disturb them. Thank God, Calcutta can now boast of at least one pair of lesbians who dare to kiss openly." This created a minor uproar in our neighbourhood as people rose from their seats and craned their heads to catch a glimpse of the daring lesbian couple in action. Afraid of causing pandemonium in the auditorium, we slithered out of our seats and scurried to a side door for a quick exit.

After the sublime and soporific Rabindrasangeet we went to Kalamandir to see a thunderous, fast-paced jatra, the most popular and exciting theatrical performance of Bengal. "Bandit Queen Champa" had all the necessary ingredients to pull the crowd: coarse comedy, dazzling gold and brocade costumes, suspense, heart-catching dialogue, gun fights, murders, four full-throated songs, one titillating cabaret and most important of all, a fairly predictable storyline that unabashedly glorified the bandit queen's tyrannical outbursts of violence. Mrs Basak was stunned by the spectacle and plugged her ears with her fingers whenever the deafening orchestra, dominated by the violin, came alive to heighten Champa's turbulent emotions. "Very interesting," she murmured with evident relief when the curtains came down amidst a thunderous ovation from the audience.

I was thinking of taking her to another good Bengali play but Mrs Basak gave me a mild shock by asking me to take her to a football match. "Oh no, I can't do that for my life," I protested. "Our football fans are so unruly."

"But, darling, how can I claim to be a true Calcuttan without going to a Mohan Bagan versus East Bengal match? Don't worry about me. Calcutta crowds are generally chivalrous, aren't they?"

I nodded, though I myself had never ventured to the stadium. On my request Tama not only managed to get the passes through her footballer brother, she also agreed to accompany us. A match between the two giant clubs, Mohan Bagan and East Bengal, would have been an ideal occasion for Mrs Basak to visit the Eden Garden stadium, but we had to depend on potluck and settled for a quarter-final league match between Mohan Bagan and Mohmedan Sporting.

There was no separate enclosure for women, so we had to sit with a group of Mohan Bagan supporters, though Tama and I managed to insulate Mrs Basak from the crowd by occupying the seats next to her on either side. Gripping a small iron rod which I had picked up from a construction site, I assumed the role of Mrs Basak's bodyguard, watching out for potential molesters and bottom pinchers, but mercifully the chivalrous football fans around us merely turned their heads to gawk at the memsahib and only one scruffy youth with a markedly concave face confided to his leering mate that he would like to lick the memsahib's rosy cheeks and find out if they were made of Amul butter or maska. Fortunately, the referee blew his whistle for the kick-off and everyone's attention was immediately focused on the field. For the first time I saw Sushil Bhowmik, the famous striker of Mohan Bagan, in action, but I was not at all impressed by his performance. He played old-style soccer, dribbling too much and indulging in fancy long shots from the midfield that either went over the bar or were blocked by the half-backs. To my great amazement, Mrs Basak instantaneously became a Mohan Bagan fan and clapped enthusiastically whenever one of their players entered the opponents' penalty area.

"Very disciplined crowd," said Mrs Basak as Tama and I escorted her out of the stadium like a VIP, my iron rod ever ready to strike at any dirty hand that dared to touch Mrs Basak's body.

After this exciting introduction to football, it was only natural that Mrs Basak would want to see one of our fund-raising exhibition matches which we were playing at that time with some high school boys' teams. These mixed matches were Mrs Mookerjee's brainchild and they had proved very successful indeed as they never failed to attract a fairly large crowd. Backed by our Luckme sponsorship and emboldened by the good pickings from these mixed matches held on every Saturday and Sunday, Mrs Chaudhury had finally declared that from the next football season the club would pay each player a monthly fee ranging from three hundred to five hundred rupees depending on one's performance in the competitive matches. As a Triple Star I naturally expected the top rate, but one could never be sure with our tight-fisted treasurer.

Mrs Mookerjee looked very pleased when I introduced her to Mrs Basak as "Madam Treasurer". Maxine caused quite a flutter among the juvenile spectators with her body-hugging, charcoal-grey jersey dress (with fitted bodice and drop-waisted full circular skirt), plaited silver bangles, giant-sized hooped earrings and a wide-brimmed straw hat. After the exchange of pleasantries, Mrs Mookerjee began her well-tried dirge about the club's financial difficulties and how the patronage of a few socialites like Mrs Basak could help the club attain its full potential within a short time. The way our cross-eyed treasurer fawned on the memsahib, I could see that she was angling for yet another handsome donation from the Basak coffers. Miss Nag, of course, chided me for bringing a "stinking sample of the decadent British bourgeoisie" to distract the crowd, but when I protested vehemently, pointing out that Mrs Basak had already taken a big leap towards the proletarian lifestyle by consuming telebhaja from a pavement stall, thereby risking her life, and had also attended a league match, Miss Nag softened a bit and conceded that with the rise of American neo-colonialism and Russian revisionism, the moribund British imperialism no longer posed a serious threat to the working class and world revolution, and if what I had just said about her was true, then she should be cultivated carefully for future exploitation. And yet, when I requested Miss Nag to upgrade me to the forward line so that I could show off my superior skills in dribbling and shooting before Mrs Basak, she summarily rejected my request which, she pointed out, smacked of petit-bourgeois inconsistency. The keenly-contested match ended in a draw and to my ill-luck, during the tie-breaker, I spurned the only chance I had to prove my shooting ability by kicking the ball right into the hands of Kalighat High School's goalkeeper. Kalighat eventually won by a goal and received the trophy from Mrs Basak's fair hands amidst clappings and wolf-whistles from an exuberant teenage crowd of ten thousand. Mrs Basak then promised Mrs Mookerjee a donation of five thousand and this prompted a hushed consultation between the treasurer and the secretary whereupon the latter conferred there and then the honorary vice-presidentship of Rani Jhansi on Mrs Basak, ignoring her mild protests.

While Mrs Basak enjoyed tea with Mrs Mookerjee and Mrs Chaudhury in their pavilion, I had to face a barrage of incisive questions from my teammates regarding my friendship with the pukka memsahib. No one really bought my story that I had befriended her during my brief stay at Rose Valley and some of my teammates made me furious when they advised me that I shouldn't have any qualms about milking this white Kamdhenu, the mythical cow whose udders never dried up, as her people had done the same to our country. Even weepy Leena, the congenital pessimist, congratulated me for hooking a raghob boal, a gigantic fish, and three-question Utpala was so impressed by my intimacy with Mrs Basak that she forgot her questions and whispered excitedly in my ear: "Lucky dog! When are you going to London with your memsahib?" I could fob off the others with vague replies and clever rejoinders, but not Tama who had discovered my actual relationship with Mrs Basak on the day she had accompanied us to the stadium. "You get into scrapes so easily, Hem," she reminded me when we were alone. "Are you sure she won't ditch you?"

"Absolutely," I assured her.

"But be careful. If Mr Basak comes to hear about it . . ."

"He already knows about it but he is not the least bothered about our relationship because he is happy with his Lola."

"Still, there is always a fear of scandal, particularly when a woman from a big house is involved. I think you two shouldn't hold hands in public."

"Good advice, darling. I will remember that."

I had not committed any crime, I thought, so why should I behave like a thief? After two weeks, Mrs Basak would go to Darjeeling for Christmas and I would be left alone. Naturally, we wanted to stick together as much as possible but it seemed that some of our friends didn't quite appreciate our togetherness.

*

Mrs Gulmohar narrowed her eyes suspiciously when we entered her flat hand in hand but she preferred to give us the benefit of the doubt, or so it seemed. She was annoyed at the way her dearest friend had thrown up her coveted post on the spur of the moment and had signed that suicidal resolution which would sound the death knell of the CLC. I had already warned Mrs Basak about Miss Jhajoria's Brahmastra and I knew that she wouldn't associate herself with the club under any circumstances, and yet I felt very sad when my proud and spirited memsahib muttered rather meekly about the necessity of yielding responsible positions to the younger generation. Mrs Gulmohar shook her head stubbornly and said, "Don't talk rot, Maxine. I have already requested Mrs Jeejaboy not to accept your resignation in a hurry and she has agreed. She has also promised me that she won't put the outrageous Bakkhali resolution before the next GB meeting before she has had a proper talk with you. In fact, she has been trying to contact you on the phone. Where have you been? You aren't available at home or in your gallery; you don't even go to the golf course. I was frantically trying to contact you the day before yesterday about that piano recital by Paul Stuart at Kalamandir next Wednesday, but Chinta told me you had gone to see a football match somewhere near Tollygunj. I thought she was trying to pull my leg, but now I can see . . ." Mrs Gulmohar broke off and gave me a nasty look. I reciprocated with an impish grin.

"We are busy exploring Calcutta these days, Gulu darling," I said sweetly. "Radha is very keen to catch up on our Bengali culture and I am trying to familiarize her with Bengali theatre, Rabindrasangeet, jatra, football matches and what have you. Next week I will take her to a kite-flying competition and a P.C. Sorcar magic show." Mrs Gulmohar looked horrified as if I had taught her best friend to play with dirt and drain muck.

"I don't believe a whit of what that monkey jabbers," she declared haughtily. "But darling, you look so different. For God's sake, don't spoil that girl too much."

Mrs Basak smiled at me indulgently and said, 'I don't know who's spoiling whom, Gulu, but I must be frank with you. I like Hem too much and enjoy absorbing whatever she has to offer. I do love her, Gulu."

Mrs Gulmohar's big saucer eyes popped out of their sockets and her mouth fell open. "That's impossible!" she cried. "Didn't you yourself assure me that you have no lesbian feelings towards her?"

"I vehemently object to that offensive term, Mrs Gulmohar," I protested.

"You may consider us as a couple with the same gender orientation. SGOs for short," suggested Mrs Basak primly.

"We love each other and nothing can change that," I declared, and to demonstrate my love for Mrs Basak, I smacked a kiss on her cheek, making her blush.

"For God's sake, allow that poor woman to breathe freely!" cried Mrs Gulmohar.

"Radha darling, do you have any trouble in breathing?" I asked Mrs Basak, throwing my arm gallantly around her waist.

"Hem loves fun," said Mrs Basak cheerfully and begged her friend to bring tea for us.

"You will ruin each other," prophesied Mrs Gulmohar darkly from her kitchen. "You two are going against nature."

"I think we shouldn't thrust ourselves on our conservative friends for a while," whispered Mrs Basak. "From tomorrow we will spend our evenings in my house, achha?"

"Splendid," I said. "You have such a lovely garden and a lily pond too."

*

But rather than wasting our precious time in the garden or by the lily pond whispering sweet nothings, we spent the last few evenings making love in Maxine's big four-poster with the chintz curtains fluttering in the cool evening breeze. Confronted with the undulating expanse of her warm naked flesh laid out before me like a gorgeous wedding feast, I felt like the starved and somewhat confused jackal in the well-known fable who couldn't make up his mind as to where he should start when too many corpses unexpectedly turned up at the mouth of his lair. After considering several options I finally decided to devour my lover's succulent flesh exactly in the same way a poor bustee boy would approach his once-in-a-blue-moon rosogolla: start licking at the periphery and slowly work his way to the core so that the delicious sweetmeat would last for at least half an hour, if not longer. I neatly divided Mrs Basak's curvaceous terrain into four erotic zones — face, breasts, abdomen and vagina, and identified the cores of these areas in her lips, nipples, navel and clitoris respectively. I worked very methodically on each zone with my mouth and tongue, starting from the periphery and working slowly towards the core which, of course, received my special attention and lingering treatment. The strenuous exercise made my lips and tongue almost numb even before I had reached the end of my journey but the intimate knowledge that Mrs Basak immensely enjoyed my oral lovemaking goaded me on till she had had her spasms and clamped her thighs tight around my head, almost suffocating me with her ardour. After one of her earth-shattering orgasms, Mrs Basak drew me to her bosom and whispered in my ear: "Darling, who says the Indians lack a scientific approach?"

I soon discovered that Mrs Basak could match my passion and uninhibited lovemaking, particularly after she had had a tot of brandy. She didn't even mind a role reversal, playing the top girl quite enthusiastically, though she preferred the passive role, protesting occasionally in feigned horror, "Slow down, you brute! You are hurting me" while I continued my frenzied lovemaking, whispering hoarsely that I wouldn't stop till she was pregnant with twins.

"Don't you want to know a little more about the infamous Florrie Heggs?" asked Mrs Basak one evening when I was trying to paint an unidentified flower and two buds on her breast with her Chanel eyeliner, moistening it occasionally with my spittle.

"I am not Miss Jhajoria," I reminded her sanctimoniously. "I have no interest in anybody's past. I am concerned only with the present."

"Ah, I can see that. Never knew you have such artistic talents, darling. Why, that boob already looks like somebody else's, maybe a Bantu woman's. Now, take a short break from your artistic endeavours and hear the Heggs saga. I want to unburden my heart."

"Shall I give Miss Jhajoria a ring?"

"Don't bother," said Mrs Basak as she pulled me forcibly to her side. "That private detective must have already sent her a sackload of information on my past, including that salacious bit about how Madge, the neighbour's girl, and I lured a tom into my bedroom with a tuna one Sunday morning when everyone had gone to the church and encouraged him to lick us to our first orgasms at the ripe age of nine or thereabouts."

"Very explosive material, that, but I think our patriotic Miss Jhajoria is more interested in your M16 connections. She thinks you are plotting to bring back the good old Brits to rule us for another two hundred years."

"I think Harriet will need a generous clipping of my bush to complete her research in that direction."

"But I can't allow that desecration, darling, because I have artistic ambitions concerning that region. I am going to paint it pink."

"Good heavens! Floral tits, pink pussy . . . what next?"

"Red rump decorated with tantric motifs and fertility symbols."

"Enough! Why don't you do something artistic with my ugly stretch marks? Now Hem, don't divert me when I am in a mood to unburden myself." Mrs Basak reached for her packet of Slims, lighted one and affected a reflective mood. "Do you fancy living in a two-bedroomed house called *Mon Repos* in the nondescript East London suburb Lovingdale Gardens which ought to have been called *Hell's End*?" she asked me almost with a challenging look.

"Yes, why not? It sounds quite good to me, even a little romantic."

"I am surprised to hear that from a budding artist. In my ears it never sounded anything but ordinary and preposterous. And what do you think about the name Florrie, may I know?"

"Wonderful. It suits you."

Mrs Basak pinched my bottom. "You devil! It seems you are quite prepared for a ghastly tale, aren't you?" Mrs Basak explained that Mon Repos was actually a drab, semi-detached house with a pocket-sized kitchen garden where her father Freddy Heggs, the shop assistant, could be seen toiling very hard on Sunday mornings to raise green peas and vegetable marrows in a competitive spirit with their immediate neighbour Ernie Clarke, the grocer, who owned an identical semi-detached with an equally preposterous name *Exmoor*. His daughter Madge was Florrie's best friend and classmate at Lovingdale Comprehensive and they shared their little secrets as much as the neighbourhood tom for a bit of forbidden pleasure. Poor Madge ended up marrying Jack Woodey, a junior chemist at Quaker Oats, after a long and tedious affair with the elder Carter boy Nobby, a garage mechanic who lived down the lane in a slightly less preposterous semi-detached called *Seven Oaks* which could at least boast one mountain ash at the front. Florrie had an elder brother called Rick and two younger sisters, Rosie and Susie. Rosie died in a car accident in Spain while holidaying with her married boss, one Mr Wolley, who had helped her to achieve her life's dream of becoming a hairdresser. Susie, the youngest of the three sisters, was clever enough to emigrate to Australia when she was seventeen and the last Mrs Basak had heard of her sister she was living a sedate and comfortable life with her three kids and twice-divorced, prematurely bald husband Andy who owned a chain of icecream parlours in Melbourne. Mrs Basak hadn't heard (and wouldn't like to hear) anything about her brother Rick after his second prison term for dope peddling and she scrupulously avoided any contact with her parents when she visited her country, though she had recently learnt from her friend Madge that Mr Basak had visited the old couple during his last business trip to London and, in the good Indian tradition of a dutiful son-in-law, had helped them with some money without her knowledge.

"Well, that's a thumbnail sketch of the eminently forgettable Heggs clan," said Mrs Basak and smiled wryly.

"But the sketch remains incomplete until you say something about your mother," I pointed out.

"A grave omission, I must admit. The poor woman came from a lower-middle-class family; her father was a primary school teacher in Richmond and therefore she had every right to consider herself a cut above my working-class dad."

Mrs Heggs, it appeared, tried her best to impress her neighbours and her husband's friends with her cheap crystal glasses, second-hand Royal Worcester dinner service, a few prints of Turner, Constable and Picasso displayed prominently in her sitting room and, above all, her laboured Oxford accent. She never missed an opportunity to mention to her neighbours her family's close relations with Baroness Trestleton of Mugbury and Sir Peter Gumsey, the third earl of Lupinsville, even though Florrie had never known her poor mum to receive any invitation from her aristocratic relations. To groom her daughters for a better future, Mrs Heggs took them to the Tate Gallery and the Victoria and Albert Museum, local theatres, the Chelsea Flower Show and even introduced the girls to the pleasures of Italian opera (though Mrs Heggs herself was reared on Gilbert and Sullivan) at the Royal Opera House. The girls however preferred to hang around Oxford Circus or go to the local disco where they met all the neighbourhood boys — Rick, Nobby, Ted, Roger and the rest — whose charms began to pall as the girls grew up and discovered new pastures.

Mrs Heggs was a churchgoer and sometimes took her daughters along. Florrie was in the church choir for a couple of years, primarily because she loved wearing her black gown and the soft black cap and assuming a solemn and virtuous air. On one occasion, after singing a solo "Give me men to match my mountains," Mrs Tidd, the butcher's wife, sidled up to her and whispered in her ear: "Don't worry, darling, someday you will definitely get a man to match your mountains." On another occasion, while coming down the churchyard path, Florrie overheard something that completely changed her outlook of life. It was Mrs Davidson, the bank manager's horsey wife (who lived in a double-fronted house called Beaconsfield in the posh Pevensey Park), who said to her companion: "Ah, that plucky little woman flaunting her new pair of gloves . . . what's-her-name?" Mrs Grange, the doctor's small, birdlike wife responded with a chuckle: "Mrs Heggs, of course. Very *refeened*, isn't she?" "Not quite quite," observed Mrs Davidson. This little exchange stung her like wasps and she vowed then and there to do something pretty fast to elevate herself from her shabby working-class existence.

Mrs Basak got out of bed at this stage of her narrative to grind out her cigarette in the cut-glass ashtray and fetch a bottle of brandy from her bedside cabinet. She poured herself a large one and returned to the bed. I thought she needed that drink to finish her grim story, but she sat on the edge of the bed, nursing her drink, and looked at Huda's

'Piccadilly in the Rain' very keenly as if she was seeing it for the first time.

"You haven't finished your tale," I reminded her.

"You have heard the rest from Miss Jhajoria, haven't you?"

"Yes, but that was from Harriet's cryptic cable."

Mrs Basak shrugged and took a sip. "Well, that church gossip opened my eyes to the harsh realities of life. I knew the tortuous road to Highlife Hall, my ultimate destination, didn't pass through Lovingdale Comprehensive, so before I finished school I dropped out to try my luck in the big bad world."

But it appeared that London had very little to offer to Florrie, the great adventuress, and, for the time being, she had to be content with a twenty-five-pound-a-week job in a Bloomsbury bookshop frequented by students and some respectable Oxbridge dons. Soon, Mr Coville, her squat and congenitally morose boss, lured her to bed with a promise to double her wages. Florrie wasn't quite innocent about her potential and had never felt any qualms about supplementing her meagre pocket money by allowing the schoolkids to fondle her twin assets behind the gym for a bob. Mr Coville went much further, earning the rare distinction of deflowering a sweet sixteen at the age of fifty-six. He loved nibbling her bush like a goat and encouraged Florrie to drop her aitches even though she was not a true Cockney. However, when her employer started showing a morbid interest in anal sex, Florrie hooked Alan Potsby, a young don from Balliol (with whom she had flirted on several occasions across the counter), and moved to the city of dreaming spires. Alan rented a restored seventeenth-century cottage for her on Cattle Street, and taught her the basics of art, music and architecture. He introduced her to his friends as Maxine and, after a little research in his college library, fabricated her fictitious Devon origins right down to her illustrious, Norman-chasing ancestors. They had become quite close and Florrie had been expecting Alan to propose to her any day when he dropped her all of a sudden in favour of a cute Russian emigrée, Nina Gubsky, whom he introduced to his friends as a Romanov closely related to Czar Nicholas II. Maxine, the dethroned Devon aristocrat, found it possible to maintain her elegant lifestyle only by picking up a few rich undergrads from the King's Arms pub. If Mrs Basak was to be believed, she had bedded a whole generation of Oxonians, including a dozen dons and at least one priapic provost who always presented himself in the persona of Mr Boggis, a travelling salesman passing through town. Despite his false goatee and wig,

Florrie had no difficulty in tracing his Oxford origins from his Drucker's boots, Hall's coat and his queer habit of counting his strokes — which once reached the incredible figure of three hundred and forty-seven! — in Latin.

"And how did you meet Mr Basak?" I couldn't help asking. "Gulu says you met him at an Oxford and Cambridge boat race."

"That's another fib I had to concoct for the consumption of my Indian friends. Of course, Gour himself suggested it. Actually I met him on Guy Fawkes' night. I spotted him in the crowd because he was so devilishly handsome. He looked somewhat foppish in his brocade waistcoat while most of the boys wore sports jackets, flannel trousers — jeans were not so popular at that time — or cavalry twills. It wasn't what they call love at first sight, for Gour already knew about my profession and I was not unaware of his reputation as a womanizer, particularly when my clients from Magdalen were chortling with delight that a handsome Indian boy from their college had accomplished the incredible feat of laying Lady Hamilton, a very snobbish Oxford socialite, and her daughter Madeleine within a week of his first visit to the Hamiltons' mock-Tudor house. Still, it was a great relief for me when Gour proposed that he take me on as his mistress and, like a perfect gentleman, paid off my numerous bills for food — which I always ordered from the Bath Place Hotel — rent, gas and stuff. I was not a big spender but these bills piled up every month just because those poor boys from the Commonwealth countries like India, Bangladesh and Sri Lanka, who constituted the bulk of my regulars, banged me on credit and I had to maintain a Fucking Register for keeping the individual accounts and chase those boys up in their digs for payment during the first two weeks of the month when they were supposed to get their monthly remittances from home. Anyway, Gour had plenty of money and I had beauty and considerable experience in simulating orgasms and we had some glorious days together, travelling around Greece and Spain, and when I finally told him about my real background, he didn't bat an eyelid and revealed that he already knew Alan and his research into my Devon forebears. That was when I started loving Gour in earnest. He took me to Yorkshire, right up to Selby, my ancestral place which, I discovered, had very little to attract a visitor. Well, I must confess that we were a happy couple, even after Gour discovered my expertise in realistic moaning within a year of our marriage. In fact, everything went fine till . . . till that bitch Lola trapped him."

From her glowering eyes and gnashing teeth, it was obvious that Mrs Basak held Lola, and not her husband, primarily responsible for her estrangement. Lola the home-wrecker! For a fleeting moment, I was tempted to tell Mrs Basak that she could now rejoice as Lola had already deserted Mr Basak to shack up with a TV film director. But I dropped the idea as I felt that it was a touchy subject which I shouldn't broach as yet.

*

One evening, just two days before Mrs Basak's departure, in the privacy of her bedroom, I went down on my knees and proposed to Mrs Basak in the right proper way: "Will you marry me, Radha?"

"A hundred times, darling," said Mrs Basak without any hesitation. "But both of us have already tied our nuptial knots."

"Doesn't matter. We can marry a second time. If Draupadi could keep five husbands, surely you can keep two."

"But who's going to solemnize our marriage?"

"A priest, of course. I will make all the arrangements."

I bribed an emaciated, hungry-looking Kalighat priest to solemnize our marriage in his own house and invited Tama and Mrs Gulmohar to attend the ceremony as witnesses. I didn't really expect the latter to turn up, but she did, probably out of curiosity or her love for Mrs Basak, though she declared haughtily that she was present as a mere observer and not as an accomplice in our illegal marriage, and she wouldn't hesitate to give evidence against me in court if and when the opportunity arose. As we sat before the holy fire, sprinkling ghee and chanting unpronounceable Vedic mantras (Mrs Basak merely moved her lips) I couldn't help remembering my first marriage with Babu. It had been torture because it had been arranged totally against my wishes. But this time I thoroughly enjoyed the elaborate marriage rituals, particularly the exchange of garlands and the obligatory sapta-padi which required us to circumambulate the holy fire seven times with the corners of our saris tied together in a knot to symbolize our eternal union in this life and the next. At the end of the ceremony, the priest handed me a small conch and asked me to dip its narrow end in a crucible of consecrated vermilion and mark the parting of my newly-married wife's hair red with the conch. But I refused the conch and took out a blade from my purse to nick the tip of my finger and streak Mrs Basak's hair with my own blood. While Mrs Basak merely gasped in horror, Mrs Gulmohar gave a shriek, calling it a barbaric act, but Tama staunchly supported my heroic gesture and the priest, satisfied with his hefty fee, nodded his approval. Before we left the priest's house, I made him write a certificate to the effect that he had duly solemnized our marriage according to the Hindu rites in the presence of two adult witnesses. Later, I gave a xerox copy of this vital document to Mrs Basak, keeping the original.

*

The evening before Mrs Basak's departure, we took a boat from Prinsep ghat and asked the boatman to row us upstream towards Baranagar. To protect ourselves from the chilly Ganges breeze, we had taken with us a blanket which also afforded us ample opportunity for friendly gropings. The pale, crescent moon creeping up over the forest of chimneys on the Howrah bank looked so fragile and unreal that it reminded me of the stencilled, studio-made moons illuminated by twenty-five-watt bulbs that provided the necessary ambience for a moonlit romance in those third-rate old movies I had once enjoyed with my schoolmates. The gaunt, elderly boatman, who sported a pointed beard and a skullcap, rowed in a leisurely fashion, spitting occasionally on his palms for a firm grip on his oar. He predicted a bumper crop of maize and mustard if the present chill continued for another fortnight, but we were hardly interested in crops and patiently waited for a chance to join our lips which came when the boat passed under the gigantic Howrah Bridge. We pulled apart, breathless and panting, just as the boat emerged on the other side, our moist, burning lips hankering for a more lingering kiss.

Unable to interest us in agriculture or the weather, the garrulous boatman finally observed, "Tell you what, ladies, I haven't seen such a good friendship between a pukka memsahib and a native woman in my thirty years of boating on the Ganga. Why, you two are even sharing the same blanket like two sisters! Inshallah!"

"Pray for my friend's good health and smooth delivery, chacha," I said as I stroked my companion's lower abdomen under the blanket. "It's her third, but still we need Allah's doa blessings."

"Hem, please!" begged Mrs Basak in a whisper.

"I perfectly understand your concern for your friend, dear," said the boatman, pulling his grey beard. "When is her child due?"

"She is in her third month. I hope it's a boy this time."

Mrs Basak pinched my arm, but I ignored her.

"Don't be too confident about a son," warned the boatman. "Take her to Pir Badrulla's mausoleum at Chuchra and tie a consecrated red thread to a branch of the holy peepul tree on the bank of the sacred talab tank behind the mosque."

"You rogue! Can't you ever speak the truth?" hissed Mrs Basak and bit my earlobe.

"My friend wishes to have twins," I translated Mrs Basak's remonstrance in my impeccable Bengali. "Should she tie two red threads?"

The boatman laughed. "No, dear, that's not how things are done there. She will have to pay the resident mullah to offer a special prayer for her at the mosque and then offer food and alms to the poor. In all you won't have to pay more than two hundred rupees."

"Thank you, chacha, for your valuable advice. Now, please turn the boat. My friend shouldn't be exposed to cold for long in her condition." I gently pressed my palm on Mrs Basak's abdomen and whispered, "Radha darling, why don't you have another baby? Your golden womb is grossly underutilized. Look, I won't mind if you requisition Mr Basak's valuable services for a few nights."

"Stop talking rot, Hem," chided Mrs Basak. "This time I am going to Rose Valley to get my divorce and not to get laid by that lech."

"Oh darling! That will be really fantastic!" I cried. "Living like man and wife at last! Why, that's what I have been dreaming about all these days. But why didn't you tell me about your plan earlier, my pet?"

Mrs Basak smiled coyly. "I wanted to give you a surprise, darling. In fact, I decided to split up with Gour when you streaked my hair with your blood and made me your wife. That's the precise moment when I realized that I can't live without you."

"Oh darling! How I want to kiss you . . . I suppose I shall have to wait till we go under the bridge again. But Radha, how will you manage without your rich and influential husband?"

Mrs Basak shrugged. "No problem. The gallery earns me about ten thousand a month and I have some savings too. I hope I will be able to obtain a fairly good alimony from Gour and we will manage pretty well. Of course, we may have to move to a modest three-bedroomed flat."

"But we need a cook and Chinta too to keep house for us," I pointed out.

"Chinta alone will suffice, darling," Mrs Basak assured me. "After all, we aren't going to throw any big bashes. We shall entertain very few people at home."

"That's right. You will occasionally invite Gulu or Mrs Walters for tea and I Tama for potluck."

We talked about furniture, curtains, wall hangings and all the other paraphernalia of housekeeping and by the time we reached Prinsep ghat our new flat, preferably located in Central Calcutta, had been well-furnished and was ready for occupation.

Before she dropped me at the gate, Mrs Basak hugged me tight against her bosom and buried her nose in my hair. "You will never leave me, Hem, will you?" she murmured.

"Not for my life, Radha," I assured her. "I have achieved my dream and I am *so* happy. I will be glad to take an oath in the name of Kali or give you my promise of eternal love and fidelity written in blood."

"God! You shouldn't spill blood at the drop of a hat. I believe you completely."

"Thanks, darling, but I have my own fear. I know so little about watercolours and Italian opera. Suppose you come across a highly attractive girl, well-versed in all branches of art and literature?"

Mrs Basak laughed and brushed her moist lips teasingly against my cheek. "Don't be silly. Love doesn't necessarily flourish between people of similar tastes, does it?"

"I told you once that opposite poles attract, remember?"

"But we are not opposite characters, darling. Florrie and Hem have so much in common. We have seen the worst, haven't we? To tell you the truth, I started seeing you in a new light after you went to the jail for my foolishness and I learnt about your horrible past from your good friend."

"I now understand why people often say 'Whatever God does, He does it for our good.' "

Mrs Basak begged me to stay the night with her and see her off at Dum Dum airport the next morning, but I declined the offer, saying that I wouldn't be able to bear the agony of parting and would rather go home.

"I shall write to you every day," promised Mrs Basak as I got out of her car, after a long and passionate parting kiss.

"That will be splendid," I said, pressing her hand. "I will answer all your letters, darling, though I am not a good correspondent like Miss Sil."

We laughed and parted in a cheerful mood.

But, in the middle of the night, I woke up with a groan. What a big fool I was, I thought. I hadn't kept any keepsake from Mrs Basak, not even one of her perfumed lace hankies, let alone a snapshot of her sweet face, to make this long separation bearable.

"Oh my God, I am such an ass!" I moaned, tugging at my hair in utter agony.

"A belated but correct self-appraisal," said a voice in the dark.

I switched on the light and found Paromita watching me from her bed with a faintly bemused smile.

Twenty

My dearest,

I arrived here around noon in the midst of a light drizzle that looked
like the prelude to a torrential downpour. The faithful Sarla and my
other servants greeted me at the gate with a fanfare which included
garlanding and conch-blowing and, as usual, Lord Steyne and Becky
joined the revelry. The sad part of this glorious homecoming is that
none of my own people has turned up as yet to help me weather the
Christmas ordeal. Of course, everyone apparently has a valid excuse:
Gour rang me up from Delhi to inform me that the winter session of
Parliament has been extended by a week to clear some pending bills
and he would reach Rose Valley just in time to cut the Christmas cake
and lend his baritone to the communal singing of "Jingle Bells". Varsha
cabled earlier, warning me not to expect her this year as she needs
time to acclimatize herself to her new surroundings (I forgot to tell
you that she has since broken up with Rob Roy, left Somerville and
crossed the Atlantic to join Roberta Wisdom University, Idaho,
which is renowned for its feminist studies). And Tee has graciously sent me a postcard from St Catherine's to assure me that she
would arrive on the twentieth with some hollyberry leaves and
accompany me, in place of Varsha, to Sherpa Gomong's shop on
the Mall to buy some twinkling stars, silver bells and tinsel to
brighten up the spirit of Yuletide. In the meantime, how does a lonely
memsahib kill her idle hours? Vrindaban, our old gardener, has the
right answer: "Rose Valley needs a water garden with a trellis-
work bridge, memsa'b," he told me. I nodded and even dug out a back
issue of *Good Housekeeping* to offer him a work plan for the water
garden.

After the weather clears up, I intend to bring out my painting gear and do a landscape, but I wonder if the gods will ordain a dry Christmas this year. How I wish you were here with me to enliven my gloomy hours with your little antics! I will be eagerly waiting for your reply in the next post.
Love

Radha

*

Calcutta
20 December

My sweet Radha,

Your letter brings me great joy and peace of mind after a miserable day and a restless night. I am not at all used to writing letters, so forgive me if you find them rather sloppy. *I love you so much*, darling, and I can't bear this separation though it's only a short one. I hope everything goes smoothly and according to plan and you return to Calcutta unscathed by the first week of January so that we may start living like a married couple right away. You must face Mr Basak boldly and ask for divorce at the earliest opportunity. If Christmas deters you, catch him on the 26th or 27th at the latest. I have a hunch that despite those skirmishes she has had with you, Teesta will ultimately support you. I am however not so sure about Varsha, but you must take both of them into your confidence as soon as possible and convince them of our irrevocable relationship sanctified by the priest. If they express any doubt or cynicism, don't hesitate to show them the xerox copy of our marriage certificate. Once the girls are on your side, Mr Basak will have no other option but to hand you the divorce on a platter. Live and let live — that should be our policy.

There isn't anything more to write about except that Tama has sprained her ankle in a tackle, so I have taken her place as a winger for the first time. Miss Nag is however far from satisfied with my performance and grumbles about my petit-bourgeois indecisiveness in front of goal. But how can I concentrate on my game when my soul is hovering around Rose Valley, wondering how my beloved Radha is going to come out of it all in one piece?
Yours forever

Hem

P.S: Send me a lock of your hair, darling, and a snapshot in a revealing dress that shows your gorgeous curves in full splendour. I desperately need something to go to bed with.

*

22 December

Darling Hem,

Please find enclosed in a twist of paper a lock snipped from the top of my head. I have no revealing photograph with me at the moment, darling, but since you sounded so desperate, I stuffed one of my peekaboo nighties into a polythene bag and rushed to Mr Singh's Sunlight Studio on the Mall. The old Sikh photographer looked quite shocked when I emerged from the dressing room in that sheer clinging thing and he shook his head censoriously, muttering in Punjabi *"Hai Rabba! Memsa'b nu ki hoya!"* (Oh God! what has happened to the memsahib!) when I insisted on striking a seductive pose before the camera with my chest thrust out, flashing a come-hither smile, my palms planted provocatively on my hips. He thought I was slightly off my rocker, but when I told him that I needed the photo to present it to my dear husband on my birthday, he grinned, showing a set of large yellowish teeth, and turned on the arc lamps.

Don't trouble yourself with gloomy thoughts about our future, darling, it's going to be rosy all the way. I am one of those dour English women whose soft exterior betrays a hard core. Even if my daughters don't side with me I am determined to terminate this meaningless alliance that has humbled and degraded me for so long. I now realize that Gour got me cheap, like one acquires china in a jumble sale, to enhance his social status and produce two fair-skinned children to perpetuate the famous Basak race even as he continued with his lechery, openly.

Darling, I too need something in bed to remind me of you. A snapshot in your football shorts will do. It was really foolish of us not to go to a studio immediately after our marriage and get some of what they call "marriage photos" in intimate poses, for a keepsake.
Yours always

Radha

*

Darling Radha,

I feel much better after kissing your hair which is so soft, lustrous and sweet smelling. In return, I am sending a recent snapshot of me taken on the Maidan during our mandatory stretch and bend exercises. Separately, I am posting you my old gold and orange school jersey which still retains my B.O., though it may appear very strong to your delicate English nose. You may wash it gently in cold water and dry it in the shade and I hope that will dilute Hem enough for your taste. I am anxiously waiting for your revealing photo, but in the meantime do send me one of your well-worn bras and a sheet of paper with a dozen clear imprints of your divine lips, including a pout and a toothy grin. I sound quite crazy, don't I? But darling, that's how I am and have always been.

I wish you all, even Mr Basak, a very happy and merry Christmas. A million kisses, darling

Hem

*

26 December

Darling,

I am still reeling under the Christmas fever and have not yet been able to open your parcel which arrived this morning. I have stashed it away in a box and will open it in private, but with Tee around and the servants continuously bothering me for one thing or other, I may not get an opportunity within the next twenty-four hours. There have been some positive developments during the past two days which I must tell you about.

Tee arrived on the evening of the 23rd as promised and Gour on the 24th. For Christmas, Gour gave me a copy of *Parliamentary Humour*, compiled by a veteran Parliamentarian, and a dazzling, mirror-studded, ghagra-choli along with a box of colourful ornaments made out of cowries, wood and stonebeads. The ornaments are just tolerable but I am afraid that tantalizing dress will have to be given away to Sarla's teenage daughter Kunti who has a taste for such gaudy outfits. Mercifully, Tee presented me with a set of lacquered bangles which I'd love to flaunt at an ethnic party. When we were alone, Tee gave me a sharp look and teased me: "I say,

Maxine Basak, what's happening to you? You look as if you are on cloud nine or an angel has brought you some terribly good news." I tried to look solemn and censorious but couldn't quite bring it off. "Doesn't your old mum have a right to enjoy good health and a bit of *joie de vivre?*" I said, but she is too clever to be duped. Later, she came to my room and gave me a suspicious look. "Are you in love, Mum?" she asked with deep concern. I was actually waiting for such an opportunity and lost no time in telling her that she was right, that you are the woman I love and, that I was going to ask her dad for a divorce within a day or two. Tee was stunned and cried, "Oh no! How could Hem do this to us?" And then she started crying like a baby and I had a tough time convincing her that our marriage had gone sour when she was only three or four and I was tired of putting on a smiling face for the benefit of the Basaks. I also assured her that my door would always remain open for my children. I think Tee understood my predicament (she, of course, knows about Gour's illicit affair) and my bitterness, for she slowly wiped her tears and slipped out of my room without a word to join Gyan and Bhairon on the veranda to help them put together the Nativity tableau.

For Christmas dinner we had invited only two families. The boisterous Khannas and the obsequious Ghoshes. Dressed in her rustling silk outfit, Teesta sat demurely like a bereaved princess, maintaining a stony silence which prompted Mrs Khanna to enquire rather indiscreetly if she had had yet another fight with me.

After dinner, Tee came to my room and said, "Mum, can't you give all of us, including Dad, one more chance?" Obviously, she thought that her bad manners had partly contributed to my decision. "I will definitely improve, Mum," she assured me, clasping my hand. "And so will Dad. If we don't . . ." "You have already improved a lot, darling," I assured her, "but your dad, I am afraid, is incorrigible and you know that. It's in the family. I only want to be free and live my own life, that's all." And to assuage her hurt feelings, I added, "I am really very proud to have reared you and Varsha, though I can't claim I have been an ideal Indian mother."

"Nor have we behaved like angels," said Tee and gave me such a beseeching look that I had to turn my face away to avoid her eyes. I felt relieved when she kissed my cheek and bade me goodnight.

Tomorrow I will have to accompany Gour — for the last time, I am quite sure — to Kalimpong to help him buy a set of handmade silver spoons with dragon handles from Sakya Kazi's antique shop and some rare orchids, particularly the exotic Cymbidium, from a good nursery. Gour is very keen to present these items to his party boss on his birthday, presumably to pave his way for a Deputy Ministership in the next Cabinet reshuffle. I could have refused the Deputy Minister designate and asked him straight away for a divorce but, with the servants trailing me around throughout the day, it was impossible. I have therefore decided to utilize this unexpected trip to Kalimpong to press my advantage. I know you will pooh-pooh my lack of courage but give me just another twenty-four hours, darling, and I will see it through.

I enclose two sheets blotched with my messy lip imprints even though I am not sure if you will be able to distinguish between a pout and a pucker!

Yours ever

Radha

P.S: I have aleady despatched a Lejaby bra which Gour brought from London last year when he was there to promote Rose Valley tea. It's two sizes too big but when I pointed out this simple fact to my dear husband, he grinned shamelessly and said, "Grow into it, darling." Anyway, I have worn it a few hours for you. Sorry, darling, I haven't been able to collect my photo from Sunlight Studio so far because there has been yet another skirmish between the Gorkhas and the BSF personnel near Chowk Bazaar and a dawn-to-dusk curfew has been clamped on the town. I hope the situation will improve within a day or two.

*

28 December

Darling Radha,

I was sick waiting for your letter but when it finally arrived, it brought very little solace and much apprehension. I won't get a wink of sleep till I get your next letter. If he refuses to give you a divorce, you just pack your things and leave Rose Valley. Don't enter into an argument or quarrel with him. We need to be very careful when dealing with a crooked politician like Gour Basak. If you think my presence is necessary, don't hesitate to send a telegram. There is an overnight bus service, commonly known as the Rocket, which takes about twelve hours to reach Darjeeling. I feel sorry for Tee but she could always come and stay with us during her vacations.

Many thanks for your ten lip imprints. I have been able to kiss you a hundred times, shaping my lips carefully to fit yours. I am however sorry to complain that your Lejaby bra has been a great disappointment. Why did you put so much talc in your cups? Do your nipples really hurt? I always thought they are tougher than mine. I wonder if it's yet another obsolete English ritual that you memsahibs have been blindly following since the good old days of Queen Victoria. I am cribbing about it because I couldn't get even a whiff of your intoxicatingly sweet-and-sour B.O.! Rush me a pair of your soiled panties, darling, and for God's sake don't deodorize them with Gala of London. I can't tell you how much I miss the warmth of your loins and the fishy aroma of your femininity.
A zillion kisses
Yours forever

Hem

*

30 December
Darling,

I am thrilled to inform you that yesterday, while we were in Kalimpong, I finally managed to give him the notice of divorce. I had half-expected him to throw a tantrum, but he accepted the news with stoical calm and asked me for a couple of days to think it over. I have allowed him forty hours, making it crystal clear that I won't change my decision under any circumstances. Darling, I wish I could give you a blow-by-blow account of my historic Kalimpong trip, but the messy days are here again and what with the cramps and the heaviness around the abdomen I don't feel like putting pen to paper.

I am sorry that my bra was such a disappointment. Anyway, I am sending what you have demanded, along with my revealing photo on the back of which I was tempted to scribble 'Florrie the Vamp', but on second thoughts I left the space blank for you to write something nastier.

I wish you and your friend a very happy New Year.
Yours always

Radha

*

Radha dearest,

Happy New Year! At last the letter that made me jump with a triumphant cry: "Bravo! She has done it!"

Radha darling, you have shown the extraordinary grit and courage of a pukka memsahib, just like the celebrated Mrs Trent of CLC who didn't hesitate to get a talaq from the nawab of Azimgunj when she had finished with him. And that brings me to a sensational bit of news which you will definitely relish even though you no longer aspire to the coveted post of President. Yesterday, on my way to the Maidan, I visited the club to hand over my resignation letter to Mrs Jeejaboy, collect my wages from Mrs Malhotra and say goodbye to Toad, Minoti and Mrs Abraham. Imagine my great surprise and joy when I learnt that Miss Jhajoria had vanished from her Lake Gardens home in the wee hours of 25th December, barely an hour before Lalbazar dispatched a posse of policemen to her house in pursuance of an Interpol Red Corner notice ("Locate and Arrest") received by them. Apparently, Miss Jhajoria had been smuggling Indians into Britain and Germany for quite some time with the connivance of her London-based beau Mr Ravi Tandon of the East-West Video Centre and another crooked fellow called Jim Handa who operates from Birmingham. Stunned by the scandal, Mrs Jeejaboy has fled to Hong Kong to absorb the shock in the comforting company of her sister, leaving the charge of the club to Mrs Mahadevan (Mrs Walters, Mrs Gulmohar and several other senior members refused to accept it). Mrs Mahadevan is maintaining a stony silence about the scandal and has been shooing away hordes of cub reporters and gossip columnists pestering her for details with her characteristic high-pitched shriek: "Aai-aai-o! I know absolutely nothing about Miss Jhajoria's misdeeds. Go and find out from her young friends." But Miss Babeja, Miss Chaki and the other young Turks are reported to have gone on long vacations to unknown destinations, leaving no forwarding addresses. While some senior members detect the dirty hand of Mr Thapar behind this scandalous incident, there are others like Mrs Walters who believe (though they won't say so in public) that you have rightly exacted one last revenge on your arch-rival by informing Scotland Yard about Miss Jhajoria's clandestine operations. Miss Sil, the great correspondent, has risen to the occasion (and done her penance for throwing in her lot with Miss J.) by publishing an angry letter in the *Statesman*, questioning the patriotism of the non-resident Indians. She is expecting rejoinders from London and New York and hopes that this could lead to yet another long-drawn debate reminiscent of her historic battle with Professor Morton on the Bengal famine. But the news that will really warm the cockles of your heart is that Mrs Walters and Mrs Gulmohar have already started a signature campaign to force you to withdraw your resignation and take over the helm in this great crisis.

"We must get back our old, reliable Maxine to weather this storm," Mrs Gulmohar told me. "I am going to write her a letter within a couple of days." I assured her that I would convey her feelings to you, but, darling, if you ask my sincere opinion, I'd advise you not to make a hasty decision, particularly when the club is drawing so much flak from the press. What's more important to you and me at the moment is to get your divorce from your boorish husband. You must enforce the deadline strictly and if you hit any trouble, do send me a telegram and I will catch the Rocket to be at your side and help you out.

I am thrilled by your delightfully shocking photo. You look so young and ravishing, darling, that I feel like rushing to Darj just to hold you tight against my bosom and smother you with a flurry of kisses. I am afraid your panties haven't come up to my expectations as they look and smell like clean laundry. After a thorough scrutiny I could trace only a very faded stain of menstrual blood! And that reminds me of your tide. Do send me one of your used pads. I can't bear this agony of separation any longer, darling, and need something strong like *that* to feel your presence and hold myself together.

A trillion kisses, darling.

Yours forever

Hem

*

My dearest,

I know you will be angry with me, but how can I act irrationally? Well, I had to extend the deadline for another twenty-four hours because, responding to a call from Gour, Varsha has arrived this morning and I couldn't force Gour to hurry up when he insisted that he must take his older daughter into his full confidence before taking any decision. After all, we are — were, to be more appropriate — a family and everyone needs to be consulted. Darling, you must forgive me for this little delay in executing my plan. I am however quite confident that I shall ultimately win this battle. As you had rightly predicted, Tee has promised to support me. I am however not sure about Varsha because it seems that Roberta Wisdom has given her a new identity and I fear that I may find her unreliable in my hour of crisis. She has dropped her South London stutter and acquired a nasal Idaho twang which I find very irritating. She has got an Afro hair cut, wears five-pocket jeans and workshop shirts with bizarre messages, smokes Virginia Slims, addresses me as "Maxie baby" or "Hon", peppers her sentences with "Shucks" and "Gee-whizzes" and occasionally cries "Yo!" which, I discovered, is the ultimate all-purpose exclamation, much superior to our old, out-dated "Wow!".

At this very moment Varsha is having a closed-door meeting with her dad and Sarla has just brought me a chit from Gour which says that he would like to consider my "case" at a family gathering to be held in the library right after lunch. I may not be as courageous as Mrs Trent, darling, but trust me, I will fight it to the bitter end, come what may.

I am really shocked by your demand. You are impossible, Hem! How could you even ask for that dirty thing? Still, since you sounded quite desperate, I am sending it, but please throw away this particular piece of rubbish as soon as you have satisfied your curiosity.
Love and kisses

Radha

P.S. I have lost interest in my water garden. All that remains of my ill-timed venture are a heap of earth and a trench filled with brackish water.

*

My dearest Radha,

I have a hunch that the devil is up to some tricks. I can see that he is scared of a split-up because he realizes that this could stymie his political career. I have great faith in your fighting abilities but my sixth sense tells me that Mr Basak might use the children as pawns to thwart your future plans. It is therefore very important that you should have a heart-to-heart talk with Varsha and see if you can win her over. If she is a true feminist, she ought to take your side and help you get out of this mess. If she still veers towards her dad, bribe her with a good dress or some money. If you can't get her support, you should at least ensure her neutrality.

Radha darling, you can't imagine what mental agony I am passing through these days. My heart is with you in Rose Valley and I feel like rushing to Esplanade and boarding the superfast Rocket but I am holding myself back as I don't want to complicate matters at this stage. Please don't hesitate to send me a telegram if things hot up. I have already taken a vow to offer a goat to goddess Kali of Kalighat if she blesses you with a smooth divorce.

Your pad has cheered me up a little. You have bled well, darling! I can see the exuberance of your period and it shows that your forebodings about an early menopause are all nonsense.

I will be waiting for your next letter with bated breath.
A zillion kisses.
Yours in this life and the next

Hem

*

5 January

Darling,

I know this letter is not going to end your acute anxiety about me but increase it manifold, particularly when you realize that due to certain sudden and unexpected developments I am now stranded in Rose Valley against my will. I say "sudden and unexpected developments" but they were not really so as I discovered later. I must give you a detailed account of what actually happened at yesterday's family gathering, so that you can understand the gravity of my problem.

The moment we were closeted in the library after lunch, Gour cleared his throat, directed his gaze at the wall clock as though he was trying hard to control his emotions and then gave a little speech: "Dear children, I have considered your mother's demand very carefully and have arrived at the painful realization that I have no moral right to deny her what she wants from me. I won't go into the details of my many acts of omission and commission, but suffice it to say that I haven't treated her well during the past ten years and have thereby given her grounds to divorce me."

"Yo!" cried Varsha. "Gour has at last decided to come clean about his little peccadilloes." Gour frowned a little even as he continued his pompous speech:

"Dear children, twenty years ago, on an unusually bright March morning, I fell in love with a beautiful English lady at the Oxford and Cambridge boat race. Twenty years later, due to my lack of foresight and my over-indulgence in sensual pleasures . . ."

"Mr Basak!" I interrupted, "May I request you not to shock my innocent girls with the unsavoury details of your personal life?"

Gour took the reprimand in good humour and said, "Sorry, Miss Heggs. That shows how much Mum still cares for her innocent babes even though she is going to desert them forever."

"Now Gour," said my feminist daughter icily. "Cut that sentimental crap and come to the point. You gotta tell us how much cash you are going to cough up for alimony."

"Fifty thousand a year," said Gour.

"Peanuts," said Varsha and lit up. "A respectable woman needs at least two lakhs a year to maintain herself in these days of high inflation."

I felt elated that Varsha had finally taken up the cudgels for me in real earnest. Maybe Roberta Wisdom wasn't that bad after all. Gour glowered at Varsha and cleared his throat. "Well, dear, that really takes the fillings out of my teeth. All right, I can go up to one lakh, provided I am allowed a decent alibi. As an MP I can't accept adultery as a suitable ground for divorce."

"What alibi would you prefer then?" I demanded.

"I suggest that *you* accept the charge of adultery."

"You talk like a MCP, Gour Basak," snapped Varsha.

"I won't accept the charge of adultery," I said stubbornly. "I have always been a chaste wife, unfashionably chaste for a woman of my social standing."

"Your fault, Miss Heggs," pointed out Gour with a hideous smirk. "I gave you permission to take a lover when . . ."

"Please Dad!" cried Tee who had been listening to our argument with a dazed expression.

"Mr Basak, I won't allow you to wash your dirty linen in front of my children," I said sharply. "May I know what you have decided to set aside as my share of the property?"

Gour shrugged. "Ah, yes. I knew you'd come to that sooner or later. Well, Miss Heggs, you get Basak House stripped of its paintings, furniture and other valuables."

"What about your stocks and shares? And the tea garden?"

"I am sorry but I can't divide any of these assets."

"Fine. In that case I won't accept anything below two lakhs a year."

"Impossible! I have heavy liabilities in the form of two grown-up daughters for whose education and upbringing I have to spend a lot. I will also have to arrange suitable dowries befitting my status for their marriages."

"You haven't given a true picture of your assets and liabilities, Mr Basak," I pointed out. "I happen to know your yearly income from your tax returns, but if you are not willing to accept my legitimate demands, I will ask my solicitors to take care of my interests. In any case, I am not going to accept the charge of adultery."

"Mum knows how to drive a hard bargain, doesn't she?" observed Tee with a sarcastic smile.

"She has to, kiddo," said Varsha and turned to me. "Stick to your guns, hon, and wrap up the deal in another ten minutes."

"I think we are wasting our time unnecessarily," I said. "I want a firm and final reply before I talk to my solicitor."

"I feel you ought to give Dad a chance," said Tee who seemed to have undergone some brainwashing, for she had earlier assured me of her unstinting support.

"Chance?" I cried. "Chance to mess up my life again for another twenty years? Tee, you are now old enough to know that men and rabbits don't change their habits."

"Come on, Mum," pleaded Tee. "He has sown his wild oats and he is now past his prime. I don't think he can pick up girls so easily now."

"Don't talk rot, Tee," chided her father. "You must realize that your mum doesn't love me any more. She loves Hem who, I think, is a wonderful woman though it's a pity that she hasn't any money."

"And what is your reaction to that barb, Miss Heggs?" asked Tee pointedly.

"I hate people who weigh everything in life in terms of money," I said emphatically.

"But the fact remains, Miss Heggs, that love escapes through the window when the unpaid bills start piling up," said Gour with a malicious chuckle.

Unable to stomach his vile insinuation, I spat out: *"I hate you!"*

"But I still love you, Miss Heggs," said Gour shamelessly.

"Enough of that disgusting lie!" I cried. *"You never loved me.* Even while you courted me at Oxford, I knew you were carrying on with Lady Hamilton. You only lusted after my body, Gour Basak, and once you were satiated, you ran after other women. It's as simple as that."

"All right, two lakhs!" announced Gour.

"Yo!" exclaimed Varsha and gave the victory sign with her two fingers. Tee burst into tears. Varsha offered her her hanky but Tee wouldn't accept it. I was going to thank Gour for his generous and gentlemanly gesture when the devil exposed his bloody fangs. "Before you set out on a victory procession with your daughters, may I point out, Miss Heggs, that my grand offer is conditional? I am afraid you'll have to accept the charge of adultery."

I declared that I would return to Calcutta to consult my solicitor and left the library in a huff.

An hour later, when I came out on the veranda with my two boxes, I found a spectacle for which I was not at all prepared. A line of prostrate human bodies blocked my way up to the stairs, with Tee at the front and the old gardener Vrindaban at the rear. Varsha was conspicuously absent.

"You can't leave us like this, Maxine memsa'b!" sobbed Sarla from her vantageous middle position.

"We won't let you go, memsa'b," proclaimed Bhairon, the old limping bearer who has served the Basaks for over four decades.

"Please memsa'b, you are our father-mother," whined Bachhan Singh, our Gorkha durwan.

"Get up you fools! You can't obstruct Miss Heggs' passage like that," said Gour rather indulgently from his chair placed strategically behind a giant fern, his face hidden behind the pages of *Investment Times*. "The memsahib can call the police and get all of you arrested. Don't forget that she is an English lady and doesn't care much about our Indian sentiments and loyalties."

"The police can't touch us!" piped up Tee. "This is a purely non-violent demonstration."

"Inshallah! We shall fast unto death!" threatened Nazir Mian, the cook.

"Tut-tut!" clucked Gour as he rose from the chair. "Miss Heggs, I am extremely sorry for this unprecedented mutiny in Rose Valley." He took out a piece of paper from his pocket and handed it to me. "Here is my solemn undertaking for future loyalty, fidelity, good behaviour and the rest as dictated by the leader of the pack, Miss Teesta Basak. Of course, I signed it under duress . . ."

I tore up the paper, threw it on the prostrating figures and marched back to my room to decide my next move. Obviously, it was Gour who had persuaded Tee and the servants to put up this human blockade. I don't think a British MP would ever stoop so low as to block the passage of his estranged wife. Upset by Gour's skulduggery, I retired to my bedroom but the devil requisitioned Sarla's services (with a handsome bribe, I suppose) and started bombarding me with a flurry of sentimental love letters to rekindle the sweet memories of our honeymoon on the Greek island of Kos and our numerous vacations in the French Riviera and Southern Italy. In one letter, he had the temerity to propose a long vacation in Mexico where, he glibly assured me, we would rediscover our lost love amidst the Mayan ruins! Of course, I tore up each and every letter and returned them to the sender to show my spite, but after the fifth the devil changed his tack and started sending me small presents beginning with a packet of Benson & Hedges, then the latest Barbara Taylor Bradford novel, *Act of Will*, thereafter a bottle of my favourite Chanel perfume, and when I returned all three, he shot his last arrow: a pair of gold crystal drop earrings. It's so difficult for a woman to return such exquisitely crafted Cartier jewellery, but I had to do it for you, darling. The way he showered me constantly with gifts only shows that this time the devil has come to Rose Valley well-prepared to woo me. After these devastating overtures, I couldn't trust myself any longer and locked myself in, ordering Sarla to serve my supper in my bedroom as I didn't want to face Gour across the dining table. I thought that after all those refusals he must have got the message and wouldn't dare to disturb me. I was therefore quite shocked when I went to get a book from the library and discovered Gour sitting in his deep leather chair with a thick volume. Before I could retreat, he darted around the table and pounced on me, kissing and molesting me savagely. Had I not forcibly pushed him away and run out of the library, he could have easily raped me on the sofa. After this horrible encounter, I no more consider myself safe in Rose Valley, not even with so many servants around me, for all of them have been bribed. Even Varsha, my only supporter in the house, is avoiding me and I suspect that she too might have been won over with some bribe.

Darling, I am now virtually interned in my own house and I need immediate help to get back my freedom. I have already composed an SOS message which I'll dash off to Amnesty International, the British High Commission and Mrs Thatcher in case Gour turns violent and makes yet another attempt to rape me. I won't send it off till I hear from you. But if I don't get a reply from you within the next forty-eight hours, I will understand that this letter has been inter-cepted by Gour and in that case I shall go on a hunger strike, though I am not at all used to starvation. I will be anxiously waiting for your reply.

Yours forever

Radha

*

[EXPRESS TELEGRAM]

REACHING DARJ WITH TAMA ON SEVENTH EVENING STOP WILL START RESCUE OPERATION SOONEST STOP WATCH OUT FOR SIGNALS AND MISSIVES STOP DON'T GLOBALIZE ISSUE AS YET FOR TACTICAL REASONS STOP LOVE

HEM

Twenty-one

Tama clambered down from a fork of the banyan tree and reported, "Not a single light up there. Rose Valley seems to have gone to sleep rather early."

"In that case we should start Operation Black Thunder right now," I said. "Let's do a quick survey of the boundary walls and choose the side which is unguarded and easily accessible."

"But, Hem, I am freezing. Let's have a cup of tea before we go for the assault."

"Not a bad idea. We have everything with us."

That was true. In the three hours we had in hand before boarding the Rocket, Tama and I had purchased all the rations and accessories required for a week-long siege. We had stuffed our backpacks with packets of rice, dal, dried peas, tea, cheese cubes, biscuits and a few other essential items like water-purifying tablets, torch, candles, matches, plastic mugs, a kettle and a saucepan. Tama had judiciously borrowed from a local mountaineering club some trekking gear – a collapsible tent, ropes, picks, a pair of sleeping bags and trekking shoes with thick rubber soles and a light grip. Outside Darjeeling bus station, we hired a horse-drawn ekka buggy and reached the outskirts of Rose Valley after sunset. We promptly set up camp and then Tama scrambled up the old banyan tree to find out if there were any lights in Mrs Basak's bedroom, so that we could assure her of our presence by pelting a stone at her windowpane, then communicate through torch signals (three rapid blinks for "How are you?", two for "All Clear!" and one for "Danger!"). But the absence of light in Mrs Basak's room made me slightly apprehensive. It was quite possible that Mr Basak had intercepted my telegram and, armed with the foreknowledge of our arrival, had locked up Mrs Basak and was now lurking somewhere in his garden with a gun.

The ground being wet and cold, it took us about fifteen minutes and a bout of coughing and sneezing from the smoke to prepare two cups of lukewarm tea, but when I took a sip of the tepid concoction, I couldn't help wrinkling my nose as it tasted like the abominable Ayurvedic cough syrup my mother used to dose me with when I was a child. Tama made a face and spat out the tea at once and then both of us turned over our mugs on the reluctant fire which seemed happy to be extinguished with a gush of acrid smoke.

"I think our first move after entering Rose Valley should be to capture Nazir Mian in the kitchen," I said, "and force him to serve us some orange pekoe tea with hot crumpets. Now let's inspect the fortifications and decide from which side we should launch Operation Black Thunder."

A quick survey revealed that the boundary walls of Rose Valley were studded with multi-pronged iron spikes which couldn't be avoided even with the help of our trekking gear. A peepul tree growing close to the south face of the boundary wall finally provided us with a reasonable opportunity to get over the wall without being impaled by those terrible spikes. We hammered several big nails into the thick trunk and managed to climb up to a fork and from there crawled along a horizontal branch which conveniently reached over the wall to the other side. We tied a rope to our sturdy branch, fabricated a big loop at its loose end and tested this crude contraption to satisfy ourselves that it wouldn't give way under our weights. Then I flashed my hooded torch at the ground below to have a clear idea of the terrain we were going to land on.

"We are in luck, Tama!" I whispered excitedly over my shoulder. "We are right above Radha's water garden. We only have to take a good swing and then drop on to that nice little hillock of dug-out earth. A soft landing and no bruises."

"But we have to be perfect in our timing, Hem," cautioned Tama. "If we drop early we will hit those flowerpots and if late, it's that ditch with the murky water that awaits us."

"We are footballers, Tama," I reminded her. "We never miss our cues, do we? I will go first. You just follow me. OK? Now, the countdown – three . . . two . . . one . . . zero!" Off I went, swinging like Phantom in Denkali forest, and dropped on the hillock. Perfect landing, but . . . a clod of loose earth under my feet gave way and before I could exclaim "Hai Ram!" I skidded into Mrs Basak's abandoned lily pond with a big splash. As I waded through the knee-deep, ice-cold water and scrambled on to the other bank, I heard rapid footfalls advancing from the far end of the wall. I signalled "Danger!" to Tama with a rapid blink of my torch, fell flat on my belly anticipating gunshots, and crawled into a lantana bush for cover, my teeth chattering as the biting cold seeped through my tight wet jeans. A little later, the stocky Gorkha durwan Bachhan Singh came running up, flashing his powerful torch like a searchlight. "There!" he cried triumphantly as his torchlight picked up my trail emerging from the lily pond and mysteriously vanishing into the lantana bush. I tried to retreat further into the bush but one of my legs got stuck in a creeper and as I struggled to get it free, I shook the whole bush, making my presence as clear as daylight.

"Come out you rascal!" barked an enraged Bachhan Singh as he prodded the bush savagely with his lathi. "Come out at once or you will get a hiding which you will remember in your next ten lives."

Getting a good thrashing at the hands of that muscular Gorkha durwan would in no way help the cause, I thought, so I crawled out of the bush and raised my hands to signal complete surrender.

"It's *you*!" cried Bachhan Singh jubilantly and grabbed my wrist. "As they say, burglary is the best profession in the world till you are caught." He chortled merrily and looked at my tight jeans and leather jacket with some curiosity. "Well-prepared for a break-in, hun?" And he twisted my hand a little.

"Let go of my hand, you goon!" I cried in pain. "I am not a thief."

"Tell that to the police who have been trying to catch you for the last six months."

I guessed that Bachhan Singh had mistaken me for a notorious female burglar who seemed to have earned a reputation in the neighbourhood and had been successfully evading arrest for some time. "Look, I am a friend of your memsahib, Mrs Basak," I told him. "So, you'd better treat me like a lady."

"You can't hoodwink me with your big lies, woman," growled the irascible durwan. "Come along!" He almost frogmarched me around the house to the front veranda and pressed the bell. "Catching a petty female thief is far below my dignity," he grumbled, "and I don't expect a good baksheesh from the memsahib this time, but still I must do my duty."

Sarla opened the door and scowled. "Bachhan Singh! I will get you sacked," she shouted imperiously. "Many-many times sahib told you not to bring dirty-shirty hitch-hikers and other riffraffs to this house but your thick head can't remember a thing."

"This is no hitchhiker, Sarla!" cried Bachhan Singh indignantly and squared his shoulders for a showdown with the maid. "This is the notorious thief they call Flat-footed Kamini. Burgled Makaibari estate the day before yesterday and now she was planning to rob our house! I caught her hiding in a lantana bush near memsahib's abandoned ditch."

"Lily pond," corrected Sarla.

"You have got a very efficient durwan, Sarla," I said, doffing my hat with a smile. "I hope you haven't forgotten Mrs Mitra."

"Arre! So it's you!" cried Sarla and turned on the durwan. "Bachhan Singh! You fool, she is one of the two lady guests memsahib is expecting."

"But she didn't come through the gate!" argued Bachhan Singh stubbornly. "She climbed the wall and jumped into that ditch . . ."

Sarla rounded her eyes and struck her forehead with her fist to indicate bewilderment. "Hai Bhagwan! Climbing over those sharp iron spikes! Mrs Mitra, you are such a naughty girl. Where is your friend?"

"Waiting on the peepul tree for my all-clear signal, I suppose."

"Bachhan Singh, go double-quick with a ladder and bring down Mrs Mitra's friend safely. No roughtalking and armtwisting, achha?"

"Never heard of a decent woman climbing tree like a langur monkey and jumping over a spiked wall when there is such a big gate for a proper entry," grumbled a thoroughly flabbergasted Bachhan Singh even as he retreated to run an errand that he obviously considered much below his dignity.

"Why did you do that, Mrs Mitra, when you are expected here?" asked Sarla as she led me to the sitting room.

"Just wanted to give your memsa'b a surprise," I said sheepishly. "Is she all right?"

Sarla pouted. "God knows what dain witch has possessed our memsahib lately. She is bent on deserting our poor sahib while he is trying his best to win her heart with loads of lovely presents and sweet letters. I hope you will give right advice to our memsa'b and stop this madness."

Mercifully, Sarla and the other servants of Rose Valley were still in the dark about the actual cause of their memsahib's sudden madness and therefore it was only natural that my role in Mrs Basak's tribulations, as envisaged by Sarla, was that of a friend-cum-matrimonial counsellor. "I will talk to her," I assured Sarla vaguely and perched on a cane stool in her newly-furnished ethnic corner as I didn't want to spoil Maxine's plush sofa with my soiled jeans.

Two minutes later, Maxine, wrapped in her favourite red baku, flew in like a frightened bird and flung herself on my bosom with an agonized moan. But as I held her face between my palms and tried to kiss her, she moved away, whispering, "Not now, darling. There is no dearth of peeping Toms in this house."

"Mr Basak's spies, you mean? Did he make any further attempt to . . .?"

"Not here, darling. The walls have ears. I will tell you everything later, in private." Mrs Basak suddenly assumed the role of a dutiful hostess and scanned my dress. "Jesus! Hem, you look like something the cat dragged in. Go to your room, the one you had before, and change into something less quixotic. I can lend you some woollens if you need them."

*

An hour later, fresh from a hot, refreshing bath and fortified with woollens, I joined Tama in the sitting room for tea, which was served with some sizzling pakoras and pastries. She looked very athletic in her jeans and green cable-stitched sweater while I preferred to look rather homely and sober in my pink salwar-kameez and hand-knitted cardigan.

"Poor Maxine," said Tama, shaking her head gloomily. "She will have to leave this big, well-furnished bungalow and her dozen servants."

I frowned. "No sacrifice is too big for love, Tama."

Tama was going to say something but stopped short as Mrs Basak entered the room and sat daintily on a sofa opposite me. While she poured tea, I saw her blush as she felt my intent gaze on her face. "We may have to stay in a hotel for a few days, darling," she whispered, handing me a cup and saucer. "Gour says he has an old friend in the real-estate business who could probably help us to get a nice flat in Stephen's Court on Park Street."

"Have we to depend on that creep even after you leave him?" I said haughtily.

"Oh no, I just thought . . ." mumbled Mrs Basak and broke off as she met my glare.

"He wants to keep tabs on us, darling. Can't you see that?" I pointed out. "We can surely find an apartment without anybody's help, can't we?"

"It's not that easy to get a flat in central Calcutta these days," said Tama, sipping her tea with a slurp that made me wince in acute embarrassment.

"Don't talk rot, Tama," I chided her. "As they say, you can even buy tiger's milk in Calcutta if you have the money."

"That's true," nodded Tama and she reached for the plate of pakoras with an unseemly eagerness which I considered very uncivilized.

"Of course, we have money, haven't we?" I said turning to Mrs Basak.

"Yes, darling," responded Mrs Basak. "Gour has finally agreed to fork out one and a half lakhs."

"I think that will be adequate, darling, though two lakhs would have been better," I said and leant over the table to plant a kiss on her cheek. Tama choked on her pakoras and gulped her tea with another loud slurp. I watched her with distaste and cursed myself for bringing her to the rarefied atmosphere of Rose Valley. "Tama, would you mind if we retire to an adjoining room for a private talk?" I said, throwing a meaningful glance at Mrs Basak.

"Not a bit," said Tama and reached for the plate of pastries.

*

Once we were alone in the library, I held Mrs Basak by the shoulders and looked deeply into her translucent green eyes because, from the moment I saw her I had a disturbing feeling that she was trying to avoid meeting my eyes. "Look at my eyes, Radha," I said, trying to sound normal and cool though my voice sounded tension-ridden even in my own ears. Mrs Basak looked up timidly, her eyelashes fluttering.

"Did that scoundrel take you to bed?" I demanded.

"Jesus, Hem! How could you even imagine such a ghastly thing? Don't you trust me, darling?"

"I trust you completely, Radha, but after your last letter I naturally started worrying about your safety in this house."

"I shouldn't have written that letter," said Mrs Basak. "I was panic-stricken and behaved like a chicken. Chee!" She shook her head and moved away to the window, stricken by remorse. I walked up to her side and held her hand. "There's no need to chastise yourself, darling. I am glad you wrote that letter. Now, tell me, did the devil make any further advances?"

"Of course he did, but today he was surprisingly subtle and . . . devious. This morning he sent me a basket of orchids and ferns with a note apologizing profusely for his boorish behaviour in the library and begging me for a last 'darshan'. Yes, that's the term he used, as if I am a saint like Mother Teresa."

"And you granted him the interview?"

Mrs Basak pouted and looked hurt. "I had to, Hem. You can't refuse a dying man his last wish, can you? After all, we have been man and wife for over twenty years . . . and besides, I wanted to find out if he had changed his mind about my alimony."

I flung my arms around Mrs Basak's waist and smacked a kiss on her cheek. "I am sorry, darling. You did the right thing."

"I am not so sure," said Mrs Basak with a sigh. "He wheedled me into accepting one and a half lakhs."

· "Don't worry, darling, we'll manage," I assured her.

"But I'm worried Gour won't let us live in peace. He is now so crazy about me that he might even kidnap me."

"Oh no, he can't do that, risking his political career," I pointed out. "I bet he hasn't got his oats ever since Lola ditched him."

"You are probably right, but that's not the only reason behind his wild behaviour. I suspect he has somehow discovered that I am now sexually more responsive than ever."

"Impossible! He is not a clairvoyant."

"But he can put two and two together, my dear," said Mrs Basak. "It was that dubious Harley Street sexologist who drummed into his head that a brief lesbian affair could cure my alleged 'orgasmic impairment'! Funny, isn't it?"

"You are mine forever, Radha, and no one is going to snatch you from me," I declared and drew her to my bosom.

I was busy reclaiming her body with my scientific and circular lovemaking when Sarla's voice rang out: "Dinner ready, memsa'b. Everyone waiting for you and your friend."

"Tell them we are coming," shouted Mrs Basak and dislodged my head from her crotch with a gentle push. "Don't forget to splash some water on your face before you sit down for dinner," she whispered.

"Is my attendance at the table absolutely necessary?" I asked.

"Not really, darling, but I would have to explain your absence to my family, particularly Gour, and that would be very embarrassing. I don't want them to think you are a coward."

"In that case I shall attend the Last Supper."

*

I had braced myself for some hostile glances from Mrs Basak's daughters, particularly Teesta, and some barbed comments from Mr Basak, but the latter not only greeted me very cordially like an old friend, he also insisted that Tama and I should sit on either side of him, probably to show his estranged wife that he had the equanimity and good sense to act the dutiful host even under the most trying circumstances. The girls just managed to be polite though I could guess what lay simmering beneath their cool exteriors. The lavish five-course dinner, starting with garlic and leek soup, progressed very smoothly. As the bearer removed the dishes and Nazir Mian served the second course, Mr Basak proudly announced that the dish we would now relish was Pan Haggarty, a typical Yorkshire dish prepared by Mr Basak himself in honour of his departing wife. I had a momentary fear that Mr Basak would use the Pan Haggarty as the prelude to a savage unmasking of his wife's true identity, exposing her, warts and all, to her daughters. But mercifully, Mr Basak restricted his culinary talk to complaints about the non-availability of good bacon, hard cheese, oregano and thyme, all of which, he informed us, were essential ingredients for a zesty dish of Pan Haggarty. While Mrs Basak affected a mild interest in her husband's panegyric on the robust homeliness of the Yorkshire dish, her daughters looked intrigued. I couldn't however fail to notice that Teesta had started darting defiant, if not challenging, looks at me and was even frowning now and then at her plate. I felt genuinely sorry for Teesta as I had a soft spot for her. Varsha however showed no sign of anxiety and tucked into her food quietly like a good girl. Mrs Basak, on her part, tried her best to look normal and relaxed, though her slightly high-pitched orders to Nazir Mian and Gyan in between the courses betrayed her edginess.

When his much-vaunted Pan Haggarty failed to cheer up the diners, Mr Basak decided to regale us with a couple of parliamentary jokes (e.g. "The other day a shiver ran along the Government benches, looking for a spine to run up"). Tama was highly impressed by Mr Basak's tongue-in-cheek style and repeatedly called him "Sir" as if she was still at Champaboti and he was our venerable president. But, disappointed at the lukewarm response from his audience, Mr Basak soon started talking shop. He proudly informed us that in the recent Calcutta auction the entire consignment of Rose Valley's prestigious hand-picked tea had been snapped up by a German company, Derteeladen, at the record-breaking price of Rs 9100 per kilogram. This made Teesta groan and Mr Basak abruptly broke off, mumbling apologetically: "Sorry, my dears, I think I am disturbing the meal." It was now Varsha's turn to regale us with stories about the latest Hollywood blockbuster, *Ugayya, the Queen of Zalbub*, which had taken America by storm.

It suddenly dawned on me that Mr Basak's jokes and Varsha's tale of primitive feminism were not primarily meant to entertain the guests but to divert a distraught Teesta who seemed to be choking back her sobs with a herculean effort to avoid making a scene during the meal. I was therefore not at all surprised when, taking the cue from her husband and her older daughter, Mrs Basak took her turn to divert Teesta by reminiscing about the elaborate Christmas rituals she had enjoyed as a child in her palatial home in Devon. It always began in the first week of December, we learnt, with a feverish search in the box room to locate the dress box stuffed with Christmas decorations. The excitement heightened as the postman brought in sackloads of parcels and Christmas cards, the latter to be neatly arranged on the drawing-room mantlepiece. Maxine and her younger brother Peter were entrusted with the job of putting holly behind the pictures and hanging mistletoe from the lanterns in the hall. On Christmas eve, carol singers carrying star-shaped lanterns on poles came round and they were always invited in for a cup of hot cocoa and slices of Christmas cake. On the day itself she enjoyed the morning service in the village church and relished slices from the giant plum cake, though the Christmas dinner always seemed to her more of a ritual. The turkey with chestnut stuffing was all right but the rich and dark Christmas pudding doused with brandy and brought flaming into the dining room was indigestible. She and Peter however enjoyed the crackers, wine and almonds. Boxing Day was less remembered for thank-you letters and more for upset tummies or headaches.

Having entertained her family with her Christmas story (even Mr Basak nodded approvingly, and probably marvelled at his wife's story-building ability), Mrs Basak thought it fit to revive the Yuletide spirit more tellingly by doling out slices of her leftover Christmas cake to all present. Sarla brought in the chunk of dark brown cake studded with almonds and raisins, and Mrs Basak deftly cut it into thin slices and then passed the tray around. I took my share and pushed the tray towards Mr Basak who picked up the smallest piece and passed the tray to Tama who unashamedly claimed two pieces.

"Thanks, but I think I have had enough of *that*," said Varsha with a cynical curl of her lips when the tray finally arrived in front of her. It was odd, I thought, for the feminist Varsha to refuse the cake after staunchly supporting her mother in the family gathering.

"Well?" said Mrs Basak dryly with the hint of a frown. "And Tee, do you also refuse my Christmas cake?" No one missed the acerbity in Mrs Basak's voice and the challenging look in her bright green eyes. Teesta hesitated and looked at her father who gave her a nod and a vague smile whereupon she picked up a piece and crammed it into her mouth, choked, and burst into tears.

"Hey kiddo! Don't be a crybaby," said Varsha. "You are now a grown-up. Here, take a gulp and control yourself." She pushed the jug of water towards her sister, but Teesta was inconsolable and refused to be comforted.

"Come on, darling, take it easy," coaxed Mr Basak.

"There are, in fact, quite a few advantages in living with a one-parent family," observed Varsha, pouring a drop of water on the still-smouldering cigarette in her ashtray. "I will explain that to you after Maxie baby leaves us."

"Poor thing. She hasn't got a drop of English blood in her veins," remarked Mrs Basak in a slightly bantering tone. "Why, at her age I was a plucky girl, capable of taking any kind of fence on my pony. In fact, at around thirteen English girls become self-reliant and totally immune to the distressing trauma of family break-ups. Can you believe, Hem, when Uncle Henry walked out on my Aunt Priscilla to live with that bit-part actress Val" (she shot Mr Basak a sidelong glance) "my cousin Maud — she was only ten at that time, mind you — merely shrugged and said, 'Good riddance, Mummy, now we can watch telly all evening and eat nothing but crisps. I hope that bum won't come back and pester you again for roast beef, chilled asparagus soup and crème brulée.' Well, that's the *real* English blood."

Teesta suddenly sprang to her feet, pushed back her chair and screamed; "*I hate you and your English blood*!" She brushed aside Varsha's comforting arm and Mr Basak's sympathetic cluckings and stormed out of the room, bringing the dinner to a grinding halt just before the dessert.

"I think I should go and talk to her," said Mr Basak and left the table, murmuring "Sorry" to no one in particular.

"Excuse me, everybody, I think Gour will need my help," said Varsha, getting up.

"I bet Gour has blackmailed her," said Mrs Basak as soon as Varsha left the room. "Have you noticed the change in her? She even refused my cake!"

"Very intriguing," I said, reaching for the untouched bowl of banana pudding. "Very strange behaviour for a feminist, I must say."

"I suspect that Gour has threatened to stop funding her costly American education, in case she openly sided with me."

"I think, Mrs Basak, you should talk to your younger daughter," said Tama. "She needs comforting."

"She is already fifteen and she must learn to cope with her problems," said Mrs Basak stubbornly.

"That's right," I nodded. "After another two or three years she will have to choose a husband and start a family of her own."

Nazir Mian politely asked if coffee should be served.

"How thoughtful of you, my dear!" said Mrs Basak with evident relief. "I badly need something to cheer me up a bit. I am *so* sorry you two had such a disturbed meal."

After Tama had gone upstairs, I dragged Mrs Basak back to the library and kissed her passionately, cupping her breast with my hand. She responded ardently to my advances but I could feel that she was tense, worried and slightly distracted. "Darling, we have to leave Rose Valley at five sharp to catch the early morning flight from Bagdogra," she said, releasing herself from my clasp. "I don't want to face my distraught family again at breakfast."

"That's a very sensible approach, my dove," I said and pinched her cheek. "Tell Sarla to wake me up at four with bed tea. I am such a late riser."

Mrs Basak accompanied me up to the landing where we parted with a soft goodnight kiss.

*

I had just finished rubbing some cold cream over my cheeks and was going to slip under the covers when I heard a soft tap on my door. Radha! My heart leaped in joy and anguish as I rushed to the door and threw it open — only to step back with a stifled cry: "Teesta!"

"May we come in?" said Teesta, her eyes red and swollen. I thought her sister was behind her, but it was Lord Steyne and Becky who slipped in, wagging their tails and sniffing at my legs.

"Please come in," I said and stepped aside, fearing that she might pounce on me for snatching her mum. But Teesta seemed to be in a sober mood and she headed directly for the rocking chair in the corner, picking up Becky on the way. "I am so sorry for spoiling your meal," she said, flopping into the chair.

"Not at all, my dear," I assured her. "Tama and I came upstairs only after we had had our dessert."

Teesta leaned back and started rocking slowly, hugging the dog tight against her bosom as if it was a pillow or a hot water bottle. "I no longer blame Mum or you for this disaster because it had to happen like this," she said in a preoccupied manner. "Dad didn't care enough for Mum and I always tormented her. God has now rightly punished both of us for our sins."

I was taken aback by Teesta's penitential mood. This was certainly not the cheeky, fun-loving girl who had burst crackers in the school chapel and waged war with the nuns to smuggle *Judge Dredd* into her dormitory. "Don't torture yourself like that, Tee," I consoled her. "You are in no way responsible for this . . . this unfortunate development. I know you are at heart a good girl, even your mum knows that."

"But I never gave her any peace of mind and she always suffered for me," lamented Teesta inconsolably.

"But mothers tend to suffer more for their girls than their boys, don't they? You have now reformed yourself and Mrs Basak appreciates that. I can show you her letters praising you."

But the remorseful Teesta mumbled something about God punishing her for her misdeeds and started crying silently, awakening in me a sudden spurt of maternal affection. I rushed to her side and pressed her head against my bosom.

"Sorry to intrude on this very intimate scene, Miss Maradona," said Varsha, who seemed to have been lurking in the corridor and had sneaked into my room bang on time to deliver her line like the all-knowing Vivek in a tragic jatra play. Stung by her sarcastic tone, I whirled around and said sharply: "I will be happy if you leave us alone for a few minutes."

Varsha shrugged and fumbled in her pockets for her cigarettes. "Sorry, hon, but I gotta talk to you and I thought I'd better say it right now or it will be too late."

"I don't want to hear any more of your shitty feminist garbage," snarled Teesta as she sprang to her feet, dislodging Becky from her bosom in the process. "You ought to have stayed at your fucking Roberta Wisdom instead of coming over here to complicate matters for all of us. And let me warn you, if you call my mum Maxie baby and dad Gour I'm gonna pull out your tongue with a pair of tweezers."

Visibly shaken by her sister's threat, Varsha promptly discarded her newly acquired Idaho twang and her feminist air. "Come on Tee, you are thoroughly worked up. Look baby . . . sis, I mean, I have come here right now to say something very important to Miss Maradona."

"I prefer to be addressed as Hem," I pointed out.

"Sorry Hem, old habits die hard. Now, let me tell you something which you should think over very deeply before you elope with Maxie . . . er Mum. Don't you think that her reminiscences of a happy Christmas in her Devon home and then offering the Christmas cake to everyone are somewhat intriguing?"

"Now Varsha, if you start talking about your Psychology 420 class and what your feminist teacher Mavis Blunt told you about third-world women, I'll have to repeat my threat."

"Let her finish, darling," I said, wiping Teesta's tears with my hanky.

"I think Mum wanted to give us an indirect hint that she still cherishes her hearth and home."

Now, it was my turn to demolish Varsha's dubious psychoanalysis. "Of course, every woman loves her home and children, Varsha," I pointed out. "But you can't expect a self-respecting woman to put up with a sham marriage and an unfaithful husband for the rest of her life."

"I agree with you, Hem, but I must also tell you that this rift between the two developed primarily because Mum refused to move to Delhi when Dad won a seat in Parliament ten years ago. You can't expect a dashing, handsome guy of thirty-three to live a celibate life in a place like Delhi, can you? That's how Lola appeared on the scene. I don't think this would have happened if Mum had joined Dad and lived in Delhi."

"But she couldn't. She had her gallery and her club," I pointed out, though my argument sounded rather hollow in my own ears.

"In that case, she shouldn't claim that she has always been an obliging and dutiful wife," reminded Varsha.

"And what about her moanings that she has been an unfashionably chaste wife in the mould of Sati-Savitri?" demanded Teesta savagely. "I have seen her flirting with Huda on more than one occasion."

"It's a friendship between two artistically-minded people and nothing more than that," I pointed out confidently, though I myself had never dared to ask Mrs Basak any questions about her relationship with Huda.

"I don't blame Mum for her little affair with Huda," said Varsha magnanimously, "but I must admit that I never imagined her capable of falling in love with a young, sporting woman like Hem."

"I'd rather accept Hem as Mum's beau than Huda or some other awful male with artistic or literary pretensions," said Tee with characteristic candour.

"Thanks, Tee," I said. "I am afraid you girls have to accept the sad reality that your mum and dad have split up for good and they can no longer live together as husband and wife."

"I don't believe that," said Teesta. "With Lola gone, Dad is now determined to patch everything up with Mum."

"There can be several reasons other than love for a man to patch things up with his wife," I pointed out. "The prospect of becoming a Deputy Minister is just one."

"But it looks like genuine love, Hem. Dad has sent her heaps of love letters, flowers and presents during the past forty-eight hours," Varsha said with a shameless glee that would definitely make the budding feminists of Roberta Wisdom hang their heads in shame.

"But your mum has refused them all," I reminded her.

"Not all; she accepted the flower basket Dad sent her this morning," Tee pointed out. "And they talked for over two hours in Mum's bedroom and when she came out, her face was flushed and glowing."

"I am sure they necked," said Varsha, grinning.

"I bet they have made love for the first time in ten years," said Tee with a cool confidence that made me shudder. Remembering how Mrs Basak had tried to avoid meeting my gaze, I knew I couldn't rule out the possibility.

"Well girls, what you want to imply is that your mum and dad love each other very much and I am a fool, chasing your mum for no good," I said to bring this disturbing discussion to a close.

"Oh no, she loves you too; we know that," said Varsha.

"I know Dad fancies you a lot," said Tee. "He has a very special look for you."

"And that makes the situation extremely complicated," observed Varsha.

"Why don't you live with us, Hem?" suggested Teesta.

"No, Tee, you can't really invite Hem to join a *menage à trois* which will be no good for any of us."

"So what do you want me to do?" I asked.

"Give Dad a chance, please!" said Teesta, pressing my arm beseechingly.

"And what about you, Varsha?"

"I wish I could cry like Tee and forget it. I don't know . . . I really don't know what to say. I only want to go back to my college. I feel you should do what you think best. Come on Tee, we should say goodnight and let Hem have her forty winks."

The sisters picked up the dogs, one each, and kissed me goodnight. At the door, Teesta turned, clasped my hands and gave me one last, long pleading look before she vanished down the corridor with her sister.

That was the precise moment when I took my heart-wrenching decision.

*

Half an hour later, as I came downstairs clutching my box, I found Mr Basak in the sitting room, pretending to read a journal.

"Cheer up, Mr Basak," I said jovially. "You have won the battle."

"Only half the battle, my dear," said Mr Basak with a mischievous twinkle of his eyes. "I have only got back my principal. Now, I will fight for my interest." From the way his eyes bored into me, I knew that he had neatly calculated me as his accumulated interest on an undisclosed investment about which I hadn't the faintest idea.

"You'd better forget me, Mr Basak," I advised him without rancour.

"I can't. I am pretty sure that we shall meet again."

I smiled wryly. "Not in this world, Mr Basak."

"I am very optimistic in matters of money and love."

"Lust would be a more appropriate word," I corrected. "Anyway, take good care of your principal, Mr Basak, or you may find yourself bankrupt one day."

"I will do that, my dear, I assure you."

"Thanks and goodbye," I said and walked towards the door.

"Wait!" said Mr Basak, rising from his chair. "I will drive you to Bagdogra and put you on the Calcutta plane."

"Thanks for the offer, but I'd prefer a leisurely trip on the Old Granny," I said.

"But it's too early, my dear. The train is at five-thirty."

"I can spend a few hours in the waiting room. Moreover, it won't be safe for you to keep me under your roof even for a minute. You understand?" I enjoyed the hint of an alarm in Mr Basak's eyes even as he laughed.

"I will remember your great sacrifice, Hem," he said rather solemnly.

"Don't mention it," I said and opened the door.

"Wouldn't you like to leave a message for your Radha?"

"I am not good at writing parting messages, Mr Basak. She will understand. Kindly tell Tama to take the trouble of carting back my

317

backpack to Calcutta . . . and would you please arrange for a car to take me to the station as quickly as possible?"

"I will drive you to the station."

But I again refused Mr Basak's offer and requested the services of his chauffeur, Narbahadur. I even foiled Mr Basak's attempt to give me a farewell kiss on the veranda and joined my palms to offer him a namaskar in the traditional Bengali style.

Bachhan Singh came out of his sentry box to open the gate, darting a suspicious glance at my box, probably wondering if I had finally managed to hoodwink his master and steal some silver from the dinner service. He condescended to salute me only when Narbahadur arrived at the gate with the black Land Rover and got out of the car to open the door for me. I acknowledged the midnight services of these faithful Rose Valley retainers with a gentle nod and a smile and then looked back for the last time at the red brick house, the well-manicured lawns glistening with dew drops, the tennis court, the flower beds and the hanging orchids and ferns on the wide semicircular veranda. I felt a sudden squeeze around my heart but I took a deep breath and checked myself. "You must not break down, Hem," I warned myself. "Not here, in front of these lowly servants. You are a footballer, a veteran fighter and a true proletarian who has really nothing to lose in this big bad world."

I kept my cool throughout the journey on the twisty hill road that zigzagged through the picturesque tea gardens slumbering under a pale moon, holding my head high like a proud princess leaving her castle incognito after a palace coup. I even remembered to offer Narbahadur a baksheesh of ten rupees which the silent and solemn-looking chauffeur pocketed with a little bow. "Ma'am, shall I take you to the first-class waiting room?" he asked courteously. "No, thanks. I'll find it myself," I said. "And thank you for this excellent midnight trip, Narbahadur." He retreated with another bow and a minute later I heard him drive away.

The platform was totally deserted, but across the railway tracks I spotted a motley group of Nepalese coolies huddled around a fire. I walked the length of the platform and found my way to the second-class waiting room where in the dim light of a naked twenty-five-watt bulb I stumbled on half a dozen slumbering beggars, including a leper, a one-armed cripple and a hunchback with a big lump about the size of a golf ball dangling from his cheek. In a dark corner, I also spotted two smelly goats, a meditative bull and three shaggy but well-fed dogs curled into three furry balls. They opened their eyes the moment I entered the room and gave a low growl. I made a soothing noise to pacify them and padded across the room, picking up a crumpled sheet of a three-day-old *Ananada Bazar Patrika* on the way to spread it on a vacant iron bench near the back wall. I used my box as a footstool, wrapped my shawl tight around my shoulders and leaned back to get some sleep. But the chill seeped through the numerous cracks and fissures in the corrugated tin walls, forcing me to draw up my legs and hug them tight against my bosom to stave off the biting cold. After holding on to this uncomfortable yogic posture for about ten minutes, I realized I wouldn't be able to sleep till I warmed up my feet. So I got up from the bench and surveyed the animal kingdom to find out if it could offer me any succour in my distress. I finally selected the smallest and the cleanest of the three fleecy, pug-nosed dogs, picked it up in my arms and darted back to my bench. The doggie emitted a whimper of protest but as I pressed it against my bosom, it raised its muzzle to sniff my neck. I had a little difficulty making it understand that I wanted it to curl up around my cold feet, but after a few rehearsals it finally agreed to play its assigned role as a footwarmer.

I woke up after about three hours' fitful sleep and came out of the waiting room, carrying the dog in one hand and my box in the other. Swaddled heavily in their woollens and furs, the passengers had already started arriving and a couple of tea vendors seemed to be ready to warm up the early birds with their morning cuppa. I walked to the ticket counter and bought my second-class ticket for New Jalpaiguri from a somnolent clerk who pointed out that I would need a ticket for my dog; I assured him that it would not be a part of my luggage. However, I took my night's companion to a teastall and treated it to a crumbly rusk, but it rejected my offering after a cursory sniff.

"Raju is very choosy, didi," said the Bhutia tea-boy with a grin, revealing a funny-looking gap in his teeth. "Give him some milk and see how he slurps it in the twinkling of an eye."

"Are you sure it's a he?" I turned the creature on its back and confirmed its gender. Of course, it was male and therefore it had a right to be finicky about its breakfast. So, I bought Raju a hundred grams of milk in an earthen tumbler and he lapped it up greedily, wagging his fat bushy tail in gratitude. "No need of that, my dear," I said, stroking his back. "You have saved me from chilblains and in exchange I have offered you milk worth a rupee. We are even now." And with that little speech I left the pup and walked to the other end of the platform to sit on a bench and wait for the Old Granny to chug in. I had a pleasant surprise when I found Raju coming along the platform towards me, sniffing the ground as though he was hunting for a particular smell. I half-expected him to ignore me and latch on to the well-dressed gent with the fur cap sitting on the bench next to mine, but Raju stopped near my bench and started sniffing my feet and wagging his tail. That gave me a pang of joy and also a little alarm. This was the time I needed a drop of English blood, I told myself, and I got up from my seat and strode away, but after walking a few steps I looked over my shoulder and found Raju doggedly following me. "No need to over-react," I chided myself. It was only a dog, a stray dog hankering for a pat and maybe a little more milk. Most probably it would meet a sudden and violent death under a speeding lorry while crossing the road or, worse still, continue living a wretched life on this railway platform, fighting other dogs twice its size for food and shelter. Poor creature! Let it enjoy my company for a few more minutes.

I returned to my bench, picking up the pup on my way, and put it by my side. It sniffed my hand, gave it a good lick and then sat on its haunches with a proprietorial air, like a trusted bodyguard. A little later, when a bigger dog passed my bench, Raju aggressively thrust out his muzzle and barked, but the majestic piedog merely snarled and sauntered away.

Ten minutes later, the Old Granny chugged in, wheezing and coughing, belching out spumes of white smoke that smelt of wood and tar. I sprang to my feet clutching my box, patted Raju for the last time and joined the crowd rushing towards the slowly-moving toy train to jump into a coach even before it came to a halt. These were the moments when my arduous training in sprinting, with or without a ball, came in handy. I elbowed my way through the crowd, swinging my box energetically from side to side to clear my path, and executed a perfect gate vault which would have been appreciated by Miss Nag if she had been there. I found myself inside an almost empty coach and grabbed a window seat, then I looked contemptuously at the unseemly crowd still jostling on the platform. My attention was immediately diverted by an American couple shooting our train from the platform with a movie camera. The lucky passengers who had been able to get the window seats craned their necks out to see the spectacle and, if possible, get themselves immortalized by occupying a second or two in the film. A few of them even flicked their combs to set their hair while others fidgeted with their tieknots to ensure that they were not caught unawares by the prying camera which was panning slowly from right to left and back to shoot the stampede against the backdrop of the vintage steam engine with its blue saddle-tanks.

The Old Granny had given a terrible shriek and had started to steam out of the station when my roving eyes spotted Raju sitting forlornly on his haunches under a fruit vendor's wheelbarrow, his small black-berry eyes desperately trying to locate my face in the fleeting windows. That was the precise moment when the devastating realization of losing Maxine forever pierced my consciousness like an arrow, wrenching my heart with an indescribable pain. I pressed my nose hard against the cold glass pane, frantically trying to see a last glimpse of that wretched dog and started whimpering like a wounded animal.

Postscript

I was planting some brinjal saplings, Pusha Purple variety, at the back of our rebuilt cottage when I heard the postman's familiar cry: "Didimoni, chitti!"

"Throw it on the veranda, Ramu!" I shouted, certain that the letter would be for Paromita. She was on the mailing list of numerous voluntary organizations all over the country and the letters, pamphlets and invitations poured in from far-flung places like Delhi, Madras and Bangalore in a steady trickle throughout the year. Letters naturally drew my Gandhian friend's immediate attention while the pamphlets and brochures gathered dust in a corner of the veranda. In her absence I burnt some of them for making tea or warming up milk and Paromita didn't seem to notice, though once in a while she would ask me if I had seen an important booklet on "Power generation from Biogas" which she had received from an organization propagating a solar cooker and other esoteric devices using non-conventional energy. I would of course shake my head vigorously and feign innocence though I could distinctly remember that I had burnt that precious booklet a few weeks before to boil up a glass of milk.

Apart from sporadic missives from Babu informing me about his steady progress in "reading-writing", the only letter I had received during the past six months was a picture postcard sent by Mr Basak from Hotel Krystal, Cancun, Mexico, showing the Pyramid of Kukulkan at Chichen Itza. Mr Basak had informed me that Maxine was pregnant and she had decided that if she gave birth to a daughter, she would call her Hem! I also learnt that Maxine had finally agreed to leave Calcutta and settle in Delhi with Mr Basak and in due course she would open a new art gallery in the capital. In the true tradition of the Basaks, the palatial mansion at Belvedere, Alipore, would be handed over to a trust as a charitable maternity centre.

Unfortunately, I no longer possessed that beautiful postcard showing a wonderful specimen of Mayan civilization, for Paromita wouldn't allow me to keep anything that even remotely harked back to my disastrous love affair with Maxine. She took this hard decision one night when she found me crying inconsolably, clutching a small bundle of letters and other mementoes I had received from Maxine. Paromita snatched the bundle from my hand, doused it with kerosene and made a bonfire of my life's most precious possessions. Still, every evening when I lit the wicker lamp under the holy tulsi plant, I never forgot to send up a silent prayer to goddess Sasthi for Maxine's smooth delivery. I even fancied that the child she was carrying was not Mr Basak's but mine. Surely, our long and passionate lovemaking sessions in that majestic fourposter couldn't go to waste! In my wildest daydreams I even imagined that her child would have a dusky complexion or some other tell-tale physical characteristics to link it unmistakably with its real father. Sometimes I also felt an irresistible urge to dash off a love letter to my Radha, but I checked my impulse, remembering what Herodotus had told us aeons ago: "One can't bathe twice in the same river."

After I had finished planting a straggling row of brinjals under the scorching June sun, I washed my soiled hands and feet at the pump and came back to the veranda, thoroughly exhausted and drenched with sweat. I flung my spade in a corner of the veranda, snatched a gamcha towel from the line and slumped in a deck chair, activating the noisy pedestal fan with a kick. While wiping the sweat from my face and arms I noticed the white envelope flung by the postman lying under the table. I bent down and picked it up out of curiosity as it looked somewhat different from the mail Paromita normally received. And different it was! I blinked my eyes in disbelief as I saw my name neatly printed on the cover. The letter came from the office of Craig & Crawley, a firm I had never heard of before. I hastily tore the cover and took out the letter, printed neatly on Sunlit Bond with the Craig & Crawley emblem embossed in gold at the top. My hands shook with excitement as I read the following:

Dear Mrs Mitra,

In pursuance of the decision taken by our Board of Directors in its last meeting, we are delighted to offer you the post of Assistant Manager in our organization. You will be initially taken on probation for a period of one year at a consolidated salary of Rs 1500 per month and on satisfactory completion of the aforementioned probation, you will be placed on the time scale of Rs 2000 – 100 – 2600 – E.B.– 150 – 3500. You will also be entitled to house rent and other allowances admissible to our junior officers.

If the above terms and conditions are acceptable to you, would you please report to the undersigned on any working day, between ten and twelve, along with your certificates and testimonials?
Yours sincerely,

N.K. Datta-Roy
Administrative Officer

This was most strange and very intriguing, for I was damn sure that I had never applied for a job in that organization. I checked the date at the top right corner to assure myself that I had not been made an April fool, for who could believe that a pukka sahib company would offer such a plum post to a non-matriculate without any test or interview when a million unemployed graduates were frantically hunting all over Calcutta for clerical jobs? Mr Datta-Roy had asked me to meet him between ten and twelve, but so great was my curiosity to get to the bottom of this mysterious offer that I dragged out my box from under the bed and pulled out my favourite boutique-print, chocolate and yellow silk sari that I had once set aside for interviews.

*

Craig & Crawley, I discovered, was located in a renovated three-storey red brick building on Bankshall Street, a stone's throw from my first workplace, the Writers'. The pretty Anglo-Indian receptionist, who flaunted her cleavage rather aggressively through her carefully unbuttoned top, gave me a long, hard stare when I produced my letter and requested an appointment with Mr Datta-Roy. She asked me thrice, in three different tones, if I was really Mrs Mitra and when I passed this strange test, she shrugged and condescended to ring Mr Datta-Roy. Then she summoned a bearer to escort me upstairs, realizing belatedly that the times had changed and she would have to show courtesy even to scar-faced probationers in boutique-print saris.

"Welcome to Craig & Crawley, Mrs Mitra," greeted Mr Datta-Roy, a short, rotund gentleman with a bald pate and a pencil-thin moustache. He occupied an enormous leather chair behind an oval-shaped secretariat table with just one slim green file in his "out" tray.

"Thank you very much for the offer, sir, but I don't think I had applied for this post," I said as I took a chair.

"Sports quota, Mrs Mitra," explained Mr Datta-Roy, smiling. "Earlier, we used to take only golfers and snooker players, but we have now decided to move with the times and take on people from other disciplines as well. Of course, I must mention that we have choosen a sportswoman because UNO has declared this year as 'Women's Year'."

Long live UNO! Long live Craig & Crawley! They must have sent one of their directors to watch this year's Hazrat Mahal Cup matches at Gorakhpur where, fortunately, we had been able to retain the prestigious Cup after a tough fight with Manipur Girls. In my elevated position of striker, I had given a very good performance, though our victory came through the tie-breaker.

"What are my duties here, Mr Datta-Roy?" I asked, suddenly assuming the cool and confident air of an Assistant Manager in Craig & Crawley.

"Playing football, mostly," said Mr Datta-Roy without the slightest hint of humour. "Our sporting executives aren't expected to attend the office regularly."

"I think that will suit me."

"But, as I often tell them, there's no harm if they take a little interest in office work and sign a few letters and vouchers now and then so that by the time their sporting careers come to an end they can do justice to their senior positions."

I nodded. "Not a bad idea, Mr Datta-Roy. I think I'd love to sign a few letters now and then if I don't have to read them as well. I hope I won't have to muck in with my junior staff too often."

Mr Datta-Roy looked impressed by my snobbery. "Very rarely," he assured me. "You may smile and wave at them from a distance at office parties and annual get-togethers. Would you like to work in our Export Division, Mrs Mitra?"

"Certainly. I do enjoy going places. By the way, what do we export, Mr Datta-Roy?"

"Tea, of course," said Mr Datta-Roy.

"Ah, tea. That's something very dear to my heart. I don't want to brag, Mr Datta-Roy, but I do know a thing or two about tea and its processing. In fact, I once visited Rose Valley to write a book on that subject. Incidentally, the Basaks of Katwa are very close friends of mine."

"Naturally," said Mr Datta-Roy with a smile which, I thought, had a hint of sarcasm in it.

I frowned and gave him a sharp look. "Well, Mr Datta-Roy, if you have any doubt whatsoever about my claim . . ."

"Oh no! How can I harbour any doubt, Mrs Mitra, when Mr Basak is on our Board?" said Mr Datta-Roy with a mischievous twinkle of his eyes. "After all, it's he who recommended your name."